RECKLESS
HEARTS

HEATHER VAN FLEET

sourcebooks
casablanca

Published by Sourcebooks Casablanca, an imprint of Sourcebooks, Inc.
P.O. Box 4410, Naperville, Illinois 60567-4410
(630) 961-3900
Fax: (630) 961-2168
www.sourcebooks.com

Printed and bound in Canada.
MBP 10 9 8 7 6 5 4 3 2 1

To Chris: my first and most favorite rugby boy.

CHAPTER 1

Collin

"Damn it, Max. How many times do I have to tell you not to mix the reds with whites when you're washing clothes in hot water?"

I tossed the laundry basket holding my newly ruined rugby jersey on top of the dining room table. It landed with a thud, knocking down one of the musical toys my nine-month-old daughter, Chloe, loved.

Raising a baby daughter with a couple of guys is a lot like being a marine. It's an intense experience that requires constantly being all-in just to save someone else's back while he manages to save yours. It smells like shit ninety percent of the time, and every time you move, another body is up in your space. But you do it because you love it. There isn't any other option but to live and breathe it. In my life, my daughter—and the guys who helped me through—were all I needed.

That, and maybe a cleaning lady.

I spun around on my untied cleats, the sound of

"Mary Had a Little Lamb" playing in the background as I rushed toward the breakfast bar to grab Chloe's diaper bag.

In the hallway to my right, my roommate—and certified laundry screwup—Max stood grinning, holding my girl in his arms. Dressed and ready to go, thank Christ, she sported a tiny green Carinthia Irish Rugby jersey her aunt Lia had made for her when Max, Gavin, and I joined the intramural club a few weeks back.

"You yelling at me, Colly?" Max kissed the top of Chloe's head, probably holding her on purpose 'cause he knew I wouldn't lay into him with Beaner in his arms.

With a thumb in her mouth, she snuggled closer to her pseudo-uncle's chest, still half-asleep from her nap. My throat grew tight as I took in her gorgeous face. Lucky for Max, the anger I'd been harboring disappeared with that one look at Chloe.

My daughter was my world—my peace, my rock. And even though the past eight months hadn't been picture perfect for us as a family or as far as life went, we were good as a unit—me, her, and Max, along with Gavin, who lived in the attached duplex.

Except that none of us could do laundry to save our asses.

"What were you thinking?" Glancing at the clock on the wall, I dropped the diaper bag on the floor next to my rugby bag and grunted. "Now the thing's pink and green, which means the guys are gonna rag on my ass all day." On the table sat a stack of five diapers. I grabbed a couple and shoved them into the bottom of the diaper bag, along with a few toys.

"Where's your spare?"

"Dirty."

Max set Chloe inside the playpen by the TV, then handed her the bottle I'd made up a few minutes back that'd been sitting on the coffee table. "Dude, pink is kick-ass."

I shot him a look. "Watch your mouth."

Ignoring me, he walked over to the basket, thumbing through it for a pair of socks, taking his time, chatting like a little kid, and acting like we weren't fifteen minutes behind schedule.

"You've got the pink-for-breast-cancer thing going on, like the *Save the Ta-Tas* T-shirts." Max picked his jersey—the one that had managed to stay green and white—out of the pile, then shoved it inside his rugby bag on the floor next to mine. "Then there's pink bubble gum that never loses its flavor…" He waggled his dark eyebrows and jogged over to the breakfast nook that separated the dining room from the kitchen. He tossed two Gatorade bottles my way. I caught both, tucking them in my own bag, along with my *pink*-and-green jersey.

"*Finally*, there's my favorite reason that pink is cool. Wanna hear it?"

Not really. But I shouldered my duffel, along with Chloe's diaper bag, and waited for him to finish anyway. When he didn't say squat, I sighed and finally said, "Jesus, don't leave me hanging. I won't be able to sleep at night without knowing why it's *cool* to have a *pink*-and-green jersey."

With a smirk, I turned to face him again, just as he tossed me the baby wipe container. I caught it one-handed and shoved it into the side of Chloe's bag.

"Mock me now, but I'm serious. Pink lip gloss looks hot as hell when it's on a woman's lips. Especially when those lips are wrapped around the head of my—"

"Shut it." I pointed a finger at him, glancing back at Chloe. Wide baby blues stared back and forth between us, watching, waiting, almost like she knew exactly what we were talking about.

Max shot his hands up in defense while I sat on a chair to tie my cleats.

"Just saying. Pink is a good color." He winked at Chloe. "Adds character. Right, Beaner?"

Eyes damn near sparkling, she babbled something or another from around her bottle, her blond hair sprouting all over the place. Before I could bitch about Max using my daughter against me, Gavin came busting through the front door, sandy hair hanging over his eyes. Any longer and he'd have the old Justin Bieber hairstyle beat.

But then I saw what he was holding and froze, while trying to ignore the snorts coming out of Max's nose.

"New car seat's ready." Gav kicked the door shut behind him with the bottom of his foot, meeting my stare.

Max laughed harder, reaching down to grab Gav's jersey this time. He tossed it at him, a perfect shot that landed on his shoulder. Like Max's, Gavin's was also still green and white.

"What?" Gav looked back and forth between the two of us, his lip curling as he set the *hot-pink* car seat down on the floor. "Quit looking at me like that."

Teeth gritted, I stood and tied the string on my rugby shorts.

"Nice choice of seat colors, don't you think?" Max

smirked, pointing toward the car seat, before he took off out the front door, car keys spinning around his finger.

I rolled my eyes and shoved my bags at Gav. He took them, trying to defend himself as he said, "You told me to get a new car seat, so I got one. Chloe's a girl, and girls like pink. What's the big deal?"

"Colly's just struggling with his masculinity today. Nothing new," Max hollered from outside on the porch.

Ignoring my asshat of a best friend, I pulled Chloe out of her playpen and smiled as I tossed her in the air. The sanity that came with being a dad definitely outweighed the occasional insanity of my two best friends.

I buckled her into her new seat. Gav had already messed with the straps, adjusting the things to the perfect size. He was a genius like that, a certified master of all things safety and organization. He'd been that way from the second I met him in basic training six years ago.

"You going to fill me in?" He grabbed his cleats by the front door and tied them to the strap of his bag.

"You don't wanna know," I said, setting the handle of the car seat, now filled with my girl, over my forearm.

Gavin grunted something under his breath, then nodded before heading toward the door. I followed, not ready to face my teammates in my fucked-up jersey but more than ready to play.

"What's this?"

I rammed into his back on the threshold, Chloe's car seat digging into his ass. She let out a happy squeal and grinned up at me, bare feet kicking the air.

"What's what?" I glanced over his shoulder.

His hand was in my bag, humor lacing his words as

he said, "Think you need to borrow my other jersey."
He yanked the collar of mine out, a rare grin on his face.

I shut my eyes and yelled out the front door, "It's
pink, Max."

"Real men wear it," he yelled at me from the street
before getting into his car.

Scratch my earlier thoughts. I needed my daughter, a
cleaning lady, *and* a new roommate.

"Get the hell over here, Colly," Max yelled from where
he was sitting on the side of the pitch, his hands frantic
as he waved them in the air at us. A few seconds later,
the whistle blew, signaling the end of game. The
guys who weren't helping to gather up the equipment
jogged toward the stack of twenty-four packs set up on
the sidelines, leaving me and Gavin with Jonathon, the
club's owner.

"Christ, Montgomery. You're a bloody good player."
Jonathon slapped me upside the shoulders, wearing a
wide smile. He'd organized the team years ago when he
first moved to the States from Ireland, and now he was
on the hunt for someone to take it over. Think he was
looking at me to do it, but I wasn't ready.

"Thanks. Felt really good out there." Normally, I
played to relieve a little stress and bond with my buddies. But today reminded me how much I still needed a
competitive challenge in my life.

Max yelped, then fell back onto his hands as Maggie,
Jonathon's daughter, stood over him laughing

Grinning, I nodded at the guys once more before I
ran off the pitch myself, wordless and knowing what I'd

find when I got there. Max didn't do diapers, at least not the number-two kind.

"She exploded," he explained, his eyebrows raised and his normally dark face paling. He looked to Maggie, like a ten-year-old could solve his problems. She watched Chloe during games when my sister couldn't be there to do it.

Everything throbbed on my body. Neck, shoulders, back, the cleat marks on my face... But not a damn thing could take down my mood as I squatted next to my girl.

"Da, da, da, da," she squealed, clapping her hands.

Max stood and took a few steps back, already sneaking away. "Just can't do it, man. Sorry."

"He said he was going to puke." Maggie giggled, slapping her hand over her mouth.

I winked at her. "No doubt he did."

As I reached for the diaper bag, Max said, "Thanks, Colly," then took off, probably to flirt with one of the rugby groupies—the hot chicks who followed the single team members around after the games.

Gavin came up alongside me after that, running his hand over the top of Chloe's head while I stood holding her. She reached for him, but he leaned over to kiss her nose instead of taking her. The guy loved Beaner, but she terrified him to no end.

"You coming to O'Paddy's with us?" Jonathon wrapped his sweaty arm around his daughter's shoulder. Her nose curled in disgust, but she didn't move away.

"Not sure." I shrugged and set Chloe on my hip. She laid her head on my damp shoulder, playing shy as Gavin did peekaboo with her.

It was hard for me to go out after games with the

rest of the team. Not when I still had to wake up in the morning to be a parent, hangover or not.

"We'll be there." Gavin nodded once at Jonathon, then at me. "Max is staying home with Chloe, and you and I are going out for once."

I raised my eyebrows. "That so?"

His face was smug with a secret. Like me, Gavin normally preferred the quiet house to a loud bar, so this was new coming from the guy who talked less than I did.

"Damn right you're going. Not a choice for our MVP to ditch out on the after-party." Another dude on the team—had to be freshly twenty-one—sidled up next to me. I barely knew him, but he was a good guy.

He tossed Gavin a beer, offering me one too. "No thanks," I said. I'd never drink with Chloe in my arms.

Jonathon laughed, head thrown back. "Ah, so glad it's not gonna be me this time. The wife would have my ass." And with that, he grabbed Maggie, along with the newbie, and headed back toward the pitch to grab the rest of the equipment.

I turned to Gavin. "What was that all about?"

"Nothing." He scrubbed a hand over his mouth, hiding a smile.

"Doesn't sound like nothing." I frowned.

"You'll see."

Before I could ask what he meant, a squeal distracted me. Chloe reached for the air, trying to grab the crispy, red and yellow leaves blowing in a swirl around us. Her blond curls blew wildly in the wind, brushing against my cheek. I inhaled, the scent of baby lotion invading my senses and calming me.

Gavin, the everyday hero, grabbed a leaf for her. He

motioned at Max across the way, green eyes squinting. "How does he do it?"

Like I knew there would be, a small circle of women was gathered around our best friend, laughing and pawing at his shoulders.

"No clue." I shook my head, not jealous exactly, more curious like Gav was.

The three of us all had something we were good at. Max was a people person, always on the hunt for a new woman to entertain. He worked odd jobs, never sticking to something longer than a few months. But he had the ability to make people laugh and feel comfortable.

Gavin was the type who worked to take care of others—to keep them safe and healthy. He was an EMT and an ex-medic from our days as marines. Quiet, yeah, but honorable, someone who'd always have your back.

Then there was me.

I wasn't rich. Didn't have a job that satisfied me past paying the bills and the mortgage, and putting food on the table. There was no woman in my life that I could kiss when I needed to or hold in my arms when life got to be too much. But I barely had time to breathe, let alone date, so that was the last thing on my mind.

Bottom line? I did the best I could with what I was given. Anything else was just details.

CHAPTER 2

Addison

IF THERE WAS EVER A NIGHT IN MY LIFE WHEN I COULD'VE used a blindfold and earplugs, it was as I stood in O'Paddy's bar witnessing the hellish experience that was my first rugby after-party.

"What in the hell *is* this fuckery?" my best friend, McKenna, slurred, while her fourth rum and Coke in an hour spilled over the rim of her glass and onto the floor.

"How about *you* tell *me*?" I moved to sit on the stool I'd been leaning against, then propped my elbows back against the bar. "Since you're the one who chose this bar in the first place. Remember?" Scowling, I took a sip of my beer, ignoring her huff from my left. As the cool liquid slid down my throat, I scanned the massive display of male thighs on the dance floor just a few feet away.

One. Two. Three… At least fifteen pairs, by my count, all covered in matching black shorts that barely covered their goods. White numbers and the words *Carinthia Irish Rugby* were written across the backs of the guys' but Kenna's giggle was capturing my attention. Turning, I found her petting Mr. Hottie's chest. But for the first time in all the years we'd been running around together, the guy she had her sights set on wasn't taking the bait.

Interesting.

After the blond on Number Six's shoulders was dropped to the floor, despite the numerous groans from nearly every man in the room, he disappeared into the crowd like a ghost—unreal, untouchable even. Kind of like any man I found attractive nowadays. Bumping into my shoulder, Kenna—sans man and with frown on her face—turned her attention to the rugby crew like I'd done. "You ready? I'm not going to find what I need here tonight, sadly. I mean, where's a good lay when you need it, huh?" She frowned, eyes squinted into drunken slits.

I rolled my eyes. "I don't think what you need is here anyway. Trust me." I patted the back of her hand, pulling her toward the door.

"Don't coddle me, Addie. I'm not a child," she mumbled, tilting, tilting, tilting some more…

"Whoa." I grabbed her around the waist, yanking her to my side. "I'm not coddling you. I'm protecting you." My voice cracked. "You asked me not to let you do anything stupid tonight, remember? Taking home some random drunk in a bar qualifies as stupid."

"Fine." She sniffled, wiping at the wet mascara now dripping down her cheeks. "We'll go." Side-by-side, we fumbled our way forward, Kenna's eyelids drooping with every step we took. The girl was breaking my heart. Her stupid ex-boyfriend… If I had it in me to murder someone, he'd be my first victim.

"I'll make us hot fudge sundaes and put something funny on for us to watch at your house, okay?"

She nodded, wiping at her damp cheeks some more. "No chick flicks, right?"

My chest tightened. "Of course no chick flicks. I promise."

"Wait." She froze, eyes widening. "Gotta pee, first." Her mood shifted as she spun around.

"Do you need any help?" I asked.

Swaying to the left, she propped herself against the wall, red dress rising high on her thighs. "Gotta be strong. Paul said I'm weak. Weak girls go to the bathroom with their friends. I'm not weak."

She wouldn't let this go, not with the mention of *him*, so I nodded and curled my toes inside my boots so I wouldn't follow. "Fine. But if you're not back in five, I'm coming in after you," I called after her over the now-blaring music.

Rubbing my hand over my forehead, I sighed. If only I'd had enough guts to keep her home tonight in the first place. I loved her to pieces—wanted her to be happy more than anything else—but this wasn't the way to go about it.

Not that I was an expert in dealing with issues myself. I had a crap ton of them that I'd been avoiding like the plague lately. For one, I only had three weeks to go until my rent was due, yet I was also two days into being jobless. The preschool where I'd been working had shut its doors with no explanation, leaving me and twenty other women SOL. I would never ask McKenna for a loan. And my parents? They'd all but forgotten I existed, so that option was out.

Still…I was twenty-six years young. A strong, savvy woman with a four-year college degree under my belt. There was no doubt in my mind that I could find another job…eventually. And so what if I had to use what was left of my meager savings to pay next month's rent? That's what it was there for. Emergencies. I'd get through this. I had no other choice.

Needing to keep myself busy as I waited for Kenna, I jerked on my coat and planted myself in an empty chair just around the corner from the bathrooms. Setting my wallet and elbows on the table, I longed for a genie to grant me a wish—an IV drip of coffee so I could somehow manage to stay up late tonight to update my résumé and send it to places that bordered my hometown of Carinthia. With the school year already in session, I was screwed when it came to finding a job in any of the neighboring school systems, but I was a planner in need of a plan.

What I needed right this moment, though, was to find something that would bring in a steady stream of cash to pay for my rent, my living expenses, and the last of my student loans.

After standing in line at the unemployment office all day and scouring the Internet for hours the night before, I'd almost given up. Until the moment I clicked on an ad for a hostess at a local waffle house. Part-time hours, decent pay… It was promising and could, hopefully, get me through a few more months. It was also the first local job that appealed to me. Sure, I had a degree in early childhood education, but when you lived in a small town like Carinthia, with one elementary school and now only one daycare, the options were limited.

Just when I was ready to go looking for Kenna, a voice interrupted my musings—all deep and hoarse—sending a bout of goose bumps up and down my arms.

Voice porn. That's exactly what it sounded like.

"You do realize its eighty-some degrees in here, right?"

I grabbed my wallet and set it on my lap. But when I attempted to swivel around in my chair to face him, he—whoever *he* was—placed his hands on the table along either side of my waist, keeping me from moving.

I stiffened, readying my elbow to drive back into his gut. "What are you doing?"

"Saying hello." Warm breath caressed my cheek as he lowered his chin to my shoulder. Not touching, but just enough to crowd me. The scent of beer and after-shave invaded my senses, and I couldn't help but inhale, latching on to the scent with all sorts of shame. A still-faceless creeper should not make my tummy tumble like an overloaded dryer.

God, I needed to get some even more than Kenna did.

"Well, you said your hello. Now say your good-bye. I'm not interested."

I dragged my gaze down his arms, eyes widening at the sight of his hands.

Strong fingers. Fingers with nails as clean as my own. The same set of fingers I'd seen wrapped around the thighs of the girl on the dance floor.

Oh God. Of all the guys to approach me, it had to be this one?

"Can't help myself," he whispered. "How about I help you out of this coat?" I tightened my hold on my wallet as his hand grazed the lapel of my jacket.

"Do you happen to know what personal space is?" I gritted my teeth, warm, yummy smell be damned.

"Hmm…" Tugging a section of my hair away from my shoulder, he trailed one of his fingers down my arm until his fingers were back on the table. "Not when there are pretty ladies like you—"

"Save it." I shivered, warning bells dinging inside my head. "I don't do strangers at the bar."

"Neither do I. Lucky for you I'm just looking for some conversation."

I highly doubted that. "I don't have time for a chat. Now if you'll excuse me"—I stood and nudged one of his arms out of my way, ignoring the rattle of laughter against my shoulder—"I need to go find my friend." I glanced around him toward the bathroom, avoiding his gaze.

"What does your friend look like?" He cleared his throat, sexy voice gone and all business as he moved to sit on the other chair at the table. Was it my imagination, or did he sound nervous?

Still, it wasn't any of his business, but… "She's blond, real tall, skinny, red dress. Drunk off her ass."

"Ah. One of those, huh?" He sighed, the sound all high and mighty—knowing too. I hated self-righteous men more than any other kind. "Need help looking for her?"

"If that's some kind of skeezy pickup line to try to get me alone, then…" I blinked, hating myself for failing in my attempt to stay composed when I finally met his dark gaze.

Holy. Hell. This man took gorgeousness to another level—to orgasmic at first sight. Blue eyes, dark hair, dark brows, pink lips, and…dimples?

Damn, damn, double damn. Why'd there have to be dimples involved?

"Not that desperate, sweetheart. Trust me." He scowled.

Ah, so it would seem Number Six was easily offended.

"Sorry. That came out wrong." I shrugged one shoulder, not really sorry at all.

His lips twitched. "That so?"

I nodded, needing to avoid looking into his eyes. But the alternative was his mouth, which was gorgeous too. Or his chest, which was big and bulky and...

Who was I kidding? This man was straight-up eye candy all over.

"You're forgiven." He winked before grabbing my hand. "Now, follow me."

"What are you doing?" I dug my heels into the floor as he tried to pull me along behind him.

"Finding your friend."

"I'm perfectly capable of finding her on my own, thank you."

He pursed his lips. "No denying that." He glanced back at the bar. "But it looks to me like your *friend* needs more help than you can give her."

"I..." Blinking fast, I looked to where he was pointing, finding the Duhamel-Tatum hottie from earlier, a protective arm wrapped around Kenna's waist and walking our way.

"Damn it." I cursed, shoving past Number Six. "What happened?"

"Hey, girl." McKenna wiggled her fingers, her head flopping to the side and onto the hottie's shoulder. "Found my future baby's daddy." She giggled and tried to cup her hands around her mouth as she whisper-yelled, "He just doesn't know it yet." I shook my head, humiliation for her burning my cheeks. If I'd been more vigilant tonight, kept her home and safe in front of the TV with wine in one hand and Ben and Jerry's on her lap, then we wouldn't be in this position.

"Jesus, K. What happened?" I stroked my hand over her sweaty forehead.

"I found her outside the bathroom taking her dress off." Duhamel-Tatum Man's full lips pursed as he shot McKenna a brief look. "She said she was hot."

"I am hot, and you want me. Don't deny it." Kenna grabbed his chin and pulled his face closer.

He frowned, studying her for a second before looking at me again. "What do you want to do with her? It's not safe for her to be here like this."

As my hand fell away from Kenna's head, I rubbed my other hand over my own forehead, trying to push back the impending headache brewing inside. "I—"

"Gavin will get her home." *Gavin*? Number Six squeezed the *Gavin* guy's shoulder.

I stared back and forth between the two men, not knowing where to look first. The difference in their appearance was more than obvious—Six was all dark and mysterious, Gavin quiet, contemplative, and serious—yet they were both delicious in the same way. Big, hulking, powerful types who could very well have been Hollywood's next bad boys. All this hotness would've been so much fun to ogle, if it weren't for the giggles and moans coming out of my best friend's mouth.

"No. I'll take her home." I sighed. "Can you get her to my car, maybe? I mean, if you don't mind…"

I pulled my lower lip between my teeth, almost kicking myself after the question left my mouth. I didn't know these two men. And just because they were good-looking didn't mean they were quality.

Gavin opened his mouth as if to argue, but Six cut him off, eyes narrowed as he jerked his head toward the door. In the end, the two hulking beasts became Kenna's and my chaperones.

Pushing past the crowd of college kids standing outside, Number Six moved with both grace and power. Shoulders back, head high—commandeering the way. With no other choice, I followed him, Gavin on my heels, leading Kenna. Her snorting laughter cut through the night—the only sound I could hear other than the thundering of my heartbeat inside my ears.

"Which one is yours?" Six asked over his shoulder, pausing for me to catch up.

"Last in the row. Ivory-colored Volvo." The eighties kind, I'd failed to mention.

Six found it regardless, motioning for Gavin without a second thought. "We'll follow you back to your place. Make sure you get home okay." He moved to open my door, while Gavin settled Kenna into the backseat.

The closer he got to me, the more panic brewed inside my tightened chest. Damn, he was tall. "No." Absolutely not.

It was bad enough that I'd brought them out here by myself, without a single can of pepper spray on me. No way would I let them follow me all the way home. Still, I didn't want to come across as a paranoid loon either.

Six glared down at me. "Unless you've got some serious muscle hidden under that coat of yours, I can't see you lifting her up and getting her home on your own, especially if she passes out."

"I don't even know you guys."

I slipped behind the wheel, needing a barrier from this guy. Fast. But when I went to shut the door, he grabbed the edge and crouched at my side. I swallowed, the intensity in his eyes too much.

"Name's Collin Montgomery. I'm a former marine, and I work nights as a security guard downtown. Grew up right here in Carinthia, Illinois, did two tours of duty in Iraq, and am back home for the first time in eight months. My parents are John and Patty, my sister's name is Lia, and I live with my two best friends. First one's Gavin St. James"—he motioned toward the Duhamel-Tatum hottie on the other side of the car— "and the other's Max Martinez, who's at home, probably sleeping." His dark eyebrows pushed together as he spoke. "I'm not a rapist, or a murderer, or some sort of sick bastard that gets off on picking up a woman at a bar to fill my sexual desires on a whim."

I frowned. Hadn't he just tried to pick me up inside?

Still. My excuses were waning. And, truth be told, I already knew he was a good guy. Call it my gut intuition or whatnot.

One of his dark brows rose. "Good enough introduction for you?" His lips twitched. Again.

I shivered as the cool October air brushed through his wild mane of black hair and into my car. That breeze was the only sign I needed. "Okay." I nodded once, attempting to play down my rising nerves. "But are *you* fit to drive?"

He smiled—big, powerful, and the first genuine one I'd seen on his lips. "I've only had two beers all night."

My face warmed. "Oh."

"We good to go now?" His dark eyebrows rose in question.

"Yeah, we're good."

"Wait here for us then." He tapped the roof once as he stood.

"Fine. I'll wait." I started my car, the motor sputtering in protest.

His eyes never left mine as he took a step back, not even when he called for his friend over the car roof.

"Good girl." And then he winked at me.

It was the wink that pushed my foot to the pedal, and the cockiness in his words that forced me out of the parking lot the moment he and his friend turned their backs on me.

Tires squealing in my wake, I hightailed it home. No way would a pair of dimples sway me to the hot-man dark side.

CHAPTER 3

Collin

JESUS CHRIST, MY HEAD HURT.

I jabbed all ten of my knuckles against my temples, trying to ease the tension. Chloe wailed from her room next door, and if I didn't miss the hell out of her, I would've thrown the pillow over my head and let Max deal with her. It *was* his idea to swap early mornings out between the two of us.

I glared at the alarm instead, cursing the time. No wonder I felt like ass. It was only five a.m.

"*Janie's got a gun. Janie's got a gun.*"

My eyes narrowed at that song and the voice singing it.

"*What did her daddy do? What did he put you throoooooough?*"

Damn, Max. The guy sang like a bird, but his musical choices were as jacked up as our living situation.

"*Aerosmith*, you dumbass?" I pounded on the wall.

"*They said when Janie was arrested, they found him*

underneath a train," he sang louder, probably trying to piss me off.

Groaning, I swung my feet over the side of the bed. Thighs burning from yesterday's match, I pulled on some sweats, wincing.

Coming to a stop outside Chloe's room, I took my time easing the door open, leaning against the frame as I stared in through the dark space. Max, decked out in a pair of white boxers with hearts all over them and nothing else, was dancing in circles with my daughter in his arms.

Couldn't help but grin at the view. And the sounds of Chloe's giggles? Fucking stretched my chest so tight it damn near hurt to breathe.

We'd come a long way in the eight months we'd been back in the States and living together to raise my girl— Max, Gavin, and me. And a hell of a lot further from the time we spent together as marines.

The three of us met in boot camp six years ago, just dumbass college grads with no real clue of where to go in life, or what to do when we got there. No plans. No ideas. Just wanted to serve our country—and find ourselves along the way. Somehow we got stuck together for the remainder of our enlistment. Whether by chance or what, it didn't matter. We were a team from the second we met. Had each other's backs during raids and helped each other get our shit together during evacs. We were always brothers. Always friends. Always equals too.

But out of everything that happened during our time overseas, they'd been the only two people able to get me through the loss of Chloe's mom. Not with big gestures or even kicking my ass, but by silently standing by me and picking up my slack when I almost didn't make it out during our last raid. Sure, I could've taken leave then, but one look at those two assholes and I *knew* I couldn't walk away.

After officially being discharged to First Civ Div, Max and Gav suggested the three of us move in together after we got back to the States. Because the thought of raising a one-month-old baby on my own freaked me the hell out, I agreed, no regrets.

And there we were: three dudes and a baby, living a life that reeked of dirty diapers, dirty socks, and dirty dishes every hour of every day. But it was *our* life. And we were good with that.

"Really, jackass?" I took a step into her room. Chloe, blue eyes bright and wide, squirmed when she saw me from over Max's shoulder. The girl was a work of art that mirrored her mom—and meant everything to us all.

"Hey, I don't screw with lullabies. This is strictly a rock household, man. You get me?" Max glared at me, but the second Chloe started to bounce in his arms, his head swiveled back to her, and his face about melted. Girl was magic, I swear to God.

I grinned. "You change her, yet?"

He stiffened. "Yeah, about that…" He cleared his throat, walking toward me, arms outstretched, Chloe's feet dangling in the air as she giggled. Dude wouldn't meet my eyes as he finished with, "I think I hear my phone ringing. Could be my mama or something."

"Save the crap." I yawned, reaching for my girl.

"Sorry, man. Haven't even taken my morning piss yet."

Chloe wiggled in my arms, tucking her tiny hand in the back of my hair. Her clothes were wet, and if I wasn't so damn tired, I would've kicked Max's ass.

Guy played the fun uncle. The one who danced and sang. Cooked like a master chef too. It was my job to do diapers and all things dad—feeding her, bathing her, the hard stuff—while Gavin preferred the technical, safety BS to anything else. Putting up gates, childproofing the cabinets in his part of the duplex and ours, making sure the car seat was installed the right way. The three of us worked together to do the impossible: taking on the duty of dad to the only person who kept me sane after coming home from Iraq. "Hey, pretty girl." I kissed her on the nose, setting her on the changing table.

"Da, da, da, da."

I smiled, tickling her as I changed her diaper and clothes, ignoring that I hurt all over, and that my eyes were burning from not taking out my contacts last night. I was living on two hours of sleep, but hearing those words leave her little mouth made it all worthwhile.

"You wanna go see Aunt Lia today?"

As I brought her close to my chest, she bounced and giggled in my ear. Her soft curls brushed against my skin, smelling like the fancy shampoo Gavin had bought to wash her hair with.

Five minutes later, with a grin still on my face, I set her in the playpen on the floor of the living room, turned on some early-morning cartoons, and shuffled into our kitchen. Eyes half-closed, I managed to make her a bottle and flip on the coffeemaker.

Feet scuffled in the kitchen, followed by a grunt as Max shoved himself up onto the counter. "What you guys got planned for today?" He kicked his feet against the cabinets. I didn't know how he was always so cheery in the morning, but he'd been that way since we all met in boot camp.

"*Chloe and I* are going to Lia's place for breakfast."

Max straightened his elbows, freezing in place with his hands flat against the counter. A grumpy-ass look crossed his face at the mention of my sister's name. "Well, shit. Guess that means I'm not invited."

I shrugged, not denying it. "Said she has to talk to me. Not sure what's up." I took a sip of my coffee, grabbed Chloe's bottle, and headed back into the living room to sit with her.

"Something wrong with Lia?"

Setting my cup on the table, I reached for my girl and brought her onto my lap. "Hell if I know. She's all over the place these days." Chloe leaned back against my chest and pulled her thumb into her mouth.

Max sat in the chair next to the couch and stared down at the floor. It was too early in the morning to deal with his pouty ass, especially when I was in a piss-poor mood myself.

After the match yesterday, for the first time since we'd started playing in the intramural rugby league on the weekends, Gavin and I had headed to the after-party at the bar.

But fuck, what a big mistake that was. Going to the bar, finding that girl? I knew I was in trouble when I first saw her sitting at that table rooting through her wallet. Little thing looked both terrified and bored at the same time.

I dreamed about her too. Dark eyes, dark skin, curves galore… Hell, I didn't even think I'd caught her name. But none of that mattered when my life revolved around being a dad and working nights. My plate was too full for anything else

Max cleared his throat. "What time did you guys get in last night?"

I lowered a kiss to the top of Chloe's head. "Don't know."

"Have fun?"

"Sure." If you can call being strung tight by the balls over some luscious woman fun.

Silence fell between us, which meant Max was either thinking or brooding. Guy never just shut up because he wanted to. When I opened my mouth to ask him about something—anything to get off the conversation of last night—he broke in with, "You met someone, didn't you?"

I flinched, not a lot, but apparently enough for him to notice.

"Hell yeah, you did. Who was she?" He sat up straighter, wiggling his eyebrows. "What'd she look like? Tight ass? Short? Tall?"

"Come on, man," I hissed, thanking God Chloe was still too young to understand what the conversations between her uncles and me were about.

"What?" He grinned. "She hot? You get her number? Do her in the bathroom of the bar?"

"What am I, twenty-one? A damn frat boy?" I maneuvered Chloe to sit on the cushion next to me and handed her the bottle. "Don't think so."

"What you are, my friend, is a desperate piece of shit who needs a woman every once in a while. That's all I'm saying." He held his hands up in defense.

"Yeah, and then what happens in the morning?" I

shook my head, disgusted with myself for even considering it. "Do I let you cook us a big *family* breakfast and then say, 'Hey, by the way, *wanna meet my kid?*'" I grunted and grabbed the remote. "Not gonna happen."

"No. What you do is cuddle with her a little bit, make her feel special, make her come a couple times, then tell her she can't stay the night. That you've got to get up early or something like that." He shrugged. "Believe me, there *are* girls out there who love one-night stands."

Truth was, I did miss having a woman in my bed. It'd been well over a year since I'd last had sex—eighteen long months in fact. But unlike Max, I'd never once screwed a girl just because. Never even kissed a girl I didn't feel something for. The bottom line was that sex wasn't something I took lightly.

Max beamed, his dark forehead crinkling with lines. "Would hate for you to miss out on some good pussy, man."

"Jesus, give it a rest." I slouched low and listened to Chloe babble as some big bunny named Harry moved across the TV screen.

"You wound me." Max pressed his palm over his heart, still smiling.

I knew his truth though, knew the shit he hid behind. The three of us each had our issues, but together we made it work. That was all we could do.

CHAPTER 4

Addison

WITH THIRTY MINUTES TO SPARE BEFORE MY INTERVIEW, I sat across from McKenna in our usual booth at the Java Java Hut coffee shop, drinking the forgive-me mocha she'd bought to make up for Saturday night. June's Waffle House and More was on the other side of the street. I could see it through the window from where I was sitting, the golden sign boasting, *The perfect breakfast for the early riser*.

Hands wrapped around my mug, I inhaled the chocolate steam. Three days ago, I'd thought that this was what I wanted—a temporary, easy fix for my lack-of-money problem. But the simple thought of dealing with truckers and grumpy old men on a daily basis, rather than the four- and five-year-olds I was used to, had a knot of unease building inside my chest.

Fact is, I don't do change well.

"So my flight to Maine leaves Thursday morning at seven. I'm gonna grab a taxi so I don't have to pay for parking."

I leaned back in my seat, thankful for the distraction as I sipped my drink. "You know I'll take you."

She stirred in another coffee creamer with her wooden stick. "No. You've done enough for me. It's time this baby bird spreads her wings."

I winked. "I would drop those metaphorical worms into your mouth until you begged me to stop."

Her nose crinkled. "Eww. I'll pass on your analogy, thank you very much."

I reached forward and pressed my hand over her forearm. "Seriously though. I'm worried about you."

For weeks now, McKenna had been wallowing, drinking when she could and alternating between angry Alanis Morissette music and Rascal Flatts breakup songs every time I went over to her apartment. This thing with her ex was bringing her down, and I couldn't seem to do a thing to help her get over it.

"I've already taken your advice, Addie. Now quit worrying."

"I'll never stop worrying about you. I *love* you."

She smiled. "And that is why you are the best friend a girl could ask for." She blew me a kiss and started rummaging through her purse. I knew there was nothing in there, but Kenna avoided talking about feelings like I avoided holidays with my family.

The bells over the door jingled as the Monday barista with the funky pink hair strolled into the shop. Her name was Lia, and I was pretty sure she was the most fantastic thing to ever grace this planet. Free spirited, cracking jokes, and taller than both Kenna and me combined. But in a weird, crazy way, she also scared the crap out of me with all those tats and piercings.

"Hey, ladies." She waved, a shiny new piercing in her nose twinkling under the low lights. It was cute, but I immediately wondered if it hurt.

"Hi," Kenna and I said in unison, waving back.

Besides my best friend, barista Lia was the other woman I ever really chatted with.

"You ladies are here early today." Lia tied her apron around her waist as she stepped behind the counter.

"Kenna's got packing to do for her trip, and I have a job interview across the street." I patted the front of my dress and smiled.

Lia pursed her red-painted lips. "Really? The Waffle House? You're classier than that shithole."

I shrugged. "Not many options around this town for a preschool teacher."

"True." She smiled at the next customer in line, taking their order.

Sighing, I picked at my cuticles and checked the clock on the wall—twenty minutes until my life took a turn for the crappier. "Why don't you just call your parents? I'm sure they'd hire you." Kenna glowered at me.

My chest tightened at her suggestion. My best friend knew the status of my nonexistent relationship with my mom and dad, but that didn't deter her from bringing it up time and time again. Going to them for a job would be worse than asking for a loan, and there'd be far too many *I-told-you-so's* going around.

"I'm not into chopping meat for a living."

"It's a meat *market*, yeah, but I'm sure there are positions available that don't include cutting up dead animals." She tugged at the necklace she wore, the one

I'm pretty sure she'd gotten from her ex. "Maybe you should suck it up, ya know? Go to them and say—"

"No." I gritted my teeth. "You know how complicated things are with them. Dad would tell me I was wasting my time working with children anyway, and Mom would tell me I should be getting married and having babies, that any child I take care of from here on out should come from my *own womb*." Their fifties' mind-set really messed with my head.

A chair screeched across the floor. Lia turned it around and straddled the seat, letting her blue eyes drag over my face. The smile on her lips was one part creepy and the other part knowing.

Whatever was about to come out of her mouth freaked me out already.

"I've got the perfect job for you. Can't believe I didn't think of it sooner."

"Oh God," Kenna whispered, no doubt thinking the worst like I was.

Stripper. Prostitute. Call girl. Those were just a few of the ideas drifting through my mind. Still, desperate times called for desperate measures. And for some crazy reason I trusted Lia. Which was the most important thing.

"What's this job?" I bit down on my thumbnail, leaning forward.

Lia flicked a piece of paper in her hand. "Do you trust me?"

"Yes."

Kenna kicked me under the table and I winced, reaching down to rub the spot on my shin.

Lia scooted the paper in front of me and tapped her matte-black fingernail on it. "Then meet me at this address at eight tonight. If you impress him, then you're good as gold for the job."

Lia stood, and my throat grew tight. "Aren't you going to tell me what the job is, at least?"

Her lips curled in a conniving smile. "Trust me. This job is perfect for you. My older brother needs a nanny for my niece, and I can promise you he'll pay you top notch."

"So, no pimps then, right?"

I cringed at Kenna's words. This time I kicked *her* under the table.

"Hey!" she groaned.

Ignoring my loudmouthed best friend, I folded the paper and put it in my pocket. "Thanks, Lia."

She nodded, and I watched her walk away, working the few customers in the coffeehouse like putting people at ease was her God-given gift—piercings and tats be damned, the girl was pretty awesome.

"You're not seriously going to go through with this, are you?"

I stood and slipped on my coat, still planning to go to my interview regardless of this new opportunity. Couldn't put all my eggs in one basket, but I could try two baskets.

Kenna followed me, huffing as we moved toward the door.

"What choice do I have?"

"Not the point. What if she's sending you into something cultish? Or…" She slapped a hand over her mouth. "What if she wants you to be her drug dealer?"

"You're insane." I yanked my hood over my head, the brisk wind stinging my cheeks as we stepped out into the parking lot.

McKenna stopped at her car, twirling her keys. I paused next to her, delaying the inevitable. "No, I'm a realist. And I *realize* that this chick—cool as hell or not—isn't normal."

"Who is normal, huh?" My eyes widened in a *duh* sort of way. "I'm half Filipino with a dad who could pass as my grandpa and a mom who's had more plastic surgery than a Hilton and a Kardashian combined—all because her *husband* told her she looked too old at thirty-nine."

McKenna cringed. "True." She settled in the driver's seat of her car, then rolled down the window. "But what happens if—"

"Stop." I pressed my hand against her door. "It's going to be fine. I am a big girl with a black belt."

"Yeah, from when you were eleven."

"Details. The point is, once a kick-ass ninja, always a kick-ass ninja." I smirked and headed across the street.

"Whatever," she hollered after me. "Don't say I didn't warn you though. Don't you dare call me collect, saying you're in jail for laundering money for the mob either. Because even though I'd fly my ass back home in a heartbeat to bail you out, I need this trip to regain my sanity."

Across the street, I turned to face her. "And I really, *really* love you for that, Kenna. Don't forget!"

I did too. So much. The two of us had been friends since college and would always, no doubt in my mind, have each other's backs like sisters.

CHAPTER 5

Collin

IF YOU LOOKED UP THE WORD *SHIT* IN THE THESAURUS, MY name—along with this entire past weekend—would be the number one synonym for it.

After telling me she needed to make more money during our breakfast yesterday morning, my sister quit on me as Chloe's babysitter. Apparently there was a new nightclub that'd just opened in town, one that promised benefits, along with a major raise and nightly tips. Lia had scored a job as a bartender there—starting tomorrow night. Of course she told me she'd help find a replacement, saying she owed both me and Chloe that. But I told her not to bother, that I'd handle it on my own. And there I was, stuck with no options as I tried to figure out who in the actual hell was going to watch my kid while I worked.

I'd ask the guys—they'd do it in a heartbeat if they could—but they had their own jobs, not to mention actual social lives.

My parents were in Arizona for the winter, so they

were out of the picture for a while. Plus, they'd stepped in and helped take care of Chloe for me until I moved back to the States, so I hated asking them for anything. Chloe's maternal grandparents lived in New York, a hell of a long way from northern Illinois. There'd been talk of them coming and staying here to be closer to Chloe, but that's all it'd been so far—talk.

What I needed was a miracle.

"Dinner's ready," Max yelled from the kitchen. I inhaled, smelling his famous enchiladas.

Chloe was already in bed, and since Mondays and Tuesdays were my only nights off, Max had skipped a date to stay home and try to help me figure some of this shit out. Gavin would be by later too, depending on when he got off work.

"So, what's the plan?" Max sat across the table from me, wearing a red-checkered apron with the words "Kiss the Cook" written across the front.

"Don't know." I rubbed a hand over my mouth. "Call some sort of service, maybe?" Like that would work. I wouldn't be able to trust a stranger with my girl. "Maybe ask to be switched to weekends?" But that wouldn't help either. Both of my buddies worked on weekends and nights like I did. Max and I just happened to have the same nights off.

"What you need is maybe one of those little, old grandmas with saggy tits so you—"

"Max." I slammed my fist down on the table. "Enough with the tits. Focus, damn it."

"Lighten up." He reached over the table and slugged my shoulder. "I'm just as worried as you are. But the difference between us is *I* know we'll find someone."

I wished to hell I could think positively like he did, but with the way things were going, I wasn't gonna hold my breath.

Right when we finished dinner, a knock sounded at the door. "You expecting someone?" Max wiped a napkin over his mouth and stood, already heading to answer it.

"Nah. Unless it's Lia coming by for leftovers."

Deciding to be useful, I grabbed the dinner plates, headed into the kitchen, and shoved them into the dishwasher. Then I ran some sink water to wash Chloe's bottles.

Some days it was hard to believe my life had come to this—all Martha Stewart, Brady Bunch. From the dirty deserts of the Middle East to dirty dishes in Carinthia, Illinois. Nothing I'd ever done could've prepared me for any of these things. Even when shit looked bad though, I knew I had it better than a lot of my brothers-in-arms. PTSD, lost limbs, some not even making it home…

Damn straight I was lucky. All three of us were.

"Collinator!" Lia danced into the room, smelling like the coffee shop she worked at.

I spun around, still pissed at her for quitting on me, not to mention that irritating-as-fuck nickname she used, but I loved her enough to accept a side hug.

"What're you doing here?" I dried my hands on a towel.

She leaned back against the refrigerator. "Nothin'."

"Liar." I propped myself against the counter, folded my arms, and waited.

"Okay, fine. I was hungry. Knew it was enchilada night, all right? Sue me." She tugged on my arm and yanked me out of the kitchen. Girl couldn't sit still. "Now, come on. There's someone I want you to meet."

"Ah, hell. You bring a douchey guy over again?"

Last time she'd done that, Max didn't let up on the sex jokes for days—or the whiskey. I frowned, thinking about the connection.

"Nope." She skipped her way down the hall, her orange stockings like flashlights lighting the way. "Brought a girl this time."

"Oh yeah?" I laughed, not surprised. My sister had a love-the-one-she's-with policy—male or female, didn't matter.

"Not like *that*." She rolled her eyes at me when we entered the living room, then shoved her hand toward the couch. "I want you to meet my new friend." She bounced in place as I took in the back of some chick with a black ponytail. Before my sister could explain, the girl turned around to face us, her dark-brown eyes wide. My mouth dropped open, and my gut went rock hard. Holy shit. It was Bar Girl, here in my house.

"What the…?"

"Number Six?" She jumped up, stumbling around the coffee table.

Speechless, I could only stare as she righted herself and moved to stand in front of me. She tucked a piece of dark hair behind her ear and then brushed both hands down the front of her outfit. Nervous, it seemed.

"You're the one who lives here? *You're* Lia's older brother?" she asked.

I narrowed my eyes. "Sorry to destroy your *serial killer* fantasies."

She cringed, then opened her mouth, only to be cut off by Lia.

"Wait…you two know each other?"

"Yeah, we know each other." I shrugged one

shoulder, trying to play it off as nothing when it was anything but.

For the past two nights, ever since her taillights flashed in that parking lot, this woman had been the star of my dreams. Dark eyes, dark hair, pink lips always pressed to mine… She was just as stunning as I remembered. I hated that she affected me so much when no woman had for a long, long time.

"Well, this is great then." Lia tucked her arm through the girl's, her excited voice damn near squeaking.

Ignoring my sister's chatter, I glanced down at Bar Girl's dress, struggling to keep from busting up laughing as I blurted out, "What're you wearing, a muumuu?" All flowery, big print with pockets along her waist. The girl was practically swimming in the thing.

Her dark eyes flared with anger, meeting mine. "It's called a sundress, thank you very much."

I grinned, already loving her sass—and hating myself for it.

"Collin." Lia smacked me across the back. "Quit being an ass."

Not bothering to apologize, I studied every inch of Bar Girl I could take in, going deaf to the conversation around me as Lia talked about my daughter. This woman was a piece of art, all curves and lines, and everything my body suddenly craved. Yeah, I didn't have the time or energy to be with a woman, but this one was like water after an eighteen-month drought, food at the point of starvation, and everything dangerous I'd sworn to stay away from.

My gaze darted to her neck, my favorite part of a woman's body. I couldn't help myself as I took in the length, the texture, the color… It was long and smooth and exposed, tantalizing, even. I licked my lips, knowing it was messed up that I could easily imagine running my nose up and down the base of her neck while I fucked her slowly, steadily… All. Night. Long.

But then my sister spouted three words that changed it all.

"*She's* my replacement, Collin."

My smile fell.

"No way… This is getting good." Max laughed from the couch, but shock kept me from yelling at him.

"Replacement." The word played over and over in my head, as well as on my tongue, yet nothing was clicking. *Replacement, replacement, replacement.*

Until it just did.

"Yes, you big idiot. Why else would she be here?" Lia shoved me once, but I didn't move.

The first woman in years to make my body sing was also the only prospect I had for Chloe's new nanny? Fate was one big motherfucker.

"No way." The words were out before I could stop them. I couldn't have *this woman* in my house, under my roof, every day, knowing I couldn't have her like my body craved. How the hell could I trust myself with her? Chloe might get attached, and then one day—when her daddy messed it up by not being able to keep his hands to himself—Bar Girl would be gone, leaving Chloe worse off than she was now. Not that she was bad off. "I'm not hiring anyone," I finally said.

Bar Girl stared down at her shoes and I followed her gaze, my eyes popping at the view. What the heck? Rain boots? I shook my head, wanting to laugh again. Wanting to rip the whole outfit off her at the same time to see what she hid beneath. But most of all, wanting to bash my head into the wall for even thinking thoughts I was in no position to think. This girl was a distraction I did not need, plain and simple.

"I didn't know. I'm sorry." She pressed her hand to Lia's shoulder. "Thank you for the opportunity, but this isn't something I—"

"Oh no." My sister glared at me, then at Max, then at the girl. "You are not *even thinking* of backing out of this, Addison."

Addison… Sweet, sexy, sassy Addison. My Bar Girl. The name fit her to a T—every clean-cut, straitlaced, muumuu-covered mysterious inch of her.

Not mine, never mine. I jerked my head once, pushing that thought into my thick, stupid skull.

"Thank you for thinking of me, but I'm going to go now."

"She's perfect, Collin." Lia tugged at my arm as Bar Girl headed toward the door. Because I was a masochistic ass, I said nothing and watched her go, getting my fill while I could.

"She's an ex-preschool teacher with a four-year degree in kid stuff. Don't let her go."

"No." One word. That should've been enough.

"Dumbass." Max snorted and went back to watching TV. I glared at the side of his head.

"Well…if you don't hire her, I will." Lia hissed and stomped her combat boot on the floor.

My jaw clenched as I met my sister's stare for the first time since Bar Girl Addison had stepped into the room. "Chloe is *my* kid, and I will hire who I want to hire, got me?"

Lia rolled her eyes and pressed one hand to her hip and the other to her chest as she ripped into me.

I tuned her out because I couldn't listen when my greedy mind needed another look at the beauty by the door. There I found her—slipping on a pink coat, her long, black ponytail falling down the middle of her back. My chest grew hot, watching as she pulled on a pair of fingerless, pink gloves. She tugged the sleeves of her coat down over the tops of the gloves and muttered something under her breath, all the while captivating me with her movements.

As much as I wanted to stop her, I knew it wouldn't be for the right reasons. Addison was an obvious hazard. The last thing I needed right then was to hire her as Chloe's nanny, especially when all I wanted was get her in my bed.

Addison

Mortification hit me hard as I fled Number Six's house. There was no way I would've shown up tonight if I'd known *he* was the potential employer.

Fate must have had it in for me. What had I ever done to deserve the bad hand that life constantly dealt me? As a kid, I'd gotten baptized. I'd always gone to church and done my homework, community work, and such throughout the years. Went to college, was a good friend to anyone who needed me. Granted, I'd made my fair share of bad choices in life, but not on purpose. And, really, who *didn't* make mistakes?

"Whoa there." Strong hands grasped my upper arms, halting me as my feet slid along the sidewalk, preventing a collision.

"Oh God, I'm sorry." I blinked and looked up. In front of me stood a familiar, hulking beast of a man. The Duhamel-Tatum look-alike, Gavin.

"I know you." He took a step back, tapping a finger against his lips. "Collin's bar girl, right?"

My face grew warm. Part two of my mortification for the night—I wasn't anyone's girl, least of all this *Collin* guy's.

"Nope. But I recognize you from the bar too. Good to see you and all, but I've gotta head home." *And as far away from this house as I can get.*

Refusing to acknowledge anything other than my Volvo sitting parallel to the curb, I dipped my chin and took off.

"You messed with his head," he called after me, his cold voice thick with animosity. "Nobody does that."

I froze like a deer in headlights, my hand hovering over the door handle. The smart thing to do would be to ignore him and find not only a new job, but also a new coffeehouse to visit. Avoid all things Number Six and his family, as well as his friends. Still, something about this Gavin guy's words gave me pause. Made me wonder in a way I couldn't help. Because, again, curiosity. "What were you doing inside my house?" He walked toward me, his eyes slit in accusation.

"Doesn't matter what I was doing." I blinked twice, going for uncaring but coming across as paranoid, I'm sure.

Gavin stood on the other side of my car and settled his elbows on the roof. "I think it does. This *is* my house."

My lips pursed. "For your information, I was invited by Lia. She told me there was a potential job for me here, but it's not going to work out."

"Huh." He tapped his fingers against the metal, the sound like the heavy pitter-patter of rain. "Why's that?"

Was it any of this guy's business? I think not. But, again, what did it matter anyway? It's not like I was going to be seeing him again.

"Because said *employer* seems to think I'm not right for the job." Which was just a theory, but the only one I had.

Truth was, I thought my asshattery the other night at the bar was why he turned me away. Taking off on the two of them after they'd helped me out. It's just that I'd been overwhelmed by Kenna's drunken state and my own bad week. Add the fact that my unfamiliar attraction to Number Six was chart-topping, and I was screwed with a capital *S*.

"Then good riddance to you."

"You don't even know me."

One half of his mouth tipped up into a sly grin. "I know enough."

"Enlighten me then, please?" I sucked in my cheek, biting down on the inside.

"You're not a fighter. You run when something scares you. Shows me enough."

"I don't *run*."

"Aren't you doing it now?" He backed away, laughing.

"I'm not running." Hell, if anything, I was simply trying to escape the crazy of all these men—this entire group of people, in fact.

Okay, fine. I *was* running. That didn't mean I liked to be called out on it.

"You are." He shrugged. "And if you get scared easily, you've got baggage, and what my family inside there does not need"—he jabbed his thumb behind him toward the house—"is some chick with issues hanging around."

My lips parted in shock. Who did this guy think he was? "I…" I had no words. No retaliation fit for human ears at least.

"Now do yourself a solid and leave."

Well, then. "Asshole."

And with what little snark I had left in me, I did what any respectable woman would do. I flipped him off and then got in my car and left.

Screw it. I didn't need the headache of dealing with these men, not when I had enough issues in my life already.

CHAPTER 6

Addison

I CRUNCHED THE PINK EVICTION NOTICE IN MY HAND, ONLY to set it back down on the table to smooth out the wrinkles. Two days late with my rent, and I'd already been served the papers.

In simple terms, if I didn't get some money rolling in soon, I would be screwed.

The waitressing gig hadn't worked out, mainly because they needed someone with experience—experience I did not have—and my unemployment check wasn't set to come for another week.

What I needed was some seriously fast cash.

I'd beg for some leeway on the rent with my landlord today and dip into my meager savings to cover what I could, but what about next month? Or the one after that? What about paying for groceries? What about paying my water bill and my cell phone bill, along with buying gas for my car?

"Ugh." I lowered my head to my kitchen table, knocking it against the wood three times.

Before I could get too worked up, I needed to eat. Like, *real* food that wasn't poor man's pizza (a.k.a. bread with ketchup and melted cheese) or bread, butter, and sugar (which surprisingly filled me up longer than anything else I ate). Oh. And coffee. I desperately needed *that* to kick-start my day, whatever said *day* promised to bring.

Futilely, I hunted through my cabinets, lip pulled between my teeth. I prayed for a miracle that consisted of the coffee bean variety, yet it did no good. Annoyance revved through me as I settled my hands along the edge of the counter. Knowing I'd have to visit Java Java Hut this morning to feed my early-morning addiction was pretty much the icing on my crap-cake.

"Stupid coffeehouse."

Things would turn around soon. They had to. Someone out there in the universe owed me something other than a kick in the ass. At least I kept telling myself that as I headed out to indulge in my single necessity.

Coffee: it made everything better.

As I pulled into the parking lot, the first thing I saw was a huge truck taking up two of the three parking spaces. All fancy hubcaps, black and sleek and shiny—a rich man's vehicle. I frowned at the audacity that some people had. Wasn't one parking space enough? I wondered if I could pull a Carrie Underwood and dig my key into the side…

Woah. Bitter pre-coffee me did not like people.

I jarred open my door, fighting against the rusted hinges while secretly hoping I'd accidentally smash the edge against Fancy Pants Truck. But that idea was struck down when I realized how not so good that'd be, since I hadn't paid my car insurance in close to six months.

Brisk, cold rain stung my cheeks, and I cursed the God of Winter for taking my warm sun so soon.

The front doorbells jingled, announcing my arrival. I shook out my hood as I pulled it off my head, droplets of ice dribbling down my neck along the way. Shivering, I yanked the thing off for good before I dropped it on the table of my usual booth—the one in the corner under the picture of a steaming cup of coffee with the quote below it saying: *If life gives you lemons, trade them for coffee*. Wishing the sentiment was factual, I headed toward the counter, flexing and unflexing my fingers to try to warm them.

The tall guy in front of me was dressed in a black leather coat with leather gloves. He tapped his fingers against the counter as he waited for the owner, Betty, to finish his order. Part of me wondered if he was the truck driver, and I had half a mind to tell him where he could shove those hubcaps. The other part had one thing on the brain: *caffeine, caffeine, caffeine*. But, still, I took in his form because I had nothing better to do as I waited my turn.

He was tall—ginormously so—and something told me I didn't want to mess with him.

"You're gonna be here awhile."

"Excuse me?" I pointed my gaze toward the floor at his question, admiring his big, black boots. *Motorcycle boots, not trucker's boots.*

"Said you're gonna be a here awhile. They only have one espresso machine working this morning."

I shrugged, looking to avoid all things talk, even the small kind. Still, when he cleared his throat, I found myself looking up—and up—at him anyway. It was obvious he wouldn't give up on the chitchat anytime soon.

"Well, hell. If it isn't the source of all evil."

My lips parted. The source? Evil? What the hell did that mean?

His dark face, high cheekbones, and square jaw made up a picture-perfect specimen. Add his closely cut, styled black hair and midnight eyes, and it was like looking into perfection—the rugged pretty-boy kind.

"Excuse me?" And now I sounded like a parrot. Next thing I knew, I'd sprout feathers and ask him to call me Polly.

"You're the root of all the evil at my house right now."

I took a step back and then another until my back collided with a table.

So…I hadn't heard him wrong then.

He laughed, looking far too amused for having just called me *evil* and the *source* of it. Tiny wrinkles curled at the corners of his eyes.

"Um, yeah, I think I'll just wait over—"

"You don't remember me, do you?" His face softened, less amused and a little sweeter. My shoulders dropped at his change, and I didn't quite feel the need to run…at least for the moment.

He smiled so widely that his perfect, white teeth practically glowed. Was he a model?

"You're Lia's friend. I met you the other night."

Nodding once, I murmured, "I know her, yes. She works here." And was once my friend of sorts until she suddenly shared the same blood as that…

Oh.

I blinked, tipping my face to the side as recognition sank in.

Yeah. So I did know this guy—Couch Man.

I shifted my weight back and forth between my feet, wondering how I'd gotten so unlucky as to run into *another* person associated with Number Six. He winked and then turned to grab his coffee from Betty. Her pale-blue eyes brightened as she waved his money away.

"Any friend of Lia's is a friend of mine." She leaned over and ran her fingers along the back of his hand. I had a feeling this guy possessed hypnotic charms when it came to the ladies—even the eighty-year-old ones.

Turning my way, he motioned me toward my booth. "Think I'm going to join you."

My eyes widened. "Um..." Damn, my vocabulary was limited this morning.

"Don't try to talk me out of it, Short Stuff. I always get what I want."

My face heated. "Y-you... I mean, I..." *And* I was done for.

He glanced over his shoulder at Betty. "Put whatever she's drinking on my tab."

Five minutes later, I was sitting across from this über friendly, sexy man having a conversation about nothing. Small talk—something I didn't typically do. We'd gone over the weather, followed by him asking me if I liked cream in my coffee and then if I had a boyfriend.

"I've got to hand it to you." He sipped his drink, stretching an arm over the back of the booth. "You know how to make an impression on people."

So it was time to get to the nitty-gritty—the *real*

reason he wanted to converse with me. Most likely having to do with me being the source of evil…and Number Six.

"How so?" I cleared my throat.

"I've got one best friend who thinks you're some sort of siren in disguise, created to lure men to their doom. And the other friend thinks you are a wasted piece of space, not worthy of—"

"Just…please, stop right there." I reached for my cup. "I came to get some coffee and look through the want ads, not get scrutinized by some guy who's only met me once." I stood and glared down at the table-top, wishing for blinders that would help me un-see things—particularly this specimen of ridiculously hot man-candy.

"Hold up now, Short Stuff." He grabbed my hand, stopping me. "You have no idea what *I* think of you. Aren't you a little curious?"

Jaw clenched, I met his gaze. "No. I don't care what you or anyone else thinks about me. So if you'll excuse me, I—"

"You don't trust people. I get it. Neither does Colly." He dropped my hand, folding his arms.

I arched one eyebrow at him, waiting. Ten seconds is all he'd get. And *that* was being generous.

He studied my face, his lip curling up on one side. "But you see, Lee-Lee said you're good people, and I trust her more than anyone else." He leaned back in his seat. "So here's the thing. I think you should come home with me today. Meet Chloe and Collin. Start fresh."

"Absolutely not."

"Why not? Heard you needed a job, and this one

would be perfect for you. Am I right? And I dare you not to fall in love with Chloe Bean." He grinned like a proud daddy. It was almost endearing that he seemed to love this *Collin* guy's daughter like his own. But even though the idea was tempting, I knew it wouldn't work out. Not when it came to Number Six. Sliding out of the booth, I fumbled through my purse, hands trembling so badly I dropped my bag. All the contents scattered across the floor and under the table. Lip gloss to tampons, anything and everything important—and humiliating—was now on display.

"Damn it." I fell to my knees, trying to sweep the stuff up with my forearm, only to be stopped short when he crouched down to help me.

"Jesus." He laughed.

"What?" My face heated.

His eyes locked with mine. "You're more nervous than a whore in church, Short Stuff. Something on your mind?" An unnerving grin sat on his lips.

"What's wrong is that I have a problem with being called a whore and evil within the span of fifteen minutes by some guy I don't even know." His face fell. The guy had the audacity to look like *he* was the victim here. I huffed once, stood back up, and yanked my half-zipped purse against my stomach. "I'm leaving. And you"—I jerked my now-empty coffee cup his way, and a few remaining drops of cool liquid sloshed against my wrist—"will leave me the hell alone."

And with that, I left the coffeehouse and jumped into my car.

CHAPTER 7

Collin

I SNEERED AT MAX AND JABBED AN ELBOW INTO HIS RIBS.

"You son of a bitch!" Groaning, he fell back against the couch cushions, probably more pissed my team scored the winning try than about my cheap shot. Some days, rugby on the Xbox was fiercer than on the pitch for the two of us.

I tossed my controller onto the coffee table and stood, stretching my arms over my head. What could I say? Success was sweet, cheating or not.

"Shut the hell up." Gavin staggered down the hall, dark circles under his bloodshot eyes. Guy looked like he'd seen better days, that's for sure.

Max shook his head and stood next to me. "Try not to stay out 'til three in the morning getting pussy next time."

"I was working, you idiot." He flipped Max off and went into the kitchen, then headed back, a bag of chips in hand.

"Ah, that's right. You live to work, and you work to

live." Max grabbed a handful of chips and stuffed them into his mouth.

"At least I can keep a job longer than two months."

Max's smile fell. "I'm working two jobs right now, you idiot. Chef *and* waiter."

"Real-life goals there, Maxwell." Gavin moved to sit in a chair at the dining room table.

"Least I get some ass too. When's the last time you had sex?"

"None of your business." Gavin kicked Max in the shin as he sat beside him.

The two of them fought like brothers, while I was their constant referee. Problem being, I wasn't in the mood to deal with it this afternoon.

Over the past two weeks, I'd used all the vacation time I had left to stay home and watch Chloe, which meant tonight I would've been screwed if Lia didn't have a rare night off. Tomorrow, on the other hand…

I stuck Chloe in her high chair with some Cheerios and walked toward the kitchen to get her lunch ready. As I waited for her baby food to warm up in the microwave, my thoughts went to Bar Girl Addison—like they'd been doing since the night she ran out of my house. I couldn't help but wonder: was she like one of those hit-and-run ladies Max talked about? Or maybe she was like me and Gav, commitment-prone but too damn busy—not to mention picky—to just find someone to take the plunge with.

Not that it mattered either way. The girl was out of my life for good. She was nowhere near out of my head though, and that was scary enough right now.

I walked back to the dining room, smiling when I

heard Chloe's giggles echo from the table. Something like a monkey or a dying baboon sounded from there too. Stopping at the end of the hall, I found Gavin on the chair in front of Chloe, trying to coax the cereal into her mouth, while Max stood behind him, yipping and bouncing from foot to foot.

"You're an idiot." I laughed, secretly wishing I could be as carefree as Max was. The goofy ass made everything in life seem so easy.

"She wouldn't eat. Max thought it'd help." Gavin gave me a tentative grin, one that said *save me*. Chuckling to myself, I leaned over and kissed Chloe's hair, shutting my eyes as she pounded her little fists against the tray. I inhaled through my nose, taking in the soft baby smell that was my little girl.

Fifteen minutes later, I was in the shower and getting ready for work when the door slammed open against the bathroom wall. I peered out from behind the curtain, expecting Max or Gav, but found Lia instead.

"The hell are you doing?" I scrubbed a hand down my face to get the water out of my eyes.

She sat on the closed toilet lid, frowning. "We need to talk."

I moved back into the shower, pulling the curtain closed. "It couldn't wait until I got out?"

"No."

I rolled my eyes. The girl could've gone off to Hollywood and been an actress if she wanted—that's how dramatic she was.

"Well, talk. You've got five minutes, maybe less."

"Fine. I'm talking."

I laughed.

"You know, Addie won't even come in to see me at the Java Java Hut anymore. I mean, she's one of the only girls who understands me, but you had to go and run her off."

I stiffened.

"Can't you just call her and—"

"Damn it, I'm not calling her. Don't even have her number. *You* go to her place and see why she's stayed away. Not my job to play girlfriend mediator."

She groaned. "Why can't you give her a second chance?"

It'd been the same thing for a week now: Lia either calling to rag on me or coming by to trap me with her guilt-ridden words. I was getting damn sick of it.

"She's right, man."

I blinked, whipping the shower curtain back a little at the voice. Max stood against the wall with his arms crossed at his chest. "Get out," I told him.

I glared back and forth between the two of them, not liking the knowing looks on their faces, then moved back under the water.

"I'm not leaving," Max grumbled.

"*We're* not leaving until you agree to call and at least apologize for being a jerk," Lia hissed.

"You scared her that night, Colly. Did you know that?" It was like a tennis match, the ball being hit back and forth between the two of them, almost like they'd planned this sabotage—which they damn well could've.

Except that what Max said made my heart skip. *Had* I scared her? I frowned at the idea. If anything, I thought she was a sassy cat, all bite and attitude.

Or maybe that was her front?

"Didn't scare her," I said.

If anything, *she's* the one who scared me. All sexy and wide eyed and warm as she blinked up at me… Then I thought of her body. Again. Even with her in that dress, I wanted to lick her. But licking was off limits because the girl was unlickable. I mean, damn. She would taste good, I'm sure. Smooth skin, probably like warm sugar… I shut my eyes, imagining her hot hands on my cock in the shower, instead of the water.

"Dude, you jacking off in there or what?" Max snorted.

God damn it. "No. Now would you two get out, please?"

"Need to finish getting one off?" Max laughed.

"Eww, gross," Lia groaned, a slap sounding against skin.

"Ouch, woman, cut your claws."

Lia laughed. "All the better to scratch you with, my dear."

I leaned my forehead against the tiled wall and groaned, not seeing any way out of this other than doing what they wanted. "Christ, would you both just get out of here? Let me shower in peace. If you do, I'll call her when I get out. Promise."

"Pay up, ten bucks. Knew he was jerking off in here."

More skin slapped against skin. "Quit talking about my brother's sex habits. And I didn't bet you a dime."

I pinched my lips together, not wanting to smile, especially since I'd just given in, but the two of them together—all vinegar and oil—made for some damn good entertainment, even though it was happening in the bathroom with me and about me.

Once the door closed, I leaned back and squeezed my eyes shut to try to get the vision of the sexy woman out of my head. Had enough of her in my dreams at night and even before I went to sleep. Visions of her bent over my bed, naked, begging for me to take her…

Damn it. Showers were off limits. They had to be. Because having this girl invade my thoughts in all aspects of life wasn't right.

A little while later, I was dressed in my work uniform and sitting on my bed with a couple of hovering idiots on either side of me. One of those being my sister. "So, what are you gonna say first?" She bounced on the bed next to me, looking like an eight-year-old kid.

"I'm not fifteen, Lia. I know how to talk to a woman."

Max laughed, knowing how much of a lie that was. Again, I hadn't actually *been* with a woman in eighteen months—not many choices when you were off in the desert dodging bullets and avoiding IEDs. And even before that, Amy had been the only one.

Since college, the two of us had always been close. Best friends to fuck buddies, to…something more. But the second I heard her voice on the phone when she told me she was pregnant—eight weeks to the day I'd last been home on leave for my uncle's funeral—I'd promised her we'd get through it together.

Except I lied and, three months into Amy's pregnancy, I chose another six months of deployment rather than heading home. It wasn't a normal situation, but to me, it was the only logical choice. My only real duty at the time had been to stay with Gavin, Max, and the rest of our unit until the end. Part of me didn't care if I'd missed Chloe's birth. Not because I didn't want to be there or didn't love Amy, but because, for nearly six years, my life had been with my friends, making sure everyone in our platoon came home alive. Together.

My brothers meant more to me than anything else back then. And things at home were, in my warped mind, a fantasy. Something I didn't have a moment to think about—didn't see or experience either. Then the accident happened, and my time as a marine came to an end soon after that. But instead of coming home to start my life with my new family, I came home to a casket and a child I didn't even know.

My hand tightened around my phone at the thoughts messing with my mood.

Fuck me sideways, would I always be such a selfish man?

A hand slapped my back, jarring my eyes open. "You all right?"

I turned toward Max, nodding. "Yeah."

"Good. Here's her number then." In his hand sat a business card decorated with white-and-black lettering. Addison's name, number, and personal information were written across the front.

"Where'd you get this?" My gaze flew back and forth between the card and Max's smug face.

"Ran into her this morning when I took your truck to get coffee. It fell out of her purse." He grinned, unashamed. "We had one helluva chat."

Lia elbowed him in the ribs like I'd done earlier. "You messed her all up, according to Betsy. She ran out of that place like the devil was riding her ass."

Max groaned, rubbing his side. "Damn, you Montgomerys are abusive."

"What'd you say to her?" I stood, my protective instincts flaring to life. Didn't like the fact that he'd been alone with her—let alone talked to her. Not because I was jealous. At least, that's what I was telling myself.

He shrugged. "I *may* have insulted her. But not on purpose."

"Jerkface. She's my *friend*." Lia stood, shoving past Max to go out into the hall.

"Lee-Lee," Max pleaded. "Come on, I didn't... She caught me by surprise, is all." He threw one hand up and then let it fall to his side.

"I've gotta make this phone call. Go make sure Gav's not losing his mind with Chloe out there, would ya?" I offered up a sympathetic smile to Max, placing orders like we were still neck deep in Taliban fighters.

Nodding once, he left the room, his shoulders sagging. The guy was a lovesick puppy when it came to my sister.

I took a deep breath and let it go. It was time to man up and do what inevitably needed to be done—pride, nerves, forever blue balls be damned. I'd gone through interviewee after interviewee, yet none of them were good enough for my girl. Which meant Max and Lia were right, no matter how much I didn't want them to be.

The sexy woman I couldn't stop thinking about might just be the answer to my biggest problem.

CHAPTER 8

Addison

W HEN I DIDN'T RECOGNIZE THE NUMBER ON MY PHONE, I
jumped to answer it, thinking it might be about one of
the twenty jobs I'd applied for. But when my loud and
obnoxious ringtone earned me a dirty look from the
librarian, I was forced to answer with a soft "Hello?"

A throat cleared as I half ran, half walked to somewhere more private.

"Addison?"

I stopped, frozen in my tracks right in the middle of the
travel and tourism section. Eyes squeezed shut, I pressed
my palm against my neck, nervous. "This is she."

A breath of air shot through the phone. "Come back
for a real interview, would you?"

I cradled the phone between my chin and shoulder,
wiping my suddenly sweaty palms across my jeans.
"Um, who is this?"

Of course I knew who it was. I'd recognize his
voice anywhere. But his demand left me feeling not so

gracious. So bossy and arrogant, like I'd just up and do what he wanted, when he wanted, where and how he wanted it done.

"Collin Montgomery. Met you at the bar. You know my sister, Lia."

"Uh-huh."

He cleared his throat again. "So, would you?"

"Would I what?"

"Come over for a second interview. I'd like you to meet Chloe. I'll cook dinner."

Trailing my finger over the book spines, I thought about his proposition. No way did I want to give in so easily—not even when I was coming up empty on the job search. But to drop everything at his beck and call wasn't something I envisioned happening either.

Still, I was desperate.

"You there?"

"Yep. I'm here." I popped my lips on the *p*, pulling out a book. The title was *Twenty-Five Tropical Houses in the Philippines*.

"Soooo...you good for tomorrow then? Tuesday. I don't work Monday and Tuesday nights. They're my only nights off. Your hours would be six at night until six in the morning, Wednesday through Sunday."

"That so?" I paused, shifting the book back into place. The coolness of the books' covers calmed me as I moved my fingers over their spines. "Not sure."

He said something then—something soft. An apology, maybe?

"What was that?" I leaned my back against the wooden bookcase, sliding down to the floor. Pulling my knees to my chin, I tried to smother the grin in my voice.

There was something pretty fabulous about making this guy squirm.

"I said I was sorry. Damn it."

"For what, exactly?"

He groaned. "For being an ass the other night."

"Okay. But…which night?" I nibbled on my thumbnail.

"Which night," he snorted to himself. "Fine. The night we met and the night at my house. That good enough for you?"

As good as I could expect, I supposed. "Okay."

"*Okay?* What do you mean, *Okay?* Don't you think you owe *me* an apology too? You ditched out on me and Gav the night at the bar *after* we helped *your* friend to the car."

I *had* run out on him, sure, but what did he expect me to do? Fall to his feet and say thanks to the Big Guy for bringing Number Six into my life?

No. It didn't work that way.

"I did, yes, but you're too overwhelming and abrupt. Cornering a woman in a bar and basically feeling her up. Who does th—"

He laughed. "Feeling you up? Oh, don't think so. You'd *know* if I were feeling you up. And you would *like* it."

My face grew hot, and I threw a hand over my eyes to hide…something. Damn. This guy. The simple thought of his hands on my skin, doing what he said I'd supposedly like, wasn't an image I could escape either.

"But I *am* sorry if I *overwhelmed* you. I have that effect on people sometimes."

I pursed my lips. "No doubt you do."

He laughed again, the sound warm and much too

inviting. "Won't happen again though. An oversight on my part."

I nodded, because my voice had pretty much gone extinct. Sure, this guy, Mr. Macho Number Six, was hotter than Hades, but he was also ornerier than a porcupine with a bad temper. And for him to know my truth, how just the thought of him made my skin tingle, would give him power over me that I'd never hand to anyone.

"We can pretend we never met. How 'bout that? You're just a woman in need of a job, and I'm just a guy in need of a nanny."

Ah, there it was. The *official* title: His Daughter's Nanny.

"Fine. When? Give me a time, and I'll be there." For an interview only, of course.

"Tomorrow night at sex."

My eyebrows shot up. "Um, excuse me?"

He grunted. "I meant *six*, not sex. Shit." Something fumbled on the other end of the line, like maybe he'd dropped the phone. Unable to help it, I giggled.

"You still there?" He sighed. "And that fuck-me comment… You know I didn't actually mean for you to—"

"Yes. Duly noted. Not what you meant. Got it." I lowered my forehead, slowly knocking it against my knees twice. Knowing he wasn't all-the-time suave made him more human to me. And *that* made him even more attractive than he already was.

"You there?"

"I'm here," I whispered back.

"Yeah. Fine. Tomorrow, six. Chloe will be here, and my roommates will be working. They work nights too. It'll just be us three. That good for you?"

No. "Yes. Six is perfect. I'll be there."

"Fine, good," he snapped. "I'll be…here."

Snappy and clumsy Number Six was a lot more entertaining than broody, moody, I'm-the-boss Number Six.

"Collin?" Saying his name felt intimate. But it's not as though I could continue calling him Number Six—especially if I got this job.

Wait. Did I even *want* this job? I mean, I knew I *needed* this job—

"Yeah?"

I sighed. "Thank you for giving me another chance."

For a good ten seconds, he didn't say a word. And neither did I. Other than the pounding of my heartbeat in my ears, the whirring of the heating units above was the only sound around. After another moment passed, he finally sighed too.

"You're welcome. I'll see you tomorrow night, Addison."

"Addie," I cut in, sitting up straighter, wincing at my abruptness and not even sure why it mattered. "Call me Addie, please."

More silence.

"Collin?"

His voice was low, sensual. I shivered at the sound. "Yeah, okay, Addie. I'll see you tomorrow."

For a good ten minutes after I got off the phone, I sat there, backside numb from the hard, carpeted floor, shoulders aching from leaning against the wooden shelf. Still, the only thought on my mind as I twisted my hands around my cell phone was: *Have I just sold my soul to the devil?*

And if so, how much would he charge me to give it back?

CHAPTER 9

Collin

THIS WASN'T RIGHT, THIS NERVOUS TENSION COILING INSIDE my stomach. I'd been through shit no man should go through, yet never once had I felt the need to puke my guts out like I did now.

I paced the length of my kitchen, hands sweating.

So what if I had a sexy-as-sin woman coming over to my place? I knew what to do, how to talk to her, how to make conversation. I wasn't a moron when it came to women. But then Chloe babbled from the kitchen floor, and I remembered what this was really about.

"Not a date." I repeated those words in my mind a good number of times as I pulled my casserole mess from the oven. Cheese oozed over the top and I burned my finger, cussing as I dropped the pan on the counter-top. *Cook dinner, my ass*.

"All right, little girl. You ready for this?" Chloe's fist was wrapped around a wooden spoon she'd been using to pound against the tile floor. Smiling, I scooped her up in my arms and brought her with me into the living room to sit on the couch…and wait.

Fuck, if I didn't hate waiting.

"This is for the best, ain't it, girl?" I leaned us back against the cushions. Chloe immediately started crawling up my chest until she had her hand in my hair. Her tiny fingers grabbed the ends, and I leaned my forehead down to touch hers. "Yeah, baby. We've got this."

A soft knock rapped against the door a second later, and Chloe jerked away from me, arching her back like some sort of gymnast. Heart pounding in my chest, I wrapped my arms around her and stood to set her in her playpen.

I felt like a damn fourteen-year-old kid about to go out on a date for the first time. Half-hard, knees weak… If I'd had on boots, there's no doubt I'd have been shaking in them.

I opened the door, struck in the chest by the beauty standing before me. "Addison." I exhaled.

I leaned my hand against the frame, needing the stability to stay upright.

Tonight she wore a knee-length, striped skirt and a fitted white sweater beneath her unbuttoned, pink coat. I could easily make out the outline of breasts, her body like an hourglass that I never wanted to end. I swallowed once before meeting her gaze.

Not a date. Not a date.

Even in the near dark, I could see the flush on her pretty skin. The way she wrapped her hands anxiously around her purse at her waist had me realizing something important: I made her nervous too.

Good.

"Hey, can I come in?" She smiled and lifted one hand to wave, like I stood twenty feet away instead of two. It was cute. I could deal with cute.

"Yeah, shit, sorry." Other than a quick nod and those three words, I didn't say anything else.

Struck wordless by a woman. Gav and Max would've had my ass for that.

I moved back, arm to the side in invitation. Raindrops stuck to her clothes and hair. There was one on her cheek, just below her right eye, and I had to tighten my hands into fists so I didn't reach up and brush it away.

She wore a beanie hat and those same pink, fingerless gloves that looked like something my grandma would've sewn back in the day. "It's getting nasty out there." She shivered.

I nodded, helping her take her coat off, my fingers grazing the back of her neck as I did. She watched me the entire time, eyes hooded as I hung her coat on the closet door.

She cleared her throat. "You have a nice home."

Shrugging one shoulder, I started to lead her into the living room, my hand hovering by the small of her back. She shivered. Again. The soft smile grazing her pretty, pink lips about messed me up. But I decided I liked it more than I hated it, so it could stay.

Not sure what that meant, but I'd figure it out later.

"How long have you lived here?" Those big, brown eyes batted, her dark lashes brushing slowly against her cheeks.

I blinked.

Two times.

Then three.

"Collin." She snapped her fingers in front of my face.

"Eight months."

She nodded and bit down on her lip, and all I could think to myself was, *Let me do that for you.*

My stomach dropped at the thoughts raging through my head.

Not a date. Not a date. Not a date.

"Chloe's in there." I motioned toward her playpen, needing this beautiful, forbidden creature to stop looking at me like she thought I was the chocolate to her sundae. One snap of her fingers, and I would've been exactly that if she'd ask me to—no hesitation.

I think I liked her better when she hated me. For my sake, I hoped she still did.

Her shoulder brushed against my chest as she moved into the living room. The scent of warm vanilla came off her hair, filtering through my nose and hitting me like a sledgehammer. My throat went dry as I watched her move, all ballerina steps—fluid, natural, graceful— but with something else I couldn't describe. Something all Addison.

I squeezed my eyes shut. *This is fine, right? Thinking the thoughts but not acting on them?* I wasn't doing anything but admiring a pretty lady who was also a prospective nanny for my daughter.

Not a date.

"Hey, peanut." There wasn't a lick of hesitation in her words as she crouched down next to my girl in her playpen. Right away, I liked that about her a whole lot. It's something a good *nanny* would do.

"We call her Chloe Bean, or sometimes Beaner." I took a few slow steps toward the couch. "She was a

month early, looked all shriveled when she was born."
At least from what I could tell in the pictures.

"Bean, huh? That's cute." She pressed her palm flat
against the webbed material of the playpen, grinning.
Chloe lifted her little hand and did the same. "How old
is she?"

"She'll be one at the beginning of January."

"Can I…?" She stood and motioned down toward
Chloe.

I froze, not sure how I felt about letting this stranger
touch my girl. Knew it was going to happen eventually,
yeah. Just didn't expect it to be so soon. All the other
interviewees I'd brought in didn't even look at Chloe, let
alone want to hold her.

Still, what else could I do?

"Go ahead. She's weird around people she doesn't
know. Might cry."

But I ate my words, watching in awe as Addie picked
her up, carried her to the couch next to me, and plopped
her on her lap like it was the most natural thing to do.

"She's gorgeous, Collin. Looks just like you."

I stiffened. No, she didn't look like me. At all. Blue
eyes, yeah, but her pale skin and blond curls were both
from her mother.

Needing off the subject, I turned to Addison and
asked, "Hungry?"

"Starved, actually. I haven't eaten all day." On cue,
her stomach growled, making her face turn all pink once
more. I glanced down at her stomach.

Her sweater slipped off her shoulder as she moved.
My gaze snagged on her collarbone. Tan skin, smooth,
perfect…likely the rest of her body was just as stunning.

She didn't seem to notice my looking, thank God. Instead, she had my girl on her lap playing peekaboo. And giggling.

Jesus, if she could handle this, why couldn't I?

I thought back on my last months in the marines. Training with my men for combat, gathering and evaluating intelligence on the enemy—I developed offensive and defensive battle plans, for Christ's sake, so what was my issue with this one woman?

I rubbed a hand over my face, flustered and screwed.

Orders…I needed to give orders. That's what I was used to, what I had to do to keep myself in check.

"Bring her in there, and put her in her seat." I lifted my chin and pointed toward the dining room. When she kept playing with Chloe, ignoring me, my jaw clenched. "Did you hear me?" I stood and walked toward the kitchen to grab the casserole I'd nearly burned my hand off on before she got here.

"Ever hear of the word *please*?"

I glared over my shoulder at her, finding a smug smile on her face as she stood. Chloe clung to her hip and side like a spider monkey, already mesmerized as she grabbed and pulled on the end of Addison's ponytail.

"You do know the definition of that word, don't you?" Her lips twitched.

I narrowed my eyes. "I know it enough."

At my words, she winked at me—*winked* at me— only to waltz into my dining room like she owned the place. On the way to the table, she patted my arm and whispered, "Good. Because without manners, there are no life rewards."

And with her ponytail swinging back and forth behind

her back and her cryptic tone still ringing through my mind, she set my girl in her chair and then sat down next to her—in *my seat*, damn it.

How the hell I'd ever survive this night—let alone the nights to come—was beyond me. With all the training I'd gone through, all the combat I'd seen, from boot camp to the desert, to the throes of war and the sight of constant death, there wasn't a single thing I could've done to help me prepare for this woman.

CHAPTER 10

Addison

TWO HOURS IS WHAT IT TOOK FOR ME TO GET AN EMOTION out of Mr. Broody Pants that wasn't irritation or rudeness. And *that* was only because I'd dropped a glob of tomato sauce down the front of my sweater. Apparently the errors of my unfortunate ways gave Collin the sudden gift of laughter. And *man*, did the sound both make me mad and bring out the flutters of something unfamiliar in my stomach at the same time. Because seriously, any man with a laugh like that was a seductive demon in disguise.

Now I was sitting on his couch, dressed in some oversize rugby hoodie, while my sweater ran through his dryer. My fingers twitched in anxiousness on my lap as I waited for him to tuck his daughter into bed. His amazing, adorable, cherub-faced daughter with whom, after five minutes in her presence, I was already wholeheartedly in love.

As Collin shut the door to Chloe's bedroom a few

minutes later, I sat up straighter, burying my hands in the front pocket of his sweatshirt. His lips were tight; his head was down. I almost asked if he'd eaten something sour, but I thought better of it as he frowned at me.

Seriously. What had I done to tick him off now?

The arrogant, playful—albeit still broody-looking—Number Six I'd met at the bar was MIA. This sweet father and mean-mugging man was someone I didn't know what to do with.

"Let's talk." He took the recliner adjacent to me, hands clenched.

"Yeah. Let's." I gulped, trying to will away the trembling in my voice.

He leaned to his right and grabbed something from the end-table drawer. Glasses. Dark frames, matching his dark hair, which would only make his blue eyes pop. I blinked at the view.

Lips still pursed, he settled the glasses on the bridge of his nose. No way would I admit it out loud, but with those glasses, this arrogant man with a daddy sweet side had officially checked off another swoony box on my hot-man list.

Nerdy glasses equaled a weakness I couldn't even handle.

At my thoughts, I stared down at my skirt, attempting to think about flowers and rainbows—not hot, sweaty sex in his bed down the hall.

Focus, Addie. Focus.

"You've got questions?" He leaned back in his seat, holding a piece of paper in his hands.

Nose scrunched, I leaned forward and settled my elbows on my knees. "Not really. I mean, is she allergic to anything? Does she have favorite foods or a specific list of snacks that she's supposed to eat or not eat? Just kiddo things."

A vein bulged along his temple. If at all possible, he looked tenser than ever. One thing was certain on my end: I sure as hell didn't appreciate his roller-coaster mood swings, especially when we were supposed to be starting over.

"No, I'm not talking about Chloe. I'm talking about her mother."

I stiffened.

Wow. Okay. Where was this coming from? I mean, I assumed he and Chloe's mother weren't on good terms if she wasn't going to be watching Chloe for him when he worked. But then, what did I know?

"You don't have to talk personal stuff with me." I shrugged.

His jaw locked. "Kind of do if you're going to be my daughter's nanny, don't you think?"

"Okay, then. So talk." I flung my hand out in front of me. "Tell me about her. What's she like?"

"She's dead."

I cringed. "Oh God. I-I didn't know. I'm sor—"

"Stop." He stood, his six-foot-something frame hovering over me before he moved to the sliding glass doors that led to a deck outside. "Didn't tell you to get sympathetic on me. Told you because you needed to know."

My throat burned as I swallowed. Why *did* he want me to know anyway? Was he hiring me? Because I didn't get the distinct feeling he wanted to from his behavior this evening.

Most of the night he'd kept to himself, watching

me—watching Chloe and me together. I never once thought I had this job in the bag, which was why I was seconds away from a good night...before he'd come in here and dropped *this* bomb on me.

A sick part of me was curious about Chloe's mother, and the sad part was, it wasn't because of Chloe. More for the sake of her father.

He turned around and leaned his back against the glass door. "Met Amy in college. We were best friends." I watched his Adam's apple bob up and down as he swallowed. His eyes, so light, were the most expressive part of his body. This time, they went glassy. "Feelings were never supposed to get involved." He scrubbed a hand over his face. "The plan for me was to enlist after college, and she'd been fine with it...until she wasn't."

His hard eyes filled with a depth I'd yet to see in him. "I left anyway and she waited. Told me she loved me. I said it back." He sighed, a sound that sent shivers up my spine. "I mean, four years and we never bothered with the words, but the night before boot camp she's spilling her guts to me."

He stared off in the distance. In a way, I wasn't sure if he realized he was *spilling his guts* to me, the potential employee. But because I hated to see him suffer—or anyone else, for that matter—I stood and moved forward, touching my toes to his. "Sometimes a person doesn't know what they want until they almost lose it."

He frowned at me, lips locked for the longest time before he finally whispered, "Guess you're right."

I nodded, not expecting him to let it go so easily and waiting at the same time for more of his story. Only, it never came. Instead, Collin studied my face, a perusal with his eyes that both petrified me and made my throat dry.

Then he spoke, and his soft words crackled. Sexy. "You gonna do this, then?"

I swallowed and clenched my sweaty hands. "Depends on what *this* is."

His nostrils flared, the insinuation in my voice coming out in all the wrong ways.

God, what was wrong with me?

He licked his lips, studying me from under hooded lids. That look and his tongue alone made me want to run fast and far from this guy and his doom and gloom. Yet at the same time, my pulse spiked and every single inch of my skin seemed to overheat. What would happen if I moved closer and pressed my mouth over his? Would he respond? Pull me close? Cup the back of my neck or grab my hair? Either way, I'd be okay with it, as long as it happened.

At the thought, I took a quick step back, unable to contain the shivers dancing up and down my arms. Goose bumps scattered across my already sensitized skin as I moved, while everything inside me remembered what I was here for. A job. Money. A way out.

"I should go." To keep my sanity safe, I walked to the closet where my jacket was hanging, the words *run, run, run* sounded like a siren in my ears.

"You know what I meant, Addison."

Oh, I did all right. And it had nothing to do with the warmth suddenly pooling between my thighs.

"When?" My voice cracked.

"You start a week from tomorrow. It's five days on, two days off. I expect you to be here on time."

Unable to look back at him, I caressed a string

hanging from the end of my jacket sleeve. The sensation of the fabric was a reminder that Collin could most definitely shred me to pieces. Of course I was smart enough to know one didn't mix business and pleasure. Not to mention that the pink eviction notice on my kitchen table at home reminded me how much I needed this job.

"Then I'll be here."

His bare feet slapped against the tiled floor as he moved away from the glass doors. He stopped a foot behind me, reaching for a piece of paper setting on the table to my right. My lower belly warmed as his arm caressed mine and I shifted in place, squeezing my thighs together. This man had the ability to obliterate me with a single touch. And the crazy part was, I suddenly craved that obliteration more than my next breath.

"Two things. You get two hundred and fifty a week, paid out on Fridays."

"That's too much for—"

He pressed his hand against my upper arm, his chest now flush with my back. I shut my eyes and inhaled through my nose.

"Take it. If I could, I'd pay you more."

I nodded, not wanting to argue. With Collin, I knew I would need to pick and choose my battles.

"Also, need to know if you're safe to be alone with my girl before you start."

"Safe?" My voice wavered.

With his other hand, he tapped a knuckle against the paper on the table. The heat of his chest nearly burned through his hooded sweatshirt now. I reached for the sheet and he took a few steps back.

"Need to run a background check on you."

I pulled it to my chest and turned around to face him, but I still couldn't meet his gaze, my eyes flitting from his chin to his chest. "Reasonable enough."

I'd worked in a day care and knew what happened in the field. If our roles were reversed, I'd definitely be doing the same, no questions asked. There were too many crazy people in this world for someone to just trust a random person they'd only met a few times.

He cleared his throat, and I finally lifted my eyes to meet his, expecting the same nasty look on his face that I'd seen on and off all night. What I saw instead was something different—and unnervingly sexy for comfort.

"That gonna bother you at all?" His eyes were softer, his lips relaxed and slightly parted.

"What, that you want to run a background check on me? Absolutely not." I swallowed, wanting him to move even farther away because I liked his nearness far too much.

"Nothing you need tell me before I do?"

"Nope." Nothing to keep me from doing my job, at least. Clean and clear, with not a drop of bad to my name. The things hidden in my past had nothing to do with my ability to be his daughter's caretaker. Things like that didn't show up on background searches; they were tattooed on my heart.

He nodded, the movement slow. Every second he stood there, his eyes seemed to pierce me, his gaze never wavering from mine. God, he had this intensity I hated but was drawn to at the same time. Part of me wondered if his constant hardness was a cover for something else he wasn't willing to share with just anyone.

Before I could count to three, he moved in again,

his hot breath against my cheek, his eyes on my mouth. If I stood on my tiptoes and pressed my hands to his chest, maybe I could finally get past wondering what it'd be like to kiss him, taste him, feel his arms around my back, grazing my backside, curving around my ass as he pulled me against his—

A piercing wail sounded from down the hall. A baby. *Collin's* baby.

"Shit." He winced and took two steps back. "Shit, shit, shit."

I jumped at his pained expression and harsh words. "Is she okay?" I bit my lip, wanting to comfort him, to ask him if *he* was okay. His face paled as he lowered his chin.

I blinked, the sound of Chloe's cries bringing me back to the here and now. My stomach, a wretched ball of nerves, bounced and jiggled with the beat of my heart.

"C-can I get her?" I moved away, careful not to touch him, just barely glimpsing his nod.

Instead of following me, Collin stayed frozen in place, watching me. Not knowing how to take him, I turned the corner of the hall to walk to Chloe's room, not bothering to look back.

CHAPTER 11

Collin

"FUCK." WHAT HAD I ALMOST DONE? WHAT WAS I thinking?

The answer was obvious: I'd gotten distracted. Pretty girls and their pretty lips were pretty little teases to my underworked cock. Simple as that. Add in the fact that this one was good with Chloe, and I knew exactly what my brain had been thinking.

I wanted to kiss her.

I wanted to touch her.

I wanted to take her against my table, ass up, cock thrust so deep in her warm pussy I could feel it in the back of my throat.

"Shit," I muttered, pacing outside Chloe's room.

Five minutes had passed since Addison walked in there, and I couldn't find the balls to go in after her. Got so distracted when she asked to do it herself that I hadn't thought twice about letting her. Wasn't a good thing, especially since I liked the thought of her holding my baby—rocking her and loving on her like I did.

My chest grew tight at the image, and I shut my eyes, pressing my hands against the doorframe. Jesus. I wasn't supposed to like this shit. Was supposed to be *comfortable* with it, not *like* it.

On that note, I jerked my head back and reached for the handle, opening the door a half second later. With my fingers wrapped around the knob, I hesitated, watching my biggest fears unfold. Addison was leaned over the railing of Chloe's crib, rubbing her fingertip across my girl's temple…just like a mother.

Too stunned to speak, I backed out of the room and leaned against the wall in the hallway. I squeezed my eyes shut, trying to wash the image from my mind.

I couldn't watch this.

I couldn't like this.

I couldn't, shouldn't, but did.

"Hey. What is it? What's wrong?" Addie was there by my side when I reopened my eyes, her dark eyes filled with worry as she searched my face.

I sucked in a breath as reality hit me. Dear God… it was happening. For the first time since Amy died, a woman was getting to me—one I barely knew. And the worst part of it all? I wanted to get to her too.

To curb the anxiety brewing hot inside me, I grabbed Addie by the wrist and marched her to the door.

"Hey, watch it." She clawed at my hand, only making me want to hang on tighter.

"What is your deal, Collin?"

"It's time for you to go." I kept hold of her arm, but not as tight, and grabbed her coat, shoving it against her chest.

"What'd I do this time?" She lifted her chin—always lifting her damn chin. Taking pride to a level I wasn't even capable of most days anymore.

"Nothing." I let go of her arm, my hands itching to grab her and pull her close.

Instead, I walked to the door and unlatched the lock.

"Oh no. Don't think so, buddy." She threw her coat and her hat on the floor, crossing her arms just under her breasts. "If I'm going to work for you, we need to set some ground rules."

I tightened my hands into fists, fingernails digging into my palms. One step forward, then two, and she was in front of me, one eyebrow arched. Her curled lips saying *I won't back down*. And damn I didn't want her to. She messed with me, all fire and sass. And it made me fucking hot.

"You are the most ungrateful son of a bitch I've ever met in my life, and if you really and truly want me to be your child's *nanny*, then you better cut the attitude or else I'm gonna—"

"Stop talking." Couldn't help myself. I had to do it. So I grabbed her waist and yanked her to my chest, while clutching the bottom of her shirt with my other hand. Eyes wide and lips parted, I took what I wanted and kissed her. Hard. Unforgivingly. Relentlessly.

And holy shit.

I mean, holy.

Shit.

That kiss was so much. But it wasn't enough—never would be enough either. Not until I had her against the wall, touching her anywhere she'd let me touch her. Skin on skin. Just once, that's all I'd ask for. I wasn't a greedy man, just needy and desperate for the only woman who'd ever mind-fucked me before she actually fucked me.

Fighting against every instinct I had, I used my tongue to explore, only to feel her arms wrap around *my* neck and her fingers dig into my scalp in response.

With her reaction, my restraint snapped in half.

I walked her backward. She obliged, hands desperate and tight as she clung to me. Warm body soft against mine, pliant and so damn sexy. Almost as needy as my own.

My knee went between her thighs as I pushed her back against the door. She moaned against my lips, the sound going straight to my cock. Her tongue was wet, my brain was fuzzy, but I needed this. I needed *her*.

I lifted her higher, her legs going right around my waist. She sucked my tongue into her mouth, and I lowered my hands to her ass, squeezing. The skirt she wore rode up higher and higher as she writhed against me, until nothing but her panties pressed against my jeans. She shivered as I rocked her pussy up and down against my cock.

Hot. Tight. Warm. That's exactly how I imagined she'd be if I sank inside her.

She tipped her head back, bumping it against the wood. Her breathing was frantic, her chest rising and falling in time with my own. I lowered my mouth to her neck, kissing and sucking her skin. She tasted clean, fresh, and I groaned low in my throat, wanting nothing more than to bite her, mark her. Make her mine for just one night.

"Collin," she whispered, her body trembling as she moved. I rocked her harder against me, sure I was going to come from the friction of the movement alone.

"Please," she cried out, dry humping my cock like it was all she'd ever need again. And if this was the last woman I ever made come, I'd damn sure not regret it.

"Ain't gonna stop. Wanna make you feel good."

I'd been an ass all night to the girl. The least I could do was get her off…and enjoy myself at the same time.

She leaned forward, whimpering as she buried her forehead against my neck. I shut my eyes, blocking out everything around us and inhaling her hair, a smell I'd never forget.

Sweat dripped down my temples as I guided her up and down my length. My hands, as greedy as my lips, now digging tighter into her ass over her skimpy panties.

"Jesus. Addie."

She shuddered at my words, moving faster, softly crying through what I knew was a quick release.

Damn, did I love that sound. Hadn't realized how much I'd missed it until it came from her. And I wanted to hear it again, until she cried out my name next time, loud as hell so the world would know I'd been the one to do this to her. For her.

But then her breathing slowed and she kissed my neck, the sensation light and soft. Too intimate. Too much.

And that's when the high came crashing down, hitting me as hard as a truck.

I'd just dry-fucked my daughter's new nanny against the front door.

And I liked it.

"I shouldn't have…" I let her go, wincing as her body slid down the front of mine.

Face hot, I took a step back and looked up at the ceiling. Couldn't meet her gaze, couldn't face her for fear of what she'd look like. Sated or happy, pissed or confused…didn't matter. I wouldn't find out.

Yeah, it was too late to go back, but if I ignored her, then maybe she'd think it meant nothing to me. Just two consenting adults who'd…

Shit. Who was I kidding?

"Collin, I—"

"Should go, yeah. It's getting late." I turned and picked up her coat and stuff on the floor, my knees weak, my cock hard and aching.

One step later, I was back in front of her, still not meeting her eyes as I held her coat out. She didn't move to take it, just stood there. I could feel her gaze on me, her confusion, her tension too. The heat coming off her body was like a warm blanket I never wanted to take off.

"Coat. Put it on. It's cold out there." I motioned for her to take it, looking at the door behind her, knowing I'd never be able to look at it the same way again.

She inhaled once, blowing her breath out a second later, the sound like nails on a chalkboard.

But her shaking hands as she reached for her coat finally forced me to look at her face.

She wasn't supposed to be shaking. Was supposed to be sated and satisfied. And her dark eyes were filled with a blank emotion, one I understood all too well. One that twisted my gut even worse than when I'd been waiting for her to show up tonight. She wore a mask, hiding her true feelings, which meant she was either pissed at me or hurt. My guess was both.

"See you in a week." I swallowed hard, knowing I was being a douche, knowing I'd crossed a line I couldn't uncross.

"No."

I narrowed my eyes. "What'd you say?"

"No, you *won't* see me next week." Her movements were jerky as she slipped on her coat and hat, then her gloves. I loved those damn gloves.

"What do you mean? I thought we had a deal."

"That deal is null and void now," she growled.

"You're kidding, right?" I knew she wasn't. I'd screwed up, big time. I took a step forward, reaching up to cup her cheek but stopping short when she stiffened. "I'm sorry."

"I should have known this is why you wanted me over. To prove just how *not desperate* you are by keeping it in your pants. You're a twisted asshole, you know that?"

And then she was gone, opening and slamming the door in my face, leaving me behind and even more messed up in the head than before.

CHAPTER 12

Addison

Two and a half weeks went by without a word from Collin, not that I was expecting him to call. If anything, I wasn't ever expecting to see or hear from him again. I'd avoided the Java Java Hut altogether for fear I'd run into one of his cronies, or possibly his sister.

Luckily, June's Waffle House had called me, saying they were desperate and willing to train me, so the waitressing gig was a go. Carinthia's one and only greasy-spoon diner wasn't my dream job, especially since I made crappy tips and minimum wage. But I was surviving, and even though I was barely getting by, I wasn't suffering for naught. Once I'd pleaded my case with my landlord and told him my issues, he'd told me he'd give me another week to find a job. And once I did, I'd have to show him proof of employment and agree to pay in weekly installments over the next few months until I got back on my feet. It'd be rough, but at least I wasn't on the streets.

Today, I'd worked ten straight hours. Thursdays weren't the best for tips, but I'd gotten my first paycheck, so that was something.

Exhausted, I sat in front of my TV, prepared to do a little binge watching on Netflix. It was cheaper than cable and played some of my favorite classics. It wasn't five minutes into me time, though, when I received a call.

"This Addison?"

I leaned forward to grab the remote, then turned down the volume. "This is."

"It's Gavin. Gavin St. James, Collin Montgomery's friend. Remember me?"

"Um, yeah…?" I had no idea what to say or why he'd call me in the first place.

"I've got a problem."

And then I heard it. The unmistakable sound of a baby crying in the background.

"Everything okay? Is that Chloe?" I stood, my skin crawling as I walked into my kitchen. The clock on the microwave said eleven, and with it being Thursday, I knew Collin was at work.

"I don't usually watch her alone. I mean, I love the kid like my own, but babies kind of freak me out."

He cleared his throat, the sound of his breath heavy and echoing over the line. I could hear him talking to Chloe, his voice soft and shaking. Something *was* wrong, but why in the hell was he calling me about it?

"Gavin?" I grabbed my keys off the table and pocketed them. Phone between my cheek and shoulder, I snagged the ponytail holder from around my wrist and threw my hair up in a messy bun.

"I need some help. I, shit, I think she's sick, and

I can't get hold of anyone else." I heard him again, speaking in softer tones, the sound making my heart beat fast and my stomach twist. She cried, then coughed hard, and then he muttered, "Fuck!"

And that's when I knew. My instincts had me running toward my front door and slipping on my tennis shoes. I was out of my apartment and down the steps in less than twenty seconds. Then in my car in less than three.

"She just puked all over me. *Ahh, Beaner. I'm sorry, kiddo.*"

"Have you called Collin?" In the driver's seat, I put my phone on hands free and drove quickly from the parking lot onto the street.

"*So gross,*" Gavin mumbled. Not only was Chloe hysterical, but she was coughing too.

My hands tightened around the steering wheel. "Have you called her dad?" I repeated.

"No, damn it. He left his phone at home. I have no way to get ahold of him."

Anger pushed the words out as I said, "If you can't handle watching a sick baby for one night, then why are you doing it?"

"Because she wasn't sick when I started, and I was the only one available to watch her. *You* are the one who ditched out on him, remember?"

My eyes went wide. *What the what?* No telling what kind of bullshit Collin had been feeding his friend, but that didn't matter—Chloe did. "Keep her upright. Don't lay her down. And do *not* leave her unattended, no matter what." I clenched my jaw, fighting against the frustration pulsing through my veins.

Collin was the one who'd kissed me first. Collin also initiated the hump-a-thon against his door. Not to mention he then basically tossed me to the side like a used condom, breaking my pride and pissing me off.

"Keep her upright," Gavin panted. "Don't leave her alone. Got it."

"Can you call Lia?"

"Her cell phone's disconnected and I don't know the name of the bar she works at either. Max is out of town for family stuff, so I'm it." He groaned, and Chloe began to cry again. "Shit, I can't do this." At his words, I immediately pressed my foot harder against the gas pedal.

"You don't have a choice," I grumbled, running two yellow lights in a row. "I'm almost there."

"Thank you," he whispered, the words barely audible.

Two minutes ago he was bashing on me, and now he was thanking me. I wondered if Collin and Gavin drank from the same water—the roller-coaster-of-emotions kind.

I hung up and parked on the street a few houses down from theirs. It was a quiet, family neighborhood, something I hadn't really noticed when I'd come by the other two times I'd been here. There again, I wasn't the type to pay attention to detail either.

Chest tight, I walked up to the door and lifted my hand to knock. But before my knuckles hit the wood, the door was flung open, making way for a frazzled, messy-haired man covered in sweat and a red-faced baby with tears rolling down her face.

"Hey, peanut." Without meeting Gavin's eyes, I reached for Chloe, throat tight when she immediately snuggled against my chest. She was hot, and not just sweaty, but fever-hot and shaking. I'd worked around children enough to know when one had a temperature.

I pushed past Gavin and headed into the living room. Memories of what had happened at the door behind me tried to push their way inside my head, but Chloe's little fingers grabbed my hair, distracting me. She hiccupped, squirming, her skin like fire at my touch, and I nearly melted at the feeling—how she relaxed so easily in my hold. Her little heart raced as fast as mine, and I felt my eyes burn with tears.

"I'm going to take her pajamas off. I want you to look for a thermometer. If she has a fever, you'll need to get ahold of her pediatrician to find out what we should give her and, if anything, how much of it we should give." There was no way I was going to give her anything without a professional's opinion. No telling what her father would say—or do—if I did.

"Okay," Gavin whispered in a rush. "She's got meds for teething in the bathroom, I think. And a thermometer in her room in a basket with all her diapers."

"On it." Still not looking in his direction, I made my way toward her room. There was only one thing on my mind—making the little girl in my arms comfortable.

"Hey, sweet thing. I'm gonna help you feel all better, okay?" I lowered her onto the changing table in her room, wincing as she grabbed and tugged at my hair. Instant tears filled her big, blue eyes as I let her go. Not wanting her to cry, I reached over and grabbed a stuffed animal off her rocking chair, laying it next to her for a distraction. And even though I knew I sang like a dying hyena, I began to do it anyway as I slipped her onesie off.

Five minutes later, she'd stopped crying but Gavin was still MIA and her shaking was only getting worse. Her eyes were wide as she studied me in the nearly dark room, but there was a sort of vacancy in them at the same time.

Not finding the thermometer, I decided I was done waiting and walked out into the dining room, Chloe snuggled in my arms. Through the breakfast nook, I could see a shirtless Gavin on the phone in the kitchen, yelling at whoever was on the other end.

"…and I don't care if I have to come over to that bastard's house and wake his ass up myself. Somebody has got to call me back, damn it. And soon." With an angry growl, he slammed his cell phone down and dipped his chin. He'd yet to meet my eyes, but I couldn't exactly move away from watching him.

Not knowing what else to do, I eventually whispered, "Everything okay?"

He jumped in place as he looked at me through the breakfast nook. "Fine." He straightened his back and walked out of the kitchen. "Is she okay? Did you find the thermometer?"

I swallowed hard. He looked fierce, but in a protective way. "No. Did you get hold of the doctor?"

"No. Just the answering service."

"That's who you were just talking to?"

His jaw flexed, but he stayed quiet and bent over to kiss Chloe's temple. Her head was on my shoulder, her hands curled in my hair.

"I'm sorry, Chloe Bean, Uncle Gavvy is so sorry."

I had a feeling he was saying sorry for a lot more than just her not feeling good. There was something about this Gavin character that broke my heart and made me almost fear him at the same time.

"Listen, I don't usually panic. I just…" He took a step back, rubbing both of his hands over his face. "I can't handle it when things don't go my way, ya know? When I can't fix something…"

I nodded for his sake, not knowing what to say. This man obviously had some underlying issues. From what I remember Collin telling me, this guy was an EMT, an ex-medic, for God's sake. One would think he'd be a little more in control when it came to a child with a fever. Before I could even begin to dissect his issues though, his cell phone rang.

Shaking his head, Gavin ran back toward the kitchen, composed and determined once again.

"Okay, sweetie, we can get through this," I murmured to Chloe, swaying her in my arms.

I walked toward the couch in the living room, sat down, and pulled a blanket over both of us. Her little body still shivered, even as she snuggled against me.

Gavin came back into the room, his brows pressed together and a pad of paper in his hands. "Without a thermometer, we can't tell if she has a fever, so I'm going to run to my place and grab one. We're supposed to hold it under her arm and then add a degree." He seemed to be reading from his paper, tone controlled, his composure in place. "If she has a fever, we're to give her a teaspoon of baby ibuprofen, and then the fever should go down within a half hour."

I stroked the back of Chloe's head, releasing my bottom lip from between my teeth. "And if it doesn't?"

He met my stare, his eyes blank. "I don't have a clue."

CHAPTER 13

Collin

THE FIRST THING I NOTICED WHEN I WALKED INTO MY HOUSE that morning was how quiet it was. There was no TV on. No clanking of dishes or rattling of toys. Wasn't like Chloe not to be awake at this hour, since she was always up at six, no matter what time she went to bed the night before.

Frowning, I undid my belt and slung it over the dining room table. Needed to piss but needed to check on my girl more. No telling how last night went with Gavin. And since I'd been a dumbass and left my phone at home, I'd had no way to call and check on them. Still, if he had any issues, I knew he had Lia's number on hand for backup.

It was the first time Gavin had stayed alone with her without Max here to help. But Max had to go out of town for some family stuff. And because he'd been the one taking care of my girl whenever I worked, since he was now between jobs until next month, I was stuck without another option. Up until Gavin stepped in. Surprised the hell out of me too. Never once had he offered to watch her by himself, always insisting someone be with him, just in case. But Chloe loved him and he was responsible, so that's all I needed to know to feel good about leaving the two of them alone.

Burned-out and tired from the night, I slumped down the hall to Chloe's room, feet nearly dragging. I wasn't the type to need a lot of sleep, but sometimes a nap was in order when I worked nights. I wondered if Chloe would let me sneak one in.

The door to her room was ajar, and a soft snore that wasn't hers came from inside. The hinges creaked as I pushed the door open. My eyes widened at the view. On the floor, sleeping, was Gavin, while in the rocking chair, with my girl pressed against her chest as she moved back and forth, was the last person I least expected to see.

Addison.

Hands clenched at my side, I whispered, "Addie? What are you doing here?"

Her eyes popped open, all wide and surprised, yet she didn't stop rocking—just looked at me with hooded lids as she rubbed my baby's back.

I took another step closer.

Gavin grumbled and sat up, rubbing his eyes with the back of his knuckles. "Good morning, dumbass," he hissed and then stood. Eye to eye, he met my stare, more pissed than I'd ever seen him.

"What the hell did I do?" I took another step toward Chloe—toward *her*.

"Out of the room. Now." Gavin grabbed my arm, pulling me back.

"No. I wanna see my daughter. Get off me." I pushed him away, reaching Addison. She stiffened at my out-stretched arm, but her protective hold on my daughter had my insides twisting the most.

"You don't wanna do that, man," Gavin warned. "We just got her to sleep like a half hour ago. She's been up all night."

Jaw locked, I glanced at Addison again. Her gaze was down this time, watching my girl with softened features. My heart skipped. Seeing her like that made me feel things I shouldn't.

My fingers itched to swoop my baby up and hold her against me, but then Gavin pressed his hand against my shoulder, his voice hoarse.

"Give her time to put Chloe down. I'll explain in the living room."

Instead of doing like Gavin asked, I watched Addison, daring her to look at me again.

But she never did.

Scared out of my mind, I followed Gavin into the hall and went to sit on the couch with him.

"What's she doing here? What happened?"

Gavin turned to face me, dark shadows under his eyes and anger like a bomb ready to explode in his stare. I swallowed hard, not having seen this look on his face before.

"You forget something last night?"

"Yeah, my phone."

"And, what, you couldn't come back and get it? Call me from a landline and let me know?" Gavin rubbed his hand over his throat. The guy looked like shit.

"Damn, I'm sorry. It was a long-ass night, and the

department's phone lines were down. You had Lia's number if something went wrong. Why didn't you call her?"

He scoffed and stood up. "Yeah. That number she gave you? Disconnected. Couldn't get hold of anyone. All Chloe did was cry and cry. She wouldn't stop. And then she started puking and shaking. About broke my heart because I couldn't do anything for her."

"What's wrong with her?" My insides burned in fear as I took in his face. "Tell me." I turned, ready to go back in Chloe's room, but Gav grabbed my arm.

"Nothing anymore." His jaw flexed back and forth. "Called Wonder Woman in there. She took care of things." My nails dug into my palm at the mention of Addie. "Found her number on the fridge. Got desperate. She came. Fixed things. End of story."

"Shit. I'm sorry, Gav." And I was, so damn much.

He threw his head back and rubbed a hand down over his face. "It's fine. I mean, Chloe's obviously better now, but six hours ago I was seconds away from taking her to the ER. All that puking and crying..."

I shut my eyes and lowered my chin to my chest. Chloe had *never* been sick before. Nearly ten months old and hadn't even had a cold, for God's sake. So what were the odds it'd happen on the night when Gavin watched her on his own for the first time?

"You should've gotten your ass in the car and driven down to my work. Told me. I would've left and come home."

I knew as soon I said the words how much of an idiot I sounded like. No way would I want him to drive my screaming baby to see me, not when she didn't feel good. As much as I didn't want to admit it, he'd done the right thing by calling Addison.

"Are you *that* dumb?" Her voice sounded from behind, an angry whisper that had me cringing.

I turned to face her, ready to say my piece, man up, and apologize, but Gavin jumped in between us.

"Thank you for coming by and helping me out. Couldn't have gotten through it without you." Before I could call him out on the flip of his mood, he had his hands around her waist, hugging her to his chest.

My back went ramrod straight, and I bit the inside of my cheek, wondering what the hell someone had done with my best friend. Gavin wasn't a hugger, yet there he was, hugging the one person he'd sworn was no good for me *or* Chloe.

Addison's tentative, tired eyes met mine when he stepped away from her, only to wrap his arm around her waist from behind. Surprisingly, it wasn't contempt that I saw in her gaze but relief and exhaustion.

Gavin's hand cupped her hip, holding tight, from what I could tell. His fingers dipped under the edge of her shirt, and I gritted my teeth, wondering what he'd do if I pulled each one of them back inch, by inch, by inch…

I blinked a couple of times and then refocused on Addie. Only, her eyes were wide and sparkling, and those pretty pink lips I'd kissed were pulled into a smile—a smile that wasn't for me.

Jealousy wasn't an emotion I was used to experiencing. But as I watched Addison snuggle close to my best friend, I realized that emotion was hitting me hard and fierce—straight in the gut.

Worse yet? I had no clue how to handle it.

"I'm gonna go get some shut-eye." Gavin finally pulled away, his arm going slack at his side. "See you later, Ads?"

My throat burned as I swallowed. *Ads*? What was this *Ads* shit?

Ignoring me, Gavin left for his duplex, leaving *Ads* and me alone and five feet away from each other. It was quiet. Tense. She didn't move, and neither did I.

Well, until I couldn't take it anymore.

"You shouldn't have come here." I'd turned into a liar. If anything, I was thanking Jesus and all his special men for allowing this woman to say *Fuck you, pride* and come take care of my sick daughter. But I wasn't about to admit it. Not when all I wanted now was for her to leave…or beg me to push her up against that door again.

"Sounds to me like you should've thrown my phone number away, not *plastered* it to your refrigerator."

I took a step closer, unable to help myself. I might not have wanted her there for the sake of my sanity, but my body had other plans. "Forgot to throw it out. My mistake."

She snorted, the sound too damn cute not to grin at. And therein was the problem, because *everything* this girl did was cute. Which was exactly why I'd been on the phone with a nanny-finding service that specialized in *old* nannies—the grandma type. Just like Max had recommended. Not the kind with perfect asses, perfect smiles, and perfect lips that parted in an *O* when she came hard against the outline of my cock rocking against her.

I shuddered at the thought, squeezing my eyes shut, willing the memory to leave me alone. For good.

"You should be glad you forgot." She crossed her arms. "*He* can't handle being alone with her."

She motioned her head toward the front door. I knew who she meant: Gavin. But the woman didn't know a thing about him. "Why do you say that? He's my best friend and loves my girl as much as I do. Would kill or be killed for the people he loves—always."

"There's no doubt in my mind that's the case, Collin. But he's not right in the head. Anyone can see that." She tapped a finger against her temple. "I think...I think maybe he needs to see a counselor or something. I mean, isn't he an EMT?"

"Yeah, so?"

"Soooo...then shouldn't he have known what to do with a sick kid?"

I took a step back, gut going hard at the revelation.

"Not rocket science, you know," she added.

Fuck. I knew Gav was having some issues, just didn't know how bad they were. Movements jerky, Addison reached for her coat. "Doesn't matter now. Chloe's asleep, and her fever is finally down. The doctor said to alternate between Tylenol and ibuprofen every four hours if it comes back."

Dumbly, I watched her move around the room. My world was completely warped from this new reality she'd just dropped on my head. Gavin... Jesus, why had I not noticed the signs? As his former superior, as his best friend, I'd been failing him, too focused on my own shit to help with the issues he was so obviously suffering from.

"...and I'd suggest taking her to the doctor today too. She was pulling at her ears a lot, so she might have an ear infection."

I grunted—fucking *grunted*—because everything this woman said was right. Still, I didn't stop her when she grabbed the door handle and said, "You're welcome by the way, asshole."

CHAPTER 14

Addison

FOR THE FIRST TIME SINCE I'D STARTED WORKING AT June's Waffle House, the restaurant was packed. Except it wasn't a group of senior citizens in there for the Tuesday meatloaf special. Nor was it a bunch of rowdy teenagers hanging out after school. This particular clientele was a team of thirteen very large men—all wearing familiar-looking black shorts and knee-high socks.

Carinthia Irish Rugby players.

Either this was a sign from God that I needed to pack up shop and move to another town altogether, or I needed to find myself a man to get my thoughts off one particular rugby player.

Samantha, the twenty-one-year-old waitress who worked with me three evenings a week, swept over. "Sweet Jesus, I think I'm in love." She pressed two fingers against her lips, darn near giddy.

I rolled my eyes, knowing exactly how she felt. The

difference was this time I knew what I was getting into when it came to these men.

"They don't bite." I shrugged, not entirely believing my words.

Lick, taste, kiss on the other hand—not to mention dry hump against doors—that was a whole other story. I blinked away the image my brain had produced, hating how it was always so fresh in my mind.

No matter how much I told myself not to look for him, I scoured the four booths and the men they housed, doing just that. No way did I actually *want* to see him there, especially when I was pretty positive I hated him. It was more like damage control, a way to prepare myself if I needed to duck and run. Luckily for me, Mr. Broody McBroody Pants was nowhere to be found.

"Do you want me to take one of the booths for you?" Eagerness shadowed Samantha's voice as she bounced up and down on the balls of her white tennis shoes.

"Have them all." I winked and then paused. "Except for the one closest to the register."

Her bright eyes twinkled with excitement. Samantha was most definitely a man-getter. If she saw a man, she went and got him, no second thoughts and absolutely no regrets.

Shoulders back, ready to face the firing squad, I zeroed in on the guy looking at me with brown, come-hither eyes. Max was an attractive specimen of a man. You'd have to be blind not to notice, but he was best friends with the enemy. Thankfully, the enemy wasn't here, so I could at least attempt to be civil for the sake of tips. I had nothing against Collin's friends, but there was no telling what kind of BS the guy had said about me after our *interview* nearly three weeks ago.

"Well, look at you, Short Stuff." Max stood when I reached the table, wrapping his arms around my waist and swinging me in a circle like we were long-lost best friends. "Gettin' sexier every time I see you." He tugged on my apron as he put me down, his arm still semi-wrapped around my waist. "Nice digs, by the way."

I grimaced. And because I didn't do well with hug-gage or compliments, I gave a nod and an awkward pat on his shoulder in return.

"What can I get you guys?" I swallowed my nerves and looked at the blond sitting across from Max. He was attractive in a cocky-bastard way. He knew it too and seemed to want the world to take note. Blue eyes, white teeth, clean workout clothes—unlike his team-mates' dirty and holey clothes. A pretty college boy. I'd met enough of them in my life to know.

"How about a platter of *you* served with me on top?" The guy winked. Max set his hand on the table and groaned.

"Um, no. I'm not on the menu." My jaw clenched as I glanced toward Samantha. She was getting her flirt on, happy as a little lark.

"If I was cooking, you sure as hell would be. Put you on my table, spread your legs—"

"Does that really work for you?" I zeroed in on Blondie again.

His gaze perused me from head to toe. "Every time, pretty lady. Every. Single. Time."

I laughed—snorted really—but it wasn't the type of laughter you'd mix with humor. This guy was asking for trouble, and it'd come in the form of my foot to his head, if he wasn't careful.

"Leave her be. She's already been claimed." Max leaned back and folded his arms over his chest with a frown.

"And what is that supposed to mean?" I tapped my pen against my ordering notepad.

His lips twitched. "Nothing."

Oh God. He knew, didn't he? Collin's doing, I was sure. Probably pushed the story past acceptable limits for the sake of his pride too.

Ugh. I really disliked men. All of them.

"Excuse me." With narrowed eyes, I tucked my ordering pad into my apron and turned toward the counter.

There, I met June's gaze as she scrubbed down the tiled countertop. "Not your break time." A warning lit up her stare, as well as her words. One that said *Don't mess this up, or you're fired*. And because I was in desperate need of the money, I'd do just about anything to keep her happy.

Smile forced, I lowered my chin to my chest, hating how I felt more like a scolded child than a grown woman. But still, I blew out a breath and decided on a different path to take. If I switched a table with Samantha and let her handle Max and Blondie, this night might be more doable after all.

I turned back around, ready to do so, when the bells over the front door jingled and pulled my attention away.

"You have got to be kidding me," I whispered, asking the invisible God in the clouds if he had a death wish for me. Because being anywhere near *him* made my chest combustible.

No matter how much I told myself I never wanted to see him again, I couldn't help but react to Collin's presence. He commanded a room, the whole former-marine package written in his stature. Thick, black hair that curled at the ends. His smile and the dimples accompanying said smile. Then there were his square jaw and imperfect nose, both somehow making him look even more perfect than he already did.

I sighed in an attempt to even out my breathing. Whether Collin knew it or not, he made me into someone I never wanted to be: a bumbling, teenage-crushing idiot who took pleasure in getting near a fire—especially when the flames were of hot-man intensity.

"No way." I turned my head, finding Blondie now standing beside me. He followed my line of sight, a sneer on his lips as he said, "You and Montgomery?"

I stiffened.

Move, punch, kick, slice: the words were like little reminders screaming in my brain.

Yet I couldn't move away because that would draw unwanted attention from Collin. So when the guy pressed his hand against the small of my back as I turned to face the counter once more, I stayed as still as I could, praying he'd get the hint.

"Don't touch me," I hissed through my teeth.

Blondie cleared his throat, nodding toward Samantha instead of heeding my warning. I glanced over my shoulder to see what he was motioning to. Grin wide, eyes alight, she pawed at Collin's arm.

Then terrible, horrible, no-good Number Six, in all of his monster-height glory, leaned in to whisper something into her ear. She giggled, pressing her hand to his chest, and a sharp stab of something hit me in my stomach.

Did they know each other? Had he dry-fucked *her* against the door?

I looked down at the counter again.

"You gonna take that, pretty girl? Gonna let him lead you on while he dicks around behind your back?" I flashed a death look toward Blondie, finding an irritating smile flashing on his face.

"I don't know what you're talking about." I turned to face him full-on, chin high. "Now, if you'll please take your hands off me, I'd very much appreciate it." Around his blue irises, the whites of Blondie's eyes were red, almost like he was on something—drugs, maybe? From a distance, he looked put together. Up close like this, he looked scary.

His lip curled. "You need a real man. Not someone who—"

"Sit down, dumbass." Max was there, grabbing Blondie's arm, disgust and boredom clouding his face.

"Nah." Blondie moved in closer, tucking a loose strand of hair behind my ear. "Think I'm liking the view up here much better." His breath washed over my face, the scent of liquor and cigarettes colliding with my nose.

"There a problem here, McIntire?"

And then he was there. That voice, those words…the touch of his hand along my wrist.

Sneaky like a fox, fast like a lion on the hunt…

"Collin."

The sound of his name was like the fuel I needed to get out of this mess. So I used the interruption to take another step away. With his forehead creased,

Collin watched me move, but unlike Blondie, he looked almost...concerned.

No, that couldn't be right. Mr. McBroody didn't care about me.

"If you'll excuse me, I was just about ready to take my break."

My throat was drier than the desert in mid-July, coarser than the heaviest grade of sandpaper. It hurt to breathe, to think even.

Somehow, I managed to push my feelings away and headed back toward the break room.

"Addie," Collin called out, the sound almost pleading— but not nearly enough to keep me from walking away.

Ignoring June's annoyed stare, I moved behind the counter, untied my apron, and hung it over the rack beneath the counter.

"Taking my fifteen."

"I said no."

I froze at June's command, my hands pressed against the swinging doors that led to the kitchen.

"Samantha can handle it. And I feel sick." Which wasn't far from the truth.

"Not the point. You're my employee; you do what I say. It's not time for your break. This is the busiest we've been in months."

I shut my eyes, wishing like hell I had the ability to stop time. If I could, then I'd escape this entire place, no questions asked, no old-lady boss to tell me what to do.

At a rate below snail, I turned to face her, trying to gauge the anger in her eyes. But a smack and then a thud sounded from behind her, taking what little patience I had left and smashing it to smithereens.

"Oh God." I swooped past the counter, going straight for Collin, not thinking, just reacting.

Over and over, he whaled on Blondie's face. Blondie seemed to match him in weight and size, but Collin still overpowered him. The two of them rolled around on the tiled floor, tables and chairs crashing every which way. It was the street brawler's version of ultimate fighting, with a ring not contained by ropes or controlled by a ref. Not to mention a clear winner who was enjoying toying with his opponent.

"Stop it!" I yelled, reaching down to grab the back of Collin's jersey when nobody else would. If anything, their teammates looked almost amused by the fight— some laughing, others shaking their heads. Even Max looked more annoyed than worried.

I grabbed the end of Blondie's shirt this time as he rolled on top of Collin, but my hands slipped before I could get a good grip. Just when I thought I had a good hold on him, Blondie threw his elbow back and rammed it square into my eye.

Black and red spots danced in my vision and I moaned, falling onto my ass.

Samantha darted to my side, squatting down next to me. "Oh my God, are you okay?"

"She's fine." June moved in from my left, whipping her apron off. "And all of you need to get out of my restaurant before I call the law." She clapped her hands, and just like that, the men split apart, fighting over.

How did she…?

"And you"—she jabbed a finger in my face while I blinked, confused—"are very much fired. Pack your things and don't come back." Her lip curled in distaste as she motioned her hand toward the men. "Bringing this sort of foulness into my business. How dare you?"

My swollen eye watered, and my lips parted in shock. "June, come on. It wasn't my fault." Panic pushed a knot into my throat, choking me.

No, no, no. If I lost my job and what minimal money I was receiving, then I'd wind up right where I had been two weeks ago.

"Please. Just give me another chance. I didn't know they were going to be here or that this would happen, I swear to—"

"Save the excuses and go." She hovered over me, hands on her hips. With white curls of hair hanging over her forehead and dark-shaded glasses covering her blue eyes, the woman looked like the Abominable Snowman's even more evil twin.

From day one, this lady had had it out for me, looking for any and all excuses to fire my sorry ass. Dropping dishes: *That's money out of your paycheck.* Losing orders: *Stay after work and mop the floor.* Getting orders wrong: *You're a lunatic who probably can't even read.*

Yeah. So maybe I wouldn't be too bent out of shape over losing this job. But still…I so, so needed the money.

A growl pulled my gaze toward the guys. Max had his arm around Collin's shoulder, talking in his ear.

Collin, on the other hand, stared murderously at Blondie's back, just as he, thankfully, tucked his tail and ran out the front door.

Max took a step back as Samantha moved to grab a white towel off the counter. Hurried motions led her to Collin's side, where she pressed the material to his

bloody temple like it was the most natural thing to
do. Not amused, I watched her speak to him, her full
lips pulled down in a frown. Another pang of jealousy
swirled in my stomach, and I wanted to look away.
Except that I didn't. I *couldn't* was more the case.
Regardless of the fact that I'd just been slammed in
the eye and lost my job, the only thing I could focus on
was Collin.

And I hated him for that reason alone.

I reached for the seat of a nearby booth to pull
myself up, but two strong arms hauled me off the floor
instead. An overpowering sensation had my insides
going warm at Collin's sudden nearness, but the dizzi-
ness accompanying being vertical made it difficult to
focus on his face.

One hand stayed on my waist while he raised the
other as though to touch my face. I flinched, not fearing
his touch, but fearing the way it would make me feel,
and he dropped it away at the last minute.

Now that I was upright, he took a step back. "Are you
okay?" Eyes fierce, he studied me, ingraining me in his
mind, it seemed.

I shook myself from the trance he'd pulled me into
and opened my mouth to speak. But it was a failed
attempt because the sudden rush of blood flow that
pushed against my temples made my knees buckle.

"Addie," Collin murmured, wrapping his arm around
my waist again.

I jerked my chin up, staring at his mouth first, then
his tongue as it slipped out to wet his lips. They parted,
and I found myself moving closer, my body suddenly not its own. Regardless of the people crowding

around us, regardless of the pain smashing the inside of my skull, and regardless of the fact that I'd just lost my job, I couldn't help but feel like I was right where I should be. The heat of his chest burrowing into me brought safety and warmth—a protection I'd never felt in another man's arms. Even though I should have been raging mad, I couldn't help but lose a little piece of myself to Collin Montgomery. And for one single, solitary moment, he made me feel like I was the most precious thing in the world to him.

But then a throat cleared somewhere to my right and I looked up, meeting Collin's heated stare. Did he feel it too? "Your eye…" This time he did reach up, the touch of his calloused finger gentle as he rubbed it over what I knew would already be a bruise.

"I'm okay." Not really, but even with my life falling apart around me again, one touch from this unnerving man made me feel as though I could take on anything.

I've never been the type of woman to feel an instant connection to people—mainly because my parents didn't teach me how to be soft and loved growing up. Being in their world meant strict rules and no heart to soften the blow that came with life's crap. I don't think they meant to do it on purpose, but that's the way it was with them. Dad was closed off from the world, while Mom was disconnected from me as a mother, expecting me to grow up as an uncoddled woman.

"Jesus, Short Stuff. That's one hell of a shiner you've got there."

Collin didn't let me go. If anything, his grip tightened at Max's words. "I'll survive." I smiled at Max, feeling unexpected tears sting my eyes. As if he knew about the war battling inside me, Collin pulled me even closer, the hands I'd fantasized about since the night I met him melded into my waist.

My heart skipped, and my chest grew tight. I wanted to breathe but couldn't—which meant I needed him to leave. "You have to go. I just got fired, and it's your fault."

"That's fucked up." He sneered. "I'll talk to your boss, I'll—"

"*Good-bye*, Collin." I looked at the door, willing him to walk out of it and refusing to meet his stare. His offer to make nice with Boss Lady was…sweet, but I knew she was too stubborn to back down now.

Turning around, I could feel his eyes like fire on my back. But because he didn't need to see me break down, I refused to stop and continued toward the break room to grab my stuff.

The thump of shoes sounded behind me, followed by the jingling bells above the front door. In turn, my stomach dropped at the noise and my heart thundered harder than it had just seconds before.

It should've been a relief knowing he'd left. Yet I couldn't fight the sense of disappointment that lingered inside me. I didn't have time to think about what that meant though, not when I had bigger issues.

Once again, I was jobless.

I rummaged through my purse to find my keys. The sudden urge to blubber created knots in my throat.

"Addison?" Samantha stood in the hall just outside of the breakroom as I left.

With my purse slung over my shoulder, I turned to

say a quick good-bye. Even though I barely knew the girl, I still felt an odd sort of kinship with her.

Sympathy flashed through her eyes. "Are you sure you're okay?"

"Fine." But my equilibrium said otherwise.

She cleared her throat and shuffled her feet against the old tile. I knew little about this woman other than that she was in college and liked guys. But right then and there, I knew something was on her mind. "So...do you know that guy Collin well?"

And there it was.

"Yes." I squeezed my eyes shut. "I mean, no. Not really."

"Um, so you two aren't, you know...together?"

I shook my head, too quickly to be believable. "*Him* and me? Hell no. Nope, nope, nope. Not in a million and a half years."

But maybe two million? Ugh.

Her eyebrows rose. I tried smiling to make up for my weirdness, but the pinching in my temples kept getting worse, so my attempt was meager.

She bit down on her lip and glanced back over her shoulder. "Because I kind of just asked him out." She twirled a lock of her hair. "I just, like, wanted to make sure you two weren't..."

I was standing there on the verge of tears—jobless, with a bruised eye—and she wanted to talk *men* with me? God, I was too damn old for this—although at twenty-six, by most standards, I was supposed to be in my prime.

But still

My lips parted to tell her what I knew she wanted to hear—that Number Six and I were never together, and I didn't want *anything* to do with him. But even thinking she was going to go after what I never would have — *never wanted, right?* — irritated me to no end.

"We used to hook up on occasion."

"Um, wow. *You?*" Her nose scrunched up and I bristled, my nails digging into my palms.

What in the hell did that mean?

"Yep." Wow. Talk about comebacks.

And what was so wrong with the idea of *me* and *him* being together in the first place? I was a good-looking woman — albeit a little short and with a few extra curves here and there. So what if Collin was a drop-dead gorgeous man with piercing eyes and lips a girl would *kill* to have? I could totally have him — if I didn't like and respect myself so much.

"Well…" She chewed on her bottom lip some more, probably wanting to ask me if she could hook up with him now. Which was a big, fat *N-O*, mainly because I wanted to ruin his life like he was ruining mine.

If evil was a contagious disease, then I suddenly seemed to have contracted the worst case of it.

"Yeah, you don't want him, trust me."

"Why's that?" Her blue eyes were bright as she batted them at me. She was so innocent. So *not* the right person for Collin — not that I was or anything.

Good God. I was going to go straight to hell for this, wasn't I?

"He can't exactly, you know…perform."

"Really?" She scratched at the side of her head, confusion pulling her brows together.

I nodded. "He said it was his disease. Something about—"

"Disease?" She squealed, shuddering. Deep inside, I was sure all her future orgasms were crumbling into tiny, withering dreams at the thought. The worst part of it all was that I had nothing against her.

But I did have something against *him*.

"Yeah, real shame too."

"Eww, I will pass on that then. Thank you for the warning."

For a moment, I *almost* felt bad for lying, especially when I thought back to the way his finger had stroked the bruise by my eye and the softness I'd seen in his normally hard gaze. It was the warm, protective Collin I'd seen with Chloe—the one I couldn't resist, the one making me twisted up inside. Eventually Samantha left, waving at me from over her shoulder with promises of meeting up soon.

I headed toward the back alley, burying all thoughts of Collin. I had to focus on what was most important: my need to figure out my life's woes once and for all.

CHAPTER 15

Collin

THE PARK WAS QUIET TODAY—A GOOD PLACE TO JUST SIT and think, push my girl in her swing, and hang with my guys. We'd done this every Wednesday morning for months.

Chloe squealed as Max shoved her black bucket-like swing. Gavin sat on a bench, coffee in hand, looking down at his newspaper. And while normally I'd have been tickling Chloe's feet or sitting in the swing next to her, I couldn't find it in me to do anything but stand there, stare at the clouds, and think about dark eyes and pink lips.

"You thinking about panties over there, big guy?"

I locked eyes with Max. The smug smile on his face was wide as he pulled Chloe out of her swing.

"What're you talking about?" I took a step forward, tugging Chloe into my arms. She bounced and giggled, slapping my neck in excitement with her knuckles.

"You heard me." He laughed. "I see it, man. You still

can't get that girl out of your mind." He shook his head, disbelief something fierce in his eyes. "She's good, man. Sweet, smart…hot as absolute hell too. I mean, I know you like her, so what's holding you back?"

"He's scared," Gavin grumbled, still hiding behind his newspaper.

"The only thing I'm scared of is not being there enough for my girl. Chicks are a dime a dozen, and this girl"—I pressed my lips against Chloe's temple and shut my eyes, holding her against me—"will only be little once. No time to waste on relationships that may or may not work out in the end."

"Who said anything about relationships?" Max sat down in the sandbox, scooping up some sand with a bucket he'd found. Chloe watched, smiling, as he poured it out.

"Not gonna get involved with a girl when I don't have time."

"You were never supposed to *get* involved with her in the first place, remember?" Gavin dropped his paper against his knees. His jaw clenched. "She was supposed to watch out for your kid, be the nanny. That was it."

Yeah, I knew he was right—he always was. And no matter how many old ladies I had in our place inter-viewing for the position, I still couldn't find someone that equaled Addison. Didn't help that I couldn't get the image of her in the rocking chair, holding my sick girl, out of my head.

"See? She's perfect, man." Max sighed, taking off his shoes and socks. "No denying it."

"What the hell are you doing?" Gavin stood from the bench and moved to stand beside us.

"Feels good. Like a trip to the spa. You guys should try it out." Max shrugged, curling his toes into the sand.

"You know how many cats probably come here and use that box as a pisser?" I laughed. Gavin did too.

Uncaring, Max dug his feet deeper into the sand, as if to prove a point. Chloe giggled, reaching for him. "What do you care? It's my feet. If something feels good, I'm gonna do it."

Chloe screeched, slapping my mouth, as if to say *Let them talk, Dad*.

"If shit feels good, then you've got to analyze the pros and cons of going through with it." That was Gavin, always *analyzing* everything.

"Nah, jump on it. Make said shit happen. Life's too damn short to worry about things like cat piss." Max kicked the sand up with his toes. Chloe squealed and clapped in turn.

"But you could get a disease," Gav continued to argue. "Get sick and die before you get to do the things you want to do in life."

Max shrugged, making weird-ass faces, which made Chloe laugh.

"You guys done psychoanalyzing the sandbox?" I asked, tossing Chloe up and down in the air. Her giggles were loud and infectious. She was prettier than the lake sitting in front of us and warmer than the sun shining above.

"You done being an idiot?" I turned toward Gavin, finding his angry eyes on me. In his hands sat a ringing cell phone, and on the screen was a name.

Her name.

"Why the hell do you have her number on your phone?" My shoulders tensed.

Max stood, probably sensing my tension. When he reached for Chloe, I handed her to him, no questions asked.

One half of Gavin's mouth lifted into an asshat smile. "Wouldn't you like to know."

My throat went dry, my voice cracking. "Yeah, I would. Gonna tell me?" I moved closer, folding my arms over my chest. The phone kept ringing, and my palms itched to grab the thing and toss it into the water.

I swear to God, if he answered, I'd kick his ass.

If he didn't, I'd probably still kick his ass.

Head tipped to the side, Gavin slid his hand over the ignore button. My jaw clenched as he pocketed the phone. "What happened with you two, by the way?"

I hadn't told either him or Max about that night. The damn door that'd forever haunt me. Didn't need them ragging on me about things I couldn't control.

Who was I kidding? In the deepest part of my mind, I'd known exactly what I was doing when I kissed her. When I spread her legs and lifted her skirt so she could rub herself all over my cock. Seeing her all hot and bothered was hotter than anything else I'd experienced in my life, but I regretted, more than anything, the way I'd treated her afterward.

"Did you fuck her?"

Lips pulled back into a snarl, I growled at Gavin. "No. Haven't had sex in over a year."

Of course I could've lied to Gavin, staked a claim that wasn't even meant to happen. But I didn't want them to know what had happened between Addie and me. It was my personal fantasy, and I didn't want to share it with anyone, especially not those two.

"I call bullshit." Gavin jabbed his finger into my chest.

"Me too." Max laughed, bouncing Chloe on one of his knees while packing sand into a bucket with his free hand.

"Amy was the last one. Haven't had the time to be a dad and nail women. You guys know that."

Gavin laughed. "You've been an ass since the night you interviewed her, Colly. Snapping at everyone and anyone who so much as breathes a word about her."

"Don't forget fighting off assholes to protect said *girl*."

Ignoring Gavin's pressing stare, I focused on Max. "You would've done the same thing."

"Fuck yeah, I would've." He settled Chloe in between his knees, handing her a shovel. When she tried to put it in her mouth, Max grunted out a no and tossed it over his shoulder. "You just beat me to it."

"You guys have something else to say, then just say it." I threw my hands up in the air before crossing my arms over my chest.

Slowly, Gavin pulled out his phone, handing it over. "Call the girl. You know as well as Max and I do that *she's* the reason you're all messed up right now."

"No." I frowned. "I'm fine."

"The hell you are," Max grumbled, brushing sand off his hands.

"If you don't call her, I will," Gavin added. "You said so yourself: Chloe needs a female around the house, and since you can't seem to pick someone from that old-maid nanny service, the two of us will hire *her*."

I stared down at the frosty grass, thinking of a million excuses for why I couldn't call her.

What if Amy wouldn't have liked her?

What if she screws up?

What if she leaves and it breaks Chloe's heart?

What if she leaves and breaks mine?

I pinched the bridge of my nose. Nope. Wouldn't go there. Not again. Maybe *never* again. "I don't know if I can."

"She's perfect." Gavin's words were soft, but I heard them all the same. And as I watched him walk back to the park bench to grab his coffee, I realized what was really going on. My best friend—the one who'd sworn off dating because it'd mean inevitable change—had a thing for Addison.

Too stunned to call him out on his shit, I barely registered his phone ringing in my palm. But the second I looked down and saw *her* name flash across his screen again, I knew how damn right he was.

The reason I hadn't picked a nanny for Chloe yet was because I'd already made up my mind. And she *was* perfect in every way. I just needed to remember who exactly she was perfect for.

"You going to get that?" I looked at Max, finding a smile on his face.

Before I could nod, I slipped my finger over the answer button and brought the phone to my ear, watching as Chloe tossed a handful of sand behind her and into Max's face.

Screw my pride my dick and heart too. This was one sacrifice I should never have been afraid of. Not when it was for Chloe, the girl I'd do anything for.

Addison

I was sitting on my couch, surrounded by two piles of unfolded laundry, when I decided to give Gavin a call. I'd been trying to contact him off and on all morning. He told me he had a job lined up for me if I wanted it, only this time he swore it had nothing to do with Collin. But I'd been unable to get hold of him.

Ever since the night he'd called me when Chloe was sick, Gavin and I had become pretty decent friends. He'd call me at random, asking me about things having to do with Chloe when Collin wasn't around and he needed advice. And since I wasn't necessarily okay with him watching her alone, especially knowing how he'd been that night, I offered my help in any way he needed it.

He answered on the third ring. "Hey, Gav. You busy?"

"Not Gav."

My face warmed at the sound of Collin's voice.

"You there?" he asked.

"Um, yes. I need to speak with Gavin, please." *Keep breathing, keep calm. You've got this.*

"But I need to talk to *you* first."

I clenched my teeth. "May I talk to him, please?"

"Nope."

I threw my head back against the couch and groaned. "Why not?" If he was going to be short with his answers, I would be short with my questions.

"Need to talk to you about something first. Told you that."

Could've sworn I heard the words *Needs to eat your pussy is more like it* in the background, but my mind was scrambling like the eggs I'd cooked for breakfast.

"Shut up, asshole," Collin barked.

I spun a loose string around my finger. "What did you just say to me?"

Total déjà vu.

The wind slapped against his speaker. "Are you driving?" I unraveled the string from my finger and bounced my knee. "Because in the State of Illinois, it's illegal to drive and talk on a cell phone unless it's hands free."

"Damn it, no. She's putting that shit in her mouth." He grumbled something else, and the sound of baby giggles tugged on my already floppy heartstrings.

I couldn't help but smile as I thought about Chloe. I'd only been around her twice, but I kind of missed the little thing.

"Not driving. Just playin' at the park."

Playing at the park. Why did the image make me grin? Collin pushing Chloe in her swing, her little baby legs bouncing up and down as he did.

"Why are you calling Gavin anyway?"

"None of your business." My smile fell. "Can you just put him on?"

"I told you I needed to talk first."

I rolled my eyes. "Fine. Then talk."

"Gonna take you out tonight."

Shock pulled me into an upright position, and I stood so fast that a pile of clean towels fell to the floor. "Um, take me out?" I scrambled to pick them up.

"Gonna apologize. Again. Buy you food, return your sweater too. If you have plans, then cancel them."

"Uh, no. Don't think so." At the simple thought of seeing him again, my stomach dipped in both excitement and unease. "You're not going to pull that in-charge bullshit on me. And besides, what makes you think I want to see you anyway?"

"You don't wanna see me, sweetheart?"

I slapped my hand over my eyes. *Sweetheart?* Seriously? "No. I don't want to see you, *pumpkin*. Not when you got me fired from my job the other night with your ultimate-fight-club thing." I blew out a quick breath. "Besides, I just…can't."

"I need a better reason."

"Are you serious right now?" What was with this guy and his incessant need to be an asshole?

"Dead serious." He laughed. "I'll be by your apartment at six to pick you up. Dress casual. Gonna take you to dinner, and then we're gonna talk. You're going to get a free meal and an apology. Can't get much better than that, am I right?"

How did he even know where I lived? "I-I—"

"You're excited about seeing me, aren't you?" His voice went low and scratchier. I shivered and dropped onto the couch with a harrumph. Speechless and mesmerized, I couldn't help but sigh at the guy's holy-shit phone-sex voice. "Bet you've been thinking about me too."

I bet he'd make millions as one of those 900-number operators.

The line went silent, but I swear I could hear his lips part. Swear I could hear him smiling on the other end too. I wanted to see his smile again, especially those dimples. Both of them.

Because I was a glutton for punishment, I finally relented. "Fine. Six. Don't be late." And then I ended the call like a kid. But not before covering my mouth to hide my smile.

CHAPTER 16

Collin

I'D ALWAYS BEEN DRAWN TO THE WAY A WOMAN SMELLS, the different fragrances they put on for different moments in their lives. But the thing about Addie was that she didn't smell like she'd doused herself in expensive perfume or slathered on a load of fruity lotion. What she smelled like, sitting in my truck, was something I couldn't describe, other than delicious perfection.

"Nice truck."

Even though I knew this wasn't a date, I still felt like I had when I'd gone out with women in the past. Only this time, it was worse because it'd been so long since I'd been alone with a chick who wasn't my mom or sister.

"How old is it?" She rubbed her fingers over my dashboard, caressing it.

"Six months." I shifted in my seat.

She pulled her hands into her lap and knotted them together. Like always, she looked gorgeous, especially when the moonlight hit her face just the right way through the windshield. The windows were both down, and the temps outside were cold, but she didn't complain, didn't even shiver as her long hair blew across her face.

"And it rides really good too. Smooth, unlike most trucks I've ridden in." She fidgeted some more, staring out the window. Didn't like her so nervous. Hated the tension stirring between us too.

"You scared of me?"

She whipped her head around, looking at me. "What? No."

"All you've done is wiggle since you got in this truck. Wanna tell me why?"

Her lips parted, and my heart thundered in my ears. I needed to keep my shit together and get us to dinner in one piece. Looking at her lips wouldn't help with the cause.

"I'm not scared of you, Collin."

"Anyone ever told you you're a bad liar?"

She bit down on her lip, hiding that pretty grin. "Anyone ever told you you're an asshole?"

I laughed. "Plenty of times by plenty of people, sweetheart. Not only in English but in Arabic and Pashtun even."

"Can't imagine why." Her body seemed to ease up the more I talked. Maybe that was the key—she needed me to lead the conversation. I was good with that. If I wanted to get back into her good graces, I'd have to play nice.

"Tell me about yourself."

Her knee bounced in place. "Not much to tell."

"Don't be modest with me." I got off the interstate and drove straight through town. "Behind those pretty eyes, there's a story to be told."

She laughed then—the full-on belly type. I liked the

sound so damn much. Liked even more that I was the one who caused it.

"Not sure what your game is, Number Six, but flattery and feigned interest won't get you where you think you're going to go."

"And just exactly where do I wanna go?" I pulled into the parking lot of the old drive-through restaurant. It wasn't the classiest of places, but the milkshakes were awesome and I loved the burgers.

"Don't make me spell it out for you."

I laughed this time, liking her smile like I liked her laugh. It was genuine and real, something I hadn't seen much of. "Fine. I won't push, but you've got to be honest with me about shit."

"Why?" The question was softer this time, and my throat closed off at the emotion in her words.

"Because I need you. And I was a damn idiot for letting things get as far as they did between us."

By the time I pulled up behind the line of cars waiting to order, she'd shut down on me again. Her lip was between her teeth, and her knees were pulled up to her chest. I wanted fun, easygoing Addie back, not the nervous one. With this girl, it was like I took one step forward and about fifty steps back. It wasn't like the moments I'd spent with Amy, or any other woman I'd ever been around for that matter. And that scared the hell out of me. Different wasn't predictable.

A Garth Brooks song played over the speakers. I reached over to turn it down, but she grabbed my arm, eyes bright. "Good song."

I pulled my hand away, studying her profile. God damn, she was beautiful.

"Didn't think you'd like real country. Most of the women I've known prefer all that Taylor Swift shit." I shuddered, fearing the day Chloe would want to listen to it too. If I had my way, she'd grow up with a steady diet of Garth and Aerosmith, a little bit country and a lotta rock and roll.

"Taylor technically started out country." Addie leaned her head to the side, her eyes teasing. "And just so you know, I'm secretly a country girl at heart."

"That so?"

"Yep. Growing up, I spent a lot of time listening to my dad's old record player in our attic. The guy was big into Hank Williams and all things country music—Elvis Presley too." She stared out the windshield.

"Nice. A little Presley never hurt anybody."

She shrugged. "I didn't mind it. George Jones and even a little bit of Willie every now and then didn't bother me."

"That right?" I grinned wider.

"Yep." She stared down at her hands, her voice almost longing.

You can tell a lot about a person by the type of music they like, but with this girl, she was more of an eclectic mix of all things, a puzzle even—one I was dying to piece together. But this wasn't the time, nor was it the place to do it. And when I'd said I wanted to get to know her, I didn't think she'd actually buy into it. There again, I liked hearing about her, even something as simple as her music choices.

I leaned back against the headrest and exhaled, "Haven't been here since I was a kid. Mom loved bringing us here on Friday nights for root beer floats."

"I grew up in Matoona." She looked out the passenger-side window.

"Yeah?"

She nodded.

"Huh, who would've thought? I grew up in Carinthia. We were almost neighbors." Matoona was only a short fifteen-minute jot on the interstate.

She nodded again, still looking out her window.

"You're hungry, right?"

Her head snapped back to me. "I could eat." She shrugged and then laughed as she said, "Probably more than you can."

My eyebrows rose. "That a challenge, sweetheart?"

Her lips twitched. "Depends on the wager."

"Didn't take you to be the betting kind." The cars ahead of us moved and I followed, hating to break the moment if I had to stop and order.

"On occasion I'm good for a wager." She smiled, softer this time, but it was there, and that's all I wanted.

"All right. Then let's do this."

Her eyes sparkled. "What are we *doing* exactly?"

"Whoever eats the most food wins. Burgers, fries, milk shakes. You good with that?"

She set her feet on the floorboard of the truck. "Oh yeah." Her grin grew wider.

"Good." I wiggled my eyebrows at her.

She tapped her finger against her chin. "But before I agree, I need to know the stakes."

Okay. I could do stakes—not to mention I could win, hands down. This woman had nothing on my eating skills.

"I win, you come back to work for me and watch Chloe for real this time."

Her lips parted. "I don't know if that's a good idea."

I held my hand up. "Hold on now. Let me order. Then we'll discuss this."

"Collin, for real. There's nothing to discuss. We obviously can't be around each other on a level that's professional." She sounded so fucking sad, her voice all soft.

I couldn't look at her for fear I'd beg, but she was blowing me off already, and I didn't like to be told no—not when I really wanted something. And I *really* wanted this woman in my life.

As Chloe's nanny.

And yeah, maybe even my friend.

After ordering a bag full of food, I pulled into a parking spot toward the back of the lot and waited for them to bring it out. Not wanting to scare her off, I decided on a different tactic. One I was sure she'd respond to.

"Hear me out. If you happen to win, I'll leave *you* alone. For good."

She bit her lip, meeting my gaze. Those dark lashes fluttered against her cheeks, and my dick immediately hardened. I needed to move, adjust, but I couldn't tear my gaze away. Couldn't pull my eyes off her.

When she looked away first, my chest tightened in disappointment. "Do you want to know a secret, Addison?"

"Do I have a choice?"

The slow curve of her lips sent my pulse into action. "You always have a choice, sweetheart."

"Not true. Sometimes, you don't have any options. Sometimes, you have to take what's given and deal with it."

I laughed. "Always so serious."

She folded her arms over her chest, slouching lower in the seat. "I don't have a sense of humor."

"Bullshit." I laughed harder. "Now, can I tell you my secret or what?"

"Is this a tell-all? Because I don't know if I feel comfortable enough to—"

"Christ, woman. Would you let me finish before you go all judgmental on me?"

She clicked her tongue against the roof of her mouth. "I'm not a judgmental person."

"Yes, you are."

"Excuse me?" she scoffed, pressing a hand over her chest.

"This was a bad idea." I turned away, gritting my teeth. One second we were laughing together, and the next she was getting all empty on me. I didn't get this woman, but the scary part was, I wanted to—and not just for Chloe.

I'd admit that to no one though.

"I don't like to party with the rugby team. I don't go out, hardly at all. I prefer to hang out and just do stuff like this." I motioned around us. "I like being around people, but not when they're all performing like circus drunks."

She tipped her head to the side, studying me. "But what about that night at the bar when you approached me?"

"Ahh, well, I was feeling braver than usual." I smirked.

"Something tells me you don't usually have a problem picking up women. I mean, Samantha was into you at the restaurant and she's gorgeous, so I figured you two…"

"Would hook up."

She bit her lip. There'd be a hole there soon if she didn't stop.

"No. Believe it or not, I haven't been with a woman since Chloe's mom."

And why was I telling her this? My sex life had nothing to do with hiring her. Had nothing to do with a friendship either. Yet it was still important to me that she knew. No doubt she thought I was a player. Thing was, I'd never been the type, not even in high school and college.

Just when the silence couldn't get any worse, a knock at the window rattled through the truck. With it was a skinny, teenage girl wearing braces and holding three bags of food I was no longer hungry for.

Addison

I watched Collin flirt with the young girl serving the food. Her cheeks were pink, and she was eating up every word he said. It should've been my service to women of all ages to tell them to run as far away as they could. Because if they didn't, there was no doubt in my mind that they'd be sucked in, never to be released.

He rifled through the bag, searching for something. In a flash he had out four burgers and two large fries.

"I'll set the rules." I grabbed my food from his hands and set it in my lap, needing a distraction from the heavy talk.

"What're you talking about?"

"This…eating contest. I set the rules." I motioned toward the food.

One side of his mouth curled up into a smile, enough so I could see his dimples.

Be still my heart. I will not lose my cool over the dimples tonight.

"Hit me with them rules, sweetheart."

I rolled my eyes at his pet name for me. He'd see how *sweet* I really was after this.

"No drinking water to wash things down. We do it dry."

One of his eyebrows quirked. "You like things dry, don't you?"

I reached over to slug him in the shoulder. "Screw you." But I still laughed.

"Dry it is." He settled the food on the console in between us, his smile never leaving his face. It was irresistible really, and I couldn't help but stare at it while he opened the burger wrappers and set them in his lap.

"First one done wins?"

I grinned stupidly. "It's on."

"Ready?" His lip curled into a sardonic smile.

I nodded once. "Ready."

He cracked his neck back and forth, rolling his shoulders. If he were standing up, there was no doubt in my mind that he'd be bouncing on his toes like a boxer.

"On your mark…" he whispered.

"Why are you whispering?" I whispered back.

"Habit," he grumbled. "Now stop interrupting me." One lone giggle slipped through my lips. He rolled his eyes at me but smiled anyway. "Get set…"

"Oh my God, hold on." I pressed my hand to my mouth, giggling harder this time. If I didn't get it out now, I'd probably spit my food out all over his jeans.

"Jesus, woman. You need mental help." But he laughed too, and soon we were both laughing for absolutely no reason, and it was the best thing I'd experienced in a *very* long time.

"Fine." I held my hand up a few minutes later. "Let's do this. I'll count down from five."

He pursed his lips. "What, you don't like my version of a countdown?"

I reached over and jabbed him in the ribs, forcing a grunt from between his lips. "Nope. Mine is better. And…five-four-three-two-one-go." I shoved the first bite of burger in my mouth.

With a quarter of it gone, pride radiated through my insides. I glanced at Collin, finding his gaze on me. Shock and amusement both registered on his face, and I shoveled more food inside in return. I chewed, and chewed, and chewed some more… But then, like a snake devouring a mouse, he shoved an entire sandwich inside his mouth. And I'm not talking about a tiny McDonald's burger either. This thing was double patties with onions and ketchup and everything under the burger sun.

"Jwweeesus." I gaped, talking around my own packed-full mouth. He winked, and holy hell…even making a mess, he looked sexy.

In response, my competitiveness snuck in, and I piled a few salty fries inside too, along with the last of my burger. I snuck a peek at Collin again, finding him frozen, watching me as I unwrapped my second sandwich.

"God damn, that's hot." Ketchup slipped over his lips, and a small piece of lettuce stuck to his chin. I winked at *him* this time, taking a nice, big bite.

Unlike Collin, I wasn't going to bother wasting

energy on talking. Instead, I kept eating and chewing…
until finally my stomach began to churn. Regardless, I
shoved a handful of salty fries into my mouth, chomping, no longer caring about manners.

Damn it, I ate like a champ, and I'd win like a champ
too. I had to.

Minutes passed, and droplets of sweat poured down
my temples. He had the heat turned up, so I leaned
over to turn it off, swiping my forehead with the back
of my hand. Who knew competitive eating would be
so much work?

Just when I had my second burger almost gone, I
turned to look at Collin, finding him with his hands
over his stomach and empty wrappers and fry contain-
ers in his lap. Between his lips was a straw—half his
milk shake was gone too.

"Shit." I dropped my food onto my lap with a slap.
French fries spilled all over my knees and the floor.

I'd been duped.

And to think, I was stupid enough to make such an
important wager with him.

"How's the stomach?"

"Lousy."

He laughed. "I won. You know what that means,
don't you?"

I sighed, not knowing how to answer. Because for the
first time ever, I was very happy to lose.

CHAPTER 17

Collin

IT'D BEEN THREE WEEKS SINCE ADDIE AND I HAD DECIDED TO make things work, nanny-wise, and everything was running smoothly. We didn't talk about anything other than Chloe, which meant we were staying on track as far as the employer-employee relationship went.

But tonight—when I swung open the front door and saw her standing in my living room, dressed like a tempting, forbidden beauty—everything inside me flipped.

I'd frozen at the sight of her. She wasn't wearing her normal jeans or one of her comfy white T-shirts or hoodies. Instead, she wore this dress—this hot-as-fuck dress that should've been illegal. It was short and blue and hung off her shoulders, baring more skin than my cock could take.

I always managed to notice her eyes, but tonight, they stood out in a way they hadn't before. They captured me, sucked me in. She was a breath-stealer and absolutely stunning.

Then Lia had popped through the door and said: *Oh, good. You're ready. We'll meet you in the car, Collin.* Apparently my sister had invited Addie to go out with us.

Now, there I was, watching her dance under the club lights, and I somehow knew I was up against the biggest challenge in my life. I wanted Addison Booker. And I wanted her in a way that went beyond normal.

"What's your issue tonight?" Gavin nudged me with his shoulder, frowning.

I leaned back in my seat, eyes on the dance floor as my sister and Addie moved together to the beat. It was my first Friday off in a month, and whatever had possessed me to come out with these three was already jacking with my head.

"Nothing." I frowned, pulling my cell from my jeans. I flipped to Max's name and sent him a quick text asking if things were good.

He was staying with Chloe and playing Xbox with the little dude from down the street who'd just turned ten. Max told us since he was babysitting one kid, he might as well have another there with him. And because my sister was dying to hang out with Addison, she'd invited us all out.

Since I suddenly liked to torture myself, I'd agreed.

"Liar. You haven't been able to take your eyes off her all night."

I shrugged, not denying it.

"Take it you two are good?"

"Yeah." And *good* was the understatement of the century.

Gavin cleared his throat, sitting up straight in his chair. "You keeping it professional, right?"

"What's that supposed to mean?"

"It means, I wanna ask her out—wanna make sure there's no baggage needing to be packed up between you two first."

My jaw flexed, and my chest tightened so hard it hurt to breathe. Should've expected this. Just not so soon.

"Why her?" I asked, already knowing the answer. She was just shy of perfect. Anyone could see that— even Gavin, who'd sworn off relationships until he knew he'd met the one. I hated to break it to him...there was no way I'd let Addie be that woman.

"Because she gets me."

"What's there to get?"

Gavin's eyes darkened at my question, but his tone stayed light as he studied the dance floor. No doubt he was watching Addison like I was.

"You gonna answer that?" I leaned forward against the table, tapping my fingers on the wood.

"I've just got all this crap running through my mind. The bad kind." He squinted. I wasn't sure at what, just knew it wasn't the girls this time.

"You wanna talk to someone about it?"

"No," he barked, meeting my stare. "I don't need a shrink. I don't need nothing."

I held my hand up, cautioning him. I knew the signs of denial, and he was definitely suffering. A lot. And as a former marine, I still felt the need to be on guard for my boys, no matter what.

"I know someone who might be worth talking to. Remember the lady I saw after everything with Amy went down? She's a good doc."

He stood, slamming his chair against the table. "I told

you, man. I don't need a shrink. I'm. Good." He drank the rest of his beer in one shot and then took off toward the bathrooms.

"Gavin, come on," I called after him, hating how badly I'd fucked up.

"What's his deal?" Lia took a seat next to me, panting.

Expecting to see Addie next to her, I glanced up, shoulders falling when I saw only my sister.

I sipped my water, suddenly wishing I wasn't the DD for the night. "Nothing. He's just tired."

Lia grinned. "Soooo…"

"So what?"

She bumped my shoulder with her own. "Addie's pretty perfect, huh? Told you so."

Seemed like everyone had a thing for the woman. "Don't even start with the *I told you so* crap."

She rocked back and forth on her heels. "Wouldn't dream of it. Plus, she's not *my* type."

"*Everyone's* your type."

She took a drink of her blue-looking vodka, still grinning around her glass. I hated when she got like that. The girl had more secrets than anyone I knew but always seemed happy, no matter what was going on in her life. She'd been given the gift of everlasting happiness, while I stayed irritated and constantly pissed off.

"Where'd Addie go?"

"Bathroom."

"And you let her go off by herself?" I stood and headed toward the hall.

"The girl is twenty-six years old. Relax, Collinator. Think she can handle finding the toilet without my help."

"Don't most girls go to the bathroom in groups?"

"I'm not *most girls*. Don't think she is either. Now sit your ass down and relax."

In this dive bar, there was no relaxing. Fucking college town, college kids, drugs, rapists. Thoughts went wild in my head as I pushed through the crowd to look for her. She wasn't in line outside the bathroom, and I couldn't go in there myself without freaking a bunch of women out, so I went back to the table to wait, hating that I had no idea where she was. When it came to this woman, my need to protect came on strong and fast.

Minutes passed, and she still didn't show. Come to think of it, I hadn't seen Gavin either. Then I started thinking about what he'd told me at the table. How he wanted to ask her out, and that set off another round of shit-storm thoughts inside my head. My buddy was messed up right now, and the last thing I needed was for him to run Addie off. I was doing a bang-up job of that on my own.

Impatient, I stood and went to look down another little hall, searching the private rooms in the back. Still, there was no sign of her. When I didn't find her, I turned back down the main hall again, not caring as I shoved people aside and got dirty looks in the process. My heart thundered in my ears as I moved faster, sweat soaking the back of my shirt.

Maybe she'd answer the phone if I called her. Outside the main hall, right next to the dance floor, I pulled my cell from my pocket. But then I looked up and searched the room once more—and that's when I saw her. With Gavin.

Side by side, they were smiling at the bar, her laughing and pressing her hand against his arm. He was smiling too, happier than I'd seen him in a long while. The view did things to my stomach—almost tore my guts out.

"There you are, ya big idiot. Thought you were gonna lose your shit back there." I blinked, staring down at my sister. Her eyes, like mine had been, were zeroed in on Gav and Addie at the bar. But the smug smile on her face had me gritting my teeth. "Huh. Would you look at those two."

"There is no *those two*. They're friends."

"Sure they are."

I glared at her, jealousy rearing its ugly head once more. "She helped him with Chloe one night. They… talk on occasion."

Her eyebrows shot up. "Oh? Talk?"

"What are you trying to say, Lia? Quit beatin' around the damn bush."

With her hands pushed out in front of her, my sister said, "Just saying I think you might have some competition."

My throat grew dry. And sure enough, when I turned back toward Gavin and Addie, he had his hand splayed wide over her lower back, getting the laughs out of her that I wanted to get.

"Keep telling yourself you don't have feelings for her, Col." Lia sighed and patted my arm. "But if you decide not to admit it, then don't get pissed at me when I tell you I told you so."

Moving her cryptic ass forward, Lia walked toward Addison and Gavin, winking at me from over her shoulder as she sidled in next to Addie. Neither of them looked her way, both too distracted with each other to notice.

Damn sister. Putting thoughts in my head. I wasn't about to admit the truth when I told myself I had no right to feel things in the first place. Still, call me a selfish prick, but just because I couldn't have her didn't mean Gavin could.

CHAPTER 18

Addison

AFTER MY FOURTH DRINK OF THE NIGHT, I WAS FEELING pretty good. Kind of floaty, where nothing could bring me down. A happiness only brought about by vodka… and the crazy girl dancing across from me.

"Having fun?" Lia leaned in as the techno song we'd been shaking our asses to came to a halt. In its place was something slower, not a slow *song* so to speak, but something more sensual—a beat that you could move your hips to. Seductive. Warm. Exactly how I was suddenly feeling.

I hadn't done the club scene when I was in college, so this was a new experience for me. Exciting in a way. And more fun than I'd had in months…possibly even years.

"Yeah, I am." I nodded in case she couldn't hear me over the bass pumping through the speakers.

"Wanna sit?" She pointed toward our table.

I shrugged, not caring either way. One thing I'd learned about Lia was that she wasn't there to pick up men like most of the girls surrounding us probably were. She was there to let her hair down—her pink hair down—and just be free. She was a dancer, gorgeous, and in comparison to her, I felt like a frumpy schoolgirl who was ready for Sunday brunch, not a night on the town with friends.

Wait. Friends? Is that what these people were to me now?

I smiled at the thought, moving toward our table. Just before I could get off the dance floor though, a hand wrapped around my waist, and a hot breath of air whispered in my ear.

"Thinking it's my turn. Whaddya say?" Grinning, I turned around, weirdly giddy over the fact that Collin was asking me to dance.

But it wasn't Collin. It was Gavin.

Stomach in knots, I put on my best smile and said, "Sure." Even though the disappointment stirring in my chest said something otherwise.

Gavin was attractive and kind, but there wasn't a spark with him like there was with Collin. But we'd become friends over the past few weeks, and that's exactly what I needed. A friend.

"You seem happy." Gavin wrapped his arms around my waist, pulling me close.

"I am. Tonight's been fun."

For three weeks now, I'd been watching Chloe, the job becoming nothing short of amazing for me. Collin and I were getting along, and I had my friendship back with Lia. I missed McKenna like crazy, and we talked almost daily, but she'd be home soon.

For the first time in seven years, I felt almost settled. Content even.

"Happy looks good on you." Lips parted, Gavin reached up and tucked a lock of my hair behind my ear. I stiffened, taking in the dangerous look in his eyes. A look I wasn't ready to reciprocate.

"Relax, Ads."

My lips parted, but I still couldn't move. Had I read him the wrong way? Because suddenly, being Gavin's friend felt too intimate, too close.

"I'm kind of dizzy. Not sure if I'm up for a dance after all."

His lips pulled down at the corners, his eyes going blank. For a second, he looked disappointed, but it lasted no longer than the blink of an eye.

"Absolutely." He cleared his throat and motioned toward our table. "Looks like boss man might cut my nuts off if I hold you closer anyhow." He chuckled. "And I'm kind of fond of the boys."

I nodded, thankful for the moment to be over. But then I looked up and saw what Gavin had. Collin's eyes fierce. And fully locked on me.

"You guys ready? Looks like the college crowd has overrun this place," Lia grumbled, tapping her empty glass against the table.

"Yeah, sure." I smiled her way, needing to avoid Collin's death look.

"Think I'm gonna stay out a bit longer. I'll catch a cab home." Gavin took a step back from me, meeting Collin's gaze. Their stares held, and I swear the amount of testosterone in the room could have been bottled and sold to any man lacking. But then Gavin turned around, leaving Collin there with confusion clouding his gaze as he watched his best friend walk away.

Avoiding my stare this time, Collin stepped in front of Lia and me, leading us toward the front door. Lia circled a finger close to her ear and mouthed *cuckoo*, almost as though her brother and his friend's mood swings weren't that big of a deal. Maybe to her they weren't, but I felt like I was on a never-ending roller coaster of highs and lows whenever they came around.

On our way out, Lia looped her arm through mine and waved to a few people as we passed by. She was a natural at socializing. Nearly everyone seemed to be drawn to her.

Outside by the main door, a skinny, tattooed hottie with a Mohawk stopped Lia by placing a massive hand on her shoulder. He held her in place, ogling her with big, dark eyes. She looked both shocked and seduced—a look I'd never be able to master.

After a few seconds of the pair pawing at each other, Lia turned around and grabbed me by the arm. "Gah, I'm such a bitch. Addie, meet Travis. Travis, meet Addie."

Travis took punk rocker to a level that was beyond awesome. Piercings in every inch of his ears that matched Lia's. Tattoos leaving not an inch of ink-free skin exposed, other than his face, along with two lip rings and a nose ring. The two of them looked good together.

"Good to meet you." He shook my hand, his British accent luring me in. My face grew hot—even though he wasn't close to my type.

"You too."

The two of us stood in awkward silence as Lia jumped ahead. When I finally spotted her coming back, she was dragging Collin by the arm. His jaw was locked, like always, but for the first time that night, his anger wasn't directed toward me.

Lia bounced on her toes, pride in her eyes as she grabbed hold of Travis's wrist and held on tight. "Colly, meet Travis. Travis, meet—"

"The overprotective brother." Travis chuckled and let his hand dangle over Lia's shoulder. His palm hovered over her breast, and even *I* wasn't okay with that display.

A growl rumbled from Collin's throat. "And who the hell are you?"

"Collin!" Lia shoved his chest, giggling. I cringed. Family drama was not my area of expertise. "Play nice. Travis is a good friend of mine."

Ignoring Collin, Travis leaned over, whispering into Lia's ear. Her face lit up, bright as the northern lights, and the growl rumbling from Collin grew louder.

Deciding there needed to be an intervention to prevent bloodshed, I reached for Collin's hand and tucked him to my side. He jumped at the contact, eyes flashing as he studied my face. I held my breath, praying my touch distracted him enough *not* to murder Mr. Mohawk Man. If there was one thing I'd learned over the past month, it was that Collin had a temper.

"I think I'm going to stay behind. You two run along home. Make sure Max isn't torturing my niece," Lia said.

At the mention of Max, Collin whipped his head toward her. "He's gonna come looking for you, ya know."

A look of challenge spread across Lia's face—with something like fear mixed in. But because Lia was the queen at hiding things—even more so than her brother, it seemed the look disappeared as quickly as it had appeared.

"Doubt he'll find me."

Before I could say my good-bye, Lia was off, hand in hand with her sexy rocker guy, leaving me outside in the dark with Collin.

"Christ," he hissed, pulling me with him. "Can this night get any worse?"

Struggling to keep up with his pace, I yanked my hand back.

"What're you doing?" He stopped, turning to face me.

"Walking at a normal pace, maybe?" I snapped.

"You're too slow. Gotta get out of here before I do something I'll regret." He reached down to grab my hand again, but I pulled it back to my side.

"Maybe if you'd ask me politely to hurry up, then I would. But it's hard to walk in heels on this bumpy road." Which is why I shouldn't have worn the stupid things in the first place.

"Then let me help you with that."

Before I could say no, he wrapped one arm around my waist, and the other behind my knees, lifting me and cradling me to his chest.

"What the… Put me down!" I laughed, not nearly as annoyed as I wanted to be.

"Nah, I kinda like toting you around like this." He winked at me, the warmth of his breath hitting my cheek. "Makes me feel like a badass."

I snorted. "Or a weirdo is more like it." A weirdo who *really* liked being this close to her boss.

"Besides, this is a bad part of town and—"

"There *is* no bad part of Carinthia."

"Maybe there is, and you just don't know it." He squeezed my side and grinned. "Now stop talking and let me get you to the car. I've gotta get home, talk to Max... He'll know more than me about who Lia's got herself hooked up with."

Frowning, I let my chin fall to my chest, worry for my friend at the forefront of my mind. I didn't know Lia that well, but I cared about her. And if Collin was worried about her, I couldn't help but be that way too.

"What was that back in the club with Gavin, by the way?" We got to his truck door, and he slowly set me down on my feet, keeping a hand along my waist the entire time.

"What are you talking about?" I swatted my wild hair from my face, trying not to arch into his hold.

"You like him."

"Well, yeah, he's a good friend, and I—"

"Not what I meant." Two steps in and he had me backed me against the truck door, his movements slow, sure, and completely sensual. He trapped me there, his hands on either side of my body.

"W-what did you mean then?" I licked my lips, and his eyes darted to my mouth before he flicked his gaze back up again.

"You want to kiss him?"

I blinked. "Kiss him?"

He nodded.

Never in my life had I seen eyes as feral as Collin's were. Darkened by the night, with hints of blue that sparkled from the streetlight.

"There's nothing between us but friendship, so no, I don't want to kiss him."

"You sure?" He lifted his hand, trailing his finger down the side of my cheek.

My breath quickened at his touch. Goose bumps danced along my arms, my sudden shiver not caused by the wind blowing around us. The soft sound of music echoed from the bar we'd just been in, but right then and there, the loudest thing I could hear was my heart beating in my ears. "I'm sure."

He hummed, amusement and heat flashing in his eyes. "You looking at me like that goes against the rules, sweetheart."

"I didn't know there were rules. You didn't explain them to me, and I've been with you all night." My words were said on a whispered gasp, and his nostrils flared in response. He moved in closer. Only his clothes and mine separated our flesh.

"Sometimes, Addie, the rules are unspoken."

He lowered his chin to his chest. Just when one of his massive hands gripped the hem of my dress, pulling it up, and up, and up…his cell phone rang.

"Fuck." He lowered his forehead to mine and I shut my eyes, unable to catch my breath.

Fuck was right.

Job, job, money, money.

I repeated the mantra in my head, needing to remember, once and for all, that the rules he'd spoken of—the unspoken ones?—were *not* the type to be broken.

CHAPTER 19

Addison

THE MOST BEAUTIFUL SOUND WAS COMING FROM CHLOE'S room, and since just the three of us were here tonight—and only two of us who could talk—I knew exactly who the sound was coming from.

Invading their privacy wasn't one of my most respectful moments, but I couldn't help myself. Hearing Collin sing an old Willie Nelson song to Chloe was probably the sexiest thing I'd ever experienced in my life. Add that it was one of my favorite songs, and I was damn near melting by the time he stepped out of her bedroom.

> *Maybe I didn't hold you*
> *All those lonely, lonely times.*
> *I guess I never told you*
> *That I am so happy you're mine…*

On and on he went, his voice cracking as he sang the words with hoarse elegance.

Tears filled my eyes as I leaned against the door-frame and watched him rock her. It was one of those moments I'd never forget—never *want* to forget. There really wasn't anything more beautiful than a father and his daughter.

Once he was done, I decided it'd be better to announce my appearance rather than to be discovered.

"Hey," I whispered.

He jerked his head back in surprise. And were his cheeks pink? I bit my lip, trying to point my smile toward Chloe, who was tucked in his arms and already dressed in her pajamas. She yawned and laid her head against Collin's chest.

"Sorry, I didn't mean to scare you, just figured since you gave me a key…"

"It's fine." He cleared his throat and handed Chloe over with not a lick of hesitation. I loved how he'd entrusted me to be a part of her life in such a short time.

"Hey, beautiful." I brought my lips to her forehead, inhaling. She smelled like baby and her daddy. A scent so heavenly I wanted to wear it as perfume.

"She's really tired tonight. Probably won't take her long to fall asleep." He took a step back and tucked his hands into his black work slacks. His hair was damp, likely from a shower, and droplets were spilling down his temples. I sighed and looked away, trying to contain the beat of my heart.

I tossed Chloe into the air, and her eyes went wide. *Sleepy, my butt.*

The giggles coming out of her mouth proved her daddy wrong. I knew I had at least another hour of munchkin time.

"You good then?"

So entranced by the little dimples on her cheeks—
the ones mirroring her father's—I'd almost forgotten
he was standing there. So I met his stare, expecting the
normal brood and gloom, but instead finding a softness
on his face I'd been glimpsing more of over the past
few days. Ever since the parking lot incident last Friday
night, the moments we shared seemed to be shifting. He
wasn't angry all the time anymore, while I felt a sense
of peace I hadn't experienced in a long while. I'd like
to say it was from my new job security, but deep down
inside I knew the truth. Collin was getting to me.

"I'm good."

He grinned, I smiled, and between us, Chloe babbled
and beat on my neck with her fists.

A few minutes later, Collin was gone, leaving us
two girls alone for the night. "So, little girl. Tell me I
shouldn't like your daddy the way I do." She babbled
and yanked on my hair. I snorted in response. "My
thoughts exactly."

She giggled as if knowing what I was saying, so
I lifted her up high and blew a raspberry over her
tummy to reward her for being so stinking cute. Her
little laughter grew louder and louder, until all I could
hear in the house were her squeals and my weird
mouth noises.

This is exactly what I imagined mothering would be
like someday. Not that I wanted to become *Chloe's* mom;
I just more or less loved the idea of becoming a mom.

I'd always been drawn to children, even in high
school when I took child development classes and did
course work at a day care. My parents, on the other

hand, didn't find my career choices worthy, which was one of the main reasons for the distance between us.

I sighed. "You don't know how lucky you've got it, kiddo." She snuggled against me, so attuned to my words. It's crazy how an almost one-year-old had suddenly become my new best friend.

Two hours later, after I got Chloe settled down for the night in her crib, I scooped up the remote control and flipped on the DVR. The last time I was here, I'd recorded a movie and I was dying to finish it. And since the luxury of premium cable wasn't in the cards for me at home, this was my only way.

Once midnight rolled around, and I'd shut off all the lights, I sprawled out on the sofa and snuggled with my pillow and a blanket. On cue, my eyes began to close. Exhaustion was a feat to overcome now that I worked these strange hours. Luckily, I was the type of person who could snooze anywhere.

Needless to say, I drifted off quickly, completely relaxed. But right when I felt myself being taken over by my dreams, the front door flung open, making way for a staggering couple: Max and some random girl with red hair down to the top of her butt.

Taken off guard, I hid under the blanket with my eyes and the top of my head uncovered. Everything in the room was quiet, except for the sound of slurping kisses and heavy moans. Biting down on my thumbnail, I waited for them to notice me, but as Max lifted the girl onto the dining room table and proceeded to unbuckle his pants, I quickly learned they were oblivious. And I was also discovering what it was like to be an official voyeur.

And oh, what I learned.

Max liked it rough.

This girl liked it hard.

And I liked how the ceiling looked in the moonlight much more than I liked Max's butt cheeks.

"Yes. Harder, Max. God, yes. Please...harder, harder, *harder*."

I giggled behind my hand, my eyes watering so hard I couldn't contain my snort. But my laughter wasn't what broke their moment. The creak of the door and another male voice did the job instead.

"You awake, Addie? I got off early and... What the hell?" The door slammed against the wall. Up popped Max, his girl scrambling to get herself covered at the same time with her shirt.

"Colly, you're off early," Max said, doing little to make himself decent.

"No shit, moron." And then he jabbed a finger toward me. On the couch. And what did I do? I waved.

"Short Stuff!" Max waved back, taking his time to pull up his boxer briefs. "Good to see you." He winked at me, like I *hadn't* just seen his bare ass.

"Um..." I pointed down to his pants, the jeans still wrapped around his ankles, making me snort even louder with laughter.

Collin, on the other hand, didn't look a bit amused. "What the hell do you think you're doing?"

"Nothing." Casual, cool, collected, Max finally pulled his jeans up, stepping back from the girl on the table. Her face was red—I could see it even in the dark—and I offered her a sympathetic smile in return.

I stood and motioned toward the hall. "So I, uh...I think I'll just go check on Chloe then."

"Don't leave on my account." Max's grin grew wider as he stared down at my boobs in my pajama shirt.

Groaning, Collin walked into the living room, toward me, throwing the blanket I'd been holding around my shoulders. "It's late. Stay here tonight. No need to be driving home."

I should've asked him why he was home so early. Should've tried the conversation thing with him too. But instead, all I could say were two little, very unimportant words. "Sounds good."

He nodded once, a dismissal—always a dismissal with me. I felt almost as humiliated as the girl Max was opening the door for, the one he smacked on the ass as she walked out of the house.

Once I made it inside Collin's room, I stood by the door, curious to hear what went down between the two friends.

"...dumbass. And in front of *her*?" Collin.

"I know, man, but Jesus. I can't always take them to their place. And I thought Chloe was at Lia's tonight." Something hard slammed against a wall or a table. I jumped at the noise, biting my lip as I looked across the hall at Chloe's closed door.

"You're a dick."

"Screw you. We can't all be perfect."

Collin groaned. "What's that supposed to mean?"

"It means we're not all celibate douche bags. We like sex. We *have* sex. What we don't do is wait around for it like you do."

"Watch your tongue." Collin hissed, the sound sending creepy vibes up my spine. I rubbed my hands over my upper arms to fight the chills.

"News flash, asshole. This isn't Iraq. You don't get to control the situation. And you sure as shit don't get to control my sex life."

"Get out."

"Screw you. I live here. I'm Chloe Bean's uncle. I help pay the mortgage on this place, so if I want to fuck a girl in the house, I will."

"Don't make me shove my fist into your face, Maxwell."

"Don't make me call you a pussy either. Oh. Wait." Max laughed once. "You *are* a pussy. Too afraid to go after what you want. Too terrified she'll—"

There was a thud. Then a crash. And I'd heard just about enough.

It was like I'd stepped into a frat house, with two guys wrestling on the floor, furniture falling, the rugs spun in all different directions. There were no fists, just a lot of grunting and... Wait.

Were they pulling each other's *hair*?

"Knock it off!" I half whispered, half yelled, not wanting Chloe to hear her father and pseudo-uncle going at it like maniacs.

Neither paid a bit of attention to me, so I walked straight to the kitchen, grabbed two giant cups of water, and hustled back to them.

"One more chance, you idiots. Knock. It. Off." Still no response. So I did what any referee would do. I dumped the cups of water on them.

"Wooo, baby." Max threw his head and smirked up at me. Water dripped down his cheeks, over his mouth, and onto the floor. I'd got him square in the face. "Let's throw you into the mix, Short Stuff. Add a little mud and a white T-shirt while we're at it."

I lifted my chin, pride radiating through my chest. Until I got a look at Collin.

If glares could kill, I'd be a dead woman from that one look alone. His fists were clenched, not a lock of hair was out of place, and his face was completely dry.

Then he stood and water ran down from between his legs, making him look like he peed on himself.

"Oops?" With a satisfied click of my tongue, I dropped the plastic cups on the floor in front of me. Then I dusted my hands off and took a step back, arms folded over my stomach.

Max stood from the floor, shaking his hair out like a dog. "I think I'm in love." He took a step forward, eyes bright and wild. "Come here, Short Stuff." He wiggled his finger toward me, grinning. "Let me kiss ya."

My shoulders tensed. "No thank you."

"Right then. Which side will it be, Colly?" Max sneered over his shoulder toward Collin, who'd also moved in closer.

My stomach dropped at the curl of his lips.

Shit.

"Right side, brother."

"Got the left then."

I blinked, staring back and forth between the two ginormous men with my hands out in front of me. "W-what are you guys doing?" I moved until the back of my heels hit the screen door leading outside.

"Payback, sweetheart." Collin's eyes met mine, sending a spark shooting through my tummy and tunneling directly between my thighs. I shuddered, wondering about this payback…secretly wishing he'd shove Max out of the room and show me how *bad* his payback could be.

Like he knew what I was thinking, Max hung back, grinning. "It's a good thing I like you, Short Stuff. Otherwise, I'd do much worse things to you than Colly'd ever do." Max cracked his neck from side to side before he turned toward Collin and pointed my way.

The one good thing about the moment? The two of them had silently—albeit with wrestling moves and grunts—figured out their problems. The bad? Now I seemed to have a whole lot of pent-up wetness between my legs and a big, sexy man licking his lips and stalking me in the dark.

"You fight dirty." Collin hovered over me, hands on both sides of my face against the glass.

I shivered. "I didn't know what to do. You guys were fighting and Chloe's down the hall sleeping, and I didn't want her to wake up and—"

"Stop talking."

I shut my eyes. "Okay."

As he tilted my chin up and pressed a finger against my lips, he whispered, "Open your eyes and look at me, Addison."

It was the *S* in my name that did it. The way the sound rolled over his tongue. God, he could make any letter of the alphabet sound sexy.

"I'm sorry," I whispered, hoping the water incident was forgiven—although I wouldn't trade what had happened for anything.

He didn't move his finger from my mouth as he said, "For what? Drenching me and Max?"

"Yeah."

"That was the smartest thing you could've done, sweetheart."

"Um..."

"You're sleeping in my bed tonight."

My heart skipped and my voice squeaked. "I am?"

He nodded once. "I'm gonna sleep on the couch."

I gulped. "Oh." I clenched my hands against my waist. "I could stay on the couch. I don't mind."

His jaw worked, and he almost looked pained but seriously sexy at the same time.

"Not gonna happen."

For once in my life, I wasn't going to argue with the guy. I may not have known what was going on inside his mind, but I'd take what I could get, even if it meant a night in his bed without him. Collin was complicated. And I was patient. My only hope? We'd find the same end goal somewhere down the line.

CHAPTER 20

Collin

IT WAS FIVE THIRTY, AND ADDIE HAD YET TO SHOW UP AT my place. She'd always been there by five thirty on the nights I worked, never a minute late, so what the hell was her holdup?

Chloe was cutting teeth and had screamed in my arms for a solid hour. Not to mention I had a bitch of a headache. Now, to top it all off, I was going to be late for work.

Since I'd been training another guy to take over the late shift so I could go to days, I had to be there as early as I could. She knew this too, damn it.

"Trouble in paradise?"

Barging through the door, hair wild and braided in pink dreads and smart-ass mouth on her like always, my sister had the guts to wink at me. If I wasn't so thankful for her help, I probably would've called her out on it. I needed her too much to be an asshole.

"Not exactly. But I am late for work."

Apparently, whatever Lia's new job was, she could

pick and choose her hours. I'd yet to ask her about it because I was a big dickhead. Still, my brain was all over the place nowadays, and I blamed it all on Addie. The woman made me forget things, not care about anything but the here and now. It was a blessing and a curse because I wanted the girl so badly I could barely breathe whenever she was around.

Problem was that the girl in my arms needed her more.

"I don't know where Addie is, and I don't have time to wait for her either."

"Did you try to call her cell?"

"She wouldn't answer it anyway, especially if she were driving."

"Huh." Lia clicked her tongue and reached for Chloe. Right away, the little stink stopped crying and started nuzzling into my sister's neck. I groaned. What was it with women and their ability to calm babies?

"That's not like her, is it?"

"No." I tried to ignore the twinge in my chest at Lia's observation. To distract myself, I reached for my belt and strapped it on, not bothering to look in the mirror. It was time to go.

"Have her call me when she gets here, would ya? Need to talk to her about things." Not true. Just needed to hear her voice, breathe it in, know she was good. Safe.

Lia kissed Chloe's hair and went to the kitchen. She was quieter than usual, not normal. Part of me wondered if that Travis trash from the other night was messing with her mind. Max didn't know shit about the situation, so I'd have to do some investigating myself. For now, though, I had to get to work.

I was out the door five seconds later and on the main

roads in less than ten. Damn, would I be glad to have day-shift hours soon.

This wasn't my forever career; nobody wanted to be a rent-a-cop for the rest of his life. My plans were to join the PD one day. But for now, until I had the time and the money to go to the police academy, I needed to keep something stable for insurance purposes.

Traffic was thicker on the main road out of town, more so than the rush hour I usually ran into on my way to work. Teeth gritted, I switched lanes, deciding to take another way. I could still see the main road from the access road, and what I saw had my stomach churning. Fire trucks, cops, and an ambulance all sat with their lights running. And there, in the small ditch running off the side of the road, I saw a car. *Addie's* car.

"No." Panic washed over me, and my palms started to sweat as I turned the steering wheel. I did a U-turn up at the next set of lights, and my heart raced as I pushed the pedal to the floor.

If that really was her car…

Please, fucking please, *don't let it be her.*

At the thought, I drove even faster, brakes squealing when I finally slammed down on them to avoid hitting an ambulance. I shut off my truck, threw open the door, and raced like fire was in my ass toward the crowd. At the top of the ditch, I stood frozen, knees locked at the view. On a gurney fifteen or so feet ahead, sitting up and smiling, was Addie—*my* Addie.

My pulse seethed in my temples. My head ached. And no matter how hard I pushed it away, I was transported back in time to that day.

The call.

"I'm sorry. There was nothing they could do, honey. They said she didn't suffer. It was blunt-force trauma to the head and—"

"Stop it," I growl through the phone, not wanting to hear it. "Let me talk to Dad."

"Oh, Collin, please. We—"

Unable to take my mom's comfort, I scream through the line again. "Put Dad on the fucking phone. Now."

Knees against my chest, I rock back and forth, the sand blowing up in my face, the sound of my brothers talking under their breath around me. All's quiet on the front now, but inside my body…inside, I'm breaking— breaking so bad I can't think, can't speak.

"Get it together, Son. Mom and I love you, and we're going to help you get through this. But you've got to keep it together."

"Just…Dad, tell me this is some sort of sick joke."

"No, Collin Matthew. Why would we ever do something so cruel?"

Teeth gritted, I roar, turning to punch the Humvee. On contact, my knuckles bleed, but I feel no pain other than my heart ripping from my chest.

It hurts. It hurts so fucking bad…

"We'll keep her safe. Don't you worry about nothing but coming home alive right now. Chloe's in good hands here with your mom and me."

Chloe. My baby. Our daughter.

Fuck.

No!

"I'm gonna—Shit, watch out!" I toss the phone into

the sand and puke all over everything in my path until I can't breathe.

Fucking gone. Amy's gone. I couldn't save her. Left her alone so I could be here in this motherfucking desert.

Dead.

Gone.

Alone.

A hand presses against my shoulder, squeezing. Max? Gavin? "Colly, we gotta move out."

I shake my head, hot tears falling from my eyes. My throat burns so bad I can't breathe, let alone lead my unit out.

"I need to go home. Should've been there. Should've been—"

"I'm so fucking sorry, Colly. But you can't lose it right now, not when you're all Chloe's got left. One more ride out, brother, then we'll go home. All of us. This is it."

My hands were clasped behind my head and I was on my knees.

I wasn't in Iraq.

I wasn't in the desert.

Addie was alive.

Addie was not Amy.

Cold rain fell on my forehead, cooling my hot skin. Frantic, I jerked my chin up, finding Addie's eyes shut and her chin in her chest. I blew out a slow breath, taking her in as a whole, willing her to look up at me at the same time. A white bandage covered her forehead, but her lips were moving. She was on her cell phone.

"You okay, son?"

I nodded and stood as a cop approached my side. "Yes, sir."

"United States Marine Corps." The cop pointed at the gray T-shirt I wore beneath my white uniform button-down. Respect held his eyes to mine and he reached for my hand, probably thinking I was some PTSD case. "Thanks for your service, young man." And then he tipped his hat and walked away.

I shut my eyes, hating myself—hating who I'd become. More than anything, I knew I had to get myself together, and it would all start with the girl sitting fifteen feet away.

Needing to see her, I started to close the distance between us. But two steps in, I couldn't make her out over the tall paramedic standing in front of her and making her laugh. Hair down to his chin, big muscles— the guy looked like the epitome of a California surfer. I kept moving until I stood a foot behind him with my arms crossed over my chest.

I cleared my throat, sizing him up when he turned and faced me. Guy was smiling, all white, straight, pretty-boy teeth. Could already tell I didn't like him.

"Collin?"

I moved to stand by Addison. Reaching for her hand, I pressed it against my chest, not knowing what to say or do. She studied me, eyes narrowed in obvious confusion. Even bandaged and bruised, the girl was beautiful.

"I just got off the phone with Lia. I'm sorry I didn't call." Her voice shook. Paramedic Guy patted her on the arm before walking toward his ambulance. I curled my lip, watching him go.

"Why aren't you at work?"

I looked back at her. "Why am I not at work?" I squeezed her hands. "You were in an accident, Addison. I saw you down here. Wasn't gonna just keep driving knowing you could be hurt."

"Well, as you can see, I'm perfectly fine."

"Doesn't look like it."

She sighed, her shoulders drooping. Just when she opened her pretty lips to say something else, the douche bag of an EMT came back over. I looked at his name tag—Jones. Would have to ask Gavin about him.

"You ready, Addie?"

Smiling that genuine smile, she said, "As I'll ever be."

He waggled his bushy eyebrows her way and then looked toward me. "Will you be riding with her in the ambulance?"

I opened my mouth to say *hell yes*, but Addie beat me to it. "No. He's got to get to work. And you said yourself, I'll just need a few stitches, right?"

"And maybe an X-ray on your wrist."

She rolled her eyes. "It's not broken. I'm fine."

The guy rubbed her shoulders, and my lip curled. "I'm gonna ride with her."

"No." Addie batted her lashes at the douche bag. "*He's* got to go to work, *and* his car is here."

"Mind talking to my face, sweetheart?" I moved closer to her, lifting her chin with my finger.

"Go to work, Collin." She bit her lip, then rolled it between her teeth. "I'll be back over on Friday. Lia's going to cover for me tonight." She shivered, and the guy wrapped a blanket around her shoulders, only to settle her down on the gurney.

"That necessary?" I growled at the EMT again.

"Procedure." He patted Addie's thigh. "We like to take good care of our patients." He winked at her. Again. Made me want to cut his eyelid off.

"I'll see you tomorrow." She dismissed me with a wave before staring up the EMT with *my* smile. The one I wanted for only me.

I watched her being pushed away, watched her being lifted into the back of the ambulance too. And it was only when the lights flashed on top of the ambulance that I realized what had just happened.

I'd been dismissed.

And I didn't like it.

CHAPTER 21

Addison

I WAS SENT HOME THAT NIGHT, RATHER THAN STAYING AT the hospital, since I was cleared of a concussion and only needed a few stitches in my temple, along with having my sprained wrist wrapped. Granted, my car was totaled, so I had to take a cab home, but I survived, even though I felt like a two-by-four had been rammed into my neck.

To stop feeling sorry for myself, I gathered the energy to shower the stink off me and then headed into the kitchen to find something to eat for breakfast. It had been a long night of tossing and turning because sleep didn't come easily when all I could envision were Collin's wide eyes as I was being whisked away in the ambulance.

Just when I sat down with my cereal bowl, a knock sounded at my door. Thinking it was my order off Amazon or maybe one of my neighbor's little daughters, I didn't bother with the peephole. But the second

I swung open the door, I discovered how big of a mistake that was.

With his face contorted as though in pain, Collin stood there, surveying me from head to toe. He opened his mouth and closed it again, only to finally say, "Get dressed. I'm taking you out for breakfast." Uninvited, he pushed his way in, scrunching his nose the second he walked into my apartment.

"Well, good morning to you too." I fidgeted with my shirt, trying to yank it down over my belly button, even though it hit just below my breasts. I hadn't planned to do anything but lounge on the couch, so getting dressed wasn't on the agenda today. "What are you doing here?"

Ignoring me, he walked into my living room. "You're a neat freak. Might have to pay you more so you'll clean for me and the guys."

Trying not to draw attention to myself, I moved toward the table and sat down by my bowl. At least sitting there, he wouldn't take notice of my tiny shorts and shirt.

Quietly, he moved around the rooms, examining the pictures on the walls of me and Kenna. He was a nosy thing. Luckily I was too tired to argue about it.

"You two been friends long?" He tapped his finger against the glass of my favorite picture, Kenna and me on a spring-break trip to Cancun when we were twenty-one.

Forgetting that he'd barged into my apartment without an invitation, I couldn't help but smile at his question. "Since college. But it feels like a lot longer."

He grunted with one of what I liked to call his caveman noises. All the while, his fingers seemed to linger over my images in every frame.

"Where's your family?"

I stiffened with the spoon just centimeters from my lips. "They're around."

"Kind of vague."

Lips pursed, I stared down at my bowl. My family was a sensitive subject, one I didn't just openly discuss with anyone. Still, he'd shared secrets about Chloe's mom, so I owed him a piece of me too. Not sure why that was, but I wasn't going to stop and think about it.

"I don't have much of a relationship with them anymore. Not for a few years, at least."

"Why?" He turned to face me, eyebrows pushed together.

"Do you want the long or short version?"

"Short. I'm hungry." He reached down into my laundry basket and grabbed a hoodie and some jeans, not once making a comment about my panties and bra hanging over the edges.

I shoved my cereal away. "I didn't live up to their standards. They wanted me to be a part of their family business, and I wanted to forge my own path."

College, teaching, the works—normal stuff that didn't mean a damn thing to them, but meant everything to me.

"Know how it is." He tossed the clothes into my lap and turned the chair next to me around to sit in it. With his elbows propped along the back and a hat pulled down over his head, he looked like an adorable boy next door…with muscle mass.

"I did the college thing, got a degree in criminal justice. Was going to be a cop until I decided I wanted more first."

"So you joined the marines out of college then."

He rubbed a hand over his mouth and stared down at the table. "It was kind of always my plan, ya know? Just didn't tell everyone about it because I didn't want anyone to worry."

I could relate to that. "Everyone has a path in life. Sometimes you hit the ground running and do what you planned the way everyone else wants, while other times you tend to indulge in detours along the way."

One side of his mouth tipped up into a grin—a genuine grin that only added to his look today. He'd also shaved away his scruff. The scruff that I'd imagined feeling between my thighs.

My face grew hot at the thought, so I stared down at the chipped polish on my fingernails to avoid his gaze.

"What's got those cheeks all red, oh brilliant one?"

I blinked and met his stare again, not even bothering to acknowledge his *brilliant one* nickname. "Nothing. Just warm is all."

He smiled in a way I'd only seen him smile at Chloe, his friends, and Lia…not yet me.

Until now.

In that moment, I felt like I'd just been handed a pass to a special club, and Collin was the president.

"You going out in that?" His eyebrows arched as he peered over the edge of the table, eyes locked on my breasts.

I stared down at them and cringed. My God…my nipples had a mind of their own. "Let me…" Again, my face grew hot. And again he smiled when I looked back at him.

My heartbeat tripled at the view of his lips all curled

and friendly—not Collin-like in the least. What did I suddenly do to deserve it?

"Do you mind, uh…" I motioned for him to turn around with my finger. He'd already viewed what little I had on, so I'm not sure why it mattered that he looked away this time. Pride, maybe? The fact that I didn't want to *like* that he watched me move around in little to no clothing? No, that wasn't it at all.

Liar.

He chuckled under his breath but stood and moved to the living room to give me my privacy. In a rush, I ran to my room, the clothes he'd tossed me draped over my arm. By the time I was dressed, I was somewhere between being composed and completely flustered. His eyes raked over me in my hoodie and jeans when I came back out, but he said nothing as he reached for my pink coat and hat along the back of my couch.

"Cold outside."

"Thanks." I pulled the coat to my chest, shivering when his fingers grazed mine.

In the truck, Collin stayed focused on the road, only occasionally glancing my way. It was kind of like it had been the night he took me out for food. Only this time, it felt different. Not so tense—easier. Like two friends just going to breakfast. Because that's all we were: friends. Employer-employee.

We pulled up to a quiet café near the corner of Main, just one block from the coffeehouse. Hustling, Collin popped out of his door and sprang to mine, opening it with a nod. Inside, we chose a booth buried in the far corner, the one with a pink chandelier hanging over the top. He was so tall that he hit the light when he sat down, and I giggled when he rubbed the top of his head.

"You think that's funny?" One of his eyebrows arched, but his lips twitched at the same time, so I knew he was kidding. Teasing Collin was fantastic.

"Sorry. I don't laugh a lot."

He huffed. "Laughed yesterday with the paramedic."

He'd noticed that? "He was funny." I tilted my head to the side, studying his face. What would he say if I told him the truth? How Paramedic Man asked for my number, and I'd told him no because I was too busy thinking about a pair of dimples on another man.

"Yeah. Doubt it."

Aaaaand broody Collin was back.

I sighed in disappointment and decided to flip through the menu to ease the new tension. Still, I felt his gaze on me more often than not, the heat of his stare, the intensity I'd never grow used to.

Squirming, I continued to play on my indecisiveness, lasting until the waitress approached the table.

"Collin Montgomery. So good to see you in here."

At his name, I looked up, finding the prettiest brunette with the greenest eyes staring down at Collin.

Tall, thin, hair in perfect waves. My throat burned when I tried to swallow around a sudden lump in my throat. Was *this* Collin's type?

My teeth ground together and I chanced a look at Collin, finding his eyes not on the girl, but on me.

"Hey, Katy. Good to see you again."

"It's Kacey," the girl said, giggling.

Collin seemed like he couldn't care less, eyebrows arched, fingers tapping on the table. But the girl was persistent, chomping on her bubble gum and never once taking her eyes off him.

"How's Chloe Bean?"

Anxiousness rolled through my stomach like a tidal wave, but I managed to keep my gaze on the table, wondering if it were possible for a person to explode with frustration.

"She's fine, ain't she, Addie?"

I whipped my head up to see him looking at me with expectation. "Um…"

"Hi, sorry. I should've introduced myself. I'm Kacey." She reached for my hand, not a lick of hesitation on her face.

Okay. So I guess she wasn't *so* bad.

"I used to date Max."

"Oh?" I looked to Collin for confirmation, because from what I had learned, Max didn't date. He splurged on women like they were pennies he'd dropped on the ground.

Collin laughed. "Yep. Poor thing."

Once our orders were taken and drinks were served, Collin leaned back in his seat and just stared at me.

"What?"

"You thought she was a girl of mine, didn't you?" His dimples sank into his cheeks as he pulled his lower lip into his mouth.

"So?" I bristled, bringing my coffee to my mouth.

Elbows on the table, he leaned forward. "I like my women with black hair, sweetheart. Thick and long… something I can grab hold of."

Warmth built inside my tummy, trailing lower and lower, until I was forced to cross my legs and squeeze my thighs together. The look on his face as he trailed his gaze all over me didn't say he liked *all* women with black hair…just *one* woman in particular.

That *woman* being me.

Suddenly the hoodie he'd picked out for me was too much. And all I wanted to do was strip and pour ice water all over myself. And if Collin sat there and watched, maybe even decided to drink from my skin, I wouldn't hesitate to let him. He was the most confusing and infuriatingly sexy man I knew.

The rest of breakfast was torture for me, mainly because Collin made eating a form of foreplay. Licking lips, licking forks, licking thumbs… Damn he had a long tongue. A perfectly pink and well-developed tongue. His lips were fuller than my own, and if I closed my eyes, I could almost feel them against my mouth, my neck, my ear…

I needed help…and I needed it fast.

Even though his mood swings had given me whiplash in the past, I couldn't help but feel as though I was seeing a different side of him this morning. Sure, he still oozed sex, but he was also showing me a softer side of himself. One I ate up with abandon. Bottom line? I was drawn to him as a person now, which was something entirely different and more meaningful than just the sexual front.

He'd opened up to me about some things: his past, his career choices, joining the marines after graduating from college. The two of us had a lot in common—both the type who wanted to do things our way, without anyone else's opinions or thoughts to bog us down.

By the time we got back to my apartment, I had a full tummy and a happy heart, which also meant my brain was jumbled when I asked, "Do you want to come inside for another cup of coffee?"

Leaning the side of his face against the seat, Collin looked at me, eyes bright and nearly sparkling in the late-morning sun.

"I would, but Max is at home with Chloe, so I gotta get back."

I stared down at the pocket of my hoodie. Shyness took over, and for the fortieth time since he'd arrived at my apartment, I felt my face grow hot.

Collin blew out a strangled sigh, which, in turn, forced my gaze to meet his again.

"What?" I tried to smile, failing to hold back the quivering in my voice.

"I didn't expect you."

Oh. "Oh."

Fingers lifted my chin up. I didn't even know I'd looked away.

"That night in the bar, when I first met you?" He searched my face, his Adam's apple bobbing as he swallowed. "I should've known you were different."

"Different how?" Did I even *want* to know his answer?

"Different in a way that scared me."

My mouth made an *O*, yet the response I'd readied on my tongue failed to come out. "I was rude that night."

He laughed. "And I was an asshole. We made a good team."

A team? Oh God.

"Should've kissed you then too."

"Huh?" My hands tightened around my purse.

"I said, I should've kissed you. I'd thought so much about it that the night you showed up with my sister, I felt like I was dreaming. Like someone was torturing me at the same time." He stared out the front window of his truck. "I knew God had it in for me, but when he brought me you, I thought maybe I'd gone too far, fucked up too many things, ya know?"

"Collin…" The torture in his voice had me leaning across the console. When I reached for his hand, I interlocked our fingers, ignoring how much mine shook. "Things happen, bad things, good things. But we're only given what we can handle in life. I believe that."

"Then why the hell do I feel like I'm losing control every time you come near?"

I knew why, yet I couldn't explain it with words. It was emotions coming free from the soul after being trapped inside for so long. The gist of it was, being around Collin made me feel the same way.

"I swore to her grave I wouldn't replace her."

My throat closed off, and warmth burned my eyes. The guilt he felt over Chloe's mom was too much for him to bear. Is that why he pushed me away constantly? If I walked away, he might be safer. Yet at the same time, both of us might be losing something so amazing that the regret would eat away at us forever if we didn't pursue it. Still, it wasn't my choice to make.

"Talk to me, Addison. Tell me how you feel." He pushed the console up and moved closer. Our knees touched.

"It's not up to me." I moved forward to press my fingers against his cheek. Leaning into my touch, he blew out a soft sigh and shut his eyes.

"Wish I could promise you perfection. You deserve it," he whispered.

My fingers danced over his chin, his cheek, until I

settled them against his throat. His neck bobbed beneath my fingers and I leaned in closer, pressing my forehead to his. I held my breath, waiting for something I had no idea I'd been waiting for.

Him.

"I don't want perfection." I pulled back first, brushing my nose across his cheek, taking the chance and running with it. "I only want you."

And then I moved forward and took a risk, kissing him once on the lips.

CHAPTER 22

Collin

Two days had passed since Addie kissed me in my truck—a day that was now one for my record books. Not because it was the best kiss of my life, or because I'd sat there like a dumbass, unable to move as she told me good-bye and got out of my truck. It was record-book worthy because she'd done the impossible: taken my dreams and given them life with that one kiss.

She'd gained control of my heart.

I'd made her come against my door, had my hands all over her body, but nothing felt as surreal as the second her lips touched mine, which is why it had only taken me ten seconds to snap out of my daze and chase after her. Five seconds after that, I caught up with her on the sidewalk by the front of her building, and two seconds later I was kissing her again, this time pressed against the glass door, my hand in the thickness of her hair as she opened her mouth for me and moaned.

Just when I was ready to take her up on more than

the coffee she'd offered, Max called to say Chloe had bumped her head on the coffee table when she pulled herself up from the floor to stand.

Now, there I was, after a long, Saturday night at work, staring down at my new dream come to life. Lying on my couch, with her hair spread over her face and a soft snore coming out of her nose, Addison looked like an angel.

Easing down on the floor next to her, I pressed my hand to her cheek, brushing hair away from her mouth. Her tongue, all pink and sweet, darted between her plump lips, drawing me in closer. As lightly as I could, I pressed my mouth to hers, not wanting to wake her but okay if I did.

When she didn't stir at my touch, I headed into the bathroom to take a shower. It was gonna be a good day.

Last night, out of the blue, I'd learned that I was up next for first shift, Monday through Friday. And I'd be starting tomorrow. Normal hours would mean normal sleep and normal time with Chloe—and now Addie too.

Addie...

Jesus, just thinking her name, imagining her in my bed, in this shower with me... Gripping the base of my cock, I stroked it hard, shuddering when I reached the head. With my forehead and a hand pressed against the wall, I envisioned her rocking over me, her hips thrusting hard, her tiny moans, her beautiful tits on display, bouncing in place.

"Fuck." I stroked faster, needing more—needing *her*. And just before I reached the edge, the moment of truth, someone opened the damn door.

I stilled, teeth gritted, my pulsing cock aching for release.

"Collin?"

My body went stiff at her voice. Not thinking, I turned off the water, whipped the shower curtain open, and wrapped a towel around my waist.

"Holy shit," she whispered.

I grabbed her wrist and pulled her fully into the room with me, shutting the door behind her.

She covered her eyes and fumbled until she landed on the toilet lid. "Give a girl a warning before you go caveman, would ya?"

Snorting to myself, I moved to stand in front of her. "How 'bout you learn to knock?"

A noise sounded in the base of her throat. "I did knock, you idiot," she grumbled.

Needing to see her face, I peeled her fingers away from her eyes. "Look at me."

Her mouth fell open, then closed, but her eyes stayed shut even after I took her hands in mine.

"I can't."

"Why?" I asked.

"It's, um... I..."

"You got something to say to me, then say it. Don't be afraid." I rubbed my knuckles down her pink cheeks.

"Well...see, you..."

Loved how I could make her speechless. "Open those pretty eyes, Addie. *See* me."

Just when I thought I'd completely terrified her to the point of no return, her lashes began to flutter against her cheeks, and she lifted her chin to meet my gaze.

"I like those eyes on me. Want them always on me, nobody else."

"You're insane." Her jaw worked and she stood,

still facing me. "No way can you tell me who I can and cannot *look* at." She shoved me back against the wall.

Leaning closer again, I lowered my lips to her ears. "No, I can't, but when I want something, I want it fully. Completely." *And I want you.*

"So, what exactly are you saying?" Her voice was low and husky. This woman made me crazy with lust, and I wanted inside her so bad I could damn near taste it on my tongue.

"Saying that starting tonight, you're gonna stay here in my house, and we're gonna try this out. Me, you, together—officially."

"What?" Her lips twitched, and my cock jumped through the towel. She stiffened, eyes going wide, and I couldn't help but laugh.

"*He's* not in charge, you know," she grumbled, curling her lips.

I laughed harder—so hard my chest ached. So hard that after a while, she started laughing too. And I liked the sound. A lot. Liked it so much I couldn't stop myself from leaning forward, tucking my hands around the back of her head, and capturing it with my mouth.

She gasped against my lips, but like the last time, she didn't pull away. Instead, she reacted—always so receptive to my touches—by wrapping her hands around my naked shoulders. Fingernails scraped lightly across my skin and I shivered, tasting her, loving the soft moan coming through when I touched my tongue to hers.

Girl built a fire in my chest that burned through my body. Now *this* could very well be the best kiss of my life.

Not wanting to think any further, I lowered my arms and wrapped them below her ass, lifting her so high that she had to look down to keep her mouth sealed to mine. Her hands tangled in my hair when I squeezed her ass, her hair falling over her shoulders and covering both our faces.

A growl built in my throat, testing me. I wanted her to lose control. I wanted her to know what I could to do to her—wanted her to feel what she did to me. So I set her on the counter by the sink, not caring that my towel was coming dangerously loose around my waist. No way worried my cock was hard and ready for her. Wouldn't push her far—not yet. Wanted her to feel good but didn't want to screw this up either.

Another moan slipped from her lips, and because I loved that sound, I tipped her head back and kissed her throat so I could hear it loud and clear. Wanted to hear my name on her tongue.

My hands grew wild, trailing down her arms and coming to rest on her hips. She hissed as my fingers slipped under her shirt. Against her neck I grinned, needing to hear more, do more, *feel* more.

"Wanna see you, sweetheart."

She stiffened. "I…"

Pulling back, I lifted my hands to cup her cheeks. I rubbed my thumbs over her skin, forcing her to keep her eyes locked with mine. "Wanna look at you, feel you against me. I won't touch you anywhere else unless you ask me to. You good with that?"

She held my stare, unwavering, until finally she lowered her fingers to the bottom of her shirt and pulled it slowly up over her head. Cheeks all pink and sexy as fuck, she smiled at me, so shy it hurt to take a breath. Nodding once, she gave me a small nudge backward, urging me to look, to take my fill.

And, holy shit, did I do just that.

"Fucking perfect."

At my words, she wrapped her legs around my hips and pulled me close again. Those hooded brown eyes could make a grown man weep with joy when they looked at you like she was looking at me.

Then the second her gorgeous tits pressed against my chest, I was a goner.

Couldn't kiss her enough. Couldn't hold her tight enough either. Needed to claim her, make her mine, even if doing so meant something I wasn't ready for. I'd deal with the consequences later, but for now, I wanted to make her feel as good as I did.

My towel slipped to the floor, and I rocked my hips against hers. She gasped and pulled away, staring down at my cock. A grin pulled up one side of her mouth. "It would seem as though you lost something," she whispered, pressing her hands against the side of my neck. Her palms were smooth, like the rest of her skin.

"Got no control over what happens down there." I winked.

One of her eyebrows arched. "So, what you're telling me is that you need a leash for that bad boy." Her lips twitched. "Am I right?"

I laughed. "More like a saddle."

"Oh God." Her nose scrunched up, and she leaned forward to press it against my wet neck. Smiling, I stroked the back of her long hair, holding her against me. In the mirror, I could see the smooth skin of her back, and I trailed my hands down her spine, watching her shiver beneath my touch.

"Collin…" My name, all soft on her tongue, had me pulling back and looking into her eyes again.

In her stare, I saw what she couldn't say, what she was too shy to ask for. And even though I hadn't had a woman in well over a year, I knew lust and need when I saw it. Knew exactly how to ease the ache between her hips too.

"You need something?" I grinned, hoping she'd play along.

She studied me for a second longer, but I saw it all the same. She nodded, her acceptance of this, of us, was right there in the movement of her head, even if she didn't verbally say the words.

Knowing what I had to do, I moved her off the edge of the sink and then fell to my knees, bringing her tiny shorts and yellow panties along with me. Never once did I look away from her eyes, too entranced with her parted lips and pink cheeks. Her breath hitched as my fingers trailed over her thighs, and I grinned, watching her eyes go wide as I tossed the scraps of fabric behind me. Slowly, I eased my hands back up, cupping her perfect ass, only to lift her back up on the counter. Not wanting to completely freak her out, I grabbed my towel from the floor and wrapped it back around my waist.

"W-what are you doing?"

I brushed my knuckles along the side of her cheek. "Haven't touched a woman for a long time. Don't want to be distracted by my own needs when all I want to do is fill yours."

"Well, I mean, if you want to…"

"Fuck?"

Her cheeks went redder, but she still whispered, "Yes."

I lowered my forehead to hers, kissing her nose. "Baby, believe me, I want nothing more than to feel you wrapped around my cock, but this thing between us?" I motioned from my chest to hers. "I'm not gonna mess it up by going too fast. You get me?"

Her shoulders fell, and I wasn't sure if relief or disappointment coated her face. But I went with it, trusting my instincts, and fell to my knees. Eager and impatient, I licked my lips, spread her legs apart, and kissed the insides of her thighs. Back and forth I trailed my tongue across her skin, growing closer to her pretty little pussy, only to kiss around it and head over to the other thigh instead.

"Jesus," she gasped, grabbing my hair and urging me forward.

Peering up at her, I blinked, pulled back, and said, "The name's Collin, sweetheart."

Then I gave her exactly what she wanted, latching my lips onto the tiny, wet bud that had her screaming *my* name instead.

Over and over, I sucked and licked, holding her legs apart by the knees. She bucked up against my mouth, fighting and more than likely losing against the oncoming explosion inside her. Head tipped back, long hair hanging down, she was a sexual goddess bringing me to my knees in all ways.

I licked from the bottom to the top, loving how she tasted, how warm she was. Thinking of how good it'd feel to someday be buried inside her.

"Collin, please, I'm gonna…"

My stomach tightened. Just hearing her little noises made me wanna come.

Jesus, did I want this woman.

She gasped, going stiff, her hand in my hair, whimpering her soft words of surrender. But I wasn't gonna stop 'til she pushed me away, couldn't let this moment end, because if I did, I'd want more, and I'd want it now.

When she finally pushed her knees together, forcing my hands back, I looked up at her face and saw a light in her eyes. Something that wasn't there before. Something close to adoration and peace. And I couldn't help but wonder if she saw the same thing in my gaze. Because I did adore this woman. Not just her looks and the sounds she made when she came. But the way she was as a whole. A good person who loved my daughter, who loved my friends.

Question was though: Was it enough to feel this way?

CHAPTER 23

Addison

I CRINGED AS I WATCHED THE TWENTY-PLUS BODIES OUT on the green field smash against one another. Their moves were fluid and fast, but rough at the same time. Rugby wasn't something I was all too keen on watching, especially when I could see how dangerous it was from the sidelines. But it was funny how no one around me seemed to mind it, including Lia, who sat beside me, screaming her brother's name.

"You see, the games are ten times more vicious than the practices, but that's the fun of it." She jabbed her finger in the air after Collin scored what was called a "try."

Chloe sat on the blanket in between us, flipping through her books and squealing whenever she saw the dog pictures. I think I liked her baby world much more than this one.

"I don't see the fun in this." I frowned as a grunt sounded from the middle of their huge, mashed-together circle.

Leaning back on her hands with her legs stretched in front of her, Lia sighed and said, "I don't really think it's about the game as much as the bonding itself. Colly needs an outlet, ya know? Besides Chloe, Max and Gavin are his life."

I didn't know that. But I'd be happy to try to understand it. I found myself wanting to know everything about Collin, even the little details.

"Tell me how the three of them got to where they are now. Because whenever they're together in the house, it's like I'm sidelined and watching an X-rated version of *Full House* with all of their bro hugs and penis talk."

"If there's one thing I don't miss, it's their penis talk." Lia snickered, rolling over onto her stomach.

"Max is the worst of all of them. He's like a junkie when it comes to sex."

Lia frowned. "This I know." I didn't miss her sarcasm one bit. "The guy's been that way since the first time I met him a few years back. But he's also a total southern boy with all the charm, and the devoted *mama* to go along with it."

"And Gavin?"

"He's a different story altogether. Both of his parents died when he was really young, and he got flung from foster home to foster home for several years. He did earn a scholarship for his smarts, I guess, but that's about all I know."

As if he knew we were talking about him, Gavin looked our way from the middle of the field and waved shyly, a happy, unfamiliar grin on his face. The look betrayed his normally grumpy moods, but with Gavin, nothing was a shock anymore. If anything, he and Collin seemed to be bred from the same team of sperm, only Gavin was more about control while Collin seemed to lose his control easier.

"Anyway, they all wound up at the same boot camp, and the three of them somehow got lucky enough to stay together when they were shipped out."

"And Collin? I mean, he told me why he enlisted. But if he was really and truly in love with Chloe's mom, I don't understand what happened."

"Not my story to tell." She made a motion over her lips, zipping them.

When I didn't say anything else, Lia sat up and moved to sit next to me again.

"Look, my brother's been through a lot. More than any person should have to go through. But the one thing he doesn't do is keep secrets." She leaned over and kissed the top of Chloe's head. Chloe yawned, obviously needing her afternoon nap.

"He's told me about Amy, about what happened between them."

"See? He wouldn't share something like that if he didn't intend to keep you around for a while." Her lips curled up on one side, a teasing expression that most definitely ran in the family.

"Well, I love Chloe, so I do plan on being around for as long as possible. I know this isn't, like, a forever job of course, but it'll help me get back on my feet."

"Honey"—she tsked—"I hate to break it to you, but my brother doesn't look at you like an employee." My face heated as I turned to find him out on the field. Fast and hard he ran, tossing the ball behind him to someone else. God, he was gorgeous. Long, muscled legs, black hair, perfect face… "He keeps you around because he *wants* you, wants you—if you get my drift."

"Oh God." I lowered my face into my hands, forever embarrassed.

She laughed and stood. "Be patient with him though. And please don't…lead him on, okay?" Her voice grew lower, more serious.

I uncovered my face and squinted against the sun as I stared up at her and Chloe, now in her arms. "It's not him I'm worried about." In a moment—a single blink of an eye—Collin could easily crush me if he wanted to.

"No doubt you're scared. And if I were you, I'd be too." A sad looked passed through her eyes.

"Not very reassuring."

"Not meant to be." She tossed Chloe up into the air. "My brother harbors a lot of guilt over what happened with this beautiful girl's mama. Thinks he owes her a life of celibacy or something, though I don't think he ever truly loved her like a man should love a woman."

I coughed, trying to keep my game face on. So… maybe this supposed celibacy only counted toward his *own* orgasms then?

After a while, both of us grew quiet, the unspoken words hanging in the air like a deep, thick fog. I didn't want to travel through it, not when everything I was feeling was so fresh and real and amazing. Yet at the same time, I knew it was an inevitable journey I'd be forced to take if I really and truly felt something for Collin.

"Are you going to the party tonight?"

"Party?"

Lia nodded, now rocking Chloe gently back and forth in her arms. Today's outfit consisted of a black sweater

with holey sleeves and a hole for her thumb at the base
of each one. Her pants were plaid, red and black, and
the epitome of schoolgirl rock chic. She looked sexy and
sophisticated, not to mention edgy. My envy level grew
every time I saw her, yet I'd never have the guts to wear
half the stuff she did.

"Yup. It's the season-end party. Other than the big
tournament in Chicago coming up, today was their last
game until the spring."

"I'm guessing Collin will ask me to watch Chloe. I
mean, he hasn't mentioned me picking up any extra hours,
but as far as I know, he doesn't have anyone to babysit, so
I figure if he's got a party to go to, he'll need a sitter." I bit
down on my lower lip before continuing. "But what do I
know? I mean, I don't know what goes on in his head. And
besides, I need to stay home and do some cleaning, maybe
catch up on my DVR recordings, and then—"

"Christ, honey. You talk a mile a minute, and I have no
damn *clue* what you're saying."

"Um…" My lips flattened into a hard line, and I
scratched my neck.

"Anyway, you don't have to worry about babysitting
tonight. Our parents are back in town visiting. They've
already claimed Beaner duty for the night and have her
staying with them at their house." She nudged me with her
knee, a sly grin on her face as she said, "So…I'll swing
by *your* house and pick you up. Got this sexy outfit for
you to wear. My boobs aren't nearly the size to fill it out
like yours, so no doubt you'll look like a rock star in it."

Chin jerked back, I stared up at her, watching as she
snuggled now-sleeping Chloe against her chest. The girl
was like clockwork when it came to taking naps.

"Did you not just hear what I said?" I lowered my voice, not wanting to wake the baby, but several loud hoorahs sounded out in the field, each of them not touching her little ears. Guess she'd had to learn to sleep like a rock living with three men.

"I heard you."

"And what part did you not understand?"

"I understood it all, and I still don't care." She winked. "You're going with me to this party."

With tender eyes and her mouth shaped in a tiny O, Lia settled Chloe into her stroller with the sort of ease normally only a mother could attain. Truly, the girl had a gift with kids, making her a hard act to follow—even for someone with my experience.

Standing too, I stretched my hands upward, moving side to side.

Lia motioned her head toward the field. "If he wants you, he'll get you, ya know. And once he's got you, he'll never want to let you go."

"Huh?"

"Food for thought." She smiled widely.

My throat grew tight. As much as I wanted to play dumb and pretend I didn't know what she meant, I knew I couldn't. Collin was like a hurricane. When he hit, it was a take-no-prisoners, all-in sort of thing. I wasn't ready to hash out the details when it came to him and me, mainly because this thing between us was still so new—not even something we could put a label on. But someday, when the time came, I was determined to give what I could

My only hope was that I could be enough.

CHAPTER 24

Collin

"YOU GUYS REALIZE THIS IS THE FIRST NOVEMBER WE'VE spent together not in a desert?"

Max's eyes were half-closed as he scanned the dark yard around the fire pit. The guy had been drinking since three, and now he was full-on shit-faced.

Gavin and I weren't as bad off as he was, just warmed enough to take the edge off the fact that it was only forty-some degrees outside.

"This is the first time we've seen real autumn leaves in at least a year." Gavin took a sip of his whiskey. "I feel like doing one of those rubbings with a crayon and paper. Like a kid." He picked a leaf up off the ground, twirling it around by the stem.

Max shoved him with his elbow. "Only rubbing you need is over your cock by the sexy-looking twin sisters we just saw walking by." On cue, two ladies, both dressed in skintight jeans, crossed our path. Max was damn near drooling as he watched them wave and giggle, while Gavin just nodded his appreciation, smiling over the top of his cup. My two brothers couldn't have been more different.

Part of me was excited to be out with my guys tonight. Chloe was with my parents, and I was free from dad duties for the first time in months. Fresh air, good drinks, good friends, and one hell of a good time. The only thing that would make this better was if Addie were here with me—Addie who'd been ignoring my calls all night.

"Shots! Let's do 'em. Time to celebrate. Get drunk." Max's gaze followed the twin ladies as they moved our way. "Fuck the shots. I've got something much better to do."

Max was off. Thinking Gavin wasn't far behind, I turned to him, taking a sip of my Bud. "Not interested?"

He stared down at the fire, face blank. "Nah. Not in the mood." He cleared this throat and kicked some loose brush into the fire. It sparked up, flicking pieces of ash into the sky. "Your parents are back in town for the weekend, then? How are they?"

I nodded, sitting down in a nearby lawn chair. "They're good. Came to celebrate Thanksgiving with us a week early. Mom's making dinner for us all tomorrow."

Gavin grunted. Guy was about as big on conversation as I was.

"How's work?" I asked.

"It's work." He took a longer drink, draining his cup. "How's Addison? Saw her at the game today." He stared down at me, accusation heavy in his eyes.

I flinched. Was that what his issue was? "She's great, Gav." I sucked in a deep breath, ready to stake a claim I wasn't even sure I had a right to.

After what had happened between us in the bathroom the day before, too many things had been left unsaid, mainly because Chloe had woken up and distracted us both. I could tell Addison wanted to talk about things, but I wasn't ready—at least not then. Just hoped she could be patient with me.

"Told you she's a catch," he grumbled, slouching down next to me.

Hell yeah she was. "Been thinking about things with her. Pursuing something—"

"Gotta piss." Throwing his cup in the fire, Gavin stood.

"The hell?" I whispered as I watched him go. Pissed he'd run off, I followed him. "Gavin!"

He didn't look back at me, just kept going, too chickenshit to face me for some reason.

I jumped in front of him. "You got a problem?"

He froze, hands at his sides and elbows locked. Still didn't say squat though, just glared at me like I'd sprouted a horn.

"Gonna tell me what that was all about?" I pushed.

His shoulders tensed, along with his jaw, but his gaze was locked on something behind me.

Just when I didn't think I'd gotten through to him, he finally opened his mouth. "She's good. Sweet as hell, kind, doesn't need to be treated like trash. If all you want is a good fuck, then I suggest you find someone else to do it with."

Anger radiated through my body, making my hands shake. The hell was he trying to say here? What gave him the right to be Addie's new guardian? He wasn't her brother, wasn't her father either. Just a guy who'd decided she wasn't the bad distraction he'd once assumed her to be.

But I couldn't tell him what I thought of his sudden need to protect this girl from *me*, of all people, because Gav wasn't who he used to be. He'd grown edgier, angrier. I knew I had to tread carefully with my words— tiptoe like I did whenever Chloe took naps.

"You think that's what I'm going to do with her?"

"Come on, Colly. You're still mourning Chloe's mother." His eyes flashed as they met mine again. "Who's to say you can handle getting involved with another woman?"

"I don't know what the hell I'm doing." I pinched the bridge of my nose. "But, man, Gav, for the first time in almost ten months, I wanna go with my gut. Wanna feel shit again that won't have me sinking into a hole I can't unbury myself from." I let my hands fall to my sides. "But if you have some sort of problem with her and me together, then I need you to tell me now so we can figure shit out before I get in any deeper than I already am."

He jerked his head back. "Are you in deep already?"

Not even thinking twice about my answer, I whispered the only truth I knew. "Can't help it. She just... got under my skin."

"Yeah." He cleared his throat. "She does that." He sighed, looking toward the fire, a faraway look in his eyes.

"Now, answer my question, because I gotta know. You got a thing for her?"

Quick to answer, he whispered, "No. I kind of thought I did at first, but it's more that she reminds me of someone I once cared about."

Gavin had secrets, bigger than Max's and mine combined. Unlike Max though, he'd never offered them up. Just locked them all away tight. One day I feared he'd break, but it wasn't my place to be his therapist. If he wanted help, all he had to do was ask us for it. I just hoped he would.

"Truth is, I'm more worried about *you* than anything else." He looked at me again and stuck his hands into his jean pockets. "You ready for this? Especially with a girl like her?"

"What do you mean *a girl like her*?"

"Oh, come on, man." He rolled his eyes. "She's an all-or-nothing woman who loves your kid and is probably halfway in love with you already."

I took a step back, face pinched. "It isn't like that." And *love*? Where the hell did that come from?

"Then what is it? What do you want with *her*?"

I glared at him. "What do you care what I want?"

"Don't play that card, Colly. I was there the night you found out about Amy. I saw what losing her did to you too. And according to everything you've ever told us, you didn't really even *love* the girl. Addison, on the other hand, *is* the type of girl you bring home to your mom. The type of girl you fall in love with. What're you going to do if she decides she wants more than what you can give her?"

"Go to hell." I took a step forward and shoved him. Fucking did love Amy. How could I *not* love the mother of my baby?

Gavin didn't budge, just laughed and jabbed a finger in my face. "I've already gone there. Don't need an invitation back."

My head hurt. All this stress over worrying about Addie all night, seeing my parents and listening to them nag on me about Chloe needing this and that, and now dealing with Gavin and his preachy sermons about shit he had no right to talk about…

What I needed was more beer.

Ready to forget, I went straight for the keg.

"Who's running now?"

I flipped Gavin the finger from over my shoulder, too tired to listen to his knowing ass.

Yeah. I liked Addison. A lot. But what my best friend said rang truer than anything else: Addison was a forever girl. I could tell already. She was real. Funny and sweet. Perfectly imperfect. And exactly the type of woman who scared me and intrigued me at the same time.

CHAPTER 25

Addison

I FELT LIKE THE WHORE MY MOTHER HAD CALLED ME after finding my first thong in my bedroom drawer at seventeen. Only this time, Lia assured me my clothing was acceptable, since I was dressing to impress—whatever that meant.

The thing of it was, normally I didn't dress to impress anyone but myself. But there was no denying that I was eager to see Collin's reaction when he saw me all done up. Just the thought of his blue eyes raking over my body was motivation enough not to throw away the outfit I had on.

Still, the second I stepped out of Lia's car and the cold air blew against my naked thighs, I realized how much of a mistake I was making.

"This is a mistake." I froze by the closed car door, rubbing my hands up and down my arms. The thin shirt I wore barely covered my skin, leaving little to no warmth—and even less to the imagination when it came to my gigantic boobs.

The stars were out in abundance, and the moon lit the way. But the bonfire lighting up the backyard of the monster-sized farmhouse was what really drew me in.

"There is no way I'm going to let you leave after all the work I put into your ensemble."

"But this isn't me." I motioned down to my naked legs and the minuscule, barely there leather skirt that sat less than a half inch below the curve of my butt cheeks. Around my waist was a black belt that attached to the hunter-green, button-down shirt I wore. But the worst part of all was that the buttons kept popping open, and my boobs were damn near falling out of the top. To top it off, I had on a pair of heels, which made walking on the grass nearly impossible.

But I guess if I was going to look like an unsophisticated slut bag, then I was going to be the badass version.

"Who cares? You look hot, and my brother is going to lose it once he gets a look at how good your boobs look."

I eyed her punk-rock outfit from the feet up. She wore pointy-heeled, leather boots, a leather skirt like me, and a red leather corset that said goth girl meets punk princess. *How is she not freezing?* Unlike me though, she was completely at ease in her clothing, while I took uncomfortable to a whole other level.

She winked, as if knowing what I was thinking, then turned around and pulled me with her by my wrist. "Let's go find our boys."

"And possibly a hole to crawl into," I mumbled.

"This is a public party, Addie. You're off-duty and looking to have a good time. No crime in that."

Groaning, I followed her through the fence, wondering who owned this house. It was gorgeous, like

something out of a *Better Homes and Gardens* maga-
zine. The giant porch on the second floor ran the entire
back width of the house. Below it was a patio filled with
gorgeous wicker furniture. Kegs and partygoers littered
the area, the guests laughing loudly and obnoxiously.
Even a few kids were running around, tossing a rugby
ball back and forth.

Leaves crunched under my heels and my ankles
wobbled, making the art of staying upright near impossible. To my left sat a field of wheat, the stalks blowing
in the night air. I shivered just as Lia linked her arm
through mine, saving me from humiliating myself by
face-planting into the dirt.

"Haven't been to a house party in ages. Not since
my freshman year of college." Her voice was wistful,
but there was also an edge to it. On the outside, with all
her tats and piercings and funky hair, the lady exhib-
ited confidence, but beyond that, I could almost bet she
hid as much garbage from her past as I did from mine.
Maybe that's why I was so drawn to her. She didn't ask
me things, and I, in turn, kept my questions about her
to myself.

At the edge of the patio, she froze, taking in a pair of
twin sisters who looked fresh out of college. "Dumbass."

I scrunched my nose up, trying to see who warranted
the name. When I finally found her victim, I realized
she wasn't *looking* at the girls. Instead she was shooting
daggers from her eyes at the man holding the sisters in
his lap.

"Is that—"

"Max? Surrrrre is."

My eyes flicked back and forth between her and

him, confusion pulling my brows together. "Uh, are you two together?"

"No," she scoffed, answering too quickly to be convincing. "Look!" She pointed toward the fire, her voice an octave higher than what I considered calm. "There's my brother. Let's go."

"I don't see…"

Once upon a time, I could contain my emotions like a normal woman who was faced with unbelievable hotness. But that girl no longer existed. Not when all my fantasies were coming to life in the form dressed in all black. Holy cow. I mean, *holy. Cow.* It was like my sex dreams were real, brought to me by the man I'd forever think of as broody Number Six.

"Come on." Lia pulled my hand and I stumbled again, not sure if my heels or the sight of Collin, dressed in a thermal black shirt and sporting a well-loved Chicago Cubs hat, was making me so loopy. Either way, my body was most definitely unstable. "You must have magic, honey, because my brother is looking at you like a spell has been cast over him."

My face grew hot, like always. And if I'd had to bet money on it, I'd have said the world shifted a bit when Collin's eyes met mine—or, again, it could've been my heels.

"I'm gonna go chat with some old friends." Lia nudged my side and left me—no, no, *abandoned me.* Only it didn't last long, because before I could whisper his name, Collin stood in front of me, eyes like liquid fire piercing straight into me.

He grabbed my hand, pulling it to his mouth. "You've been avoiding me." He kissed my thumb.

I licked my lips. "Nice weather we're having, no?"

"Don't change the subject. Tell me why you were avoiding me tonight."

Not exactly the greeting I was looking for, but... "I wasn't avoiding you. I was taken hostage by your sister after the game this afternoon."

Hunger and appreciation filled his dark-blue eyes as they trailed up and down my body.

Okay, so maybe this outfit was going to serve its purpose after all.

"Tried to call you." He moved in closer, lifting his other hand to trace a line over my collarbone. My breath caught and my belly warmed, betraying the rest of my cold skin.

"I didn't have my phone." Actually, my phone broke, and I couldn't afford to buy a new one.

He moved his hands down my arms and laced his fingers with mine. His palms were heated, a comforting sensation I didn't know I needed. I shivered, regardless, willing him to come closer to me, to wrap his arms around my waist and kiss me until I grew dizzy with need. *Crazy* couldn't even begin to describe how this man made me feel.

To me, Collin was like a sample of chocolate, the most decadent kind—something almost forbidden. Combine that with his abilities recently displayed on the bathroom counter, and I was pretty much a lust-filled lost cause.

"Come with me." He motioned his chin toward the side of the house, pulling me along with one of his hands.

Side by side, we made our way to the edge of the small lake sitting due south of the home. Not once did he let me go, his fingers too busy tickling my palm the entire way. Awe filled my chest and I held my breath, focusing on the silver moon. It lit up the dark sky and reflected off the water like tiny crystals.

"Used to come fishing out here with my dad when I was a kid. Caught catfish to eat and bluegills for fun." Collin squeezed my fingers.

"Sounds nice." Especially since growing up with my parents consisted of the occasional pedicure with my mom when she wasn't off playing mah-jongg with her friends, while my father spent his time in front of the TV, drinking beer and watching golf—when he wasn't working at the store, of course. "Maybe someday you can do the same with Chloe."

"Plan on it." He held my gaze, a silent vow in his eyes.

"She's really lucky to have you, Collin."

He searched my face in a way that would normally make my skin itchy. Only lately I'd found myself liking his lingering stares. The sincerity in them made me feel almost cherished, something I'd never felt before.

"Tell me what goes on behind those pretty eyes. Tell me about you." He lifted his free hand and gently touched my temple.

I willed away my nerves and lifted my chin high. "Not much to tell."

Moving in closer, he pressed his fingertips against my cheek as he whispered, "Everyone's got a story, and yours is already written on your face. Just wanna see it on your lips and hear it with my ears this time." His head tipped to the side, and it took all of me not to lean into his touch. Besides Kenna, nobody ever cared enough to ask me about my personal life.

I shrugged. "Not sure where to start."

"How 'bout a game then?"

I bit my lip to hold back a smile. "You and your games." He laughed, and so did I. "Just as long as you play fair this time."

He pressed a hand against his chest and mock-gasped. "You're killing me here."

"And you, sir, are the most dramatic man I know."

Pieces of his dark hair curled out over his ears and forehead as he pulled off his baseball hat and stuck it in the back pocket of his jeans. "Then it's obvious you don't know Max all too well."

True. "Fine. You ask, I'll tell."

His eyebrows arched. "That's dangerous."

"Don't care." With Collin, the idea of playing it safe wasn't an option anymore.

"Fine. Tell me what you were like as a kid."

"I was quiet. Loved to read."

He pulled me even closer, wrapping his arm around my waist. "So, not real different than you are now, huh?"

"Nope." I popped the p, regretting how uninteresting I really was. "Bet you were a tree climber. Girl kisser and"—I tapped my finger against my lip—"a troublemaker. Am I right?"

"Close." He winked. "I was also an athlete. Loved playing football, baseball...wrestled too."

"So you were one of those tight-singlet-wearing boys?"

He lowered his lips to my ear, bringing his body flush against mine. His denim jeans brushed against my sensitized thighs, and I gritted my teeth, praying

I didn't moan at the contact. "Wore the thing better than any other guy on the team. And that was *with* my underwear on."

I laughed. Hard. Only Collin could make me hot and bothered one second, then make me laugh out loud the next. "And I bet you had a lot of fans of the cheerleading variety."

He pulled back, only to bring his fingers to the ends of my hair. Like it was made of the most delicate silk, he rubbed the strands between his thumb and forefinger. "Didn't have time for girls. Too busy with sports and the like."

Dedicated and delicious. Two perfect *d*-words when it came to a man.

"How about you? Did you play any sports?" He didn't move back. Instead, he kept playing with my hair, looking down into my eyes, and occasionally letting his gaze linger lower.

"I played golf."

"Golf." He frowned. Not necessarily an annoyed frown, more a curious one.

I held back my grimace and looked the other way. It was a sport I loved once upon a time. "Kind of had to. It was ingrained in my head since I was first able to wrap my chubby baby fingers around a club. It's also the only thing my dad and I had in common."

"You still play?"

I stared out at the pond. "Not anymore."

"Wanna tell me why you stopped?"

"My dad and I don't speak anymore and he was the only reason I played."

"Why don't you talk now?"

I bumped his hip with mine, trying to smile. "And this is the part of the conversation where I plead the fifth."

A heavy sigh filled the air, but I didn't turn to face him. If I did, then I'd have to talk about things I didn't want to talk about yet. No need to bring the newness of our friendship—or whatever this was—into a slump.

After a while, the warmth of his arm around me wasn't enough, and the cold wind proved to be too much for even Collin's massive body. My teeth chattered, but I didn't want to suggest going back to the house. For one, there were too many people there. And another? I liked being with Collin like this, regardless of the sudden conversation lag.

"Cold?" His voice cracked.

I nodded down at my heels.

"Let's get you back to the fire. Warm ya up."

Disappointment washed over me, even though I knew we couldn't be out here all night. But then we began to move, and as we walked, his fingers found mine again, connecting with them in a way that gave my goose bumps purpose.

"Where'd my sister find this getup you got on?"

"She didn't really find it." Other than the fact that she'd mentioned my boobs would look better in it than hers. "Guess it was too big or something on her and she decided I'd look better in it."

"Yeah?" He stared ahead. But the lines by his eyes had me questioning his sister's once-logical answer. "My sister is conniving." He looked down on me, his eyes alight with humor. "Don't get me wrong. She usually means well."

"You think she dressed me like this on purpose?"

His lips twitched as we approached the fire. "Not going to put it past her."

Lia was also going to be seeing the bottom of my shoe. Still, a small thrill managed to course through me every time Collin took the time to appreciate my...*assets*.

"Sit right here." He plopped down in one of those extended lawn chairs, patting the space in between his thighs.

"*Please* does exist in your vocabulary, correct?"

He frowned. "Sorry. *Please* sit right here."

I grinned at my small success and did as he asked, never once regretting it. A blanket was tucked over the back of the chair, and he reached for it, settling it over the top of my legs once I lowered myself against his chest. The fire crackled before us, illuminating the quiet area around us. There weren't many people hanging around outside anymore, my guess was from the sprinkles of rain steadily falling now, so the privacy was near perfect.

"Whose house is this anyway?"

He encircled his arms around my waist, resting his chin on my shoulder. "Club's owner."

"And who is the club owner?"

"Jonathon St. Marks is his name. He's close to forty. Has a couple of kids and a wife. Needs the club to make him feel young again."

I settled my ear against his chest, taking in the thump of his heart. "Probably a way to blow off steam too."

He lowered a kiss to my forehead. "Yeah, kind of why Gav, Max, and I all play."

At the mention of his friends, a thought plagued me. One I'd wanted to ask for a while now, but didn't feel like it was my place...until that moment.

"Why come back to Carinthia and not move to where Gavin or Max are from?"

Fingers danced over my arm beneath the blanket, and I snuggled in deeper against his chest. "Because Max was running from his past, and Gavin was trying to find his future."

"And you?" I turned completely on my side, reaching down to wrap his arm tighter around my waist. His fingers caressed my stomach, slipping between the gaps of my buttons. When the tips found my bare skin, I held my breath, consumed by his touch.

"Guess I was just trying to find purpose again."

"You'll always have a purpose in life. You're a father."

A button on my outfit popped open, and then another, until his hand slipped fully inside and flat against my belly. I did nothing to stop him.

"*Purpose* is a word with many meanings, Addie." His voice crackled. "Just one of those has to do with my daughter."

The tips of his fingers found the top of my panties, and I whimpered as he slipped his fingers just under the edge. Insanity and need had me arching backward, allowing his hand to slide lower. Other than a couple sitting across from us, everyone had filtered inside.

The cold drizzle had increased to a steady rain that coated our faces, but neither of us cared, both panting hard as his hand slipped even lower.

"Christ, you're wet."

Desire surged between my hips, and I rocked against his palm. Yet he held his fingers too high, teasing me—torturing me.

"Don't wanna share you with anyone else. Too many people around."

Needing more, needing to assure him this wasn't sharing, that this was completely him and me, alone in our own world, I tipped my head back and met his stare. "Please…" I pleaded with a whisper and was rewarded with a growl buried low in his throat. Lifting his other hand, he cupped my cheek and kissed me moments before his fingers obliged my begging and dipped even lower.

Against his mouth, I moaned, kissing him harder than I'd ever kissed a man before. Our lips, slick from rain, collided in a battle of give and take, making me forget who I was and where I was, but never who I was with.

Faster and faster, his fingers rubbed over my clit, a skillful move he mastered with little effort. It took little work for him to bring me close to the edge, but whenever I got too close, he'd slow down, kissing me softly once more.

So worked into a frenzy, I barely noticed him lowering his free hand under the blanket, but the second I felt more buttons come apart against my breasts, I came alive, burning for him, for his touch.

"So damn sexy. Can't wait 'til I taste you here." He cupped my breast, rubbing his thumb over my nipple at the same time. The fingers below my panties moving so fast I barely had time to think.

With my head tipped back even more, he nibbled on the base of my throat, not hard, but enough to sting in the most delicious of ways.

"Can't wait to be inside you. Can't wait to have you

in my bed, screaming my name as I fuck you slow, hard…whatever you need."

Dear God in heaven, why did I wait so long to make this happen?

My hips moved so fast against his hand that it should've been embarrassing, but the second the throbbing peaked into something sensational, I knew it didn't matter where we were—or even who surrounded us. There's no way I'd ever *not* let this happen again.

Other than a hiss or a whimper, I couldn't speak, let alone think logically. Holy crap, if foreplay was always this hot with Collin, there's no telling what it'd be like for us when he finally made good on his promise of sex.

"Let it go, Addie. Do it quick…"

Seconds later, his urgent words pushed me over the edge and he caught my loud moan with his mouth. The climb had been fantastic, but the outcome was a dream come true.

Until a voice rang out.

"You two done yet?"

Barely breathing correctly, I shot up, forgetting my shirt was still unbuttoned.

"Lia!"

Collin laughed and followed me upright, making sure to keep my breasts, now hanging out of my bra, covered with the blanket. His ability to stay so composed not only annoyed me, but also made me wonder what it took to make him really lose control.

"Maxwell's gotten himself in real deep this time. Gavin's got him in my car, and we're about ready to take him home."

Collin nodded, water dripping down his nose. "Give us a second."

With a wink, Lia looked at me and laughed, her shirt so wet it was now see-through and plastered against her body like a glove. "Didn't I tell you, honey? Complete and utter spell."

I groaned and lowered my face into my palms.

"Didn't *I* tell you my sister was conniving?" Collin whispered low in my ear.

He kissed me lightly on the cheek and kept me covered so I could button up. All the while, my grin stayed in place.

CHAPTER 26

Collin

I HADN'T BEEN ON A REAL DATE IN CLOSE TO FIVE YEARS. Not one where I picked up the girl, took her out, and treated her right. But instead of feeling confident, like I had this in the bag, I was more like a twelve-year-old kid with a raging hard-on and no way to relieve it.

It was two nights before Thanksgiving, and exactly four nights and twenty hours since I'd last had my hands on Addie's body—alone, without anyone around to bother us, that is. I was officially done worrying about what would happen if things didn't work out between us, done worrying about her leaving too. No matter what, I'd make her stay—or I'd die trying. Fuck all my internal debates. It was time to live again.

"Oh my God. I love this part. Haven't you seen this movie before? It's a classic." Addie's eyes lit up as she pointed at the movie screen.

It was a damn cold night for a drive-in; plus it was starting to snow. But having her in my arms, leaned

back against my chest between my thighs, was so
worth it—though I had no clue what the hell we were
watching. Hadn't been able to concentrate on anything
but her since we'd arrived. It had to be the way she
smelled. So good and sweet, like warm vanilla, cara-
mel on a sundae, fresh cookies right out of the oven.
Too hot to touch, too tempting not to eat. And as I held
her against me in the bed of my truck, my arm tucked
around her waist, popcorn in her lap, I realized that's
exactly what I wanted to do. Wanted to devour this
woman—take everything I could and leave her limp
and sated beneath me.

When I didn't answer, she turned to me, the smile
falling off her face as she met my stare. "What's wrong?"

I gulped, naming the things in my head. Number one?
She was too gorgeous for words.

"Nothing. Just finding other things to enjoy besides
the movie."

She rolled her eyes, but snuggled in closer. Her ear
against my chest, her hand on my stomach, under my
shirt. She traced lines along my abs, and I feared my
cock against her hip would scare her away. But she
didn't move. And neither did I—no way did I wanna do
anything she didn't.

But that didn't stop me from thinking about touching her the way I'd done on Saturday night. And in my
bathroom. And against my door...

Which brought me to the second thing wrong: I
wanted to strip her, fuck her, and then do it all over
again. And again after. Right here. Right now.

"Collin?"

I ran my nose over her hair, inhaling. "Hmm?"

"Thank you."

"For what?"

Took her a minute to answer, almost as if she couldn't remember the reason. "For being patient with me. I know I wasn't the kindest of people when we met, taking off on you that night at the bar like I did."

I frowned. "You've got nothing to be sorry for. Told you, I was a dick and *you* were nothing short of incredible." I rubbed my nose against hers when she angled her body to face me. "You've never backed down from me, no matter what kind of shit I gave you. Not a lot of people do that."

She scoffed. "*Incredible* is not the word I'd used to describe me. More *impatient* and—"

Not wanting to hear her excuses any longer, I pressed my mouth to hers, holding it there until she relaxed against me. When she wrapped her arms around my neck, I grinned against her lips, loving how she was putty in my hands, knowing and okay with the fact that I was putty in hers too.

"No more apologies. You got me?" I leaned back and tugged down on the base of her pink knit hat, loving it even more up close.

She leaned forward again, pressing her forehead to my shoulder. "No more apologies."

"Good." I stroked my fingers up and down her spine. Igniting shivers in her body was like winning a hard-fought battle. My reward? A beautiful girl who had me wrapped so tightly around her finger that I couldn't stop to catch my breath half the time.

After a while, my grin faded and my heart took over instead, beating like a bass drum in my chest. As she squirmed against me, her curvy hips rubbed against my cock. I gritted my teeth.

Damn, I was trying to be good—for her. A noble guy who only wanted her to be happy. But it was like she knew how to make things hard on me—how to turn me on, how to push my limits, my needs, my want for her.

Soon her lips were on my neck, wet, warm…exactly what I craved. I growled, the sound low in my chest, almost burning, my hands quick as they came to rest along her waist. Wasn't enough though; I needed more. So with the patience of a saint, I lifted my hands and grazed them across the sides of her breasts outside her sweater. The blanket covering us had slipped to our feet, leaving us exposed to the cold night air. Didn't matter. I'd always keep her warm.

Losing my patience, I rolled her over, pressing her head flat against the pillow we'd been using to prop ourselves up with.

"You keep squirming on me, and you're gonna be sorry."

She giggled as I lowered my mouth to her neck and trailed kisses over her throat.

Those giggles fast turned into moans.

She arched her back, pushing me past the hard limit I'd tried to set. "Wanna touch you so bad, sweetheart. Wanna put my lips on that pretty pussy and hear you scream my name again."

Dark, hooded eyes met mine. She looked seductive, almost drugged. Was that a dare in her eyes too? Because I would do exactly what I said, right here, right now—proud to be the man causing her screams.

"Collin…"

Panting, I lowered my forehead to hers. "Fuck, do I love the sound of my name comin' out of your mouth."

I lowered myself down over her stomach and lifted her sweater so I could kiss her warm belly. Her hands were in my hair, pushing and pulling like she was fighting with something—an angel and a devil on her shoulders: one telling her what she wanted, the other one telling her what she needed.

My job should've been to do what's right—heed the desire and side with the angel.

Then again, I never claimed to be a good man.

I'd let her decide, let her use me like a puppet and pull those strings however she wanted.

With a gasp, she pushed me up and off her. But before I could let disappointment take over, she had me on my back, rough and frantic as she reached for my zipper. Fire lit her dark eyes in the night, and her lips parted. One move is all it took her to get my buckle off and my pants undone.

"Jesus Christ," I whispered and threw my head back when my cock sprung free from my boxers. Didn't even care that it was cold.

Frozen in place, she pulled her bottom lip between her teeth while she stared at my dick.

I sat up on my elbows, alarms going off in my mind. "You don't have to do this."

She met my gaze, eyes dark and serious. "I want to."

"Have you ever sucked a man off before, Addie?"

She shoved my shoulder, laughing once. "I'm not a nun."

But I wanted her to be one. Twenty-six years old or not, I wanted to be the only guy she'd ever been with.

Her shoulders relaxed, and with both hands on my thighs, she moved closer. "Besides, blow jobs are like riding a bike."

I frowned, annoyed with her analogy. "Like you suck one dick, you suck them... Holy shit." Her mouth went down, her tongue caressing the head. With a skill I'd never seen or felt in my life, she sucked on the base from the bottom to the top.

This girl was a magician, and she'd yet to even wrap her lips around me fully.

Noises were coming out of my mouth. Low, desperate, so fucking eager that I nearly lost my mind. Didn't care who heard me though. This, right here, was the hottest fucking moment in my life, and there wasn't a thing that could ruin it.

Slowly, she dragged her lips up over the head and, with a soft sigh, lowered her pretty mouth back down. "Christ, Addie."

My words encouraged her, and she dropped her mouth even more, taking me in deeper—to the point I could feel the back of her throat. The urge to push up was so damn strong that I wanted to scream.

Sweat gathered along my neck and my temples, but I couldn't stop watching long enough to wipe it away. Instead I reached down, bit my tongue, and stroked the hair away from her forehead. She jumped, her dark eyes meeting mine. In turn she went faster, deeper, tighter.

My stomach clenched, and like she knew just what I needed, Addie brought a free hand up and trailed it around my belly button, down the trail of hair, and back up to start her luscious torture all over again.

Definitely the devil—wasn't a damn bit of angel in

this sexy woman. Addie made me wild, made me growl, made me so hard I was gonna explo—

"Excuse me."

"Gah!" Addie flew backward at the noise, ramming her ass against the tire rack.

"This is a family drive-in, so I'm going to have to ask you two to leave."

A flashlight shone in my eyes as I scrambled to cover my exploding dick with the blanket.

"What the hell are you doing, man?" I slammed my head back against the pillow, groaning.

"Sorry, but we've had some complaints about…"

I glared at him, warning him with my eyes not to say anything else. He pressed his lips together, while Addie, on the other hand, hid her face in her knees, shoulders shaking, crying. *Stupid, pimple-faced, little prickhead.*

"We're leaving. Suggest you do the same," I growled, fisting the blanket so I didn't stand up and swing at the kid.

Instead of ducking and running, he just looked from me to Addie, then back to me—a dumbass grin on his face the entire time.

"You want a show, asshole? 'Cause I'll give you one with my knuckles if you don't move."

Fear flashed in his eyes, and he took a step away from the truck. "Uh…no, sir. No. I'll, uh…" He pointed his flashlight toward the screen, then ran away, his tiny-ass tail tucked between his thighs.

"Addison, hey…" I moved closer to her, tucking my half-deflated cock back into my pants along the way. "Don't cry. He was just some dumb kid." I wrapped my arm around her back, pulling her against my side. But when I pulled her hands down, I didn't see tears on her face. I saw a huge-ass smile on her lips instead.

"That was…" She belly laughed. "The funniest thing"—she snorted—"I've ever"—she pressed her hand to her stomach and fell over onto my thighs—"been through." She sighed, but then she giggled some more, the sound so contagious that I laughed right along with her.

CHAPTER 27

Addison

BEFORE MY MOTHER DECIDED HER MAH-JONGG FRIENDS and the need for every plastic surgery imaginable mattered more than her daughter, she was actually pretty amazing.

She did my hair and nails, and took me for massages at the age of twelve because she thought it would make my scoliosis straighten out. She used to believe in holistic medicine and shots, and natural ingredients in her food. Used to make all dinners from scratch and demanded we have dinner together as a family every night at six sharp, no matter what was happening.

Having grown up in the Philippines with a super-religious family, Mom wasn't one who necessarily lived by the rules as she got older. And I liked that about her. She was a free spirit, natural, and, even though it was in her own way, loving.

But it was amazing how time, and one man, could change a person.

Mom wasn't the hugging type, of course. More the pat-on-the-back, nod-your-head type when I did something good in life. But the one thing I remember the most about the woman—prior to my falling-out with my parents—was when the two of us had *the* chat. Not necessarily just the sex and condoms, but the chat about boys who would grow to be men, and boys who would never grow to be anything but the immature scuzzbuckets they were.

As I sat curled into Collin's side on Thanksgiving night at his dining room table—Chloe on the other side of him, devouring a small piece of pumpkin pie, while Lia, Gavin, and Max sat across from us drinking beer and arguing about who would win that night's football game—I couldn't help but wonder what category my mother would put him in.

In my mind, he was perfectly flawed—perfect for me. And even though I wanted to push the thoughts of my mother's opinion out of my head, I just couldn't for some reason. Which sucked because I was so happy—happier than I'd been in a very long time. "So, I'm having a craving." I grinned up at him, trying not to ruin the night with my thoughts. I blamed it on the holiday and the fact that my parents didn't even bother to call and wish me a happy Thanksgiving. There again, I didn't bother to call them either.

"That so?" He turned toward me, nuzzling his nose against my cheek. I shivered in response like always, almost forgetting what I said, where we were, and who surrounded us.

Giggling, I managed to push him back and turned, knees intertwining with his. "Not *that* kind of craving."

He leaned forward, pressing a hand to my face. "Are we talking ice cream or strawberries and chocolate? What are the things women crave nowadays?"

Muscles, dimples—preferably two—full lips, and gorgeous, dark-blue eyes. *Those* were the things I was suddenly craving, especially when Collin looked at me as though *I* were on the dessert menu, not the pumpkin pie sitting in front of us on the table.

"Addie."

"Huh?" I blinked.

"Cravings?" His eyes narrowed, but his lips twitched too.

"Yeah, yeah, sorry. I want this dessert thing, actually. It's called bibingka. It's made with rice, coconut, and duck eggs, all wrapped in banana leaves... I had it every Thanksgiving. My mom always made it." Collin screwed up his nose, but a hint of a smile still covered his mouth as he continued to listen. "You can't find duck eggs in any of the Carinthia grocery stores. But I know a place that sells them in Matoona."

"Uh, okay." Collin scratched at his scruffy chin, the sound all sorts of sexy. I settled my arms along his knee, needing to be closer. "Doubt there's anything open right now though."

"This store is open twenty-four seven." I shrugged, my face heating at how eager I sounded. Regret hit me the moment I stared across the table, finding all three sets of eyes on us. Lia smiled knowingly, Gavin's eyes were narrowed, and Max was... Well, Max was Max, making weird faces at giggling Chloe.

My shoulders fell and I sighed, already hating that I'd even made the suggestion. This was Thanksgiving, Collin's first one back with his friends and his daughter.

The last thing he needed was an impromptu meet and greet with my parents. Parents who undoubtedly wanted nothing to do with me anymore.

I lowered my chin to my chest. "Forget I said anything. It was stupid."

He leaned forward, lifting my chin with one finger before pressing his lips to mine in a soft kiss. "For you, Addie, I'd travel to the ends of the earth just to find you duck eggs." I smiled. "Just let me clean Chloe up and put her to bed. Then we can go."

Tears gathered in the corners of my eyes when I looked away. If a man offered to drive to the ends of the earth to buy you duck eggs for some random dessert on Thanksgiving night, you knew he was a keeper.

"Come on, y'all. Let's do this thing. I got twenty on the Bears." Max winked at me as he stood, then grabbed Lia around the waist before tugging her to the couch.

Gavin groaned but stood too, his chair grating across the floor. He followed the pair and said, "You two know nothing. The Packers are in it to win it this year."

"Bullshit." Lia snorted, sipping her beer. "The Super Bowl will be dominated by the Mets. And I will laugh in the faces of you all when—"

"Lee-Lee"—Max tugged her onto his lap, arm wrapped around her back—"you do know the Mets are a baseball team, right?"

Even I knew that one.

"Well, I…" Lia's cheeks uncharacteristically turned red as Max held her face between his hands.

"And this is why you are gonna be the death of me." He kissed her on the forehead, like Collin kissed me. It seemed to mean nothing to Max as he leaned back in the seat, but Lia sat there stone-still on his lap, eyes wide as she stared at the floor.

I narrowed my eyes, catching her gaze as she stood to head to the bathroom a minute or so later. Her gaze said, *Don't ask*, but the questions in my mind were scrambling like mad.

A half hour later, Chloe was tucked into her crib, asleep, and Collin and I were on the road.

Collin tapped his thumbs against the wheel to the beat of the music on the radio, Christmas music already jingling away. A light dusting of snow fell from the sky, hitting the window like tiny crystals.

As much as I appreciated the fact that he'd agreed to this farce of a trip, I couldn't help but wonder if it was a mistake. It was seven thirty on Thanksgiving night, so the chances of either of my parents being there were slim to none. Likely it would be one of the people they'd hired since I left, or possibly my dad's cousin, who occasionally filled in when need be. Still, just going into their territory felt like I was stepping onto a battlefield.

Is this what Collin felt like when he was still enlisted? Or stuck in the bunkers of Iraq, waiting for the next IED to explode?

"Your hands are shaking."

I gave my head a fast jerk and beamed over at him, the fakeness of the smile hurting my cheeks. "Thinking maybe I had too much caffeine today or something."

"You sure?" He arched a brow. The fact he could already read me so well should've been scary. But it wasn't. Instead, it was comforting to have someone in my life like this.

"Yes, sirree." And what was I, twelve?

Hands moving over the top of the wheel, Collin stayed quiet as he pulled his truck into the lot a little while later. By then, my knees were bouncing in place and I had the window partially rolled down, face held close to it like a dog.

"Addison."

"Hmm?" I searched the parking lot for my parents' car even though, after seven years, they probably had a new one.

"Talk to me."

"I just really want that dessert, and—"

"No. That's not it." He pulled my face toward his and frowned. "If you wanted this dessert, you would have made it already, especially if it's some sort of a tradition for you."

"Not true. *But* would you believe me if I told you I don't remember how to make it and they have the recipe at this store?" I bit my lip, my excuses lamer than lame.

He sighed. "Knew you weren't telling me the truth the second you asked. But I didn't wanna upset you when we've had such a good day." He cupped my cheek, leaning forward. "You being at my place with my daughter, my sister, my best friends"—half of his mouth curled up into an alluring grin—"made this day damn near extraordinary."

"Yeah?" My stomach dipped in the best possible way.

"Yeah, sweetheart." He rubbed his thumb along my cheek. "Plus, there is no way this hole-in-the-wall convenience store will have *duck* eggs."

"Hole-in-the-wall?" What did he mean by…? I turned my head to face the store and gasped.

One glass window was boarded up, and the white

frame hugging the door hung loose on the right side.
Over the top of the door, the *B* was burned out in the
dilapidated Booker's Meat Market sign, and the trash
barrel out front overflowed with God only knew what.

"Oh hell." My throat grew dry, my chest aching.
Blindly, I reached for the door handle, scrambling
to get it open, panic as thick as chewing gum stuck
in my throat. I stepped out of the truck and didn't
glance back as I darted across the parking lot toward
the store.

This…this wasn't right. This…this…

"Addie?" A hand pressed against my shoulder,
another around my waist. I wondered if fate had finally
gone and ruined me after all.

"This is my parents' store." The words were a whisper, my lungs stinging as I tried to breathe.

Memories bombarded me.

Mom kicking me outside to color with chalk on the
sidewalk when I was ten.

Dad firing up his grill in the parking lot, selling
Mom's egg rolls for the lunch crowd.

Selling soda cans and lemonade for a quarter on the
side to make money so I could buy gum balls at the
candy store down the street.

"Let's go inside. Do what you came here to do, okay?"

"I'm not sure if I can."

Collin moved to stand in front of me, crouching
down a bit so his face met mine. "Not sure what's
brought this on, or what this place even means to you,
but something tells me if you don't go in now, you
might not go in again."

My lips quivered. This beautiful, stubborn, cocky,

know-it-all man understood exactly what to say and when to say it.

"W-will you go with me?"

He used his index finger to wipe the tears away from my cheeks. "Wouldn't let you go in there without me."

Chest tight, I grabbed one of his hands and interlocked our fingers. Moving to my side, he motioned for me to go first. Knowing it was time, I reached for the old door, ignoring the foghorn-type warning going off inside my brain.

Seven years. Seven long, lonely years. That's how long it'd been since I last set foot inside this store. Turning back wasn't an option, but neither was stepping through that door, not when my heavy feet felt like they were glued to the sidewalk. But then something magical happened. Collin squeezed my fingers and pulled me along behind him. And that's all it took for me to take those final steps.

A bell clanked against the door, and I jumped. Collin laughed softly and urged me on with his chin. In and out I attempted to breathe as I stepped inside…and ran straight into an unfamiliar man.

"We close in five minutes."

"We just need one thing," Collin interjected, the sound a warning.

The man with a unibrow and an accent straight out of Germany glared back and forth between us but made no move to stop us. When had my parents hired this guy? And close at eight? Since when? One of the last pieces of advice I'd given my parents was to run a normal seven-to-seven shift. Most of the nearby small stores did. But Mom was money hungry and thought the night crowd would bring in the most cash with their booze buying and whatnot.

"Get what you need, and let's get home," Collin grumbled, letting go of my hand to press against the small of my back. "I'm thinking we're not wanted here."

My lips parted. More than anything, I wanted to tell him this was a safe store, a safe neighborhood too. I used to sleep on the cot in the back room some nights when I was younger and my parents had to do the night shift. But he was right. Something was off. Something wasn't what it used to be.

"I just… I need to see the back of the store for a second."

"The back?"

I nodded. "Yeah…th-that's where they keep the duck eggs."

Down one aisle, then a right, then another left and we'd be there, at the cooler filled with the eggs, next to the meat counter with my dad's handwritten signs, all telling the prices per pound.

Only what I found instead was one giant wall of floor-to-ceiling coolers, all filled with beer. Wine. Wine coolers.

"Addison?"

I turned to my right, thinking I'd missed something but finding another cooler.

"Hey, let's—"

"Where is it?" I growled and turned to my left. Another cooler, this one filled with milk and juice and pop and…not meat. Not cheese. Not duck eggs. There was nothing reminding me of Booker's. Nothing reminding me of my parents.

"Addie. Talk to me."

"I…" Not wasting another second, I pushed past Collin and took off toward the front of the store. At the view, I stumbled back. The once-open cashier space was blocked by bulletproof glass and bars. How had I not noticed this when we walked in?

"Who are you?" I asked the man.

"Who are you?" he asked, his white eyebrows pushed together.

"Where are Rose and Robert Booker?"

"Who?" The man looked from me to Collin, who had moved to stand next to me.

"Addison, come on. Let's go." Collin's voice was soft, placating even. I jerked out of his hold.

"No. I need to know." I approached the man, pressing my hands on the counter. "Where are the Bookers? The old owners of this…" What was this place now? A liquor store? Convenience store? A hole-in-the-wall just like Collin had called it?

"I do not know. This is my brother's business. His name is So."

I laughed, the sound sarcastic, edgy, impatient. "You're telling me the owner, the guy who now *runs* this place, is named *So*?"

"That is what I am telling you. Now leave. I am closing the store so I can go home and be with my family."

"No," I whispered. "They sold it." Ugly tears ran down my face, yet I couldn't find the energy to wipe them away. "They sold it…" I gripped the back of my hair and turned toward Collin, willing him to understand, only to see pity and confusion in his eyes instead.

I hated pity.

"Addison." Collin moved closer, reaching for my

hand. At the last minute, I pulled it away and ran for the door. In the parking lot, he called my name, but I shook my head and said, "I can't be here."

My vision blurred as I charged toward his truck, stopping when I realized he'd locked the doors and I couldn't get in.

I settled my head against the cold window and squeezed my eyes shut to curb my angry tears. In a way, I'd known this would happen, but I still couldn't help but curse myself for thinking that they would have cared enough to tell me they'd sold the store. My father was a selfish man, and when he didn't get his way, he made sure to hurt the person who wouldn't let that happen. Like a child, that's what he was—a spoiled, pretentious child. To him, I was nothing but the extra baggage who came along with his mail-order bride. Add that I didn't bow down to his whims like my mother did or follow the career path he wanted me to, and I was all but dead to him.

"Will you talk to me now?" There wasn't a lick of hesitation in Collin's voice as he spun me around and hugged me to his chest. "Don't do well without words, Addie. I'm not a mind reader, never have been."

My shoulders shook as I sobbed. Every second longer he spoke, my body broke down, his arms the only thing holding me up.

"I know you've got secrets. Hell, we all do, baby. Nobody wants to share them. It's human nature to lock all the bad inside."

My heart skipped at his words, the feeling of shame washing over me.

"What I do know is that it's better if you talk about

the bad shit, especially to someone who's willing to do absolutely anything to make your pain go away."

My chest grew tight. The intensity, the fear, the purpose, the willingness...those things were all I could see, taste, want, desire. And they were all there on Collin's face when I finally pulled back to look him in the eyes.

No, I wasn't ready to talk about my family—not sure if I ever would be—but I was ready for more. With Collin.

With no thoughts of my family, their betrayal, and my loss, I let the rightness of Collin take over and pressed my lips to his.

Collin was my more.

CHAPTER 28

Collin

I'D BEEN KISSED BEFORE, MORE TIMES THAN I COULD count. But with this much desperation? This much need? Hell no. Not ever.

"Let's get in the truck," she whispered against my neck, biting down on the tip of my ear with enough force to send my cock into my zipper.

Somehow, in the dingy parking lot of this run-down convenience store, I'd wound up with this gorgeous woman pressed against the hood of my truck, hands beneath her shirt, cupping her breasts, and asking for things I wasn't sure she was ready to give—even if I knew I was ready to give them to her.

I pulled back, hating the distance. Knowing at the same time I had to be the one to put it there. "Tell me what you want. Meant it when I said I couldn't read people real well."

Chest moving fast, she lowered her hand and cupped my dick.

"Fuck, baby." I shuddered as she ran her palm over the zipper. Unlike the last time, her hands weren't shaking. There was no confusion in her eyes either. Just heat and need and the same desire I'd felt for her since the night we'd first met.

With a sort of strength only a priest could maintain, I pulled away and let her go.

"Come on." I took a step back, unable to look into her eyes.

At her side of the truck, I opened the door and shooed her in. She lowered her chin, probably thinking the worst of me when really all I wanted to do was strip her down right here in the cab.

Tipping her chin up, I whispered, "Not gonna make our first time happen in a parking lot. It's not right."

"Collin, I don't care where—"

"Said no, Addison. Now get in the truck before I lose my mind."

My throat burned like a fire poker was shoved down inside it, especially when she batted those big, soulful eyes at me. No way did I want to be an asshole, but this beautiful woman was emotional, obviously broken over something, and definitely not thinking straight. Sex right here was the last thing she needed. And because I respected her—who she was and her feelings—I did what she couldn't and said no. She'd change her mind anyway once we left this lot and whatever memories were eating her up.

What I wanted to do first was hear about those memories and see if she could at least give me a little insight on what caused her emotional meltdown.

After I drove out of the lot, I kept my eyes on the road ahead. "You ready to talk to me?"

"I don't want—"

"Wrong answer."

She sighed and sank lower in her seat, giving me nothing more than her stoic profile and an occasional sniffle along the way back to Carinthia. Hated her quiet more than anything. Hated losing her smile, her laugh, and even her goofy-ass jokes. Part of me thought maybe being in the truck like this would give her the chance to think and talk to me, but when I pulled up to the rugby field no more than twenty minutes later, she still hadn't said squat.

Other than a couple of streetlights off on the side road, the place was pitch-black. Thick cornfields lined the left side, while on the right sat a playground. Knowing I needed to let Max in on what was happening, I pulled out my phone and sent him a quick text, making sure Chloe was covered.

A few seconds later, I was out of the truck, after grabbing the blanket in the cab. Lips parted in a tiny *O*, Addie stared up at me as I leaned against the frame of her opened door a second later. Instead of coming right out and asking what was really wrong, this time I studied her pretty face, waiting to see if she went first. Of course she didn't even move, so I rolled my eyes and wrapped my arm around her waist, carrying her fireman's style toward midfield.

After a couple of slaps along my shoulder blades, I couldn't help but smile in success as I set her on her feet.

"Why did you bring me here?" She straightened her sweater out and then folded her arms across her chest.

All the earlier heat and need I'd seen in her eyes were gone, replaced with a familiar brokenness I still saw in my own reflection some days.

"Brought you here to show you this." I lifted my hand up toward the sky, letting the stars speak for themselves.

"It's beautiful." Loved that sound—the breathiness in her words. So open and raw and real.

"Something about being out here at night makes all the bad shit in life go extinct, even if it's only temporary, ya know? Figured I'd share it with you." I cleared my throat and tossed the blanket onto the ground, face going hot at my sentimental bullshit.

When I was done, I looked at her again, meeting her gaze and finding her eyes softer than before, her shoulders relaxed. The snow had stopped, and a soft layer surrounded us on the grass. But the blanket was thick, so she'd be safe from getting wet. Plus, I'd do everything possible to keep her warm.

"Sit." I pointed at the blanket.

"Here?"

I nodded.

"But—"

Groaning, I grabbed her around the waist and pulled her down sideways onto my lap. She squealed, all crazy-like, until I settled her against my chest and draped my right arm across her back.

With a big sigh, she relaxed against me. Her hair tickled my chin, while the scent of her shampoo put me into a state of oblivion with only Addie on my mind.

"The airport landing strip's about two miles to our west." I pointed at the lights flashing on the small runway in the distance.

"I didn't think something so simple would be so beautiful."

Nothing was more beautiful than the woman in my

arms. But spouting that line would be like chopping my dick in half, so I'd have to settle for keeping my thoughts inside for now.

"You ready to talk yet?"

She shook her head again, a slow movement against my chest.

"Someday then."

"Someday soon, I promise. I just... This is too perfect to ruin." The promise of her sticking around long enough to tell me the truth was enough for me.

"Wanna know another reason I brought you out here?" I sat up a little straighter, and she followed suit. With my finger, I tipped her head toward mine and brushed my nose up and down over her cold cheek. Her breath grew heavier, fogging up the air around her lips.

"Why?"

Slowly, I tucked my hand up under her shirt and spread it across her spine. "So I could kiss you without sharing it with the world."

She groaned, leaving me unsure whether it was because my hand was moving higher, trailing a line under her bra strap, or because I'd irritated her. Either way, I was fine with it because it meant her mind was already clearing.

"You're a fool. Nobody could see us back at the store other than maybe *So's bro*."

Strong, resilient—even after her mini breakdown, Addie was a rock, more powerful than I could have guessed. Sure, I wondered if sarcasm and joking were like her cover-up. But then again, we all had our ways of coping.

"Wonder if So's mom's name was Ho," she whispered, voice all rough and sexy.

Fighting the laughter in my throat, I whispered back, "Or maybe he had a sister named Flo." I grinned, kissing the top of her head.

"I'm going Gigolo for the dad, Piccolo for the sister, and Bob for the other brother." She shivered, finally resting her cheek against my chest. Both of her palms were on my thigh, rubbing back and forth in a maddening line.

"Bob?" I managed to get the word out, my cock so hard against her leg I was sure she felt it.

She leaned her head back and lifted her chin, our eyes meeting. With her mouth tipped up on one side, looking sexy as sin, Addie was like an offering from the gods. One no man would ever be able to refuse.

"Bob the oddball."

I shut my eyes, rubbing my forehead against hers. "The oddball, huh?"

One of her hands lifted off my thigh to run through the back of my hair. Her fingers were like silk—soft, smooth. "Every family has one. The one member that's out of place and doesn't belong. The *Bob* of the group. Like me."

My throat burned. She was giving me a hint, and it tore me up inside. What happened in her past to make her feel like she didn't even fucking belong in her own family?

Not wanting to push her, I kissed the spot to the right of her lips. "I like you as a Bob."

She grinned, letting her fingers trail lower into the collar of my shirt. "Minus the penis, of course."

"Thinking I'd go penis for you, sweetheart."

A full-on belly laugh rumbled through the air, just

as a plane roared overhead, coming in to land. Addison jumped at the sound.

"Is it supposed to be so low?"

"Yeah," I whispered, not even bothering to look. I had something more important I needed to study.

As the loud roar of the plane continued, my need for this woman only intensified, faster and harder than I'd ever known before. Like a rocket to the gut, a plane to the head, a sledgehammer clobbering away at my soul. Looking at Addie made everything right. Kissing her made everything perfect.

She turned back around to face me, and I went for it, growling low in my throat as I hitched her body up over my lap, her legs now straddling mine. No time to waste, not a moment too soon. If I didn't get inside her, I'd lose my mind.

Chest to chest, I went right for the bottom of her shirt, only letting her lips go to speak. Needed her words, her commitment to this before I took it further. Nothing was sexier than a woman saying yes.

"I need you like water, baby, but I'm not gonna do anything 'til you tell me you need me too."

Panting, she pulled back, only to grab the hems of her sweater and the T beneath to throw them up over her head. Her lips twitched, and her eyes were heated, playful, and gorgeous. "If this doesn't tell you what I need"—she wrapped her bare arms around my back, urging my shirt up this time, her nails scraping over my flesh—"then you need a serious lesson on what a woman wants."

I didn't need any lessons. Just needed the right woman to tell me how and when to—

"Make love to me, Collin. Right here." Her whispered request stirred something inside me. Maybe it was the *L*-word she used. Maybe it was the desire in her voice or the honesty in her eyes. But it was something I knew damn well I'd never let go of.

"Fuck yes."

I spun her over, pulling her beneath me, stomach tight. Not thinking about where we were or how exposed this made us, I reached for the button of her jeans, popping it open with a flick of my fingers. My knuckles grazed her pretty stomach, and I moved my mouth down, needing to taste the smooth skin. Just below her belly button, I kissed a curve, loving how she wasn't shy with her body and instead arched her back and urged me lower.

"Gotta take my time with this." Worship her like she deserved.

The broken stalks of corn nearby blew in the breeze, rustling around us like perfect music for the perfect night. The low buzz of the plane engine still echoed in the distance, sounding almost like the vibrations coming from inside my chest. Our blanket had bunched beneath us, the scratchy material nowhere near perfect enough to serve this moment. But then Addie shivered, urging me closer with her hands on my forearms and making me forget about details.

I leaned back and slipped my own pants off, gritting my teeth as the sting of cold air hit my back. "Jesus, it's cold out here."

She rolled her eyes, finally succeeding in pulling me closer. But instead of telling me *I told you so* like she probably would've normally done, she brought my face down to hers and kissed me. Kissed me so slowly that the goose bumps on my arms were no longer caused by the cold.

Groaning, needing to touch her all over, I reached back and lifted her leg, trailing my fingers from the back of her knee, up her thigh, and down all over again.

When I'd gotten my fill of her legs, I spread them wider with my thighs and devoted the next few minutes of my time to her round, supple breasts. She hissed against my lips, pulling away to throw her head back, almost like the sensation was too much. Her hard nipples were like pebbles beneath her bra—couldn't wait to get them in my mouth. Grinning against her neck at the thought, I kissed her throat, still enjoying the torture as I grazed over each of her nipples with my thumb.

Damn sure I was gonna take my time and make her remember this.

"Please, Collin. I can't… I need…" Knowing I'd teased her long enough, I rolled over onto my side, making sure not to let her go. To do what I wanted next, she needed to be near me, facing me, as close to me as I could physically get her.

Wanting to see more, to feel it all in my hands, I reached behind her back and flicked the clasp of her bra off. Like a cat, she hissed as I scooted closer, never lifting my lips from her skin. I pulled her bra straps down over her shoulders and tossed it on the blanket to my right.

"Goddamn perfect." Even in the dark, I could see the outline of her dark nipples, the curves of her rounded breasts. I kissed the top of each one, licking, tasting, until my mouth closed over a nipple.

"Oh my God," she groaned, thrusting her hips against

mine. I growled at the pressure and lowered my hand to her ass, feeling the back of her tiny panties.

Never relenting, I sucked on her nipples and caressed every inch of her backside, slipping my hand beneath the material to squeeze and thrust against her. Harder than hell, needier than I'd ever been, I said, "Fuck this slow shit. Need you. Now."

Feeling crazy, I slipped off her panties, then my own underwear, and pushed her onto her back, all wide eyed and naked flesh. I wanted inside her so bad I could taste it.

"Can't go slow, not anymore." She whimpered, sucking on my neck, my chin.

I reached for my jeans, needing no other sign. She was feeling the same way as me. Hovering over her with one hand propped by her face and my cock resting against her bare thigh, I grabbed my wallet from my pocket and searched for a condom.

Max—the good guy he was—had restored my supply the second he'd seen me and Addie together. Said I'd need it eventually, saying I was an idiot for not being prepared for the inevitable. And even though I didn't believe I'd ever get this lucky, I'd always hoped, knowing my attraction for Addie was an explosion in the making.

And now, here I was, seconds away from getting exactly what I wanted. With the woman of my dreams.

The blanket moved down, leaving her ass exposed against the damp, snowy grass and my knees on either side of her waist. My chest hurt just looking at her— knew she was the only one I'd ever want this bad again.

"Gotta fix the blanket. Don't wanna—"

"No." She brought my forehead to hers, nibbling on my chin. "I don't care about that. Just…please."

I shut my eyes, taking in her words, then pulling back to meet her gaze. And seeing her silent nod, her heated gaze, I lined up my cock and drove inside her, finding my home once and for all.

CHAPTER 29

Addison

THERE'S THIS PLACE BEFORE EUPHORIA—SEXUAL BLISS, orgasmic perfection—where you think nothing and everything at the same time. Words you can't contain, like "Oh my God, yes... Please, harder." And then there's the moment you call out your partner's name: "Collin..." But what I was fast learning as a woman with little sexual experience is that being with the right person can bring on the euphoria from the first moment of connection. Because the second Collin slid inside me, I wanted to come.

My hands were on his back, holding him in me, scratching at his sweaty skin, his tight ass. The moment of connection was almost too much, yet not enough. Collin was inside me.

Collin, my boss. Collin, my friend. Collin, my lover.

The last thing I wanted was to rush this moment and find the end so soon.

One stroke, then two, his body knew exactly what to

do to mine. Hips upon hips, skin upon skin, lips upon lips, sweat, cold, hot—I was a mess of need, and damn, it was too fast, too good, too right.

His lips grazed over mine, slow, steady, like he was barely in control.

"You're so tight."

One thrust—hard. An ache so deep in my body that I wanted to scream.

"Loving your sweet pussy, but it's been so long for me. So fucking long…"

He groaned. Another thrust, this time me pushing hard against his hips.

"Never gonna want another like I do you though. Never."

My eyes rolled into the back of my head at his words. They were so honest, and scary, and the most real I'd ever heard.

I pressed my feet flat on the grass, and he slipped a hand beneath my neck, lowering his mouth down over my chin, my neck, worshipping me. The wetness beneath me on the grass served as a reminder of the raw moment—and no matter what, I'd never, *ever* regret it.

Over and over, he thrust against me—inside me. The ache subsiding, bringing a delicious sensation of sparks throughout my body.

I scraped my hands over his backside, and he cried out, "You're killing me, sweetheart." Reaching down between us, he pressed a thumb against my clit. Sweat slicked between our bodies, the cold wind an unexpected blessing.

With a growl, he sat up, fighting mad as he straddled me across his lap. The position forced my legs wider, pushing him in deeper. And then his hand moved faster, as if this alone was his reason for moving us. My breasts rubbed against his chest, and I looked down, watching him move inside me.

"Beautiful." Like me, he was looking down at our connected bodies, a grin on his lips. But when he met my stare, his face grew tighter, his pace increasing.

I moaned, I called out his name, and in turn, he moved his fingers faster and pressed his forehead against mine.

He didn't kiss me after that, just held my gaze as he rocked me up and down and held a thumb over my clit. There were things unsaid in his stare, a promise I was dying for, but now wasn't the time for commitments.

And then it happened. He groaned. I groaned. He thrust harder.

"Addison." He lowered his chin to his chest, pressing his forehead to my lips. "Sweet. Addison." He tightened his hold, and then I came—so hard I screamed. The night air capturing my sounds. I was dying the sweetest death by orgasm ever. And it was the best way to go.

Soon after, he followed me and dropped both hands to grab my backside as he finished. Filled with awe and wonder and magic, I watched him bite down on his lip, watched him welcome the ache I'd just found.

And that was the moment I knew I'd fallen for him. Hard.

—∿∿—

I darted up from my pillow, eyes bleary as I searched the room. My chest grew tight as the sunlight spilled in from an unfamiliar window. But before I could let myself relax and enjoy the fact that I was sleeping in Collin's bed, a cry sounded out. Chloe's.

In only Collin's T-shirt, I scrambled out of bed and

went straight to her room. Only, the door was open, and she wasn't inside, her screaming coming from the living room. Panic washed over me, and I darted down the hall, the ache between my thighs reminding me I'd done more than just sleep the night before.

Instead of finding a burglar or whatever crazy person my mind was conjuring up, I found three men in different states of dress, all nailing and pounding something *kind of* resembling a piece of furniture. Chloe, on the other hand, was not crying, but squealing in excitement as she sat in her high chair, watching the three men.

Too exhausted to speak, I stayed back and watched the show before me unfold.

"No, you dumbass. When it says flat head, you use a flat head." Collin.

"Screw you. You wanna do this yourself, then do it. I'll gladly sit on the couch and watch this shit show unfold. God knows Max'll have it fucked up in no time." Gavin stood up, running a hand over his face.

"You're just in a piss-poor mood because I made you get up and go Black Friday shopping with me, so piss off." Max.

"Will you two guys just shut up? You're gonna wake up Addie."

I grinned, hiding my lips behind my hand. Lordy, Collin was sweet—respectful and always thinking of others. It's just one of the reasons I was so attracted to him. Yes, he did suffer from an occasional case of dickhead-itis when he got all domineering on me, but it wasn't something I couldn't handle.

Not to mention that just *looking* at the guy made me hotter than a sauna in the middle of the desert. With the simple bunching of his shoulders as he hovered over his white instruction manual, he stole the air from my lungs. Dressed in black boxers, no shirt, and… Oh hell, were those scratch marks down his back? I cringed.

"I don't get you, man." Max sat back on his heels. His eyebrows were drawn together in concentration, and he had on a pair of dark glasses, making him look one half sexy nerdy and the other half naughty sinister. Short, spiky, black hair stuck up all over, but it was still coated with gel from the night before. He was dressed in a white T-shirt and a pair of black gym shorts. "You have this hot-ass woman in your bed, yet you still sleep on the couch *and* choose to wake up early on a Saturday to put furniture together." Max sighed, lowering his chin to his chest. "You're making my cock hurt just thinking about it."

"Don't." It was one word, nothing more. But the second Collin said it to Max, I knew he meant business.

Confusion pulled my brows together. He hadn't slept in the bed with me? How had I not noticed him getting up to leave?

"It's called respect, you idiot. She was exhausted, and I couldn't ask her to go home so late." Collin sighed.

"Well, shit. I'm thinking you need to get on that before—"

Collin slammed his tool on a piece of wood. "For God's sake, Max. She's Chloe's fucking nanny. Leave it alone."

My jaw clenched, anger at the forefront of my emotions. I took a step back into the hallway and leaned my shoulders against the wall, stealing the quickest, sharpest breath I could inhale. There, in the narrow, empty space, I tried to pretend Collin wasn't actually *denying* me. It had to be more of a mistake with his words is all.

Benefit of the doubt, Addie. Give him the benefit of the doubt.

"But didn't you say the two of you—" Gavin.

"Can we put this thing together and just stop with the chick talk? My head hurts, and Chloe isn't gonna last much longer in her high chair." I knew the sound in Collin's voice. I could hear the exhaustion and annoyance too. I just wished I knew why. Was it because of me? Of what happened between us?

I turned to go back into his room, get dressed, and leave, thinking I'd overstayed my welcome after all. But before I could get too far, Gavin's words stopped me short. "What's on your back, man? Nail marks?"

I shut my eyes, hands clutching the bottom of Collin's shirt.

Chloe's squeals grew louder, her toys clattering on the floor at the same time. My head snapped in her direction, and *her* eyes, wide and gleaming, were locked onto my face. In all her baby excitement, she threw her arms out toward me, and I cringed and waved in response. It was pretty much a safe bet that three ex-military men would catch on to my spy tactics, but then again, what did I have to lose?

I looked around the corner once more, finding Gavin behind Collin, who was now standing.

"Nail marks?" Max narrowed his eyes and moved in closer to see. "Where?"

"His back." Gavin grinned, pointing down at the marks. "Well, hell. Now it all makes sense."

My stomach dipped, nerves eating at my insides.

"What?" Collin circled around to face them both, rubbing the back of his neck at the same time.

Max tapped a thumb against his smug smile, while Gavin scrubbed his hand up and down his face.

"Do you guys mind?" Collin's shoulders bunched and stretched as he reached forward to grab a shirt off the end table.

"Well, well, well. The dirty dog fucked her after all." Gavin looked up at the ceiling. My stomach coiled even tighter, and I pressed both hands against my throat.

Were they mad? Disappointed? I held my breath, not realizing how much I wanted their approval until that moment.

Collin moved toward Chloe, eyes narrowed as he picked her toys up off the floor and set them back on her tray. "Didn't *fuck* anybody. I don't plan to either."

Max folded his arms over his chest. "You're lying."

"Come on, man." Collin laughed, the sound eerily distant yet again.

Gavin stabbed a finger in Max's chest, the testosterone between the three of them going up about a thousand notches. Surprisingly, Max moved to stand next to Gavin.

"Don't shit where you eat, man. I've told you that. Meant it more so with *her*." Gavin.

Collin took a step back, away from the wooden planks used for whatever they were putting together. One thing was for certain: I didn't want to be a part of this. If Collin *was* having regrets over what happened, there was no way I could continue with whatever charade he was playing with me. I was already in too deep. If I sank any lower, I knew I'd drown. Not just because of Collin, but because of Chloe and his friends—his sister too. These people had become my family, and if I lost them all, I...

No. I couldn't think like that. *Wouldn't* was more like it.

And screw the tears burning my eyes and the fact that my hips and body were deliciously sore from last night too. No way would I let Collin decide what happened between us without my input. I was done standing down to appease the people I cared about. Bending to their will just to make peace I'd never be happy with. I did it growing up with my parents, at least until college came along. Meek me was over. And if Collin didn't want me, then I wouldn't want him either.

Or I'd pretend not to want him, at least.

"You know..." Shoulders back, head high, I cleared my throat and stepped into the room. Three sets of eyes flashed my way, every one of them perusing my nearly naked body at the same time. Let them be made powerless by my womanly wiles. God gave me boobs, an ass, and long legs for a reason. It was time I used them for evil.

"When I was a kid, my dad used to struggle for *hours* trying to put stuff like this together." I whipped the instructions out of Collin's hands, clicking my tongue. "And every time, I asked if he wanted my help." Avoiding Collin's gaze, I moved to sit on the floor. "But every time, he'd tell me that women were only good for cooking and cleaning and breeding children."

Somebody hissed at my words, another sighed. It didn't matter what they thought. My father was in my past, and his sexism would stay there too.

"There was this one time when I was around sixteen,

I think. I got so angry at him for telling me no that I stayed up all night to put something like this together anyway." I reached across the one and only drawer they'd managed to piece together and grabbed the set of screws to go with the flat head I'd jerked away from Gavin's hand. "And do you know what he said to my mother when they found me asleep on the floor the next morning?"

"What?" Collin.

Shrugging, as though the memory didn't sting, I grabbed the two panels of wood labeled *A* and lined them up, screwing them together.

"He told her I was a disgrace. That any girl who used tools the way a *normal* girl would use makeup and curling irons was no daughter of his."

Pride radiated through me as I grabbed the next panels and did the same thing. For the first time in almost ten years, the memory didn't make me cry. Instead, it made me angry and bitter. It also proved I wasn't going to let anybody get me down, especially not Collin. Because whether he knew it or not, I wasn't a woman he could string along at his discretion.

I was Addison Booker: a bitch when she wanted to be, and a lover when she needed to be.

CHAPTER 30

Collin

I HAD NO IDEA HOW LONG SHE'D BEEN STANDING THERE. The two things I did know? She looked sexy as hell in my T-shirt and was also on some sort of feminist rampage, which made her look even sexier. Her hair was down, stuck to the side of her face and neck, and her legs—*good God*, they were ball-breakingly gorgeous.

No way did I like the fact that Gavin and Max could see so much skin, but they knew better than to ogle her too long. I might have denied them her at first, but doing so was also guy code for "I ain't ready to tell you shit yet, so leave it be."

"—so if you even so much as *think* about telling me to leave, then back off, because I'm not going anywhere until I finish this thing. You hear me?" Screwdriver high, she jabbed it in the air at each one of us—me the longest.

My throat went dry, but I nodded, not wanting to tear my eyes away from her. Had no intentions of making her leave. She'd know that soon enough.

"Shit. Give me your father's address. I'm gonna go kick his ass myself." Gavin rubbed his hand over his forehead.

"Nah." Addie scrunched up her nose. "The man's not worth the wasted energy. Just wanted to let you guys know I'm not necessarily just some Suzy Homemaker. I may adore Chloe, do your dishes, and occasionally fold your underwear when I see it lying around—"

"You fold my underwear, Short Stuff?" Max asked. Addie's cheeks turned pink, her unspoken answer in that look alone. Max groaned and pressed his palm against his chest. "Then you stack it and put it on my dresser, don't you?" Max moved over the cardboard spread across the floor on his knees until he was crouched in front of her.

"Well, someone has to. Seriously. You guys are like barn animals when it comes to laundry. You'd think after going through boot camp and then being marines, you'd know better." She frowned. "Poor Chloe. When she learns to walk, she's going to be buried alive under all the piles you have stacked up."

"Marry me." Max pressed his hands to her cheeks. "Have my baby boys, and do my laundry, and I will make you the happiest woman alive. I swear to God."

Her eyes widened. Mine narrowed. And deep in my throat, I growled like a rabid wolf.

Gavin hooted really loud and grumbled, "You got a death wish, Maxwell?" Then he laughed harder when he met my glare, slapping his thigh as he went to the kitchen.

When I turned back to tell Max to shove his pussy words up his ass, I saw it—a nightmare come to life. Max had his hands around Addie's waist and was kissing her.

"The hell?" Lunging forward, I grabbed the neck of his shirt and yanked him back. He landed on his ass, face red, licking his lips—and that smile? I was gonna slap it right off his face.

"Aww, man." Max shut his eyes and blew out a slow breath. "Those lips. Just as tasty as they look." His eyes reopened, meeting mine in a wink as he stood and moved toward Addie again.

Addie, on the other hand, turned pale and glanced my way. Max had made her speechless.

"It's all good, Short Stuff." Max rubbed her shoulders with his hands and kissed the top of her head, like I hadn't just tossed him onto the floor. "You know where to find me when my best friend fucks up." He wrapped his arms around her shoulders and pulled her to him for a hug. Addie's pale face regained some color as she looked at me from over his shoulder. I was surprised she hadn't kneed him in the nuts herself.

A movement from the left caught my eye—lucky for Max. When I looked, I found Gavin standing next to the high chair, Chloe held out in front of him, giggling. Awkward as hell couldn't even begin to describe the man as he transferred her to his hip.

"Max," he grumbled. "Get your ass back in Chloe's room and teach me about diapers." A small, sideways smile played out on Gavin's lips.

I knew what he was doing. He was giving me the time I needed to talk to Addie, to see what she'd heard and figure out what kind of damage control I had to do. My buddies had their own ways of making things happen for me, and damn did I love them for it—even though their tactics weren't always conventional.

Max stood and walked toward Gav and Chloe, stopping to squeeze my shoulder and whisper in my ear, *"You fuck her over, I'll fuck you up, capeesh?"*

And then he was off, dancing like a monkey—literally with his hands under his armpits—toward my daughter.

"A monkey, moron? Really?" Gavin handed Chloe to Max, who took her without a second thought.

"Don't knock it, Gavy-Gav. Getting the sillies out every once in a while does wonders for the libido."

I slapped my hand against my forehead. Jesus Christ. What the hell kind of friends did I have anyway?

Once they were out of the room, I didn't waste another second and went straight for Addie. She had her back to me, shoulders tense as I approached. I wrapped my arms around her waist, nuzzling my face against the side of her neck.

"Turn around and face me." She stiffened and slowly did as I asked. Her lips were pursed in what was probably annoyance, but I didn't care. I had to kiss the memory of Max away, and I had to do it right then and there.

No man would ever touch these lips again as long as I was around.

At first she was stiff, mouth unmoving and hands at her side. But I worked my lips over hers, licking the seam and begging for entrance with my tongue. Seconds later, she melted against me, tucking her arms around my neck, opening wide. I shuddered, wanting nothing more than to wrap her pretty legs around my waist and take her against the sliding glass doors at her back.

Thinking like the smart man I didn't know I had in me, I pulled away, only to kiss her chin, her neck... "Wanna be inside you again." Had to at least tell her.

But then she shoved me. Not some gentle love pat or passionate, let-me-get-you-in-position push either. This was fire and ice, anger and hate. And out of all the looks she'd ever give me, this one scared me to death.

"So…what part of *Chloe's fucking nanny* did you mean just now, huh?" She crossed her arms under her tits, pushing them up even more.

"What?" Couldn't keep my eyes off her nipples. Seeing them poke against the material made me rock hard.

"Do you really think I'm stupid?" She took a step back.

Shit. She hadn't just heard a little of my conversation with the guys; she'd heard all of it.

"Did you think I needed a pity lay? Because there are lots of men out there who'd have pity sex with me."

I jerked my head back, stopping in place. "Pity?" And with another guy? The fuck was she talking about?

She glared at me, her dark eyes furious. But I held her gaze with my own, refusing to be pushed away. "The only thing I consider a pity is that I couldn't have you sprawled out naked beneath me all night like I wanted to."

Now I was just plain pissed. After everything we'd done, the shit I said to her, she was suddenly thinking I was some sort of douche bag who felt sorry for her?

Hell no.

"Well, I'm not deaf. Can hear perfectly out of *both* ears." She rolled her eyes—*always rolling her pretty eyes at me*. "And I heard exactly what you said to Gavin and Max."

"What'd you think you heard?"

She scoffed, tossing her hands up between us. "That you didn't…you know. With me."

Another step, then another, and I had her against the

glass doors. Her chest moved up and down, like she was struggling to breathe, but I didn't touch her. Couldn't yet, especially when I knew it'd be all over if I did.

"What's that? You're stuttering."

She motioned her hand lower, and I licked my lips. A nervous Addie was my weakness. Any more of this, and I'd do exactly what she thought I'd said I didn't do last night.

"I've got aches in places I haven't used in years, so unless I have a ghost lover who visits me in my dreams, then I know we most definitely…ya know…did *it* last night." Her cheeks turned bright red, the cutest color I'd seen on her face yet.

I pressed my hands against the glass on either side of her face and held her in place with my chest and arms. "Say it, sweetheart. Want to hear the word come out of your mouth." I licked my lips again.

"I don't want to say—"

"Please?" She loved manners, and I'd give them to her if she said the words I wanted to hear.

She huffed. "Fine. We *f-fucked*, and you said we didn't." Innocence captured her eyes, making her look far younger than she was. It also made me want to corrupt her, dirty her up again. Obviously she wasn't afraid of sex. If anything, I knew she had a wild side. So what made her so afraid to say *fuck*?

"No. Fucking is fast. Hard. Quick." I looked down at her throat, watching it move as she swallowed. I reached up, tracing her pulse, mesmerized. "What we did last night…" I lowered my forehead to hers, pressing my hands against the sides of her neck. "It was so much better than that."

She shivered, reaching up to hold my wrists like she was seconds away from falling.

"I just heard—"

I kissed the spot between her eyes. "I'm sorry. What you heard..." My chest burned as I struggled to get the words out. What was she doing to me? What was this feeling spinning in my gut and chest? This sudden obsession to be with her, hold her, comfort her...

"But—"

"Gavin and Max are idiots if they haven't figured things out by now."

"Figured out what exactly?"

I pulled back, needing to see her face, her smile. Hearing it in her voice wasn't enough for me. "I'm crazy about you, Addison. Have been since the day I first saw you."

A soft looked passed over her features. Not just a smile or a bat of her lashes, but her entire demeanor changed. Something lit a fire in her eyes, something built in her smile too. Something pushed the air out of her chest so hard that her shoulders were back, higher, more confident. She was...content. Still, she didn't say anything. Instead, she stood on her tiptoes to press her soft lips to mine. And that's all I needed—to know she felt the same way.

This kiss wasn't fast or hard. Instead, it was slow, sweet, and everything Addie was to me, and I was to her.

And for the first time in a long-ass time, I finally knew real happiness again.

CHAPTER 31

Addison

TEN STRAIGHT HOURS OF RUGBY HAD FROSTED MY BRAIN like the leaves on the early December trees surrounding me. It's not as though I didn't *like* the sport. It was action packed and held my attention the entire time. But I didn't have a clue what was happening. The one thing I *did* know? It looked painful, and every single match, someone would walk away with an injury. This last one just happened to be a cleat to Max's temple.

Which is why we were waiting outside a hospital room at Chicago Mercy Medical Center.

What was supposed to be an overnight adventure with me and Collin and his friends was—after a day of rugby tournaments—fast turning into a dull headache.

I sat on Collin's lap, Gavin on the floor to our left with a set of brothers from the hosting Chicago rugby team. They were originally from Australia but now lived nearby, traveling with an American team across the state. One was quieter than the other. I think his name was William, but I didn't know for sure. What I did know was he had green eyes and brown hair, and looked like a hero out of an erotic novel come to life. The other guy? He had a green Mohawk, all shaved on the sides but long and hanging in his eyes in the front. His name was Oliver. Unlike his brother, he was loud and funny and reminded me of someone Lia would've loved. A punk-rocker sort. His smile bared dimples— nowhere near as cute as Collin's—and I could tell he was the type that easily charmed the panties off any girl within a fifty-mile radius.

"So that's it, then. You say these lines to a woman, and it actually works?"

"Yeah. Have the ladies on their knees in no time." Oliver winked at a nearby nurse, who in turn ran into a wall.

I laughed. The poor single women on this floor. They were doomed, surrounded by these wild men. Maybe even some of the taken ones too. Someone was destined to screw up an emergency or two because of all this hotness.

Collin nuzzled his nose against the back of my neck, seeming oblivious to everything but me. I smiled and shut my eyes, clinging tightly to his hand. It was good to see him so relaxed, even though we were technically in a hospital waiting while Max got stitches.

Things between us had changed for the better since Thanksgiving, two weeks ago. We'd grown closer, more official in a way. Granted we hadn't had the *technical conversation* about what the two of us were yet. But I was as much to blame for that as he was.

"…and can I give you an Aussie kiss? It's like a French kiss, but Down Under."

"Jesus," Collin mumbled, body shaking as he laughed.

"Just watch, yeah? I'll show you how it's done." Oliver stood up, his long legs bringing him in front of an orderly pushing a cart of laundry down the hall. She had to be around thirty. Pretty yet tired-looking.

"The hell is he doing?" Gavin asked William.

"The coit's gonna wind up gettin' his nuts clobbered if he's not careful."

Leaning back, Collin shoved his legs out in front of us, pulling my back flush against his chest as he touched his lips to my ears. "What's a coit?" he asked.

William looked from Collin back to his brother, frowning. "Means asshole."

"Think I'm gonna need a lesson in Australian urban slang." Gavin leaned back, smiling, with his arms over his chest.

The conversation went on around us, but all I could feel was Collin's breath on my neck when he laughed and his hand on my thigh as he rubbed it.

"You all right?" He laughed low in my ear a few minutes later, damn well knowing what he was doing to me, from the sounds of it. His free hand tightened along my waist and he squeezed, slipping his fingers under the hem of my flannel shirt.

I laid my head on his shoulder. "Perfect." And I really was. Being here with him, in this town, in his life, made me feel like I'd found my first real peace in years.

"Taking you out tonight." He kissed my temple.

"You are, huh?" I grinned, watching Oliver but

completely focused on Collin's warm fingers sneaking
up higher along my ribs. Back and forth they trailed
over my skin in a mesmerizing pattern that made goose
bumps dance along my tummy.

"Yeah. Dinner, then we talk."

"About…?" I bit my lip.

"Us."

Inside my stomach, tiny butterflies sprang to life,
dancing and fluttering like they were caged and more than
ready to be freed. And even though I wanted to smother
my smile, hide the excitement, I couldn't.

I sat up instead and faced him, pressing my nose to his
as I whispered, "I'm okay with talking."

He ran his thumbs across my lower back. "Kissing too?"

I nodded.

"Good."

Just as my lips touched his, a loud smack sounded
from behind us. The woman Oliver had approached
screamed, "How dare you say that to me? I should have
you arrested."

Collin rubbed the tip of his nose across mine, and
even though I didn't get the kiss I wanted, his affectionate touches were almost as intoxicating.

"What'd you say to her?" Gavin laughed.

I glanced at Oliver. The cocky smile he'd worn all
day was replaced by a frown and furrowed brows. He
looked like he wanted to rip someone's head off.

"Answer him, man." William sighed, rubbing a hand
over his mouth. Unlike Gavin, he didn't look amused.

"Nothing."

"Nothing?" Gavin laughed harder, shoving him in the
shoulder. "A smack in the face was for nothing?"

"Jesus, just say it." William leaned back against the wall, chin high.

"It's never failed me," Oliver growled. "Don't understand."

"Because you always do it when you're full, that's why," William groaned.

I frowned, staring back and forth between the brothers. "Full?"

Oliver's grin turned teasing, an obvious escape mechanism from getting burned. "Full is drunk. It's what you Americans call it, no?"

"Brother, leave it." William stood, a good inch taller than Oliver.

"No, I wanna hear it. Tell me what you said to that lady," Gavin said, moving to stand between my line of sight and Oliver's.

"Told her I wanted to..." Oliver leaned back against the wall next to his brother.

"—get lost in her outback." William finished his brother's words, smacking Oliver upside the head as he sat down next to him.

Just then Max walked into the waiting room, a massive bandage covering his head and, like always, a smile across his face.

"Fuckers!" His hands shot up over his head. Then he looked at me. "And miss." He winked, and I rolled my eyes. "I am ready to get shit-faced."

Gavin shook his head, while Oliver jumped up to chest-bump him. Collin settled his forehead against my back. I couldn't stop grinning

These men were ridiculous. And pretty damn awesome too.

—◦◦◦—

"I didn't take you to be a deep-dish kinda woman."

Melted cheese dripped down Collin's chin as he tried to take a bite of his pizza. His face was an adorable shade of pink from getting windburned all day.

"Wouldn't have it any other way." I took another bite myself.

He wiped his lips with his napkin, and his dimpled cheeks puckered inward. "Very true."

The small talk was fine, but I couldn't help but wonder when we were going to delve deeper into the good stuff. He'd made it very apparent we were going to have an "us" talk tonight, but he'd yet to bring it up.

Collin's dark hair fell over his forehead as he leaned across the table to cover my wrist. My fingers twitched, wanting to brush the softness back with the tips. "Let's play a game."

"Another game?" My pulse spiked.

His lips tilted into a slow, sensual grin. "Yep. Five questions each, no holds barred, ask away. Only one pass."

"Just one pass?" I took another drink of my soda and licked my lips to keep the wetness from spilling down my chin.

An Italian ballad played softly in the background, and my chest warmed with contentment. Regardless of the fact that my dress was entirely too short, I slouched a little lower in my seat and extended my legs out in front of me. Our feet brushed, and I couldn't help but smile.

A candle flame danced between us, and the way the light reflected off his sparkling eyes enthralled my soul.

"Yes. One pass. But I go first."

"That's not fair." I chuckled, mind scrambling as I thought about what I wanted to know. There were so many things to ask and so few questions to ask them in.

"Perfectly fair, I'd say. I came up with the idea, so I ask the first set."

I leaned forward on the table, moving so our hands interlocked. Part of me did it so I could hide the sudden trembling of my fingers. He was giving me a chance to know him, so it was only fair that I was ready for him to know me too. The idea of sharing my past didn't come easy to me, but still, if we were going to be together, I wanted full disclosure, no holding back.

"Then ask away." I stared down at the silverware, too scared to see the judgment in his eyes when I told him the truth about my family.

"Favorite color."

I blinked, looking up. On his face was a soft smile. One that said *We're in this together*.

"Yellow."

"Yeah?" His eyes widened in surprise.

"Yep. It's…a happy color, ya know? Like the sunshine and sunflowers, bananas and lemons."

One side of his mouth curled up. "Lemons and bananas, huh?"

I refused to let myself grow embarrassed. I was who I was and wouldn't change for anyone. "And sunshine too. Don't forget that. It's the sign of summer."

As if he finally understood, he nodded and brought my knuckles to his lips. "I'm good with yellow and sunshine."

_____" —my pulse slowed—"what is your favorite
____?"

"Easy. Fourth of July. Means freedom. Gives me serving as a marine more of a purpose."

"I get it." And I did. A marine was a breed of human who deserved so much more than just a nod, pat on the back, or "good job." They fought for me, for America. But Collin was an exemplary man for so many more reasons.

"Tell me about your mom."

My throat went dry. "Um…" I frowned, taken aback by the sudden change in direction of our little game. I knew it was coming, but getting no warning sucked.

"You gotta tell me, Addie. I need to know what breaks you so I don't let it happen again."

A small smile crept over my lips at his sweet words. "You can't take my bad away, but thank you for wanting to try."

"I can take it away if I want to. Replace it with all good things instead. That's my plan, but first I gotta know the truth."

Letting go of his hand, I leaned back in my chair and toyed with the paper napkin sitting next to my plate.

Fine. If he wanted to hear what broke me, I'd tell him. I just hoped he didn't decide I was too much work.

CHAPTER 32

Collin

"MY MOM WAS FROM THE PHILIPPINES. SHE MOVED OVER here when I was two and married my stepfather, a Caucasian man, who later adopted me." Addie's lips pursed as she shredded her paper napkin. Not once did she meet my eyes.

"You don't know who your birth father is, then?"

She glared at the candle burning on the table. "Nope. Don't really care, either. You can't love or miss someone you never knew."

I stared down at the same candle, wondering if this would be Chloe talking about her mother in twenty or so years...maybe even sooner. Right then and there, I decided I'd do everything I could to make her *not* feel that way. "What happened between you and your parents exactly?"

die sighed. "We were close, my mom and I, but
ke, best friends close. My father was more of

a…figure who brought home money, drank beer, and occasionally told me thank you for giving him another beer when he asked." She scoffed. "For as long as I can remember, Mom let him walk all over her and tell her what to do. I mean, he wasn't an abusive man. If anything, he was more affectionate than my mother was, if you can believe it. But he was fifty when they got married and my mom was only twenty-nine, so his kids were having grandkids and I think he was just…done with having kids. I was just an addition to his wife." She bit her lip and glanced up at me, her eyes warm but her voice cold. "My father had these standards though. He said we *had* to follow certain rules to fit in with other women in American culture."

"Bullshit," I growled. As a father myself, I wanted to wring the motherfucker's neck.

"He had the fiftie's mind-set that women needed to dress properly, clean the house constantly, *and* be at his beck and call whenever he needed. *But* he also expected my mom to help with every aspect of the family business at the same time."

"Sounds shitty." My jaw flexed. It was hard to stay cool and relaxed when all I wanted to do was drive the two hours back home to first hug my baby girl and sister, and then find Addie's asshole father and make him pay.

"It was all I knew, so it doesn't bother me a whole lot. But it still pissed me off that he tried to control everything I ever did." She met my stare, finally, but her face was blank. Emotionless even. "He told me I'd never be smart enough to go to college. That I just needed to marry wealthy and pop out a couple of grandkids maybe work at their *store* when need be. Even had a guy lined up for me to marry fresh out of high school. His forty-year-old insurance agent, if you can believe that." She stared down at her lap. "The moment the guy showed up at my house during my graduation party with an extravagant and creepy number of roses, I knew I had to break ties with my parents."

Scowling, I leaned across the table and grasped her hands. "But you went to college. Got yourself a degree too. Not trying to sound like a dick, but how'd you afford it?"

She clicked her tongue against the roof of her mouth, leaning back in her seat. "Mom may have abided by Dad's rules, but that didn't mean she wanted me to be unhappy. She had money stored away that my father didn't know about." She rested her hand on her chin. "Under my mattress, buried away in old pots and pans she had stored in the garage. All her Pinoy memorabilia that my father insisted she hide away."

"Jesus," I groaned as the reality of this entire jacked-up situation sank in.

"Once I applied for school, was approved for student aid and grants, and used the money Mom gave me, I packed all my stuff and moved to Macomb. Got a part-time job on campus, another part-time job working at the on-campus preschool, and spent the rest of the time studying and getting my degree."

I frowned. "And your parents? What happened?"

She pressed her lips together for a minute before she finally said, "Dad told me not to bother coming home. after all he'd done for me, I was pretty much space to him."

"No." I leaned forward, hands going tight around the edge of the table. "You're an amazing woman who does amazing things. That man doesn't even deserve the title of *father*."

Tears filled her eyes, but Addie held her chin up, not letting them fall. "I wish, more than anything, that my mom would've walked away. But she likes the security of a steady income…and I think she feels like she owes my father a lifetime for bringing us to this country. I miss her like crazy. But I know, deep down, she's at least proud of me, even though she never once said it."

I scrubbed a hand up and down my face, fighting back the anger in my throat. "Your father was a damn fool."

"It is what it is, you know?" Her mouth twisted to the side before she finished. "I dug my grave, and now I've gotta sleep in it."

"How long has it been since you've talked to them?" I pushed the candle aside, along with the pizza, and pulled her hands close.

"The last person I spoke to was my mother, and that was a year ago when she dropped by my apartment with some Filipino cuisine and a plea to call my father and try to make amends."

"And?"

She squeezed my hands. "I told her he wasn't worth it. That I'd love to see her, even if it was in secret, but she refused." Her jaw clenched, and anger replaced the wetness in her eyes. "Claimed she wouldn't go against her *husband's wishes*, so I told her to leave and never come back. And she listened."

In a flash, I moved around the table to sit in the chair

next to Addie. The second I held her face in my hands, she shut her eyes, relaxing into me. "If your mom and dad were any sort of parents, then they wouldn't have cared what you did, as long as you were happy."

A few tears slid down her cheeks and over my hand, but she managed to smile. "Thank you for saying so"— she reached up and held my wrists—"but my parents were never typical, so I expected them to do what they did. That night when I found their store gone was a weak moment for me. I don't have many moments like that anymore. I'm better than I used to be. Stronger."

My heart thudded in my chest. "I've had those weak moments. Needed them so I could get over a lot of bad shit I've seen and been through in my life." I leaned forward and pressed my forehead to hers. "Don't be afraid of them. Not when you've got me to—"

"Collin." She pulled my face up, lips quivering, eyes still red and wet. "Can we go now?"

My shoulders fell. Apparently there were limits when it came to Addie, and I needed to abide by them. But I also needed her to know I had my fair share of skeletons too. "This isn't the end of this conversation. You can't just bat your pretty eyes and expect me to forget it. I'm not your parents, and I'm not planning on leaving you alone, even if you try to push me away. You got me?"

"I got you," she whispered, pressing her lips against mine.

Even though I wanted to believe her, I knew I couldn't. Not yet. But I was damn sure not going to push me away. I fought hard for what I wanted. w that I knew it was Addie, I'd never let her go.

Addison

"The lake froze over last winter. So much that the remaining birds couldn't find any good food sources. A lot of bird deaths and all."

Collin's gaze was pointed toward the dark water of Lake Michigan as we walked along the lakefront, yet his thoughts were a million miles away. Part of me feared I'd scared him away with the story of my imperfect family, but I knew him better than that, heard his words loud and clear inside the restaurant. Collin didn't care one bit about my past. Instead, he wanted my future. And I'd known the second he held my face between his hands back in the restaurant that I wanted to be in that future with him.

Our hands were interlocked, but because it was so cold, he tucked our fingers into his pocket. "I lived here for a while. Did I tell you that? With Amy, before I enlisted, right after we graduated from college. It was only for a couple of months."

Caught in the spell of his words and voice, I looked up at his profile. "You don't have to talk about her any more than you want to."

His brows furrowed as he stared down at the dark sidewalk. Still, he didn't speak as we walked.

"I mean, I get it. You loved her, probably always will."

In the middle of the walkway, he spun me around by my arm to face him. His fingers wrapped around my upper arms, and he pulled me against his chest. In his arms, I was safe. Protected. Terrified too because being there felt so right.

Unable to look away, I asked, "You okay?"

He loosened his hold on one of my arms and lifted his hand to trail his knuckles down my cheek. I shivered, unable to fight the goose bumps forming beneath my clothes.

"Had no idea she wanted anything beyond sex and friendship with me. We were roommates. Best friends. That's all it was to me. We dated other people and hung out to drink beer on Thursday nights after work." He tucked his hands into the pockets of his jeans, but took a step closer to me, until our chests pressed together. "Then it all changed the day before I left for boot camp." He lowered his chin against his chest. "And because I couldn't stand leaving anything behind me unfinished in case I didn't come home, I told her I felt the same way, thinking at the time maybe I did, or that when I was done with my tours, that having her to come home to was going to be what I wanted." He shrugged.

I had no idea what to say. So…I didn't speak, only gave him my ears. He needed to talk. I needed to listen.

"After I got stationed, I only came back to the States once. My uncle's funeral. And that night was the only time the two of us had unprotected sex."

"She waited for you." I bit my lip.

He nodded. "Then the next morning, I told her I didn't want her to wait for me anymore because I'd been thinking about re-upping. I told her she deserved better and to find someone committed to her. Then she smacked me, told me she hated me, and left."

"That was the night she got pregnant, wasn't it?" I whispered.

"Yes." Unwavering, he met my gaze.

"Did you love her, Collin?"

"I did."

I expected those words…but why did it hurt so much to hear them out loud?

"What happened then? How did you find out about the pregnancy? About Chloe?"

"She sold her Chicago condo, saying she couldn't afford it, then moved to Carinthia." He cringed. "Mom saw her at the grocery store one day—that's how I found out she was living in town. She asked Amy to come over for dinner, being polite. Then Amy broke down at their dinner table and told my parents and Lia about being pregnant."

"They knew before you did?" I reached up to toy with the collar of his shirt, needing to keep touching him to get through the story.

"Yep. Eventually Amy sent me an email telling me the truth, so it didn't really matter." His voice shook. So did his hands as he lowered them to my waist.

"And she wanted to be closer to your parents because of Chloe, didn't she?" I asked, the pieces finally coming together.

He nodded once, confirming my suspicions.

Amy was *so* in love with Collin that she would've done anything to keep him. Moved to a new town, made nice with his family to gain support…but he broke her heart, and Collin held some mad-crazy guilt over doing and saying the things he did to her. Still, what about her parents? Her friends?

"Where are her parents?" I asked.

"New York. They come to visit on occasion, but

it's really sporadic. They've only seen Chloe a handful of times."

He pulled me against his chest, squeezing me to him. With his chin on my head, he continued to speak even though every nerve ending in my body was rattled.

"How did Amy…" I held my breath, not wanting to ask but really wanting to know at the same time.

"How did Amy die?"

I nodded, hating my incessant need to know everything and anything.

"After Chloe was born, she moved in with my mom and dad for support. One night she told them she was running out to grab diapers, but she never came home. Died in a head-on collision."

"God…" I wrapped my arms even tighter around his waist and squeezed my eyes shut.

"Two weeks later, I finally came home."

"I'm so sorry," I whispered in his ear.

He kissed the top of my head. "I blamed myself for a long time. Like, maybe if I hadn't reenlisted, I could've been home and there for her. Maybe I could've looked into family housing and gotten transferred to be closer."

I leaned forward. "Life's what-ifs are always the things you can't control. Don't continually beat yourself up over them."

"She might still be alive though. And Chloe could've been with her mother."

More than anything, I would want that for Chloe too. But at the same time, something pinched inside me at the thought of never having met Collin or Chloe. I was selfish for even thinking those thoughts, but I was only human.

"I'm not going to say I'm sorry for your loss," I whispered. "I know it won't help if I do." Heart breaking with every word I spoke, I continued to spill my guts because there really was no point in holding back anymore. "But I am going to say you are one lucky man because Amy left you with a memory you won't ever be able to let go of. And it comes in the form of a beautiful little girl who loves you more than the Harry the Bunny and Cheerios." I pulled back to look up at him, cupping his warm cheeks. "And in eleven-month-old terms, that's pretty amazing."

Even in the dark, I saw his eyes go wide, but I kept going, pretending not to care what he thought and only knowing I had to get my words out before I lost them.

"Right here"—I pressed one hand over my heart—"I know who you are. An amazing father, an amazing brother, and an amazing friend." I blinked away the warmth in my eyes. "And I know I haven't been through what you have, but—"

Lips cut me off. Soft, commanding, and everything I didn't expect. Hands went around my waist, only to hold me up on my tiptoes. I had no idea what I'd done to deserve this kiss, but I wasn't going to complain. Nor was I going to be the one to stop it. If Collin wanted to kiss me, then by God, I was going to kiss him back.

CHAPTER 33

Collin

COULD'VE SWORN I WAS DREAMING, THAT THE HAND grazing my hip and trailing down beneath the sheets was my own. But it was too soft, too gentle.

Eyes blurred from sleep, I squinted at the clock. Three fifteen in the morning and I wasn't alone in my bed. I grinned at the thought, pretending to be asleep as the sexy-as-hell woman of my dreams wrapped her hand around my cock from behind.

"Collin," she whispered, stroking me slowly.

Took all my willpower to stay still, especially since I was more than ready to turn her over and fuck her for the third time since we'd gotten back to our hotel room. But I wanted Addie to set the pace for once, to be in control and take me the way she wanted to take me.

And damn, she didn't disappoint.

The covers slid off my body, rubbing against my bare legs as she rolled me onto my back. Her breaths were already heavy, a sure sign she was as worked up as I was. Her tiny fingers trailed over my stomach and I shuddered, unable to stop myself from opening my eyes and meeting her gaze.

Before I could comment on the thoughts going through her mind, she straddled my thighs, pressed her perfect tits against them, and took the head of my cock into her mouth.

"Damn, baby. You're gonna kill me." But death was gonna feel so damn good.

Around my dick she moaned, lowering her mouth. Slow. So fucking slow. Taking her time, loving on my cock like it was all she needed to survive.

I gripped the sheets, watching her move. The torture was almost too much. "Addison," I growled, leaning up on my elbows, chest tightening the longer I watched.

She met my gaze again, eyebrows bunched together in concentration.

"Addie girl, feels so fuckin' good."

She moved faster.

Fingers grazed the underside of my ass, and I hissed as one of them slipped between my cheeks. She squeezed and played and moaned, the vibration coursing through my dick like a sexual earthquake. Bright lights flashed behind my eyes when I shut them. In and out, I tried to breath, failing the harder she sucked. More than anything I wanted to come inside her mouth, to flip her around and on top of me so I could have her come against mine too. But damn, she was pretty with her hair all around her face and on my thighs with her lips suctioned around me, so asking her to stop wasn't something my lips and tongue could comprehend doing.

And then, like she could read my mind, she turned her body around, bringing her pretty pussy to my head, giving me what I wanted without my even asking.

Loved how she took what she wanted.

On my back, I squeezed her hips and dipped my tongue against her. She gasped around my cock, stopping for a second only to suck me harder than before.

This was heaven—the Addison kind. And I was the luckiest son of a bitch alive.

The headboard began to rock as her legs and feet writhed by my head. The sound rhythmic, the perfect, sexy beat. I sucked on her clit; she sucked on my head. I moaned; she hissed.

And then suddenly, it wasn't enough. I needed to see her face, not just hear her noises. I wanted to kiss her. Touch her breasts. Feel her eyes on me. And I wasn't going to stop until I had it.

Impatient and damn near ready to explode, I flipped her onto her back, crawled up her body, and slid inside her, not thinking of anything else.

"Kiss me, sweetheart."

Her lips met mine, as demanding as my words. Fingers pulled at the back of my hair, the pain so good I bit her lip in response. She gasped as I pulled back, her gaze meeting mine.

"Collin!" she cried out, reaching for me, needing me.

There was nothing I wanted more than this. Nothing I wanted to feel but her and me.

"Fucking love you." I yanked her up so we were both sitting, urging her to ride me. "Fucking love you so much." Those words. I'd only said them once, but

I'd never really felt them. Never wanted to feel them as much as I wanted to with Addison.

"Oh my God." She nuzzled her face into my neck, clawing at my back. "Collin, yes. I—"

I cupped her face, bringing her lips to mine. Didn't want her to feel pressured to say it back. Just wanted her to know. Needed her to know.

Hands eager to touch her all over, I reached down between our bodies, allowing my fingers to graze over her clit. She moaned, still kissing me, and I took that as my cue to go faster.

"Holy shit," she mumbled, pulling back.

I gripped her ass with my other hand, bringing her up higher, her breasts rubbed against my chest, spurring me faster.

"I can't… I need to…" she groaned.

"I know," I whispered, trailing kisses along her neck.

The sheets slid beneath my ass, granting me the ability to slow the pace while still concentrating on keeping her filled. My sudden need to possess this woman overrode my own needs as I rubbed her clit harder.

"Tell me I'm the only man who will ever fill you here"—I pressed my thumb harder against her—"again."

She hissed, arching her back. "Yes."

"Fuck, yes." Faster, harder, with everything I had left, I poured my emotions into her with every thrust and every breath until she was screaming my name.

And with her contented sigh, I yanked my cock out, spilling my release all over her thigh, hating myself for not asking if I could take her without a condom, but thankful I had the common sense to pull out. She was on the pill, and both of us were clean and had been tested, but I didn't want to take the chance 'cause nothing was foolproof.

"I love you," I whispered again, taking her mouth in my own. And for the first time in years, I could feel the promise of a forever.

CHAPTER 34

Addison

STANDING OUTSIDE THE FRONT DOOR OF HIS HOUSE, Collin wrapped his arms around my waist and pulled me against his chest. "Stay here tonight. Gonna get cold without you in my arms."

The cold wind blew through my hair and I shivered, wanting nothing more than to stay. Still, I didn't want to be too eager, in case he decided this thing between us wasn't what he wanted after all.

Regardless of my thoughts, I couldn't resist leaning forward and pressing a soft kiss to his lips. "You're so convincing." Grinning like mad, I pulled back and laid my chin on his shoulder.

He nuzzled his nose against my cheek. "I'm no poet. But you make me wanna write sonnets and quote Shakespeare just to keep you here. Better?"

I giggled. "Your bed is entirely too small."

He pulled his head back, as did I. "Got a pullout

couch. Gotta get a new bed." He grinned. "A bigger one so we can roll around in it."

I giggled. "Don't get a new one on my account. It's not as though I'm going to be living here with you."

He frowned. "Why not? Told you I loved you. Told you I wanted you in my arms every night. What else do I have to do to convince you?"

I cleared my throat, head spinning from the sudden whirlwind of this all. We'd just made "us" official less than a month ago, and now he was talking about me moving in with him?

"Max wouldn't like it if I moved in."

"Don't give a shit what Max likes." He dropped his hand, reaching for something in his pockets. "You're in our life now. He don't like it, then—"

"Stop." I pressed a finger to his lips, leaning forward to brush my nose against his neck. He inhaled hard, and I watched the tension seep from his shoulders. After kissing his throat, I pulled back. "He pays rent. You can't just decide whether or not to move someone else in. It's not right."

He opened his mouth, ready to speak, but the door flew open behind him. Collin whirled around, standing in front of me with his arms spread to the sides. I rolled my eyes and shoved him to my right to stand next to him.

"Hello, young man." A gentleman with a mustache and collared shirt lifted his chin in greeting. "Pleasure to see you again."

Collin stiffened, his jaw dropping. "W-what are you doing here?" Forgetting me completely, he darted forward and pulled the guy into a hug, only to shove his way inside the house seconds later.

"Hi." I waved awkwardly at the handsome gentle-man. The man was tired-looking, with lines surrounding his eyes and lips. Out of every emotion in the world, sadness had robbed his features the most, I could tell.

"Good to meet you. My name is Alexander." The man nodded my way, holding out a hand.

Shivering, I moved forward and gripped it. "I'm Addison Booker, Collin's girlfriend." I shook his hand, all the while thinking ridiculous, thirteen-year-old-girl thoughts.

Girlfriend.

Collin's significant other.

The woman in Collin's life.

Soon, I'd be writing his name with mine, adding doodled hearts and pink roses all around them.

I moved around Alexander, inhaling his cologne at the same time. In a way, he reminded me of my father… but with a much nicer demeanor.

When I walked into the living room, I found Collin on the couch, hugging a gorgeous older woman with white hair and bright-blue eyes. Eyes that mirrored Chloe's.

"She's so beautiful. And getting so big too," the woman blubbered, a tissue clutched in her hand by her eyes.

I locked my gaze onto Lia. Her face was pale, and her eyes were almost paranoid as she glanced from me to Collin to Chloe, then back to me once more.

My need to comfort pushed me forward, and she latched her arms around my neck, hugging me tight. "Missed ya. Wanna go hang out? Go grab some coffee? Like, now?" She laughed nervously and pulled me toward the door.

"Um…" Biting my lip, I glanced from Collin's happy smile over to the woman who had Chloe's eyes.

"Seriously, Addie. Let's go. He stole you away for an entire weekend and—"

"Lia." I pulled back and squeezed her hand. "Just give me a second, okay?" Was it my imagination, or was she trying to get me out of here on purpose?

"God, she looks just like Amy."

I stiffened, staring down at the man. Eyes soft, he crouched next to the woman.

Collin's face lit up like a star on Christmas morning. In his gaze, I saw love and adoration only a father could ever feel.

"She's definitely as gorgeous as her mother was."

I swallowed hard at his words, staring at Chloe and then the woman who held her and then Chloe again.

Like a lightning bolt shot through my veins, the reality of this situation hit me. These weren't just old friends of Collin's.

These were *Amy's* parents.

"How about we take you two out for dinner?" The woman jumped up from the couch, bringing Chloe with her. She glanced back at us, her eyes popping when she looked my way, then softening when they landed on Lia. "And Lia, dear, we'd love for you to join us too. You were our daughter's confidant when Collin was overseas. It'd mean so much to us to spend time with you again."

My stomach clenched when I glanced up at Collin. He was talking to Alexander, laughing like old friends, oblivious to the scene—and to me too.

For appearances' sake, I approached the woman,

smiling softly as I held out my hand in greeting. "Hello.
It's so nice to meet you. I'm Addison."

Her dark eyebrows rose slightly. "Ah, yes. My granddaughter's nanny. Lia mentioned that. So good to meet
you. If you haven't noticed"—she wiped her damp eyes
with her tissue—"I'm a wee bit emotional right now.
My husband and I...we haven't seen Chloe in four very
long months."

Her smile was polite, genuine even, but the awkward-
ness of the situation was making my skin itch all the
same. It was great that they were here for Chloe and all,
but the fact that they had just shown up out of the blue
was unnerving.

I glanced at Lia, looking for backup, but her head was
down—no help there, apparently. So I looked toward
Collin instead, but he and Alexander weren't even in
the room.

Lovely. A lone cat in a dog-eat-dog world. This
wasn't turning out to be a splendid evening.

"We're moving here to Carinthia to be closer to our
granddaughter. I am so excited to spend time with her.
I plan on watching her as much as Collin will let me."

Lia moved closer, reaching for my hand. Too numb
to respond, I let her take it, ignoring her silent squeeze.

"Th-that's great. She is a wonderful baby." The
words came out as a whisper, and the woman's smile
grew wider in turn.

"I worry about her is all." She leaned in close to
whisper to me and Lia, "All these men, no motherly
figure around to soften her up." She shuddered, completely ignoring the fact that I was in fact female.
And so was Lia. "It's probably for the best that Chloe

grows up around family, especially without her mother around."

Like there was a string yanking on my heart, I felt it drop inside me, the sensation so aching I could barely catch my breath. Not even Lia's hand on mine could keep me from freaking out internally.

God...what was I going to do if I lost this job? Worse yet—what was I going to do if I lost Chloe? She'd become my world in six short weeks. Same for her uncles and aunt and...Collin.

Panic had me wanting to run, and I managed to drop Lia's hand to take a step back.

"Addie," she warned, looking like she was ready to chase after me. Tie me down if she had to.

With the biggest smile I could muster, I reached out for the lady's hand. "It was so good to meet you." Her head cocked to the side in confusion, but she smiled all the same, taking it up a notch to step closer to me.

"You too, dear." Like we were the oldest of friends, she wrapped her arms around my shoulders and held me close. "It was so good to meet you."

My throat burned with a sob as I swallowed, but somehow I managed to keep it locked inside. "You too."

"Addie, don't you—"

"Tell Collin I'll talk to him later." Chin high, I glanced at Lia, nodded once, then turned toward the door.

And without a second thought, I did what I've done best in life: I ran.

—◆◆◆—

"Stupid, stupid, stupid." How could I be such an idiot? Thinking I could live up to the standards of a ghost. A memory Collin would probably *never* be able to move past.

By the time I was halfway around the block, my hands were ice cold, even shoved inside the pockets of my coat. Sniffling, with my nose almost a frozen block of ice, I made it around the corner, only to hear *his* voice.

"Where are you going?"

I moved a little faster. "Home."

"Why?" His shoes slapped against the concrete, the sound as ominous as the unsteady beat of my heart. Snow fluttered down, the early December days already brutal—the perfect theme for the moment. "Don't go. You said you'd stay with me tonight." His voice grew desperate, a sound I wasn't used to hearing.

I flinched. "I just figured you were all going out to dinner, and since I wasn't invited, it would give me a chance to go home and catch up on some things in my apartment. It's lacking TLC because I'm always at your place." I laughed. "God knows I spend my days doing more of your laundry than I do my own." I sucked in a quick breath before I continued. "And besides that, I need to go home and feed…feed…" I squeezed my eyes shut. "My cat."

Collin jumped in front of me, eyes teasing, smile smug. It pissed me off, made my blood boil. How the hell could he be so…so…*happy*?

"You don't have a cat." He moved closer, wrapping his arms around my waist and tucking my head under his chin. I blinked quickly, trying to contain my tears. No telling how fast they'd be frozen against my cheeks if they fell.

"I'm going to get one. Right now. I need a friend." Crap. Even my excuses sucked.

"You wanna get a cat?" He reared his head back, smile fading. "I don't like cats."

Well, fate was *just* fabulous, wasn't it?

"Huh. That stinks. I'm still going to get one. You can't stop me." It wasn't his fault I was in such a foul-ass mood, so why was I making this worse than it was?

"Addison," he growled, holding my chin up. "What's. Wrong?"

My jaw clenched. "Nothing."

He groaned, lowering his forehead to mine. "Not stupid, sweetheart. So either tell me now or—"

"Y-you aren't going to need me anymore. *Chloe's* not going to need me."

His gaze flitted from me back to his house. "What do you mean?"

"*Suzie* said they're moving back to Carinthia, and that she's going to be watching Chloe now. That means you won't need me."

I folded my arms over my chest, needing space. Collin didn't give it, only moving closer to hold my shoulders. "Not gonna happen."

"But she said—"

"Stop right there and listen to me. *You're* not going anywhere, damn it. You're mine. I'm yours. That'll never change. And even if they are moving here, it wouldn't matter. You're not going anywhere." He latched onto the back of my coat.

More than anything, I wanted to believe him, but something was holding me back. Whether it was our conversation in Chicago or seeing him react to Chloe's grandparents the way he did, I didn't know. For now though, I'd give him the benefit of the doubt. Why? Because I was in love with him too. And when it comes to love, you sometimes can't help but lose who you are or what you believe in, even when you don't mean to.

CHAPTER 35

Collin

"Let's go." I tugged at Max's arm to get him out of the cab.

"You're gonna get your ass handed to you." He pointed in my face, laughing as he jumped out onto the sidewalk behind me. "And I can't *wait* to see you grovel."

With his foot, he shut the cab door, then rammed into me with his head like a bull.

I roped my arm around his neck, holding tight. "It's all your dick's fault," I groaned. "Just had to get those girls' numbers, didn't you?"

One side of his mouth lifted into a grin when I let him go. "Yeah. Yeah, I did, Colly. You see, we can't *all* be pussy whipped by the perfect girl."

"Damn right you can't be." I slugged his shoulder, proud to wear the title of pussy whipped by the girl I couldn't wait to hold in my arms. "Maybe it's time you find someone to get pussy whipped by."

A funny looked crossed his face.

"Unless of course you've already found one…"
My grin fell. Maxwell Martinez, finding one woman?
That'd be a sight to see. Not to mention a damn miracle
from God himself.

"And deprive the women of the world of my body?"
He motioned a hand over his chest, back to normal
with his cheesy grin. "Hell no." He winked and headed
toward the door, two steps ahead of me.

Max and I had left the house early to drop Chloe off
where Suzie and Alexander were staying. Then Max
mentioned something about stopping by to see my sister's new place of work, which turned into an hour-long
affair of yanking Max away from two different groups
of women. Now it was after eleven, and we were an hour
late meeting up with Addie and McKenna at O'Paddy's.

This was the first fuckup I'd made since the two of
us made it official, and yeah, my balls were strung tight,
worried she'd let me have it. Still, I'd make it right if she
was really pissed—with all the good parts of our bodies.

We were celebrating tonight. I'd finally applied to
the academy, ready to take the step toward being a cop.
After I'd told Addie what I wanted to do, she'd encouraged me to apply, said she'd be there for Chloe. And
now that Suzie and Alexander were officially moving to
Carinthia, I finally bit the bullet and signed up.

"It's packed in here." Max nodded toward a couple of
ladies off to the right.

I frowned at the scene around us, thankful Gavin had
decided not to come. Guy didn't do well in crowded,
loud places like this one was tonight.

"You see her?" I yelled over the heavy bass, scanning
the room for my dark-haired beauty. I knew she was

wearing a red shirt, because I specifically remembered trying to tug it off when I stopped by her apartment earlier in the evening. I'd needed to be alone with her to tell her the news about officially applying, and then she'd kissed me senseless in excitement, which made me want to strip her naked and *fuck* her senseless. Good thing she was more of a grown-up than me and kicked my ass out to go to McKenna's place. Otherwise, we probably wouldn't have made it here tonight.

It'd been a week since Amy's parents announced they were moving to town, and even though I cherished every second with my Chloe Bean, I loved the fact that Addie's and my alone time had been amped up to more than just a spare hour here and there over the past week. Chloe's grandparents wanted to spend as much time with my little girl as they could. Still, not even the hours Addison and I spent between the sheets were enough. I wanted to spend forever making my woman happy.

"Holy shit." Max pointed across the room. "Who's the hot blond standing next to Short Stuff?" His eyebrows rose.

I shot him a narrow-eyed death glare. "Don't even think about it. That's Addie's best friend, and she's off limits."

Max put a hand on my shoulder and squeezed. "You take away all my fun."

"No, I just know how much you like to break hearts."

He shrugged, not denying it.

I stood watch for another second, memorizing the curve of Addie's ass in those jeans. The way her hips swayed as she moved to sit on the barstool made my dick go hard. Last night in her kitchen, I'd taken her from behind, my hands gripping those same hips that were making my mouth water.

God, I loved that woman. And it wasn't all because the sex was incredible either. Addison Booker had grown to be my heart and my soul. The only air I could breathe when my world had been polluted with bad shit.

"And check out the trash that just walked in." He whistled low and nodded to a guy approaching Kenna from her right.

"The hell's McIntire doing here? He's not allowed to come back around, according to Jonathon." I took a step forward, hands already tightening into fists.

Max's arm shot out in front of me. "Hold on now, Collinator. I'm not standing up for him by any means, but this is a public bar."

I clenched my teeth at my sister's nickname. Max had been spending far too much time around her, apparently.

"Let's give the girls a chance to stave him off. I don't want the soon-to-be-cop getting arrested for battery."

"Swear to God, Maxwell, if he so much as—"

"No." He jumped in front of me, dark eyes narrowed.

"No?" I arched an eyebrow.

"We're not in Balad anymore, you idiot. You. Are not. In command." He got in my face, going nose to nose. "And you sure as hell don't have to save everyone. You get me?"

I pulled in a sharp breath, glancing over his shoulder. Addie was pulling on McKenna's arm—McKenna who looked like she was one step away from beating McIntire's ass. Her hand was up in his face, a sneer on her lips. And if only for a second, I relaxed, thankful that my girl wasn't alone when it came to people who loved her besides me.

"Fine. Five minutes, or I'm showing his ass the door."

———∿∿∿———

Addison

"No. One more shot." McKenna tossed her head back, newly bobbed, blond hair touching the base of her neck. I'd never been happier to have my best friend back, but I'd really prefer she didn't get crazy wasted like the last time we went out.

"Take it easy, m'kay?" I smiled, then laid my head on her shoulder, exhausted from being up at five.

I'd been staying at Collin's more often than not, even had my toothbrush sitting inside his bathroom cabinet. I figured now that he was working days, it'd be easier for me to just sleep at his place. He'd been begging me for a week straight now to just move in, but I wasn't ready. Not yet.

"Evening, ladies."

I flicked my eyes up, disappointment setting in when I realized it was not Collin or even Max. They were late, and my anxiety was rocketing up the charts.

"Not interested." McKenna flicked her latest suitor away, not even bothering to look at his face.

"You're really taking this no-more-men thing seriously, aren't you?" I asked.

She smiled and trailed her finger over the rim of her shot glass. "It's easier, you know? I mean, if I'm feeling the need to have sex, *then* I'll try to find someone. But for now…" She chewed on the straw she'd taken from the holder in front of us. "I'm good with saying no. It's really not so hard."

I smiled. "I'm proud of you. But just remember, not all men are Paul."

At the mention of her ex's name, she looked away. But I noticed the stiff way she held the rest of her body. She could only fool me so much.

"Tell me how Number Six is doing," she said, looking back at me with a face of complete composure. Her eyes were bright and shining, her cheeks almost glowing under the bar lights.

My face heated before I had a chance to ask her what was really going on in that head of hers. And to be honest, I had no clue why I was even blushing. "We're doing really well, actually." *Except for tonight and him being an hour late, of course.*

"And how is everything workwise—for you, I mean. Still looking for something more next fall?"

I swallowed hard, hating that I was already lying to myself, as well as to Collin. Though lying by omission wasn't as bad as lying altogether. Besides, I planned on telling him about the phone call I'd received that afternoon from the Matoona School District. I just hadn't had the opportunity yet, not with his good news about applying for the academy.

Apparently Matoona had an opening next fall for a lead teacher position in one of the district's top preschools. It was one of the places where I'd sent my résumé before Collin hired me. I didn't think I'd have a shot, but when they called and asked me to come in for an interview, I didn't hesitate. It was literally a dream job for me, something I'd been waiting years for. But I was on edge about telling Collin, fearing he'd shut down on me if I told him I wanted to pursue something besides being Chloe's nanny. And now that he was committed to the academy, I felt like I might have to put my dreams aside. Sure, he had Amy's parents, but from what I'd learned about them, they weren't the best on keeping commitments.

"Work is great. I love Chloe. She lights up my world," I answered, not wanting to get into the work issue just then.

"And her daddy lights up a lot of things on you too, I'm thinking."

Even my neck warmed as I stared down at the bar, and I couldn't help but grin. "That is true."

After that, our conversation turned from me to her and what she'd done in Maine during the six weeks she was away. Besides doing a little soul-searching, she'd been applying for jobs online back in Carinthia. She'd finally decided to use her nursing degree and actually work in the field.

In a way, I was okay with Collin being late. I'd missed my best friend like crazy and would take any bit of alone time with Kenna that I could. Sure, we'd chatted on occasion throughout her absence, but it was never for more than five minutes because her nieces and nephews were always screaming in the background.

While she was in the middle of telling me about the night she'd spent with a Spanish waiter, a voice sounded from the other side of her, freezing me in place.

"Well, lookie here. Didn't think I'd ever see your face again."

Not bothering to look at Blondie from the diner, who I'd learned was named McIntire, I glanced at McKenna instead, waiting for her reaction.

"Not interested, Blondie." She curled her lip.

I couldn't help but snort. The fact that she used the exact label I did when meeting this guy said something about our friendship.

"Awww, you don't mean that, do you? I mean, dressing like that shows me you're just like your friend over—"

"Listen up, asshole." Kenna turned to face him, finger flicking against the guy's nose. "If you don't move out of my way, I'm gonna hook my fingers into your nostrils and slam your head against this bar."

I cringed at the visual. "Kenna, let's just go. This guy's not worth our time." I pushed my arm through the crook of hers.

McIntire's head tipped to the side as he studied me. "Where's Montgomery tonight, pretty girl? Get tired of you already?"

"What did you just call her?" McKenna's fingers gripped my wrist, nails digging into my skin.

I couldn't even wince at the pain, since the adrenaline coursing through me was countering it. "It's time you step away, *Blondie*."

He laughed at me, a big, whooping, boisterous laugh. Kenna curled her lip higher, and I shrugged, already knowing how weird the guy was. This wasn't anything new to me…but if Collin and Max happened to walk in and see him, the night would end before it got started.

"If you wanna keep your body parts intact, then I suggest you leave," I hissed when he finally stopped laughing.

One side of his mouth curled up. "Make me."

Before I could do exactly that, Kenna beat me to it and slugged him in the mouth like she'd been given the gift to kick ass in the span of six weeks. Eyes wide, I stared down at the laid-out jerk.

"Time to go," Kenna whispered, motioning toward a big bouncer who was already making his way over.

"But he was harassing us and—"

"It doesn't matter, Addie. This, right here"—she motioned a hand at the guy moaning on the dirty floor—"means it's our time to walk away." She shook out her right hand, yanking me forward with her left. "Plus, I think I broke my hand and am seconds away from bawling my eyes out."

Mouth still gaping, I looked at her swollen knuckles and nodded, wondering where in the actual hell this woman who'd possessed my weepy, terrified bestie had come from.

"Jesus, that was hot," a voice hollered from our right when we approached the door. I lifted my head, recognizing Max's voice but looking straight at Collin instead. The breath in my lungs squeezed tightly at what I saw.

Eyes flaring, lips pulled tight, my boyfriend looked as though he was seconds away from going postal. He glared over my shoulder toward the damage McKenna had left behind and took one step forward.

Not thinking twice, I flung my arms around his shoulders, stopping him. I kissed his ear before I whispered, "You're here."

Instantly, he relaxed in my arms, the tension seeping away like air from a balloon. "Sorry we're late." He wrapped his arms around me, fingers tangled in my shirt.

"And I'm sorry to break up the happy reunion, but

this lady needs to go before I lose my nursing license for good."

I cringed, pulling back and reaching down to link my fingers with Collin's. "I'm sorry, K."

She shrugged, sizing Collin up the way a father would size up his daughter's first date. "I will always be there for you, Addie." She looked at me and nodded. "More than any man ever will be."

Collin flinched, and my shoulders grew stiff as the silent stare-down between my boyfriend and best friend came to a head. I counted in my mind, waiting for who would say the first words, who would snap first...

"Christ almighty, you are my soul mate." Thankful Max jumped in, obviously feeling the tension too. He wrapped his arm around McKenna's shoulders and tugged her close. "The name's Maxwell. And I really could use a boxing trainer. You give private lessons?"

I sucked in a breath, waiting for her to freak out on him like she'd done with McIntire. Surprisingly, her face went soft, and she grinned up at Max. "For you, hot stuff, I'd probably do just about anything." She winked and then left through the door, swaying her hips a little more than usual.

I snuggled closer to Collin's side as we followed her and a drooling Max outside.

"Maxwell," Collin called after him, a warning in his voice. "Remember what I said."

From over his shoulder, Max grinned back at Collin, then winked at me. "Just having a little fun is all."

I walked Kenna to her cab a minute or so later, and Collin walked Max to his Uber driver not long after that. The pair went their separate directions, leaving Collin and me alone.

"Walk with me?" he asked.

"Absolutely." We could have gone with Max, but I figured Collin might need a little more time to cool down. Between McIntire and what Kenna said, I knew he was strung tight.

"I'm sorry we were late," he finally whispered, taking my hand. We walked down the street toward the park two blocks from the center of town.

"It's fine. I've missed Kenna, and we got to talk and hang a bit, just us girls."

He rubbed his thumb over mine, going quiet.

"You okay?" I held his wrist with my free hand, wanting nothing more than to hug him, to pull him close.

"I'm fine."

I frowned. "You're not fine. If you were, you would've had me in a car by now and taken me home." I grinned and tugged him across the street at the first sign of the park. "A few minutes after that, you'd be inside me in your *new* king-size bed." The one that had just been delivered today.

The first flash of a smile since we'd met up showed on his face as he followed my lead. "Would I now?"

I nodded and walked us toward the only slide there, the moonlight reflecting off the silver metal of its wide base.

"Uh-huh." I smiled, feeling brazen as I lay down on the slide, urging him to lie on top of me. Obliging, he snuggled over my body, straddling my hips, his smile still holding strong.

The space was tight, the metal cold, but having Collin this close warmed me to my soul.

I nipped at his neck. "You going to tell me what's wrong now?"

He groaned. "Coercion is not your best game, beautiful."

"I beg to differ." I kissed a path to the other side of his face, grinning against his ear as I said, "I think I'm quite skilled at coercion."

A warm laugh slipped from his mouth. "I'm startin' to think you're right."

"Talk to me, Collin."

A shuddering breath blew from his mouth as I pulled the tip of his ear between my teeth.

"Just didn't like that I couldn't be there to knock McIntire on his ass. Hate that guy. Hate having him in the same room as you."

I pushed him up a little to look into his eyes, my hands never leaving his cheeks. His need to take charge and be the big, bad protector used to bother me, but I knew now that it was just him—who he was. And even though it took some getting used to, I was starting to do just that.

"You know I'll always be there for you, right? You and Chloe are my life."

My chest warmed. "And you two are my life as well."

He shut his eyes, inhaling as though he was taking in this moment with all of his senses. After that, he kissed my forehead and I shut my eyes too, which in turn had him leaning down to kiss each of my eyelids. His warm breath was the perfect blanket from the cold air, and I wrapped my arms around his waist, needing him closer. He lowered his chest back to mine, and I could feel the beating of his heart. It was a rhythm I'd never grow tired of.

"But what happens if I'm not always there?"

"No buts. No what-ifs either." I shook my head. "Don't forget, I have been on my own for years now, and I do know how to take care of myself."

He frowned, opening his mouth only to close it again, until he finally nodded in consent.

Knowing I had the ability to calm the anxiety inside him, I pulled his head closer to mine again. "I'm okay, Collin."

"I know." He shut his eyes, the tension seeping from his body. As a reward, I softly kissed his lips. In response, they formed the perfection of a smile.

"Let's talk about what I'd be doing to you if I had you in my bed again." He tugged my sleeves, pulling my favorite pink coat off me in seconds. I didn't even have time to care before he pressed his mouth to my neck. With his free hand, he slowly undid the buttons of my red shirt.

I moaned as he splayed his warm palm over my stomach. "You'd touch me." I lifted my hips, rubbing against his.

"Where?" He kissed a path up my neck, then my chin, before hovering over my mouth.

Snow fell around us, tiny droplets sticking to his dark hair. The lone light in the park acted like a spotlight on our bodies, urging me to speak.

"Here." I grabbed his hand from my stomach and placed it on top of my breast. "You'd touch me here."

He groaned, lips still barely touching mine. I could almost taste the beer on his mouth, the mint from his toothpaste too. I wanted him to kiss me again, but I wanted to look into his eyes even more than that.

"Then what would happen?" he whispered, never moving the hand, never moving his mouth closer either. My stomach tingled in awareness as his erection pressed against my jeans.

"You'd pull the edge of my bra down"—which he

did, the lace caressing my sensitized nipples—"then you'd roll the tip of one of them between your fingers."

"You mean your nipples." One side of his mouth tipped up as his fingers skillfully worked as I suggested.

I moaned and my eyes half closed as I nodded.

Unable to help myself, I wrapped my legs around his hips, arching closer. The friction I desired to curb the ache between my hips wasn't anywhere close to what I needed yet.

Without him asking this time, I continued to speak, practically panting as I told him what would happen next. "Then I'd reach down to stroke you." I lowered my hands, undoing the button of his pants, then the zipper. With my feet, I tugged his jeans and boxers down below the rounded globes of his perfect ass. Then with no second thoughts, I took him in my hand, stroking him, just as he lowered his mouth to my nipple.

"Collin," I groaned, the new sensation overriding my ability to think.

He reached down and flicked open the button of my jeans. How he stayed upright was beyond me. But I wasn't about to complain. Not when he was in the process of stripping my panties down to my knees too. I centered his cock against me, but he made no move to enter my body, just hovered and looked—down at my exposed breasts hanging over the lace of my bra, then at my eyes, which I'm sure flickered with a heat that matched his own.

"Now is the part where you'd fuck me." I bit my lip, hoping for just that. He'd always been gentle with me, never truly losing control.

He lowered his mouth, biting at my chin, then whispered in my ear, "You done trying to tell me how to do my job?"

I froze, the nails on my free hand digging into his ass now. My hand around his erection loosened until he reached down and squeezed my fingers around the base for me.

I frowned. "Are you kidding right now?"

His lips twitched. "You're bossing me."

I narrowed my eyes. "You boss me all the time." I squeezed my hand harder, tugging up on the head of his erection. Not enough to hurt him, but enough for a warning to flash through his eyes.

"That's what I do. Take what I want."

I rolled my eyes. "You, sir, are a sicko."

He laughed, lowering his forehead to mine. "I'm your sicko, sweetheart."

I sighed, frustration diminishing as I kissed his chin, then his cheek. "That you are, Number Six."

He nodded. "Forever, Addison. I'm yours forever."

My heartbeat skipped at his words, and a lump of emotion built in my throat when I tried to swallow. It wasn't the first time he'd mentioned spending forever with me, but it was the first time I could feel it latch on to my heart. "Collin…I am so in lov—"

Then he kissed me, cutting me off, that word *forever* meaning more than I deemed imaginable for a guy like Collin, for a girl like me.

Then he did exactly what I'd wanted and sank inside me.

"Now, we fuck."

And if there was one thing Collin did well, it was make good on his words.

CHAPTER 36

Collin

IT WAS TWO DAYS BEFORE CHRISTMAS WHEN MY LIFE TOOK a turn for shit.

Hell, if I was being honest with myself, things had started going downhill the night Amy's parents got into town. I tried like hell to pretend it was a good thing, that having a piece of Amy there all the time was gonna be good for my girl. But the more time I spent with Suzie and Alexander, the more distanced Addison seemed to get.

My nerves were constantly shot, as I worried she'd run out on me like she'd done the day she met them. Her standoffish attitude since then hadn't escaped me. And other than the Saturday night we'd met up at O'Paddy's, and the nights in between we'd spent in each other's arms, I felt like she was slipping away.

One of the first things outta my mouth when my sister and I had sat across from Amy's parents back on the night they took us out to dinner was: *I love Addie*. They took the announcement well and even asked if we could all have dinner together sometime, surprise, surprise. Said they wanted to meet and get to know the girl who'd become so vital to Chloe's life.

Now there we were—the four of us—without the safety net that came with Beaner, my sister, or my buddies. *Awkward* was a damn mild word compared to what this night was turning into. Every time I looked at Suzie, it was like the ghost of Amy was sitting there with her. Judging, watching, silently waiting for Addie to screw up. It made me nervous as hell.

"So, Collin tells us you used to be a preschool teacher." Alexander slung his arm around the back of his wife's chair, Scotch glass dangling from his fingers.

I lowered my arm around Addison's chair too, slipping the ends of her hair between my fingers. Like a magnetic force, she moved closer to me, her thigh going flush with mine.

Unaffected by the round of fifty questions, she nodded and smiled, the epitome of polite. "I was a preschool teacher, yes. I went to Western Illinois University and received my bachelor's in early childhood education too."

"How interesting. I could tell by your interactions with our granddaughter today that it's a—how do I put this?—well-suited career choice for you." Suzie reached across the table and picked up her napkin, laying it back on her lap. The whole time, I could see the silent judgment flashing in her eyes.

Amy was premed.

Amy was going to find the cure for cancer.

Amy, Amy, Amy.

I tried not to let it get to me, knowing she wasn't doing it on purpose. No doubt this was just as weird for them as it was for us. Still, the tension radiating around the table was getting to me, making my shoulders stiff and my lower back burn in the hard chair.

Had nothing to feel guilty about myself—I'd finally figured that out. Addie came into my life at the moment she was meant to and filled the emptiness inside me, making me happier than anyone—besides Chloe—had ever done. That's what mattered here. Nothing else.

For the next five minutes, once the conversation started flowing, I tried relaxing. But the top button of my shirt strangled the life outta me, along with the tie Addie insisted I wear. I cracked my neck, then checked my phone at least a half dozen times under the table, hoping there'd be an emergency at home with Chloe. Not a real emergency, but something that'd give us an excuse to leave. Like a diaper nobody could change.

Only good part about this night so far was the little blue number Addie had on her body. Just short enough to be considered sexy but long enough to be classy. It dipped low in the front and back both, and she wore a pair of black heels that I planned on having her wear tonight in bed—with nothing else.

Licked my lips just thinking about the things I wanted to do to her when I got her beneath me wearing fuck-me heels. With my mouth, my hands, maybe even the tie around my neck…

Hell yes. I'd definitely use the tie.

"But I've heard the pay is really nothing more than minimum wage. That's the thing that has my mind boggled. It doesn't sound like a career path one would want

to take for the rest of their life, am I right?" Alexander
leaned forward. His wife followed suit, pressing her
hand against his shoulder. He whipped out a business
card and flicked it between his fingers, staring once at
me, then at Addie again.

"I do enjoy it though, sir. Not many people can say
that about their jobs."

My chest tightened with pride and I grinned, leaning
over to kiss her temple. She'd had to defend her career
choice for too long now—to her parents and now this
man. I wasn't about to let her continue.

"Doesn't matter how much money she makes. I'll
take care of her in the end."

Addie stiffened. I turned to get a read on her face but
stopped when Alexander started in again.

"Still. If you are going to be in my granddaughter's
life, don't you want to do everything you can to provide
for her?" His gaze was still locked on Addie's face,
ignoring me. Sure as hell didn't sit right in my damn
gut. "Find a *better*-paying job to help cover expenses?
Children are costly, and it's near impossible to raise
them on one income anymore, especially on the single
income of a police officer."

My spine went rigid.

The hell did he just say?

Addie quickly moved her hand to grip mine under the
table, her gaze zooming in on my profile. I could feel
the warning in her eyes as she stared at my face, but I
couldn't even spare her a look. No way in hell would I
let this man try to tell me what I would or wouldn't be
able to do for my daughter and the woman I loved.

"I can assure you, sir, Chloe will be just fine

financially on Collin's income. Police officers make a great living."

No matter what she seemed to say, Alexander kept. Fucking. Going.

"I'm not so sure about that, Addie. Which is why I want to offer *you* a job. I'm opening my own law practice right here in Carinthia and will be looking for a new secretary." He winked at his wife, whose face had gone white.

Addie squeezed my hand harder, and I gritted my teeth together so tightly that my jaw ached.

"I would, in fact, double your salary, offer insurance, and—"

"She won't need insurance when she marries me." I balled my free hand into a fist, inhaling to cool the temper flaring inside me. "And I sure as shit can provide for her *and* Chloe on my salary just fine."

"Collin, stop," Addie hissed.

I didn't. "Hell, if she didn't want to, Addie would never have to work another day in her life."

Addie jabbed me in the ribs, but I barely felt it.

"It's the truth." I glared at her; she glared back.

"Marriage?" Alexander scoffed and leaned back in his chair, bringing his wife along with him.

"Yes, sir. Plan on marrying her within the next year." Daring him, I leaned forward in my chair this time. My jaw clenched and unclenched like my hand as I pulled it out of Addie's hold to lower it around her thigh instead. She jumped, but I couldn't stop. Needed to touch her bare skin so I could keep my head on straight—or distract myself from freaking the hell out.

Dark eyes narrowed, Alexander opened his mouth,

probably to tell me off, but Suzie said first, "But you two have only known each other two months." She looked to me, a plea in her eyes. "You and Amy were together for much longer than that, yet you didn't ask her to—"

"*Thank you*, Alexander, for the job offer," Addie said, her words fast yet poised, just enough to break through to me. "But unfortunately I will have to pass." She cleared her throat. "I actually just received a call about a new job opening in Matoona. It's for a lead teacher position in the district-run preschool. A dream job for me, really. The pay would be that of a teacher's salary."

What?

I froze, careful not to move a muscle, not even acknowledging the fact that Addie's hand was now on my leg, squeezing—our roles reversed.

"That's…that's fantastic, Addison. I'm so glad you get to follow your dreams. N-not many people get to do that." Suzie's eyes filled with tears. She moved her chair back from the table, and the wood screeched across the floor, echoing around us in the restaurant. I was the only one who didn't flinch at the noise. "Now, if you will all please excuse me," she whispered, the sound barely reaching my ears over the roaring inside my head. "I need to use the ladies' room."

"Collin?" Addie touched my shoulder.

I shook my head, not giving a damn where we were as the words spilled out of my mouth. "You gonna leave us?" I asked Addie.

"Leave you?" She jerked back. "Why would I leave you?"

"You're gonna find a new job, gonna leave us for

something better." I know I sounded like a goddamn idiot, a child even, but everything she was saying… everything she *didn't* say… I couldn't help myself.

I pinched the bridge of my nose, the paranoia too much. I had to get out of here. Get *her* out of here.

"Well, this dinner was stimulating to say the least." Alexander chuckled and folded his arms over his coat as he looked at his watch.

From across the table, I glared at him. "Yeah. And a *big* mistake, actually." I stood and reached for Addie's arm to pull her up with me.

"Collin, stop it." Addie stood up too and pressed her chest against my arm. Not even the feel of her breasts against me could curb my anxiety. "You're making a scene."

"Don't give two fucks."

Her eyes widened. "Do not talk to me like that. I am not one of the guys from your unit. And you are *not* my father either. I. Am. Your. Girlfriend."

"I think I'm just going to go find my wife and take off. Don't worry about the meal. We will take care of the bill," Alexander said.

"No." I jerked my finger at him, then motioned for the waiter, the pain of Addie's words slicing through me. Still, I couldn't control myself. "I'm payin' for dinner."

"Really, Collin. Let us—"

"I'm. Paying."

Alexander lifted his hands in defense, zeroing in on Addie, who'd taken two steps back and was already grabbing for her coat. *No. No. No.*

Needing to hold her close, not let her go, I reached for her back just as Suzie approached.

"It was nice meeting you, Addie. And, Collin, please call us if you need anything at all."

Then they left like a storm, the aftereffects almost worse than the actual moment it all happened.

Addie turned to me, her lips pursed, more pissed than I'd ever seen her. And it scared the hell out of me. "I'll meet you in the truck."

Addison

The entire ride back to Collin's house was undoubtedly the worst moments of our relationship thus far. He was scary silent, other than the first few minutes when he'd begged for me to look at him, talk to him, hold his hand. To get him to relax, I did interlock our fingers, but I wasn't ready to forgive his behavior in the restaurant, not that he even apologized.

After that, he'd completely shut down on me, to the point that my stomach burned with uneasiness. There was one thing Collin struggled to do, and that was step down when told. If I hadn't feared that he might go off the deep end, I would've asked him to take me back to my apartment for the night. I might have loved him, but the way he pushed things to the extreme was exhausting. And there was no way I would *ever* let him treat me the way my father treated my mother.

And then there was the whole subject of marriage. How could he do that? Say what he had in front of his dead ex's parents—parents who were obviously still in mourning? I had no doubt he felt he was saying the truth, but Collin had issues when it came to using a filter for his words. Soon, I'd approach the subject of his assumption, that I would marry him within the next year. But tonight wasn't the time, at least not for me.

The lights were on in living room when we got to his place. Lia was sitting on one end of the couch, a bowl of popcorn in her lap, and Max was on the other, looking like he was seconds away from snoring. I barely acknowledged them before I headed straight back to check on Chloe in her crib.

Curled up on her side with a thumb in her mouth, she looked like the princess I always knew she was. Even with the feelings stirring inside me, I couldn't help but grin when I looked down at her. Chloe was the reason the reason I'd wanted this job in the first place—her father was the reason I stayed. I needed to remind myself of that, even though he didn't always handle himself the way he should—like tonight.

Not wanting to wake her, I slipped from the room, fingers wrapped around the door handle as I pulled it shut with a quiet click. What-if thoughts ran through my mind as I made my way down the hall to Collin's room. Had Amy not died, would she and Collin and Chloe be where we were now? My throat burned at the thought, the possibility too much to take in.

Refusing to go there right now, I turned the corner to Collin's room and froze at what I saw. Sitting on the edge of the bed, face in his hands, he looked more broken than any man should. A little of my anger slipped away at the view, my shoulders falling at the same time. But I still couldn't forget his behavior tonight like I wished I could. He'd acted like an idiot, embarrassing himself and me. Part of me realized that some of it was my fault he'd gone off like he did—me dropping the bomb about my interview. So I was going to woman up and apologize for it, even though he owed me an apology just as much.

Silently, I settled my purse on his dresser and slipped my heels off, kicking them to the side. I could feel his gaze trailing over my legs, my body too, but I wouldn't let his seduction mess with me when things needed to be said. Very *important* things.

"We need to talk, Collin." I sat down on the bed next to him, my hands fidgeting against my lap. For once, he didn't try to interrupt or touch me. Instead he just sat there, quiet, listening. "I should have told you about my interview. It wasn't right of me to spring it on you the way I did—and in front of Suzie and Alexander at that."

I waited, thinking he'd turn to me, give an excuse, tell me off, or even kiss me to shut my mouth. But he barely moved.

Clearing my throat, I kept going. "I got the call the Friday before we went to O'Paddy's. I wasn't…expecting it. I'd applied there before I even met you, before you *hired* me, thinking I didn't have a chance all along." I rubbed a hand over my forehead. "I was going to tell you, but—"

"It's fine."

I frowned and looked at his profile. His jaw ticked, the first sign of emotion I'd seen from him in an hour.

"It's not *fine*. I didn't tell you, and then I wound up blurting it out in front of your dead girlfriend's par—"

"I said it's fine." He pulled his knee up on the bed and turned to face me.

"If it's so fine, then why are you looking at me like I killed your puppy?"

One side of his mouth tipped up. "I don't have a puppy."

I groaned. "That's not the point."

"Tell me what the point is then, huh? That you wanted a new job but didn't have the guts to tell me? That working for me—being with me—was only temporary?"

"I... *What?* That's what you think? I told you I applied for that job *before I met you.* What part of that don't you understand? You're twisting around everything I've told you, and it's not fair."

He scrubbed his hand up and down his face until he finally let out a heavy sigh. "I'm not stupid, Addie. I know that you have bigger plans than just being my daughter's nanny for the rest of your life. That being with me is a stepping-stone to more. I just didn't think it'd be happening already."

"No. Just stop right there." I grabbed his wrists and pulled his hands to my neck, needing him to touch me, to remind him that I was real, not just some figment of his overexaggerating imagination. "I'm not going anywhere."

He moved closer, bringing his forehead to mine—a Collin move that I recognized as pure desperation. "I don't wanna talk anymore." His eyes shut. "Not tonight." Moving in to kiss me, he paused, less than a breath separating our mouths. "Just wanna forget tonight ever happened and wake up with you in my arms."

"We can't avoid talking." I shut my eyes at the feel of his lips as they moved to touch the corner of mine. The sensation nearly overrode my emotions, my frustration. And he was doing it on purpose. But somehow I managed to push past it. "Collin, wait. Sex and orgasms won't fix this."

He froze. "Addie, please…"

"I'm here to stay—for as long as you want me around. If I take another job, it's not because I'm done with you or Chloe. It's because I want to do more in life than just stay home and pop out babies. Not that there's anything wrong with staying home and popping out babies. Because honestly, there isn't. It's just not for me." I was rambling. Again. But that didn't faze him like it usually did, which should have spooked me but didn't because I was also on a roll.

"Tonight was pretty damn awful. I felt like an idiot trying to prove myself to those two people. And you… you just spouted off bullshit about *forever* and *insurance, a-and—*"

"Why?" He finally spoke, pulling back to look me in the eyes at the same time. I could see the pain in his blue eyes, the stab of my angry words having pushed him to a point I'd never seen. Not just sadness and desperation. But fear too. I'd never seen Collin—the big, bad, tough marine—look scared in all the time I'd known him.

"*Why?*" I softened my voice, for him and me both. There was no point in getting all worked up when it might not lead us anywhere. "You really have to ask me that?"

He nodded, just once.

"To them, I'm Amy's replacement, and if I don't live up to their standards…"

His breath fanned over my lips as he exhaled. "You're amazing, Addison Booker. And I don't care what anyone else says, especially not Suzie and Alexander."

I winced, wishing I felt the same way he did. With Amy's parents around, I felt like I had to prove myself— fill the shoes of a ghost, which was nearly impossible. Collin had insisted that he'd never loved Amy the way he loved me, but I still couldn't shake the feeling that I might not be enough. Not necessarily for him, but for his daughter.

"I'll never be her, Collin." I looked down at my lap, the sting of tears burning my eyes.

A finger pressed under my chin, lifting my head. "Good. Because I don't want anyone *but* you."

He pulled me closer, wrapping his arms around my waist. Still wearing my dress, I lay against his chest as we settled our heads on the same pillow. It was more intimate than a kiss, a touch, or a caress could ever be, but it did nothing to curb the anxiety fluttering through my chest.

CHAPTER 37

Collin

ON CHRISTMAS MORNING, I WOKE WITH ADDIE IN MY arms—spooned against my chest—and to the sound of Chloe babbling over the baby monitor.

Later in the day, Gavin came over for dinner. Lia too.

Addie and I cooked for the five of us, since Max was out of town with his family in Tennessee, and Lia and my parents were in Arizona until April. We didn't make a big hoopla out of things, but I'd wanted to make this day as nice as I could for Chloe, since this was her first Christmas.

Plus, today was the day I planned to make up for every mistake I'd made with Addison so far.

Between last-minute shopping, my job, and Addie hanging out with McKenna, the two of us hadn't been spending a lot of time together, and it bugged the hell out of me. I'd been a dick the night we'd gone to dinner with Alexander and Suzie, but I couldn't figure out how the hell I was gonna apologize without sounding like a whiny loser. Unlike me, Addie had apologized the second she'd gotten me alone that night, even though she didn't have anything to really be sorry for, unlike me. But even as she'd said the words, I knew I didn't have a clue how to say them back the way I needed to, to express how fucking sorry I really was.

She didn't complain when I pushed her to forget about things for the night. Nor did she complain the four times I'd made her come. But I felt her resistance, felt the way she closed herself off after every orgasm and moan of my name from her lips.

Bottom line? I knew she needed the *I'm sorry*, but I didn't have it in me. At least not then.

But I did now.

"She's eleven months old, yet she has more crap than I do." Lia picked up Chloe from the floor and planted her on her hip, staring down at the piles of wrapping paper flung all over the place from the day.

"She's a beautiful, spoiled princess." Gavin yawned as he stretched his hands over his head. "She deserves the world."

"You think?" Lia kicked him in the shin with a toe, grinning.

At my side, snuggled up with a cup of hot chocolate and some sort of Philippine dessert, the one with the duck eggs, Addie looked at my friends, contentment in her dark gaze. Damn, she was beautiful. That long, thick hair of hers was done up in a braid hanging down one side of her neck. I twisted my hand at the end of it, tugging it lightly to get her eyes on me.

She smiled.

"Thank you. Today was incredible." I swallowed,

overcome by her beautiful eyes as they sparkled my way—for me.

"Thank *you* for giving me the first sense of family I've had in a long time." She pressed her nose to mine, kissing my lips.

Taken aback by the love I felt for this woman, I leaned over and kissed her bare shoulder when she looked away. The big, poofy sweater she wore kept falling off her shoulders.

"You ready to open your present?" I asked.

She bit her lip, and I jumped up from the floor, heading toward the Christmas tree across the room and not waiting for her answer.

Chloe was back on the floor, crawling toward the tree, while Gavin slipped into the kitchen. My guess was for another beer. I'd not taken a drink today and didn't figure it was a good idea for what I had planned for Addie and me later tonight when everyone had gone home and Beaner was asleep. Part two of her gift from me.

At least five long orgasms.

"First, she's gotta open mine." Lia rubbed her hands together and dove toward the tree in front of me, producing a huge-ass box in the process. She shoved it against Addie's chest, smiling wider than I'd seen in weeks. My sister was so up and down lately, crying and closed off one minute, ass-kicker mode the next. A lot of it had to do with the fact that she'd been seeing a new psychologist—dealing with the bad crap from her college years. Luckily, today had been one of her better, calmer days.

"Fine. As long as she opens mine next." I turned and winked at Addie.

She batted her lashes as she glanced at me from her spot on the floor. The quiet excitement in her eyes had my gut going hard. Loved all things happy Addison almost as much as I loved all things spent and well-loved Addison.

"Fine, fine, whatever. Just open mine already." Lia jumped up and down when she stepped in front of Addie. Gavin came back into the room, a beer in one hand and a piece of leftover ham in the other.

"Oh jeez, Lia. I can't believe you got these. They're too expensive." From the giant box, Addie pulled out a pair of boots, all leather and brown, with fuzzy stuff on the inside. She hugged them close, like they were her best friends.

"They were on sale. Figured they'd be awesome for when you start teaching next year. Not only will they keep your feet warm and fuzzy, but they are comfy too."

My chest grew hot, but somehow I managed not to flinch. Had she talked to my sister about this job too? She'd had no problem blurting it out in front of Amy's parents either. And, yeah, sure, she'd tried to talk to me about it, but that was after the fact. Wasn't gonna let it get to me though. Not tonight.

"Thank you so much." Addie hugged Lia with one arm, then stuffed the boots back into the box, reaching down to grab my small, square box sitting on her lap.

Not having a lot of time to think, I watched as she ripped it open, that same excitement still in her eyes.

"Hope you like it."

She buried her hands in the piles of tissue paper I'd used, grin still wide.

Silently, I watched as she pulled out the small key

chain plated in silver. Tiny diamonds made up her initials in the center, and I studied her face as she flipped it over to read the engraving.

"'What's mine is yours,'" she read out loud, eyebrows pushed together in what looked like confusion.

I crouched down next to her, leaning forward to kiss her lips. "I'm so sorry for being a dick. I love you. Want you to be with me and Chloe all the time." I swallowed. "Move in with us." I whispered the last four words, tucking some of her hair behind her ear. "Please."

Her smile fell. "Collin…"

"Idiot," Lia mumbled. I glared at her from around Addie's shoulder, willing her to shut her mouth. Instead, she got up and grabbed her phone off the dining room table, burying her face in it.

My sister had told me to leave it be, that when Addie was ready for more, she'd tell me and make the next move. But I couldn't wait anymore. Not only did I want her because I loved her, but also because I secretly needed the reassurance that she wasn't going anywhere.

I knew I was a crazy bastard, but that didn't stop the insecurities running through my head. Even if she did decide to take a new job, I had to know that the two of us were solid. After the night we'd gone out with Amy's parents, I felt like I was grasping at straws to hold on to her. And it scared me shitless. Yeah, things between us had happened fast, but when you know…you just. Fucking. Know.

Least that's how it was with me.

"It's really gorgeous, Collin, but…"

My throat burned when I swallowed. Even when she turned to look at me, I knew I had my answer already.

And yeah, it hurt like I'd been beaten in the chest with a hammer.

Not wanting to wait another second, I tugged her onto my lap. "Not a marriage proposal, sweetheart."

She sighed and wrapped her arms around my neck. Killed me to say what I did next, but at the same time, scaring her away would hurt me more in the end. "Just wanted you to know that the option is there whenever you're ready." But that was a lie, because what I really wanted from her was a yes, or even a *hell* yes.

"You sure you're okay if I take more time to think it over? I mean, I just caught up on my rent. I feel like I should, I don't know, do it for a little while longer to prove I can actually manage taking care of myself." She bit her lip.

I pressed my hands against her cheeks and lowered my forehead to hers. Not just because I wanted to kiss her, but because I didn't want her to see me breaking. "I'm sure."

Then she kissed me, tangling her hands in my hair. I kissed her back, trying to convince myself that she wasn't saying no for forever.

"Hey, you two." Gavin whipped a blanket over our heads. "Knock that shit off."

Addie smiled against my mouth between kisses, then whispered, "It's still Christmas, and I really wanna give you your present, but I can't 'til they're all gone and Chloe's asleep."

Didn't matter that my heart was nearly breaking in my chest, my cock was already up and ready, telling my emotions to piss off.

"Let's make it happen, then."

A little hand grabbed my knee from over the top of the blanket. I kissed Addie between the eyes before I yanked the blanket off our heads and said, "Boo."

Chloe giggled, and I reached down to tickle her waist before plopping her at my side. Right away, she laid her cheek on the blanket that'd been piled up on my calf, yawning and content as she stared at the Christmas lights. I reached down to run my fingers through her curls, finding my girlfriend's hand already doing the same thing. Instead of stopping, I helped—my hand on Addie's as we moved in sync over my baby girl's soft head. These were the moments I wanted every day for the rest of my life.

Lia plopped down on the chair to our left, and Gavin sprawled out on the couch and shut his eyes.

"Who's next?" I asked, not wanting to move.

Addie sighed. "I told McKenna I'd call her before I opened her present. Might as well get that over with. No doubt it's some extravagant gift that cost a fortune."

My hands tightened around Addie's waist, wishing I could keep her close. I nuzzled my nose into her hair, groaning five minutes later when she stood. Chloe had fallen asleep against my calf, a little baby snore coming out of her nose. Then a louder snore sounded from the couch, where Gavin's eyes were shut and his arm hanging off to the side.

Like uncle, like niece, I thought to myself before looking at Addie's ass as she bent over to grab a long envelope from under the tree.

Lia was on her phone, probably texting the dirtbag she'd been seeing from that club, so I took the spare minute to get my mental state in order and grabbed Chloe to put her to bed. She didn't make a sound as I changed her diaper and tucked her in her pajamas, only whining when I had to take her thumb out of her mouth to get her shirt off. In a way, I didn't want to leave her room because that'd mean the day was over, that I'd have to feel the rejection every time I looked into Addie's eyes. She didn't want to live with us yet. I got it. But why did I still feel like I was losing her?

Out in the living room, Lia was getting her coat on. "You leaving?" I asked.

"Yeah, figured I'd swing by Travis's house before I headed home."

Any other day I'd have told her what I thought about this *Travis* guy. But I figured since it was Christmas, I'd let it go.

"You okay?" She motioned her head toward the kitchen, where Addie was talking to someone, I assumed McKenna, on the phone.

"Don't start with the I-told-you-so's."

"Collin." She squeezed my shoulder. "It's been, what? Almost three months? Don't rush it."

Didn't realize my hand was shaking 'til I ran it up and down my face. "I know. I just…I fucking love her, Sis. I don't know how to handle the way she makes me feel sometimes. Tangles me all up."

She reached for me and pulled me into a hug. "I know, Big Brother. But you have to remember that she's been through a lotta crap in her life with her parents. Give her time to adjust to being loved like crazy by a man who'd do anything for her."

I shut my eyes and pressed my chin against Lia's shoulder. "I'm trying."

She patted my back. "I know you are."

After she left, I lowered my forehead to the door. The place where it had all started between Addie and me. At the time, I thought I was just some screwed-up guy in need of a piece of ass. But thinking back on it, I knew I'd been lying to myself. I didn't know love until the second I knew Addison Booker. And if I had to wait a little while longer to make her feel the same way, I would. Just prayed she wouldn't change her mind in the end.

———～～～———

Addison

My eyes watered as I pulled Kenna's present from the envelope. A plane ticket to Maine blurred before me.

"It's one week, Addie. That's it. You told me you needed some space to get your head together."

"But that was *before* he apologized and asked me to move in with him. I feel like if I go now, he'll think I'm running."

McKenna sighed from the other end. "Isn't that what the plan was? To run for a bit until you realized that it wasn't what you wanted after all?"

"No." I frowned, flicking the paper between my fingers. "I just want to make sure is all. I love him so much, but he's so…" I squeezed my eyes shut, *Passionate* was the first word that came to mind, and *filled with love*. The way Collin reacted to situations wasn't just him being a bossy ass. It was just him being him: a man who loved hard and fought harder for what he wanted. Still,

every time he tried to tell me what to do, all I could think
was: *Am I my mother after all?* "I mean, what if I don't
move in right now and he decides later I'm not good
enough after all?"

She laughed. "No guy like Collin will change his
mind that quickly. The guy is flipping nuts about you. I
saw it that night in the bar." She huffed. "Besides that,
even if he did decide not to wait, he'd be crazy and definitely not worth your time."

I was nuts about Collin too. So nuts, in fact, that
I'd almost told him yes when I opened that key chain
tonight, though I knew deep down that I was still not one
hundred percent ready.

Being on my own for a little while longer in my
apartment and paying my own bills was for me and me
alone, not because I didn't want Collin, but because I
was looking for solidification in my life—to prove my
father wrong, though he'd never know. To be able to
take care of myself and prove to the world that, financially, I could be the person I was required to be in order
to be a stepmother to Collin's daughter some day. I was
almost there, believe me. But not quite yet.

"Just talk to him. Tell him I bought these tickets
because I want to spend New Year's with you. Because,
in truth, that's what it comes down to."

I shut my eyes. "I will."

"All right. The little nugget kids are calling. Gotta
go do the last-minute, nighttime auntie…things." She
paused a second. "Being around all these little germy
boys makes me realize that I do not want children anytime soon. Maybe never."

I couldn't help but grin. "Don't knock it yet. You

still have a lot of years left." I twirled the ends of my hair and stuffed the ticket into my jeans pocket, storing it away for later.

"Yeah, but the supply of men to help me make them is severely lacking."

This time I laughed out loud, just as Collin came up beside me to lean against the counter. "Gotta go," I said to Kenna. "Talk tomorrow."

"You're coming to Maine. We will drink all the problems away with the new year." She yelled through the phone, so loud that Collin cringed.

Holding my breath, I clicked End and waited for the inevitable bomb to drop.

"Hi," I said.

"Hey." He lowered his chin to his chest and rubbed the back of his neck.

"How much did you hear?"

"Enough." He looked at the floor, obviously avoiding my eyes.

"Collin, I don't have to go."

Silently, he leaned closer and pulled the white ticket from my pocket.

I shooed it off, trying not to make a big deal about it. "It's nothing. Just a dumb gift from McKenna. I'm not gonna go."

"New Year's?" he asked.

"Yeah, I mean, I know it's last minute so—"

"You're going."

I swallowed hard. "No. There won't be anybody to watch Chloe and—"

"Said you're going. Suzie'd love to watch Chloe. It'd probably be good for her to spend some time with her grandmother." He handed me the ticket, not meeting my stare. I stuffed it back into my jeans, ignoring the metaphorical weight against my thigh.

"Oh. Well, yeah, that's probably true..." If it was, then why did I feel like he was dismissing me? My eyes burned. Before he could look at me, I walked to the fridge to grab a bottle of water. I took a long drink, begging the lump in my throat to go away.

"Ready for bed?"

"Yes." My voice cracked. I turned around, scared to see his face, his expressive eyes. If they were blank, it'd hurt more than anything else.

Before I could get a good look, he flicked the lights off. Still, he reached for my hand, not hesitating to lock our fingers together. I took another deep breath, but my heartbeat still pounded like an out-of-control drum cadence in my chest.

Palms pressed together, he pulled me to the living room, avoiding my eyes as he flicked all the lights off along the way, leaving Gavin asleep in the living room, snoring.

The tension flowing off Collin's body had my skin burning with unease. I wanted to speak but had no idea to say. Collin was a man who always said what was on his mind, but the second he got me into his bedroom, he switched off the light and pressed his mouth to mine.

Wordless and greedy for anything he could give me, I pulled him closer, desperate for him as I grabbed the front of his shirt. He pulled me down on top of him on the bed and immediately gripped the bottom of my sweater. Still, he hesitated to pull it up, always asking before he took. When I nodded once, he drew it up and over my head, only to let his hands run down my sides. Seconds later, he worked at the button of my jeans, flicking it open and slowly slipping them down and off my body.

When I couldn't take the silence anymore, I grabbed his arms and settled them against the bed. He didn't fight me, just lay there, eyes shut. "Look at me, Collin."

The curtains on the window to our right were open, revealing the moon reflected off the new dusting of snow outside. The light outlined his face just enough that I could see his eyes when they opened, shiny and blue and filled with a dangerous emotion that nearly stole my heartbeats.

Collin was scared.

I lowered my head to his, the move he'd always done to me. "I love you, Collin."

His fingers tightened around mine. The power in his arms was no match for me as he flipped my body beneath his, then nuzzled his nose in my hair. "Never wanna lose you." The whispered words were tender and shaking.

"You won't," I said, needing his skin on mine, needing to feel his heartbeat closer.

Minutes later, he was free of clothes. Kissing me with a burning fervor, he reached for the straps of my bra to tug them down over my shoulders. Then his hand was on my breast, kneading and pulling, tugging my nipple, until his mouth replaced his fingers.

I moaned, wiggling to get my panties off. I needed him inside me. I needed to prove to him that I loved him by doing to his body what he always did to mine. But when I finally shook off the last leg of my panties, I knew he had other plans. Kissing his way down my stomach, he took his time to caress and lick my nipples, until he landed between my spread thighs.

"Collin," I cried just as his tongue and mouth crashed against me.

With a low groan in his chest, he gripped my thighs tighter, the pleasurable ache only sending me closer to the edge. He licked and nibbled, sucked, then licked again, as lightning bolts of desire and pressure pulsed between my hips.

Before I could reach the end, he stopped, leaving me gasping as I arched my back. I didn't have a moment to cry out at the loss because he was there on top of me, his erection at my center, pressing inside.

"Deeper," I hissed as he filled me. "Faster," I begged as he pushed inside a little more. Still, he was wordless, only staring at me with pain and pleasure and more love than I'd ever known.

His hips were relentless yet slow, savoring yet desperate. Never once did his beautiful blue eyes leave mine.

This man...this brilliantly hard-loving man was treating me with kid gloves. The kind that made me feel fragile. The kind that made me want to cry out with frustration but hold on to him forever.

He pushed me close to an edge I wasn't afraid of, only to pull me back from it every time. Forty minutes turned into fifty minutes, until an hour passed. All of those minutes were torture to my heart, pain to my soul, but brought perfect pleasure every second they lasted.

Finally, when sweat had coated our bodies completely and when our breaths had turned into pained gasps, I found my release, calling out his name with *I love you*. Soon after, he followed, but with the sort of finality to his cries that made tears flow down my cheeks when it was all said and done.

Collin had made just made love to me like he was saying good-bye…and I could do nothing but let him.

CHAPTER 38

Collin

"I'm going. Booking a flight at the airport, then leaving." I grabbed my rugby duffel in the closet and dumped all my crap on the floor. Then went back to my room and threw in a spare set of clothes and underwear. Back in the living room, I looked at Max, who was feeding Chloe in her high chair.

"Not a good idea, man."

"She hasn't answered my calls since she left this morning. Hasn't bothered to text me either. What if something happened to her? To her plane?" I paced the floor, rubbing a palm over my chest.

"Calm down. She only left this morning. Short Stuff's probably not even settled yet."

"I'll be back." I grabbed my keys off the end table by our couch, kissed Chloe, and took off, ignoring Max's groan about how pussy whipped I was.

"Collin!"

Was at my truck when I turned to look at Gavin on
the porch. With his shirt off, no shoes, and half-buttoned
jeans, he stared at me from the top step, the streetlights
just flickering on. "Where are you going?"

"Airport."

Gavin laughed. "Damn. You made it longer than I
thought you would."

"Fuck you." My hand hovered over my truck door,
nerves eating me alive.

She'd left not even nine hours ago. I'd been the one
to take her to the airport, the one who'd dropped her
off at the terminal. The one who kissed her so hard I
couldn't breathe.

Then she'd said to me: *I don't have to go*.

And because I loved her, knew that she needed this,
I said: *Yeah, I think you do*. Even though I knew it was
right at the time, saying that didn't stop the paranoid
sensations going through me. Did she get lost and
abducted on the way to Kenna's brother's house? Or
worse yet, was she avoiding me?

"Damn it." I rubbed a hand over my forehead, hating
the rational part of my brain for taking over.

I couldn't leave.

Had a daughter who needed her dad and a job that
relied on me.

Footsteps slapped against the cement as Gavin came
up from behind. Least he'd put on a sweatshirt.

Hands in the back pockets of his jeans, he leaned
back against the bed of my truck, just staring at me.

"What?" I barked.

"You run on two speeds in life. You know that?
Don't give a fuck, and give entirely too many fucks."

I frowned. "There a point to this?" My hand fell away from the door handle.

"The point is, if you want this girl to be yours forever, you've got to step back and let her go for a while."

I opened my mouth to tell him I didn't have a clue how to do that just as Lia pulled up to the curb. Her rusted, black Beetle rumbled and squeaked as she stopped. Pink hair pulled back, she shoved open her door and headed our way. Her black motorcycle boots thudded on the cement and crunched in the two inches of snow we'd just gotten that morning.

"Going somewhere?" She folded her arms over her stomach, smirking.

I cringed. "No."

She tucked her arm through mine, grinning. "Good boy." Rolling my eyes, I followed her inside, ignoring Gavin's laugh from behind as he held the door open for us. I was too tired to fight right now.

"Are you wearing a Batman mask?" Lia skipped into the room. Apparently it was another happy day for my sister.

"So what if I am?" Max lifted it up on his head, grinning, eyes only on my sister. "Chloe Bean loves when Uncle Max plays superhero with her."

"Jesus, you're nuts," she snorted, plopping down on the chair.

I blew out a breath, trying to keep my pride intact as I said, "I need help."

All eyes zeroed in on me, even Beaner's. The air seemed to be sucked out of the room. Nobody spoke, so I cleared my throat to try to curb the tension.

"I love her, but I don't know how to knock that love

down to an acceptable kind. The kind where I don't seem…" I winced. "Crazy." My face burned at my admission. In all my years of boot camp and missions, middle-of-the-night base evacs and raids, I'd never been more nervous than I was admitting to my best friends and sister that I didn't know how to love a woman the right way.

And what the hell did they do when I bared my fucking soul to them?

They. All. Laughed.

And the laughs weren't just loud. They were hard and so damn big that by the time everyone was done, they were all wiping their tears.

"Screw you all." I walked over to Chloe, needing her with me. At least she didn't think I was an asshat.

Lia spoke first, in between coughing and laughing. "You, my brother, are growing up." She kissed my cheek. "Very proud of you."

I frowned and wiped at the spot she'd kissed.

Max was next. "Sorry." He laughed some more and shook his hand in front of his face. "Can't talk. Laughing."

"Hardy-har." I pointed at him. "Laugh at the dude who's got issues. Just wait 'til you get all messed up over a woman." His face fell, and his eyes dropped to the floor. This was the second time he'd reacted like that when I mentioned him finding someone besides the harem of woman that he called on a weekly basis.

Gavin frowned and said, "You've got to tone it down a little. Don't get so mad when she's got an opinion about something. And when she tells you she's not ready for a step, don't jump to the conclusion that she's going to run away."

"Yeah, man," Max said after finally wiping the last of his tears. "Girls wanna be loved. Chased, even. But they don't like to be pushed."

"Never tried to push her. Just came out that way is all."

Lia walked over to me and sat on the arm of my chair. "It's all right, Collinator. It's in the Montgomery blood to get what we want when we want it." She winked. "But when it comes to the person you love, you need to make sure those wants of yours are a two-way street."

Gavin—the wise owl he was—put a lot in perspective for me, but Max and Lia made sense too. But I knew it wasn't normal for me to let things happen naturally. Not when I was used to being the one who made them happen. Still, I knew I'd have to try—for Addison. Probably had known that for a real long time.

"Holy shit!" We turned to face Max, finding him at the edge of the coffee table, arms stretched toward Chloe. My throat closed off as Lia stood and gasped.

"Da-da-da-da." My baby girl held a hand on one of the dining room chairs and waved her fist at me, a giant smile on her little face. And then she let go. Then she took a step. And then another and another, until she was in Max's arms, squealing.

I jumped off the couch and raced toward my little girl, only to swipe her from Max's arms and into my own. I tossed her into the air and laughed. "Did you guys see that? Holy hell, she just walked!" I looked at my two best friends and sister, pride filling my heart. Chloe giggled, smacking the top of my head with her hand like she was saying, *Put me down. Let me do it again.* But I couldn't. Not yet. Just wanted to keep that moment in my head a little longer.

"She sure did, Big Brother." Lia smiled sadly and turned away, but not before I saw the tears on her cheeks.

I hugged Chloe close and kissed her nose, then her head, then her cheeks. But as happy as I was, I knew the pain in my chest wasn't gonna go away until I brought my other girl back home.

For now though, I knew I had to let her go.

At least for a little while.

CHAPTER 39

Addison

"I'M NOT SURE IF I'LL BE COMING HOME TONIGHT. SO DON'T bother waiting up."

My eyes narrowed as I watched my best friend run around the small bungalow we'd been sharing for a week now. Her brother was very well off, a surgeon with more money than he could ever count. His two-story mansion-like home was less than a quarter mile up the road.

"I still can't believe you're leaving me alone on New Year's Eve."

McKenna rolled her eyes and grabbed a pair of bright-green pumps by the door. She slipped them on and said, "Sorry. I need a piece of ass, and as much as I love you, you're not quite man enough for me." She winked.

I slumped down on the couch, pulling my fleece robe tighter around my shoulders. The chilled wine and movies waiting on the coffee table in front of me were for naught, and all I could do was blink away my tears.

Of course I wanted my best friend to enjoy her last few days in Maine. She'd met a few guys, most of them of the bearded-lumberjack variety, but to ditch out on me on my last night here? Yeah, that had to go against some best friend's code. I was sure of it.

Still, I *had* been kind of a lump this week, so I couldn't exactly blame her for wanting to leave a miserable witch like me for the night.

Kenna crouched down in front of me, poured a glass of wine, and frowned as she handed it over. "Look, sweetie. I'm not trying to be mean, but you're miserable. Why don't you just call him already?"

I pulled the wine close to my chest but didn't drink it. Because drinking alone would surely bring me *past* the point of misery.

"He's avoided me all week. When I try to call him, he doesn't pick up. It's like he's just forgotten about me."

"Has he texted you?"

I nodded, staring into my glass.

"And has he told you he loves you in those texts?"

I nodded again, knowing how much I lived for those three typed words on my screen.

When I didn't move to drink my wine, Kenna grabbed my glass and sucked it down, then poured me another one and shoved it back into my hands. "He's just giving you space like you wanted him to, remember? Plus, the guy is absolutely miserable without you."

I leaned forward, resting my elbows on my knees with a frown. "How do you know he's miserable without me?"

She reached for my next glass and drank it down too. Then stood and tossed another piece of wood into the fireplace. "I *meant* he's *probably* crazy miserable without you."

"Doubt it." Of course the tiny butterflies coming to life at the mention of Collin missing me like I did him were fluttering like crazy. His touches, his kisses, the way he spoke too loudly, and loved me louder… I missed him so much I could hardly think, let alone move from the couch most days.

"Seriously. Why don't you, I dunno, get dressed at least. Maybe put on some makeup, do your hair up pretty."

"What, for Patrick Swayze in *Dirty Dancing*?" I snorted and folded my arms over my chest as I leaned back. "Don't think so. I'll probably just go to bed early, maybe start packing up the rest of my things."

"Whatever," she grumbled. "Don't say I didn't warn you."

I followed her with my gaze as she walked toward the closet. She pulled out her gray peacoat and slipped it on.

The doorbell rang, and Kenna's eyes grew wide with excitement. "Love you!"

"Yeah, yeah," I called after her. "Love you too."

And there I was…alone. The epitome of a sad, broken woman in a gorgeous log cabin up in the hills of some ski town, alone on New Year's. This had the makings of a bad romantic comedy written all over it. Except that I wasn't Kate Winslet or Cameron Diaz. My happiness was far away, and he might or might not be missing me like crazy too.

"No crying, you idiot." I wiped at my damp cheeks. "*You're* the one who needed *space*, remember?" I mocked myself, stooping to a new life low.

This trip was supposed to give me time to wrap my

head around my and Collin's relationship. But one night away from him had verified what I think I already knew deep down.

That I loved him and wanted to be with him all the hours I could, that he wasn't my father but instead a man who was overly emotional, not to mention broody, but loved me and let me make my own choices...most of the time. So yeah, I *did* want to move in with him. Pride be damned. Which was exactly why I'd put my house key on that key ring twenty-four hours after I'd stepped off the plane.

What I didn't expect was for him to actually abide by my need for space. God, if anything I needed him here more than ever. I needed his arms wrapped around me. I needed to hold his warm hand in mine. And I really, really needed to hear his laughter and feel his heartbeat against my ear.

Not to mention I'd missed a huge step in Chloe's life—learned about it in a text at that. Her first few steps, and I hadn't been there to see them.

Talk about a broken heart.

Outside the door, a crash sounded, breaking me out of my pity party. My back went rigid as I glanced at the window. A shadow flickered from the other side, indicating movement—someone was there. Suddenly my romantic comedy premise held a more thriller-horror vibe. All alone in this cabin, barely any cell service, and a trek up the road to get to McKenna's brother and family, who weren't even home.

Yeah, this wasn't creepy or anything.

"Quit hallucinating." I squeezed my eyes shut before standing.

Next to the door was a snow shovel—plastic and not really useful to take someone out, but it was better than nothing. I grabbed it, readying to whip it at a head just as I flung the door open. The whoosh of the icy air from outside burned my cheeks, but the shadow was no longer there.

"Hello?" I looked to my right, then my left, but the area was clear.

Taking a step back, I gulped. "God, I need that wine."

Frustrated and tired, I pulled the door half-closed, freezing in place when the shine of something caught my eye. On top of the small snowdrift next to the railing was a box wrapped with a red bow.

Slowly, I reached down to grab it. If there was some sort of freak out there, planting crap to get my or Kenna's attention, I sure as hell wasn't staying here to find out who it was.

Sticking the box in my robe pocket, I grabbed Kenna's sister-in-law's car keys off the rack hanging near the front door and took off down the cement stairs. Of course I didn't bother with a coat or actual shoes other than my slippers, or even my cell phone. This wouldn't be a real nightmare if I did.

Teeth chattering, I made it to the black Audi in record time, hopping in and slamming the door shut behind me. I clicked the locks, that sound the only noise I could hear. My heart raced like I'd run a mile, and my eyes bulged wide as I searched the perimeter of the cabin. Still, I saw nothing.

Until I flipped on the headlights.

"Fuuuuuck!" I screamed, slamming the car into reverse. I didn't look where I was going, just went for it, crashing against something. Hard. My head whipped forward and the air bags blew.

"Oh God." Chest tight, I barely released a breath as I glanced behind me to find a light pole coming through the trunk.

"And this would be how I die." I laughed hysterically. "Tragic death by murderous lumberjack and a light post." I could see the headlines now.

There was a tap on the window, and I screamed louder. Then laid on the horn, thinking someone would come running. But then again, nobody was home. Kenna was gone, and her brother and sister-in-law and their kids were off skiing for a few days at some resort.

The door wrenched open, and the dark shadow of a man growled. Out of self-preservation, I curled into a ball and screamed.

"Shouldn't have l-listened to my sister. Should've d-done my own thing."

I stopped screaming and sat up, knees colliding with the air bag.

"Collin?"

He lifted his baseball cap off his face. The whiskers on his chin were frosty, his cheeks red.

"Oh my God, what are you doing here?" Unthinking, I jumped from the car and wrapped my arms around his waist. He wore a thin jacket and what felt like a long-sleeved shirt beneath, but most of his body felt like a human Popsicle.

"Y-you've had enough s-space, sweetheart." My eyes widened as I pulled back and took him in from head to toe. He was shaking, stuttering, and his lips were blue.

"Where are your boots?" His feet were bare. "Oh my

God, where's your car?" I took off my robe and wrapped it around his shoulders.

"D-don't n-need this." He tried to shove it off, but I pushed his hands away and held it there, urging him back toward the cabin.

"Don't be a stubborn ass. You're frozen and hardly dressed right for this weather."

"S-says the g-girl in a r-robe."

I rolled my eyes. "Least I'm wearing long underwear underneath."

"S-sexy." He smiled, just enough to show me his dimples. I shivered in response.

The dimples: always my weakness.

"Come on, Casanova. Let's get you stripped down by the fire."

"Y-you gonna s-strip too?"

Just inside the door, I turned to glare at him, but before I could think of a smart-ass remark that didn't lead to me doing just what he'd asked, Collin's knees buckled and he fell to the floor.

"Collin!" I fell down beside him, cradling his head in my lap. "I need to call an ambulance."

He scrunched up his nose, shooing me away with a weak hand. I caught it and immediately started blowing hot air on the skin. It was so cold—ice-cube cold.

He winced but still managed a small grin. "L-like you t-taking care of m-me."

Tears burned my eyes again, but I kept blowing on his freezing skin, moving one of my hands to rub the wet hair off his forehead.

"Can you just stop with the sweet talk and tell me what happened?"

He rolled so his face was inches from my waist. If this were any other time, I'd have questioned his tactics, but I knew from how much he was still shaking that this was survival of the fittest.

"Rental car got stuck down the hill. W-walked."

"How the hell did McKenna not see you?"

"T-took a wrong turn. M-made m-my way through the w-woods."

I yanked my robe and jacket off his shoulders, trying to get him to move. But he didn't. "I've got to get you closer to the fire, Collin. There's a bad draft by the door and—"

"No." He sighed, pulling his hands away to press them under the waistline of my shirt. I hissed at the contact, but if this was the only way to get him warm, then I'd deal with it.

"Fine, you stubborn ass." I leaned my head back against the wall next to the door. Nodding once, he stayed silent. And within seconds his breathing evened out and his eyes shut.

Okay then. Guess I'd be sleeping on the floor tonight.

CHAPTER 40

Collin

IF THIS WAS A DREAM, I NEVER WANTED TO WAKE UP. ADDIE'S scent was all around me, her hands tangled up in my hair. I rubbed my fingers over her soft skin, her curvy waist, her hip.

But then I heard the sound of her moan and felt the vibration against my skin. So I opened my eyes, looked up, and found her holding me in her arms like I'd imagined, face lax in sleep.

"No dream," I whispered, reaching up to rub my finger over her nose, her forehead, her eyebrow and cheek...

Damn, did I miss her.

Her eyes fluttered open and met mine. "Hi."

It was one word, but I felt it everywhere.

"Hey." My voice cracked, but at least I wasn't stuttering. Stupidest thing I'd ever done was take the advice of my sister and McKenna. Women thought they knew romance, but what they didn't know was that their version damn near froze me to death.

"You okay?" She moved to sit up and away from the wall.

"Perfect now."

"You're here." A line between her eyebrows surfaced and I reached up again, running my finger down the middle of it. Hated seeing it there. Meant she was worried.

I'd scared her.

"Wouldn't be anywhere else." Slowly and steadily, I sat up, moving to sit by her side.

Reaching out, she grabbed my hand and pulled it to her lap. "Not that I'm complaining, but why *are* you here?"

I shut my eyes and leaned closer, pressing my forehead to hers. "Want the long story or short?"

"Short."

Only thing I needed now was to touch her. So I did. And as I told her my story, I trailed my hand along her chin and cheek, writing the words *I love you* over the surface.

"About lost my shit without you." I pulled back and found her cheeks red, her eyes sparkling too. "Was on my way to the airport the same day I dropped you off." I cleared my throat, wanting to laugh at myself for being so stupid. "Luckily Gav and Max talked me down off my ledge. Lia too."

Addie sighed and looked at the floor, almost like she was disappointed. But that couldn't be right.

"Realized what a paranoid dick I'd been the week before Christmas. So I figured the least I could do was give you what you'd asked for."

"And what was that?" She met my eyes again, testing me.

"You needed space."

"And you gave it to me." She squeezed my fingers tight.

"I did. Damn hard too, because it's not what I do. Second you got on that plane, I was at the desk, begging some poor girl who looked no older than a kid to make the plane stop. Had security called on me and everything."

"Oh, Collin."

"Told you I can't help myself when it comes to you. But now?" I sucked in a breath. "I'm damn scared to love you the way I wanna love you, mostly 'cause I'm afraid I'll wind up pushing you away."

"I called you." She cupped my cheek, changing the subject. "The second I got to this bungalow, I picked up my phone and dialed your number. You didn't answer, so I thought maybe it was the service or something. But then you texted me right back a minute later saying you were too busy to talk."

"Addison rehab. I was going through it."

She snorted. "I didn't know there was such a thing."

I leaned back and held my hand against the side of her throat. I watched as she melted into my touch, and the way her head tilted to get closer to me was everything I needed right now. "Gav told me I needed to take things down a notch when it came to you and me."

"You? Take things down a notch?" she scoffed and wrapped her arm around my waist. My hand went around hers in turn, and she laid her head on my chest, right where it belonged. "I didn't fall in a love with a man who takes things lightly, Collin. I fell in love with you. Broody, gloomy, overbearing Number Six."

She poked my stomach and I grunted. Didn't bother to push her away—liked any kind of touch she offered. But I did grab her wrist, pulling her hand to my mouth when she was done. I kissed her palm and asked, "What's with the Number Six thing?"

One half of her mouth moved up into a slow, sexy grin. "That night we met, your jersey said number six. I watched you in the middle of the dance floor."

My eyebrows rose. "Did you?"

"Yeah, I couldn't see your face. But I could see your hands wrapped around that girl's thighs." She sighed. "All I could think about was how *big* they were. Massive even."

"My hands?"

She nodded, touching my chest. "Yep. Then you held me against that table and, well…you know what happened next."

I kissed her forehead and shut my eyes, remembering what I'd thought when I first saw her sitting alone. Quiet, approachable, someone to practice talking to, someone to just…be with, if only for a few minutes while I waited for Gavin to go to the bathroom. Didn't expect her to be beautiful though. And I sure as hell didn't expect her to be the other half of my heart.

"Hate to break it to you, but six isn't my normal number."

She gasped and lifted her head. "I feel like I've been living a lie."

It was my turn to laugh. "Not sure things would've ended the same had you seen what my real jersey looked like that day."

"Oh?"

I shrugged. "Pink and green are not nearly as hot. Max messed up the laundry that morning."

As she laid her head back down on my chest, the

silence grabbed the air between us again. My eyes were heavy, but my heart was happy.

"I'm sorry, Addie," I finally said.

She tightened her hand around the bottom of my shirt, staying quiet, listening.

"I'm sorry for not being smarter. For being a jackass. For making a scene at that restaurant. For not calling you back." I ran my fingers through her hair. "And I'm also sorry for not believing you when you said you wouldn't leave us."

"Don't be sorry." She propped her chin on my shoulder and rubbed her knuckles over my cheek.

The smell of wine and vanilla meshed in the air, making my stomach go tight with need. Every delicious inch of this woman was mine, and I'd never mess that up. Ever.

"And don't you dare stop being you either. Whether you realize it or not, I *love* your crazy need to be in control. I love your grumpy moods sometimes too. What I really, *really* love is being the one to test your control and pull you out of those moods." She moved her leg over both of mine until she was straddling my waist. Chest to chest, she looked down at me in a way I'd never get tired of.

Like she wanted me.

Like she needed me as much as I needed her.

Other than grabbing her hips, I held still as she kissed my chin, then my cheek, finishing up with the tip of my nose.

"But…could you possibly fill me in on why you had to come all the way to Maine to tell me this when you could've told me before I left or even waited until I got home?" She bit down on her bottom lip, her hair shadowing our faces. "Not that I'm complaining or anything, because I am very happy you're here."

I scowled. "Lia made me do it."

Her eyebrows shot up, and a laugh popped out of her mouth. "For real?"

"Yep. But I'm not sure if losing my shoes in a snowdrift was part of the plan."

A hiss pushed through Addie's lips. "I'm sure she had good intentions if she told you to do what she did. My guess is she had no idea what you were getting yourself into. Plus, had I known you were coming, I would've come and gotten you at the airport."

"And ruin the romance?" I faked a gasp. "Never."

"The box!" Addie shot up onto her feet, almost like she could read my thoughts. She dug through the robe on the floor beside us, her smile shy as she straddled my thighs again.

My hands went straight to her ass, pulling her closer, which earned me a scowl—a sexy-as-*hell* scowl, but a scowl all the same. There were some things I'd never stop doing, and one of them was making her know she was mine.

"Want me to open it now?" she asked, messing with the red ribbon I'd wrapped around the box.

I nodded and sat up straighter, bringing her with me.

Like she couldn't wait anymore, she ripped the ribbon off of the box, lip pulled between her teeth the whole time. Couldn't take my gaze away from her long enough to think about what she'd say when she saw it, just concentrated on the happiness on her face.

She'd never looked more beautiful.

"Here, you do it." She bounced and grinned, pushing the box into my hands.

"Ain't what you think it is." I bit down on my cheek, nervous. Knew she wasn't ready for a ring; knew she wasn't the type to jump in with both feet like I was either. Guaranteed, though—just like I'd told Alexander and Suzie—within a year, she'd have my last name.

And if I had it my way, a son growing inside her too.

But baby steps—I had to learn to take them. "Okay." She rubbed her hands together like a kid on Christmas morning. Ironically, I'd planned on giving this to her on Christmas before the key chain idea hit me.

I opened the box and held it out in between our chests.

She gasped and pressed her hands over her mouth. "Is that…"

"I don't do commitment lightly, Addie. And this, right here, is like me giving you the last part of my soul I've got left to give."

I lifted the two silver dog-tag chains and lowered them around her neck. They settled against her heart, the sight nearly making my eyes burn.

"They're beautiful." She rubbed her hand over the engraved letters.

"They're dirty." I frowned.

"No." She moved closer and rubbed her nose against mine. "They're beautiful."

Deciding to pick and choose my battles, I let it go. "Told you I loved you, Addison Booker. You were mine from the moment I saw you that night in the bar. Took my head a bit to catch up with the heart, but this is me, telling you now, I am one hundred percent committed and in love with you."

Her lip quivered. "I don't know what to say."

"That's easy," I whispered. "Tell me you forgive me for being a douche bag. Tell me you won't ever take these off. And then tell me you love me too."

"Is that all?" She laughed, but tears were running down her cheeks.

I leaned forward, kissing the drops away and tasting her warm skin at the same time. "I've got a long list of stuff I'd like to do right now, including getting you naked and having you ride my cock, but I figured you needed to be romanced a bit before—"

She jumped at me, wrapping her long legs around my waist this time, all before kissing me like I was her last breath. I grinned against her lips, pulling back to see a giant smile on her face too.

"I don't need romance. I'm no warm-and-fuzzy girl who has to be wooed. I like hard sex and I like it with you, so if all you wanted was my forgiveness, I have no problem giving that to you."

"You really love me." I'd never tire of hearing those three words.

"I do." She sat up, still on my lap, as she reached around to grab something from her pocket. "And this right here…" Something silver flashed in between our bodies. Diamond initials—A. B.—there in my line of sight on the surface, and a house key dangling from the end. "…was the easiest decision I've had to make in a long time."

Grinning, heart damn near exploding in my chest, I said, "If it was so easy, then why'd you make me wait so long to hear it?"

She looked away, her cheeks going pink. "Let me

clarify that for you. What I meant to say was, *after* I got my head out of my butt and realized my reasoning for not living with you was bullshit, *then* I decided the answer was simple."

My smile fell and I sat up, holding her ass and pulling her closer. Her legs wrapped around my back, hugging my waist this time. The way she arched against my cock wasn't lost on me either—the two of us loved to fuck.

"Not bullshit. Smart." I reached up and held her face between my hands. "You don't jump into things like me. Gotta think it over, be sure you wanna take the plunge." I shrugged, wishing I'd thought this myself a week ago. "You're my opposite, my other half, and the rights to all my wrongs."

She sniffed and buried her face against my neck. "There you go, being all poetic on me." She tugged on the back of my hair.

"Can't help myself. I love you."

With a sigh, she said, "Say that again."

I kissed her neck. "I." I kissed her ear. "Love." I kissed her cheek. "You." Then I kissed nose and trailed my hands up and under her shirt. She moaned, rocking against me, lips inches from mine. Tracing my fingers along the skin at the small of her back, I waited for her words, knowing I'd do anything she wanted just to hear them come out of her mouth.

Eyes heated, searing into me, she pulled back—not to say *I love you too*, but to yank her shirt off and press her beautiful, naked tits against my chest.

"Jesus, Add—" Before I could say her name, she had her mouth on mine. A kiss that said *I need you*, a tongue battling with mine that said *I need you now*. Gasping, she pulled back, hovering over my lips when she finally said, "And I am wholeheartedly in love with you too." Another kiss on my lips, then she said, "I just didn't know it right away either."

I squeezed her against me. Holding her tight. Never *ever* wanting to let her go again.

"Collin?" I kissed a trail down her neck, loving how sweet she tasted.

"Yeah, sweetheart?"

"Do you think we could try another game? We're pretty good at those."

I tucked my nose into her hair and inhaled. "You name it."

She licked her lips and lowered her chin, a conniving smile forming on her mouth. "First one to moan is the loser?"

Not wasting a minute, I leaned forward and said, "Hell yeah," before I pulled her lower lip between my teeth. She wanted to play, and I liked to fight dirty.

Breath hot against my mouth, Addie said what every guy in my shoes would wanna hear but never get to:

"Game on, Number Six. Game. On."

EPILOGUE

Max

One month later

THE TABLE WAS A DISASTER. CAKE WAS SMASHED ACROSS the surface, and ice cream had settled into the cracks. The restaurant floor under Beaner's high chair looked like someone had emptied a pile of garbage all over it, yet none of us could stop laughing as she shoveled more food into her little mouth.

It was Chloe's first birthday—January thirtieth. And damn if it hadn't been a good night to celebrate.

"Think we shoulda taken out an insurance policy on this place." Colly leaned back against his chair, arm wrapped around Addie's shoulder and playing with her hair. "My daughter eats like Maxwell."

I flipped off my best friend and settled my arm along the back of the seat next to me.

Gavin elbowed me in the ribs. "Hands," he grunted.

"Aww, sorry, big boy. Didn't mean to lead you on." I leaned over and smacked a big, wet, sloppy kiss on his cheek.

"Christ, Max, knock it off." He elbowed me in the

ribs again, and this time I did drop my arm. Guy had one hell of a jab.

"Can you two please get along for one night?" Addie pointed at us from across the table, her lips twitching like she was fighting a smile.

"Yes, Mom." I winked and her cheeks flared red even as she rolled her eyes.

"Don't be smart, Max." Colly leaned over and kissed his woman's head. Guy was pussy whipped. And damn if it didn't make my chest all warm and fuzzy. I reached a hand up and rubbed the spot over my heart with my knuckles, not liking the sensation.

The two of them had settled into a routine over the past few months, a family of three in the most messed-up way. What started out as a nanny situation had fast turned into a fucking situation, which then led them into the complicated situation that came *after* the fucking part—a situation I was never gonna find myself in.

I'd been on the sidelines the entire time, watching the whole thing go down. Still, I wasn't too surprised they'd wound up at this point—living under the same roof, playing house, and falling in love. It was all part of a *normal* couple's life plan.

I was happy for them. Really. They deserved each other, and Chloe deserved a lady who'd love her like a mom. And it also meant—now that Addie was living with us—I'd never have to wash or fold my own underwear again. *I* was the real winner here.

"I should probably start putting the rest of the cake away." Addie sighed as she moved closer to Chloe, her face swallowed in disappointment. "Maybe see if they have any rags and whatnot so I can start cleaning up the mess."

I cleared my throat, knowing what was bringing her down. It was my job to push her back up—though I'm sure Colly had his own ways of doing that too. "Don't worry about the extra cleanup, Short Stuff." I grinned as our brunette waitress made her way across the room, her eyes sparkling at me every chance she got. "I've got an in with the waitstaff, and I'm pretty sure she'll be okay with the extra tip I plan on giving her later tonight."

I watched as she moved—all long legs, long hair, curvy hips, and a pair of tits to die for. Had I known one of my regulars worked here, I would've gotten us a better table.

"You are a disgusting man, Maxwell Martinez." Gavin smirked at me and grabbed his coat as he stood.

"Love you too, snuggle bear." I blew him a kiss as he went to hug Addie, which earned me more middle fingers from three of my five favorite people. I say three because Chloe was one and wouldn't likely be flashing it at me anytime soon, and my fifth favorite person hadn't bothered to show tonight.

Thinking I could will her here with my mind, I glanced at the door, hoping Lia would surprise us all by popping through there at the last minute. What the hell was more important than her niece's first birthday party anyway? Collin's little sister had been making herself scarce for the past month. He thought it was because of that new asshat she'd been dating, but I knew her better than anyone.

Lia wasn't avoiding the group. She was avoiding *me*. I just wished I knew why.

Addie reached for the cake box, organizing the pieces that had been cut but not eaten, just as Gavin waved good-bye and left. He had to get to work, and according to the clock on the wall, he was already late.

"Lemme help you with that, sweetheart." Collin grabbed Addie's wrist and stood, sweeping in for a back-bending kiss. I watched, smiling, shaking my head, and wondering what that feeling was they had inside to make them wanna kiss all the time. It wasn't annoying. But it was unnerving, especially since I kept getting those warm fuzzies every time I saw it happen.

"Cover your eyes, Beaner. They're gonna make you a baby brother right here in the restaurant at this rate." I leaned over and poked the little thing in the sides, not giving a shit that she was completely plastered from head to toe with cake and ice cream and God-only-knows what else.

She giggled at me and pointed a finger my way. I ate the cake off the end, and she belly laughed when I popped my lips.

Collin pulled away from Addie, grinning. "I'd be okay with that."

"Slow your roll, buckaroo." Addie pinched his cheek, then turned just as the waitress approached.

Hottie leaned over to grab something off the floor, the top of her shirt unbuttoned and ready for a feasting. I licked my lips.

"We still good for after I get off?" she asked me, batting her lashes as she stood back up.

"Sure thing, pretty girl. Can't wait."

She held my stare, giggling as she twirled a lock of her hair around one of her fingers. I watched the movement, mesmerized, until a blast of pink flashed out of the corner of my eye.

"Lia!" Addie screeched so loudly that half the restaurant looked our way.

Like I'd been shot in the gut by a stun gun, I turned, finding Lee-Lee's eyes narrowed at the waitress, then narrowing even more at me. Then my two favorite women hugged it out, breaking Lia's gaze from mine.

I swallowed, trying to focus on the hottie, but that weird-as-fuck fuzzy thing started working its way into my belly at the sight of Lia.

After a few seconds, I cleared my throat, winked at my waitress as she walked away, then turned to Lia. "You actually made it." I patted the chair next to mine. When I glanced at her brother, he looked somewhere between pissed and worried as he studied her.

Lia shoved my hand out of the way and sat. "Sorry. Not all of us can get fired from our jobs yet expect the world to magically provide for us." She winked. I knew she was going for playful, but it came across as bitchy — not Lia.

"I didn't get fired." My jaw clenched. Not my usual go-to response when I looked at this woman. "I quit."

She started to respond when Addie reopened the box of cake and all but shouted, "Chocolate okay? We ran out of vanilla."

Not wanting to ruin the almost-perfect night, I didn't latch on to Lia's bait anymore after that — just watched as she smiled and accepted the plate from Addie. I had no idea what her issues were with me right now, but tonight was about Chloe.

"Let's toast," I finally said, raising the last of my beer

in the air. "To Beaner, the only girl I'll kiss who has a mouth full of food and poop in her diaper."

Weird with me or not, Lia snort-laughed under her breath. It was short, but it made my heart skip a beat. I loved being the man she could laugh at—and with.

Mindlessly, I rubbed my free hand over my chest again, pushing the fuzzy shit away. I was getting far too soft. "And may all her birthdays be as kick-ass as this one," I finished, raising my glass higher.

"Language," Collin grunted, but then moved to grab his bottle, grinning at his daughter as he spoke. "To my baby girl. Love you more than anything else in this world."

Addie grabbed her soda next, raising it to clink with ours. Her eyes were wet as she smiled back and forth between my best friend and Chloe. Unlike us, she didn't speak, but the wordless stare and smile were enough.

Lia grabbed the full glass of red wine I'd ordered earlier for Addie. She'd refused, saying someone had to be the DD. Now Lee-Lee lifted it, not even asking who it belonged to. "To Chloe Bean, the best one-year-old ever."

"Hear, hear." I nodded, then downed the last of my beer, the cool bubbles making their way to my stomach. I looked around the table, breathing in the happiness that came from my friends. It was a combination of vanilla and cake and flowers and warm beer—the perfect scent of a family.

We weren't blood, but everything about these people was my life. And no matter what happened in our futures, I'd never once regret knowing and loving them all.

ACKNOWLEDGMENTS

First and foremost, I need to thank my husband, Chris, for being there through every aspect of my writing career. From my tears when nothing was working out right to my celebrations of the littlest to biggest things. It's been a seven-year journey for me, babe, and without your culinary skills in the kitchen, our kids would not have eaten anything but pizza and the occasional box of mac and cheese. Without your encouragement, I would have given up a long time ago. Without your ability to be the financial backbone of our family while I stayed home with the girls and my stories, I would not be where I am today. There's not a day that goes by that I regret that night in Off Limits when you first flashed me your fifteen-year-old dimples. And through all of our ups and downs, I can officially say you are my happily ever after.

To Kelsey, my oldest daughter, for becoming the most amazing mini-me ever (though I'm pretty sure you'll disagree with that): You listen to me talk endlessly about book boyfriends and, even though you often roll your eyes, you never turn your back on me when I need a set of ears. You loaned me Shay Mitchell to inspire Addie and, though we argue about the Emison ship versus the Collin/Addie ship, you don't fight me like most kids would. You, little KK, are pretty much the greatest, most amazing twelve-year-old I've ever known.

To Emma, my middle kiddo: With your crazy thoughts, your love of cheese, and your YOLO attitude, you are basically my heart and soul when it comes to keeping my chin up. You make me laugh when I want to cry; you remind me that I am amazing on a daily basis. Your love of reading inspires me to write more books, even though these are not the books for your little eyes. Still, you're the best hugger ever with the best laugh and the best smile. Yes, you test my patience with your need to constantly borrow my computer, but I have to say you are the best, most amazing, ten-year-old a mom could ever have.

To Bella, my baby, the one who inspired me to pick up reading books again when she first popped up in my belly: I knew you were going to be my endgame from the second I first saw your big, brown eyes. You gave me life and the gift of putting my fingers to the keyboard in the first place. You're the only kiddo I got to stay home with, and you quickly became my lifeline, even as a tiny baby. Fast-forward a few years and you became my helper at two, my snuggler at four, and the only first grader I know who gives motivational speeches when all I want to do is cry. God blessed me with you at a time when I didn't know I needed you the most.

To my parents, for obvious reasons: You not only gave me life, but you made me who I am today. And even though you still have to remind me to keep my van clean and clean my toilets, you are two of the best parents a girl could have.

To my agent, Stacey Donaghy: When I first signed with you, I had no idea what we'd go through to get me to where I am today. There's not a day that goes by when I'm not thankful to have you in my corner. Your FB messages give me hope and brighten my days, and your unwavering support makes me want to weep for joy. This is truly a journey I wouldn't be on without you, and I just want to say thank you again for being the best literary soul mate a girl could ever ask for.

To my editor, Cat Clyne: You took a chance on me, something I will never EVER be able to repay you for. Thank you for loving my group of crazy guys as much as I do.

To Katrina Emmel, I honestly don't know where I'd be without you. You're not only my daily sounding board and critique partner, but you are truly one of *the* best friends a girl can have. You've stuck by me and this book for over two years, and if it weren't for you, it wouldn't be where it is now. (And neither would I.) I couldn't imagine my life without you. Thank you for all you do, thank you for being who you are, and most of all, thank you for coming into my world.

To Jennifer Griswell, a.k.a Collin's, Max's, and Gavin's biggest cheerleader: Having you as a critique partner was a game changer. You give amazing advice and guidance, and remind me on a daily basis that I don't suck. You're absolutely one of my best friends, no doubt in my mind. Thank you for loving my boys—and me—like your life depends on it.

To Kasey Lane: You read this baby in a pinch for me and provided me with some amazing feedback that I will *forever* be grateful for. I am so glad to know you, have you as my publishing sister, and to be able to call you a dear friend.

To the girls in the Life Group: Amanda, Kelly,

Anise, Sam, Colleen, Tara, Stacey, and Kimberly. You accepted me even though I wasn't a debut author or even a 2016 release. I can't imagine not having you all in my life. Thank you for allowing me into your world and giving me a place to vent and squeal and find some amazing friendships while I was at it.

To my Hookup Ladies, Kelly Siskind and Jamie Howard: The fact that I get to hang with you in this group of amazingness is pretty much the best part of my days. There is never a dull moment when it comes to you two and I can't thank you enough for wanting to team with a girl who came in so late the game.

To the Twitter #amediting crew: You got me through two grueling weeks of developmental edits, then two more days of copyedits, and for that, I will forever be grateful and look forward to many more years of motivation.

To my BFB family: I may not be there as an editor anymore, but I will always be there as a friend and a big, big fan of all the amazing authors. Erin Rhew, Jessica Calla, Jenn Herrington, Ellie Siphella—you all rock in ways I won't ever be able to point out in one simple paragraph. Thank you for being in my literary family.

And finally, to the fans who've stuck with me over the past four years (I know exactly who you are, by the way): Though I've not always been the most consistent author as far as books go, you've been there to read all my words and it keeps me motivated to keep going with your likes and messages and follows. I never thought, for the life of me, that I'd have fans who enjoy my words. You make this all possible and worthwhile.

ABOUT THE AUTHOR

Heather Van Fleet is a stay-at-home-mom turned book-boyfriend connoisseur. She's a wife to her high school sweetheart, a mom to three girls, and in her spare time you can find her with her head buried in her Kindle, guzzling down copious amounts of coffee.

Heather graduated from Black Hawk College in 2003 with an associate's degree and has been working in the publishing industry for over five years. She is represented by Stacey Donaghy of Donaghy Literary Group.

Find her at heathervanfleet.com.

A SURE THING

First in the steamy Donnigans series
from author Marie Harte

Meet the Donnigans: with the oldest former-Marine brothers adjusting to civilian life, their younger sister constantly in trouble, and their youngest brother clueless about life in general, falling in love is the last thing on anyone's mind.

Being a Marine was everything Landon Donnigan had dreamed of…until a bullet sent him home with a medical discharge. When he decides to teach a self-defense class and meets sexy Ava, he realizes his combat skills are useless when it comes to his heart.

"A blazing hot, emotionally intense love story."

—Kirkus Reviews

For more Marie Harte, visit:
www.sourcebooks.com

BEAUTIFUL CRAZY

First in the Rock 'n' Ink series
from author Kasey Lane

Kevan Landry has one shot to sign the metal band Manix
Curse and get her fledging PR firm off the ground. If she
doesn't succeed, she'll lose more than her company.

Mason Dillon heads the most successful music PR firm
in Portland and has been commissioned with signing Manix
Curse. But after going head-to-head with Kevan over the
band, work is the last thing on his mind.

Forced to prove their marketing skills, the pair wages a
battle for the band. If they can set aside their differences,
they may find together they're the right mix of sexy savvy
to conquer the bedroom and the boardroom.

For more Kasey Lane, visit:
www.sourcebooks.com

UNDER HER SKIN

First in an exciting dark contemporary series
from debut author Adriana Anders

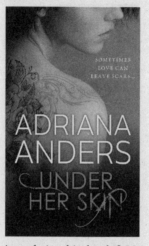

A darkly possessive relationship has left Uma alone and on the run. Beneath her clothing, she hides a terrible secret—proof of her abuse, tattooed on her skin in a lurid reminder of everything she's survived.

Caught between a brutal past and an uncertain future, Uma is reluctant to bare herself to anyone, much less a rough ex-con whose rage drives him in ways she doesn't understand. But beneath his frightening exterior, Ivan is gentle. Warm. Compassionate. And just as determined to heal Uma's broken heart as he is to destroy the monster who left his mark scrawled across her delicate skin.